Lindsey Kelk is an author, journalist and prolific tweeter. Born and brought up in Doncaster, South Yorkshire, she worked as a sales assistant, a PR, a silver service waitress and a children's editor before moving to New York and becoming a full-time writer. She now lives in LA.

Lindsey has written fourteen novels, including the *I Heart* books and the *Girl* series, as well as several standalones. A fan of lipstick, pro-wrestling and cats (although not all at the same time), she co-hosts the beauty podcast, *Full Coverage*, with make-up artist, Harriet Hadfield.

You can find out lots more about her here: http://lindseykelk.com and on Facebook, Twitter or Instagram @LindseyKelk.

Also by Lindsey Kelk

I Heart series
I Heart New York
I Heart Hollywood
I Heart Paris
I Heart Vegas
I Heart London
I Heart Christmas
I Heart Forever

Girl series
About a Girl
What a Girl Wants
A Girl's Best Friend

Standalones
The Single Girl's To-Do List
Always the Bridesmaid
We Were on a Break
One in a Million

Novellas only available on ebook
Jenny Lopez Has a Bad Week
Jenny Lopez Saves Christmas

Lindsey Kelk

One *in a* Million

HarperCollins*Publishers*

HarperCollins*Publishers*
1 London Bridge Street
London
SE1 9GF

www.harpercollins.co.uk

A Paperback Original 2018
18 19 20 21 22 LSCC 10 9 8 7 6 5 4 3 2 1

A catalogue record for this book
is available from the British Library

ISBN: 9780008239046

Typeset in Melior by Palimpsest Book Production Ltd, Falkirk, Stirlingshire

Printed and bound in the United States of America by LSC Communications

For more information visit: www.harpercollins.co.uk/green

For Rowan & Kit
One in a Billion

CHAPTER ONE

Every once in a while, everything comes together and for a single day, your life is amazing.

'Hands up if you think Annie Higgins is the most wonderful human being in the whole wide world?' Miranda yelled, lining up an armful of champagne bottles on her desk. Well, leftover Marks & Sparks cava. It was cold and it was fizzy and it would do.

Brian immediately raised his hand in the air. Modesty kept mine down but it was a challenge.

'And hands up if you're excited that we're up for not one, not two, but three very important and exciting awards?'

This time, my hand shot right up. That was an actual stone-cold, verifiable fact. They'd already tweeted it and you could not take back a tweet. Ask literally anyone.

'Our first award ceremony,' Mir said, with eyes so dreamy you'd think she was preparing for the Oscars. 'Our first mandatory fancy-frock professional event for Content. You know they hold it in the ballroom at the Haighton Hotel and everyone wears black tie and—'

'And everyone does coke in the toilets,' Brian interrupted. 'Don't you pop that cork, I want to make a Boomerang.'

Miranda wrestled with the bottle of fizz, her tongue sticking out the side of her mouth as I counted down. 'One, two, three . . .'

The bottle opened and a shower of champagne arced high into the air, dousing the office floor to wild applause. There was a reason Rodney the cleaner didn't like us. Actually, that wasn't true – there were lots of reasons.

'Such a waste,' I said, holding out my plastic cup for a pour from the already half-empty bottle.

'But it looks so cool,' Brian said as he uploaded the loop to Instagram. The cork went in, the cork came out, the cork went in, the cork came out. He had a point.

'To Annie, a verifiable goddess,' Miranda said as she filled my glass before passing on pouring duties. 'This is going to make us, you know.'

'Is it going to make us rich?' I asked, bracing my face for her big, sloppy kiss. 'In fact, I'd settle for financially solvent. Do any of the awards come with a cheque?'

She held up a finger to shut me up, knowing full well if anyone else had done that, I'd have bitten it off.

'Not interested in hearing about real life right now,' she replied. 'Today is for celebrating, so shut up and let me tell you how amazing you are. This is the start of it all for us, Annie. It's all upwards and onwards from here on in. Our little company just put on its big boy pants.'

'Big *girl* pants, I can't stand boy shorts,' I corrected,

rereading the confirmation email from TechBubble on my phone. *Content London has received nominations in the following categories: best social media campaign, best boutique agency and best new agency.* 'Do you know what? I don't even care if we win.'

Mir said nothing. Instead she slowly raised one eyebrow.

'I already feel like a winner,' I insisted. 'I don't need some industry prize or shiny trophy to validate me.'

Up went the other eyebrow.

'Just being nominated is an honour in itself?'

My best friend shook her head. 'Yeah, the problem is, I still remember when you didn't win the three-legged race at school and decked Marie Brown with a tennis racket.'

'Don't be ridiculous,' I mumbled into my drink. 'It was a hockey stick.'

'It was brutal,' she assured me. 'Very Tonya Harding.'

Somewhere along the line, I'd missed the memo about not being competitive.

'Shall we go up to the roof and celebrate properly?' Miranda suggested, gathering up the unopened bottles. 'It's such a gorgeous evening and the weather's been awful all week.'

'Mir, it's only Tuesday,' I reminded her as she walked away.

'And the first five days after Sunday are always the worst,' she called over her shoulder. 'Can you tell the boss I'll be late in the morning?'

'You just did,' I replied, chasing after her.

Just over a year ago, Miranda and I pooled every penny we had and moved Content London, our 'two girls, one laptop' digital marketing agency, from the settees in the back of Costa Coffee to a tiny corner of a very trendy new co-working space in East London called The Ginnel. The manager sold the building on stories of its 'history' and 'character', a description that roughly translated to 'people used to get mugged outside, but not any more'. Exactly the kind of place that would fascinate your father and worry your mother. Of course, that meant that after the cheap deal he used to lure us in expired, the rent was extortionate. But Miranda insisted it was worth it, for the location and the connections we could make and because you never knew who you were going to bump into at the barista station.

Because of course there was a barista station.

The best part of the entire building was the honest-to-goodness actual roof terrace. It wasn't fancy – we didn't have a bar or a sophisticated sound system or sexy, lounging furniture – but we did have a load of waterproof beanbags, someone's second-hand settee and the most beautiful view of the London skyline I had ever called my own. It was all very DIY chic but I loved it. I'd even brought in a few potted plants to hide the electrical boxes. Nothing I could do about the man across the road who liked to parade around naked of an evening, but Miranda assured me he added to the rooftop's character.

A few months after moving to The Ginnel, we expanded our work family to make room for Brian, another of our oldest friends who both happened to know his way around a website and was prepared to take a chance on a fledging company. I still wasn't sure if it was because he had so much faith in me and Mir or because we never complained about him rolling into work after ten a.m. every morning but either way, I wasn't going to complain. Our budgets were still tighter than a tight thing but we were making it work, just about.

Only puffing very slightly from the last set of stairs – I was determined to make my ten thousand steps – I put my glass down on a wooden box-slash-makeshift table and straightened up to admire the view, digging my fingers into my lower back. Even though we were right in the heart of London, and The Ginnel wasn't a very tall building, it always felt peaceful up here. I looked down, watching the tops of the red buses sail by, the tops of people's heads bobbing along to whatever was coming out of their earphones. Even the swell of competing sirens seemed softened by a few floors' distance. Plus it made for fantastic sunset skyline pics and who didn't love a sunset skyline pic? Monsters, only monsters. Whenever the weather allowed, I was up here, soaking in the Vitamin D and willing my skin to tan. But for all The Ginnel's Brooklyn hipster aspirations, we were still very much in England and I remained the same shade as your average sheet of A4 year round.

'Starting without us?'

I was settling myself down on the sofa when Charlie Wilder emerged from the doorway, his ever-present shadow, Martin Green, close behind. Charlie was one of the original tenants of the building and generally liked to swank around as though he owned the place. Martin, however, did own the place. Would that I'd had the presence of mind to mortgage myself to the hilt and buy a ramshackle, East London teardown when I was twenty-two. Fifteen years later, he must have made his money back on this place a thousand times over. I was fairly certain our monthly rent alone was more than the cost of his original mortgage payments and there were dozens more tenants in the building. He was so rich, it made me want to do a little cry.

'Start without you?' I looked at Charlie, slightly flustered on the inside but cool, calm and collected on the outside. Sort of. I could already feel myself turning red. 'As if we would.'

'What's the occasion?' Martin asked, eyeing the bottles of fizz.

'We,' Mir said, handing him a freshly filled glass. 'Are celebrating.'

Martin – commonly referred to as Miranda's Work Husband, although never to his face – took the drink with a shy smile. Yes, he could be obnoxious and yes, he wore one too many ironic T-shirts but he was also too cute when it came to his very obvious crush on my friend.

'Celebrating what?' asked Charlie.

'Did Taylor Swift like one of your tweets?' Martin asked, much to Charlie's delight.

'Tay-Tay did like one of my tweets once,' Brian said, talking into his champagne glass. 'And it was a magical day.'

'We've been nominated for a couple of awards,' I replied, tucking my light brown hair behind my ear in an attempt to look as casual as possible. 'But well done, you're very funny.'

'She's being polite – you're not funny at all,' Miranda said in a stage whisper, flashing her middle finger at the pair and dropping down onto the sofa beside me. Behind them, what looked like the entire population of The Ginnel streamed out of the staircase and onto the roof. 'What's going on? Why are you all up here?'

'We're watching the game,' Charlie answered, as though it was obvious. 'Kick off is in five minutes.'

'Oh Christ, it's the England game,' Mir groaned. 'Kill me now.'

'We're in the second round of the World Cup,' Martin replied with mock shock. 'Where's your national pride?'

'The same place as your sense of style,' she said, sipping her drink and staring straight ahead. 'We were having a nice time, do you have to ruin it with football?'

As much as she might protest, the bickering was part of the flirting. Until recently, it was all back-and-forth banter, sliding into each other's DMs and cow eyes across the coffee shop, but that was before the fateful Friday night two weeks ago when Miranda had one too many cheeky Vimtos and Martin had inhaled god only knows what and I walked in on the pair of them, snogging like a pair of teenagers in our office. But since then, nothing.

Rather than give Miranda a satisfactory answer, Martin and Charlie gravitated over towards the projector screen set-up, joining the other half-dozen men who were all stood around, observing the process, rubbing their chins and nodding.

'What's going on with you two?' I asked. 'Has he declared his undying love yet?'

'No, because he's an idiot,' she replied with a resigned sigh. 'Whatever, it's not like it's a big deal, is it?'

'Of course it isn't.' I patted her knee and passed my champagne to an empty-handed Brian as he walked by. 'You're a kick-arse queen who is the master of her own destiny and you've got better things to worry about than Martin Green.'

'Please don't call me a queen,' she said, fluffing out her amber afro. 'You can't pull it off.'

'Dope,' I replied with a nod.

'No, Annie, just no.'

Everyone on the rooftop cheered as a bright green field appeared on the giant projector screen and I felt my heart sink. There was no way I was spending the rest of the evening watching football; we were supposed to be celebrating, not punishing ourselves. Across the way, I saw Brian press his fingers to his temple and pull the trigger before cocking his head towards the exit. But before I could make my escape, Charlie and Martin leapt over the back of the sofa, Charlie pressed up against my left side and Martin glued to Miranda's right, squishing us into the very finest BFF sandwich.

Charlie flashed me a grin and I blushed from head to toe. It wasn't my fault, I was a nervous blusher and no matter how many times I saw him, talked to him, awkwardly shared a lift with him, I couldn't seem to make it through a conversation with Charlie without saying something idiotic. I always talked utter shit when I was nervous and six feet something of blond hair, big brown eyes and an annoyingly adorable lopsided smile definitely made me nervous. He looked as though he should be in an advert for outward bounds holidays in Iceland, not running his own advertising agency. And while I wouldn't necessarily say I had a crush on him *per se*, I could admit to having lost the odd half hour imagining the two of us stranded on a desert island with nothing but a bottle of tequila, a never-ending supply of Krispy Kreme doughnuts and some baby oil.

'Not a big football fan then?' Charlie asked, spreading out across the sofa and forcing me into Miranda's armpit. Fantasy Charlie would never manspread. Fantasy Charlie would have got down on the floor and given me a foot rub. Fantasy Charlie was the best.

'I used to go out with someone who worked for the FA,' I explained, snapping a hair band off my wrist and bundling up my hair. I hated the feeling of hot hair stuck to my neck in the summer. 'We went to a lot of games, I think I'm just footballed out.'

'Congrats on your award thingies, we were only joking with you before,' he said, leaning towards me as the players streamed out onto the pitch and everyone on the roof began to cheer. 'Do you think you'll win?'

'We'd better,' I replied readily, a proximity shiver running down my back. 'I mean, I'd like to think we're in with a shot to win *something*.'

And when I said something, I meant everything.

'I'll keep my fingers crossed for you,' he promised. 'I've seen so many people go in and out of that end office, really glad you're managing to make it work.'

'Thanks?' I said, folding my arms over my boobs, shrinking down into the sofa. 'We're trying.'

Charlie did not need to know about our cash-flow problemette. As soon as last month's invoices were paid, it would all be solved; the last thing we needed was word getting around that we were struggling.

'You know, I'm always here if you need any help,' Charlie offered, flexing the manly bicep that peeked out from the short sleeve of his England shirt. 'I only started up a couple of years ago and I know it isn't easy.'

I smiled, melting just a fraction.

'Actually, that's really helpful, thank you.'

I turned my attention back to the TV before I could ruin the moment. The camera zoomed along a long line of men with expensive tattoos and identical hair-cuts as they sang the national anthem. If I wanted to make a getaway, now was the time. It wasn't that I actively disliked football, it was more a Pavlovian response to having spent every weekend travelling from stadium to stadium for five long years with my ex. There wasn't another woman on this planet who knew how to find the cleanest ladies' loos at any given premier league team's home ground as quickly as I did.

But it was a lovely evening and we did have all that fizz and there would be no convincing Miranda to leave now Martin had made an appearance. And then there was Charlie. Maybe it was worth sticking around, at least until half-time.

On screen, the national anthem ended but instead of the clapping and jogging shenanigans that usually followed, the camera panned around the stands. An entire section of the stadium had taken off their England shirts to reveal bright pink T-shirts and when the camera pulled out, they formed a massive heart in the middle of the all-white-wearing crowd. All at once, the same section held up their phones until they joined together in one enormous high-tech jigsaw that read MARRY ME KARINE.

'Oh god, it's a flashmob,' I heard Miranda mutter at the side of me. 'I'd murder someone if they did this to me.'

'Point taken,' Martin whispered back.

But I was too busy staring at the screen to comment.

The words were replaced with an image of a couple on the big screen pitchside. He had dark hair and olive skin and she was tiny and blonde and beautiful. She was so delicately pretty, it looked as though her features had been carved out by unicorns. So that's what their horns were for. Eventually, the cameraman found the couple themselves and zoomed in on their corporate box. They needn't have zoomed in quite so close, you could have seen the ring from space, it was enormous. And of course, Karine said yes.

Suddenly, I seemed not to be breathing and my hands were clamped over my mouth. I leaned forward, resting my elbows on my knees, completely mute.

'Mortifying,' Martin scoffed. 'Who proposes at a World Cup game?'

'Someone romantic?' suggested a random voice behind me.

'Someone with a massive pair,' Charlie commented.

I exhaled for the first time in what felt like minutes. I happened to know first-hand that they were both wrong because it was Matthew, my ex-boyfriend.

Like I said, every once in a while, everything comes together and for a single day, your life is amazing.

Unfortunately, this was not going to be one of those days.

CHAPTER TWO

'Did she see it? Did she see it?' Brian sprinted across the roof, knocking several people out of the way as he lunged in front of the big screen. 'Annie, close your eyes. Take out your contact lenses. No, you don't wear lenses, poke out your eyes.'

I opened my mouth to say it was fine but nothing came out.

'Are you all right?' Miranda asked while Brian began unfastening his button-down shirt in order to cover the screen where the happy couple were busily waving to their thousands of new friends. 'Annie, talk to me.'

'I'm missing something here,' Charlie said, shielding his eyes from Brian's pasty torso.

'And I'm missing the game,' Martin shouted. 'Get out the way, dickhead.'

'This is bigger than twenty millionaires kicking a ball around,' he shouted back. 'That's Annie's ex. Show some respect, man.'

'Twenty-two!' Martin gasped in horror at the idea of someone not knowing how many players made up a football team. Charlie, Miranda and Brian all stared, waiting for me to say something.

'I'm fine,' I insisted. 'Really.'

There were at least three dozen people on the roof terrace, some I knew, most I didn't, but every single one of them was looking at me. If you took off my clothes, threw in a couple of murderous clowns and a box full of spiders, it was my worst nightmare come true.

'Yes, Matthew's my ex-boyfriend,' I confirmed to Charlie with a breezy smile. 'But very ex. Long time ago. Not a big deal.'

'Well, it's not quite been a year, has it?' Miranda corrected helpfully.

'Feels like much longer,' I said, pinching her thigh tightly as I stood. 'You know, I'm not really in the mood for football. I think I might head home after all.'

'We're coming with you,' Brian declared, shirt still open and streaming out behind him like a factory seconds Backstreet Boy. 'Come on, Miranda.'

Mir paused for a split second, glancing at her work boyfriend who kept his eyes on the football.

'Come *on*, Miranda,' Brian barked.

'I don't mind if you want to stay,' I told her, lying through my teeth. 'Honest.'

I would literally never forgive her.

'I'm coming,' she replied, leaping to her feet and wrapping an arm around my shoulders. 'We're out of champagne anyway.'

I noticed Martin watching out of the corner of his eye but he didn't say anything to try to stop her.

'I really am OK,' I said, sending a silent prayer up to the patron saint of friends for my bests. 'It's just the surprise. It's been ages since we broke up, sorry, since *I* broke up with *him*.'

13

'Really?' Brian scrunched up uncertain features as he hustled us across the rooftop, down the staircase to the fourth floor and buzzed for the lift. 'I thought you were the dumpee.'

I pursed my lips tightly.

'No, I wasn't. I ended it.'

Brian looked to Miranda for confirmation.

'Technically, yes,' Mir said, rubbing little circles in the middle of my back. 'She broke up with him.'

He still didn't look convinced.

'But wasn't he already—'

'Shut up, Brian.'

'And didn't you walk in on them—'

'Shut *up*, Brian.'

'The official record shows I did the dumping,' I insisted as the lift pinged open. 'And that's what matters.'

Out of the huge floor-to-ceiling windows of the fourth floor, I could see a glorious sunset breaking across the sky. It was such a beautiful evening and I didn't want to ruin it for them.

'You two should stay,' I said, slipping one foot between the lift door and the wall. 'I'm going to go for a walk.'

'No way,' Brian said. 'We're not leaving you alone.'

'I don't need a babysitter,' I insisted, putting on my resolved face. 'That was admittedly very weird, but I'm fine, I promise. Just not in the mood to go over it all night long.'

Did anyone really like rehashing their break-ups? It felt like a lifetime since Matthew and I had ended things, but seeing him on the big screen had been a shock. I'd done such a good job of wiping him out of my life, such a dramatic re-entry felt like a punch to the gut.

'As if I'm going to let you go home on your own and be upset over that tosser,' Miranda said as my resolved face faltered. 'Matthew was a wanksock, you are the best. It's like you, then Chrissy Teigen and then Beyoncé.'

'No way am I better than Chrissy Teigen,' I argued. 'Maybe Beyoncé on a good day, but never Saint Chrissy.'

She stared at me with a thoughtful pout and I offered her a genuine, if watery smile in return.

'Fine, you can go,' she said, finally. 'But you have to promise me you're not going to spend all night stalking their Instagram accounts.'

'I'm not a sadist,' I replied, stepping into the lift. 'I'm going to watch the proposal once or twice, find something he bought me and burn it, have a cry in the bath and then watch QVC Beauty until I pass out in front of the TV.'

'We can't argue with that plan,' Brian said, blowing me a kiss as the lift door slid shut. 'We'll see you tomorrow, love.'

My flat was only a five-minute walk from work – if you took the shortest route. But I was in no rush and the long way was calling me. Beautiful weather had been in short supply all summer and it felt good to feel the last rays of sun on my skin as I trotted out into the empty street. Everyone was watching the game, I realised as I peeled off my denim jacket and straightened the sleeves of my pink T-shirt, and the city was mine. Winter had overstayed its welcome well into spring and I couldn't even count the number of nights I'd stayed late at the office to keep my central heating bill down at home. Such was the glamorous life of a London gal.

15

There was something reassuring about a warm summer's evening in the city. People slowed down, they smiled, they forgot their problems and lingered a little longer, another drink, a chat outside the tube station. It was hard to be social when you were running away from the rain or hiding under your hood from an angry gust of wind. But this was perfect wandering weather. A whiff of the chip shop, the clean soapy smell of the laundrette, I could even find a soft spot for City Best Kebabs on a night like this. Or, let's be honest, any night.

I held my phone in my hand, as I almost always did, and as I turned off the main street it began to ring. I'd been avoiding checking my messages since I left the office. A cursory glance at my inbox on the way down in the lift had revealed more puke-face emojis than I'd had the privilege to see in my entire life. My friends were good people. But this was a call, not a text or a What's App, and no one called me, save my sister or my mother. This time, it was my mum.

'Annie.'

'Mum.'

'I just saw the news.'

I sighed internally and looked longingly at the fried chicken place across the street.

'You know I don't watch the news,' I replied, keeping my head down and walking on by. I had half a packet of perfectly delicious, three-day-old scones at home that weren't going to eat themselves. 'What's wrong, has the world ended?'

'Not the news-news,' she said, sighing externally. 'The news about Matthew. At the football thing.'

'Oh, *that* news,' I replied, blasé as could be. 'I saw that. I must drop him a text.'

Mum seemed surprised.

'Oh.' It took a moment to choose her next words. 'I thought you might be a bit upset.'

'I'm fine.' How many more times would I have to sing this song before everyone believed me? 'Me and Matthew broke up forever ago,' I recited. 'I'm really happy for him.'

'Doesn't feel like it was that long ago to me,' she replied. Helpful as ever. 'But that's age for you. If it wasn't twenty years ago, it was last week.'

'Mum, you're only fifty-eight,' I reminded her. 'We're not carting you off to the knacker's yard just yet.'

'You might as well,' she muttered as I hopped down off the pavement to dodge two tired-looking mothers pushing two double pushchairs. I smiled politely at the women and skipped on quickly. Miranda and Brian were all the children I could cope with for now. 'Honestly, Annie, I'm falling apart at the seams.'

It was utter nonsense, I'd never seen a midlife crisis go so well. Ever since she'd left London and moved up north, my mother had been through a complete renaissance. My dad left when I was little and Mum hadn't dealt with it terribly well, then out of the blue, she was thriving. My sister was worried she'd taken herself off to Yorkshire to die but as it turned out, we'd had quite the incorrect impression of Yorkshire. Mum had transformed from a depressed divorcée into a lean, mean needle-wielding machine. One day she was a practice nurse at our local surgery, the next she was opening the first medispa in Hebden Bridge and bringing Botox to the masses. I hadn't seen my mother's forehead move in more than two years.

'You're sure you're not even a little bit sad about Matthew getting engaged?' Mum wheedled. 'No good can come from bottling up your feelings. You'll block your chakras, and then I can't begin to tell you what kind of a mess you'll get yourself into.'

'My chakras are absolutely brilliant,' I assured her. 'All properly aligned and shiny and fresh and whatever else they're supposed to be.'

'Why don't you take a few days off?' she suggested. 'I'm going to Portugal on a yoga retreat tomorrow, with Karen? From the library? We're adding a studio onto the back of the clinic so I can teach once I've got my five hundred hours.'

The image of my mother administering lip filler while in Warrior III tickled me.

'I can't take any time off at the minute,' I said, forcing a little extra regret to my voice. 'We're so busy at work and we've been nominated for some awards, big ones, so I need to be around. I'm totally gutted though, I'm sure it would be fun.'

'You've really thrown yourself into work since you and Matthew separated,' she replied with a soft warning in her voice. 'But you must remember to look after yourself. We work to live, we don't live to work.'

'That's not it at all, I love my job,' I reminded her. 'And like I said, everything's fine.'

'That's your theme song,' Mum said before breaking into song. 'Everything's fine, everything's fine, my name is Annie and everything's fine.'

'Mum, you're breaking up,' I said, holding the phone at arm's length. 'I can't hear you.'

'Phone calls don't break up any more,' she shouted out of my tinny speakers. 'Annie?'

'Sorry, didn't get all that.' I held my finger over the end call button. 'I'll call you when I get home.' A grumpy, fat pug grimaced up at me from outside the newsagent's on the corner. 'I'm not going to call,' I confessed. 'I'm going to go to bed.'

The pug judged me silently.

They say home is where the heart is but I kept most of my other essential organs at the office. My flat was so small, you could walk from the front door to the back wall in five big steps and if I was being entirely honest, I wasn't the most house-proud of humans. Piles of ironing, piles of mail, piles of books, piles of absolutely anything that could be stacked on top of each other were dotted around the living room, creating an obstacle course of little leaning towers. Every ounce of energy I had went into my job. Home was supposed to be the place where I could switch off. Not literally, of course, that would be insane. I couldn't remember the last time I'd actually seen my phone with less than 43% battery.

Even though it was small, the flat was mine and I did love it. Little bathroom, little bedroom and a tiny open-plan living room and kitchen that might be a bit more inviting if I ever got around to buying a new settee. It turned out getting hold of an entire flat's worth of furniture after a break-up was expensive – who knew towels could cost so much? And so, instead of the beautiful mid-century modern West Elm sofa of my dreams, I made do with my sister's hand-me-down Ikea loveseat. It was too small for two people to sit down at the same time and painfully uncomfortable if you ever tried to lie down on it. Once upon a time, I think it had been white but now it was . . . well, white it definitely was not.

Carefully placing my laptop bag on top of the second-hand dresser I'd wedged in the space by the front door, I turned on the kettle before taking one giant leap from the kitchen into the bedroom and stripping off my clothes. More wine would not make me feel better. This was a night for tea. Besides, I told myself, I had nothing to feel bad about, other than the bag full of dry cleaning I'd been meaning to drop off for almost six months.

The front of my built-in wardrobe was mirrored from floor to ceiling, meaning at least once a day I had to give myself an all-over once-over. No matter how many body positivity videos I watched, I still preferred not to stare at my backside for too long. Objectively, I knew this was not a worst-case scenario situation; I liked my hair when it didn't frizz, I liked my legs and thanks to a thirty-day plank challenge, I felt strong in the middle, if not especially skinny. And who wanted to be skinny these days, anyway? Being able to see your ribs was so 2015.

'I'm happy for him,' I told Mirror Annie. 'Because I am a whole and complete person who only wishes joy for everyone in the universe.'

Mirror Annie frowned.

'Fuck it,' I muttered. 'I hope he trips down the stairs and breaks both his legs.'

Yep, that was better.

Sometimes I wondered what would happen if my flat ever made it on to *Through the Keyhole*. Who would live in a house like this? A smart, small newbuild on the outside, the hoarder-like tendencies of a Deliveroo addict on the inside. The many devices covering every available surface suggested it could be the kind of professional troll who thought Piers Morgan talked a lot of sense. The endless polystyrene cartons and pizza boxes suggested someone who didn't know how to turn on an oven. So far, so slightly worrying; very single middle-aged shut-in. But the lack of porn and huge stack of online shopping packages to be dropped off at the post office was a real curve ball. I'd lost count of the number of times I'd ordered something from ASOS only to realize, when it arrived twenty-four hours later, that I'd already ordered and returned the exact same thing a month earlier.

I plugged my phone into its charging dock, turned on the tiny TV in the bedroom and fired up my iPad, all while the kettle boiled. Time for one last circle around the socials to make sure everything was good and well with our clients. The influencers, the style vloggers, Fitspo and BoPo specialists, gamers and the mummy, travel and beauty bloggers, we worked with all of them. I'd learned more about different walks of life in this job than I could have ever come across in any other profession, whether it was how to apply perfect winged liner, where to stay on the island of Vanuatu or how to improve your vertical reach in *Street Fighter V*. Not all of my newly acquired knowledge had proved helpful yet, but who was to say when I might find myself invited to a formal video game competition in the middle of the Pacific Ocean?

As far as I could tell, all was right with the world of social media. Or at least, as all right as it ever would be, I was good at my job but I wasn't a miracle worker. I carefully avoided my own pages. Even with all the filters and blocks and mutes I'd put on Matthew's name, there was still too great a chance of seeing their happy, shining faces, and I didn't want to give myself nightmares. With a fresh mug of tea and the last three broken Hobnobs in the packet, I retreated to my bedroom. My safe, beautiful, man-free bedroom. It was wonderful, not having to explain my every move to someone the way I had when I was with Matthew. I loved not having to justify another late night at work or an after-hours cocktail. I loved eating biscuits for dinner, scheduling my own weekends and never finding softcore porn in my Netflix queue. I loved my life. Would it be nice to occasionally have someone to snuggle up to while I yelled at the TV during *Question Time*? Maybe. Would it be nice to have a second pair of hands to help bring the shopping back from the supermarket? Of course it would. And yes, perhaps an actual living, breathing man might beat creating a nest of pillows in the middle of the night once in a while, but I was very much of the opinion what was meant to be would be. My life was full and fun and I was happy. Something I couldn't always say when I was with Matthew.

Munching the last of my crumbly dinner, I turned off the TV and turned on my podcast app. *Behind the Scenes* had an interview with Mark Ruffalo. Maybe if I listened to it as I fell asleep, I could trick my brain into dreaming he was my boyfriend.

Because that was the behaviour of a perfectly happy, single thirty-one-year-old.

Wasn't it?

CHAPTER THREE

'It's shit, Annie,' Miranda growled, blinking into the bright morning sunshine. 'I feel like I just got told off by my dad for spending all my pocket money.'

We'd been to see the bank manager. It had not gone well.

'Can we just go back to the office and talk about it there?' I asked. Yesterday's beautiful weather had turned into a sweltering, sticky day and all the things I loved about London in the summertime had been washed away by the sea of sweaty bodies pressed against me on the Northern Line. 'I can't be angry and outside at the same time, Mir, it's making me feel stabby.'

There were many difficult factors in running a real business but far and away the hardest part was money. There was never enough. Every single month we had to find rent, we had to find wages and for some reason, clients kept expecting us to do things for them before they paid us. It made literally no sense. I didn't walk into Topshop, pick up a frock and flash the girl on the till a peace sign with a vague promise to get her the money within thirty days. Also, no one ever paid within thirty days. Ever.

Even though I was insanely proud of owning our own business there were other downsides too. I couldn't call in sick and take to my (non-existent) settee with a Terry's Chocolate Orange and watch an entire season of *RuPaul's Drag Race* when I was having a particularly bad day. Like today, for example.

Miranda and I started Content because we were out of other options. After spending the best part of ten years in miserable marketing and advertising jobs, me withering away at a giant agency, nursing a sense of integrity that just wasn't welcome, in a dark corner – literally a dark corner, I couldn't even see a window from where they'd shoved me – and Miranda bouncing between every company in London, we decided it was time to become masters of our own destiny. And so we pooled our meagre resources and decided to live the dream.

With hindsight, I did sometimes wonder if we mightn't have been better off just going to Disneyland for a fortnight then getting jobs at McDonalds when we came home but, you know what they say, you live and learn.

'I'm so pissed off,' Mir said, rolling up the sleeves of her oversized white shirt only for them to flap back down by her sides like an angry penguin. 'He talked to us like we were children.'

'He wasn't angry, he was just disappointed,' I agreed, wiping a film of city sweat from my forehead. 'But not nearly as disappointed as Brian's going to be when he finds out we can't pay him at the end of the month.'

'We'll work it out, we always do,' she muttered before automatically checking her phone. 'All we need is breathing room. Maybe we could get another company credit card? Or we could sell something.'

I looked at her while she angrily swiped at her screen.

'Like what? A kidney?'

'Not helping,' she replied.

'You're right,' I said, unable to stop myself from bending down and picking up the Starbucks cup and depositing it in the closest bin. 'We need our kidneys. We drink too much.'

'Didn't we start our company because we didn't want to spend the rest of our careers listening to sanctimonious old men telling us what to do?' Mir was still lost in rantland while I melted into an Annie-shaped puddle on the side of the road. 'I want to march back in there and show him just how badly I have overextended myself.'

'We don't give up and we don't give in,' I reminded her, blocking her path. I was fairly certain she wouldn't really walk into Barclay's and deck the business manager but there really was no telling with Miranda Johansson. 'That's our motto, isn't it?'

She frowned and shook her head.

'I thought it was "Yes, I will have another"?'

'We can't afford the first one, let alone another,' I said. 'Come on, let's go back.'

'Fine,' she sighed, opening up a rideshare app on her phone. 'We can work this out without the bank. I believe in us.'

'I believe I'd rather not be bankrupt by Christmas,' I told her, covering her screen with my hand. 'We should get the tube back.'

Mir threw her head back and howled out loud, attracting the attention of more than a few confused onlookers. 'But it's so hot,' she whined. 'And the station is miles away.'

'Mir.'

I hated it when she made me sound like my mother.

'Fine,' she said, grudgingly cancelling the car. 'I'll just sweat through my shirt and look like a skank all day.'

'That's my girl,' I replied, patting her on her sweaty back. 'One day we'll have drivers at our beck and call, hot and cold running drivers, ready to ferry us here, there and everywhere.'

'Hot, cold, moderate, I don't care,' Miranda said, rolling up her sleeves once more and putting her best foot forward. 'I just want to actually make some money for a change.'

It was always nice to have a dream.

'Morning.'

Just what I needed. I looked up from my important tea-making activities to see Martin and Charlie flanking either side of the office kitchen. Rather than reply, I offered a tight smile and kept my eyes on the kettle hoping it was politely rude enough to send them on their way. On the walk back to work, I'd made a deal with myself. If I managed to call in at least one invoice *and* made it through the entire day without brutally murdering the first person to mention Matthew's proposal, I was ordering Domino's for dinner.

'How are you feeling this morning?' Martin asked in a sympathetic tone of voice I assumed he usually reserved for his grandmother's best friend.

'Amazing,' I replied without looking at him. 'Thank you for asking.'

Keep your eyes on the prize, I told myself. There's pizza at stake, don't murder them.

If only they hadn't approached me in the kitchen with all its bright and shiny sharp things.

'Everyone's been talking about last night,' Martin said while Charlie hovered at his elbow, monitoring my expression. 'Must have been weird for you?'

'You don't really expect to turn on the game and see your ex getting engaged in 4K HD, do you?' I replied. Deep, calm breaths. Think of the garlic dipping sauce. 'Seems like more of a Facebook thing.'

'Seems like you're well out of it to me,' Charlie said, passing me the milk from the fridge. 'What a cock.'

They mean well, the voice in my brain whispered, *let them live and you can have garlic bread as well*.

'The only thing that's getting to me is having to talk about it, to be honest,' I said as I aggressively dunked my teabag. 'It's really not a big deal.'

'My mate Will just got dumped. I could set you up with him if you'd like?' Martin offered helpfully. 'I'll give him your number.'

They're only trying to help, do not disembowel them with a Nespresso pod.

'Recently dumped Will sounds lovely,' I said with as much grace as I could muster. 'But just because my ex got engaged, it doesn't mean I'm desperate for a boyfriend.'

The two of them exchanged a glance and I knew what they were thinking.

It was the same thing I was thinking, lying in bed, wide awake at three o'clock that morning and scrolling through Bumble, Tinder, Happn, Hinge, Huggle and god help me, even Farmers Only. As soon as you ended a relationship you were in a game of snakes and ladders with your ex, there was always someone keeping score and, right now, Matthew was winning. Any points I'd earned from technically doing the dumping had been wiped off the board by his proposing to his supposed soulmate twelve months after we called it quits.

'I'm dying of thirst, Higgins. Where's my tea?' Miranda strolled into the kitchen, having traded her oversized shirt for a cropped neon yellow T-shirt. She was the best, all faux leather trousers and fuck-you attitude. It was something I needed more of. The attitude, not the trousers. I got thrush from just looking at them.

'Martin offered to set me up with his friend,' I told her, handing over her My Little Pony mug. It didn't really go with the rest of her look but when it came to a cup of tea, Mir would have drunk it out of a lightly rinsed bedpan if it was the only option. 'Because I'm a sad and lonely spinster.'

'Are you joking?' she asked, looking astounded. 'Have you seen this woman? Annie's amazing. Any man alive would jump at the chance to go out with her. She's funny, she's clever, she's generous, she doesn't mess about and have you seen those getaway sticks? Annie, pull up your jeans, show them your legs.'

'Get off,' I muttered, slapping Miranda's hands away from my knees. 'Can I go back to my desk now please?'

'Obviously, Annie is amazing,' Charlie spoke extra loudly to make sure we knew he really meant it. 'And if it's all right for me to say so, you have got a cracking pair of legs there, Higgins.'

'It isn't,' I assured him. 'But thank you.'

'You're looking at the empress of social media,' Miranda was really on a roll. 'She's a kingmaker, best

28

in the world at what she does. The fact you even get to stand in the same room as this woman is mind-blowing to me. She's the Meryl Streep of socials. In fact, I'm fairly certain you should bow whenever you see her.'

'Yeah, yeah, she turns in a good tweet,' Martin said, looking at the door and clearly wondering how his morning had taken such a wrong turn. 'We're all very impressed.'

'What did you just say?' Miranda slammed her cup down on the table, hot tea spilling eveywhere. *She turns in a good tweet?*'

I winced as I sipped my tea. What an idiot.

Martin paused and looked at Charlie. Charlie shook his head. Martin did not take the hint.

'That's what you do, isn't it?' he replied. 'Twitter?'

'Do you even know what we do?' Miranda asked. 'Do either of you have any clue?'

Martin shook his head. Charlie apparently knew better than to react. Mir sighed sadly and gave me the look. I shrugged apologetically and leaned back against the counter to watch the show. This wasn't the first time we'd had to explain our actual jobs and I very much doubted it would be the last.

'OK, so, Charlie, say you're trying to think of a clever tagline to go on your thirty-second advert for a chicken cooking sauce?' Mir began, gesticulating wildly as she went. 'And you're dead excited because the advert is going on in the middle of *Coronation Street*.'

He nodded.

'You're wasting your time,' she said, clapping her hands right in front of his face. 'No one watches the adverts any more. They're all on their phone, inter-acting with content *we* created instead.'

'There are twenty million Instagram accounts in the UK,' I said, picking up where she left off. 'Our influencers alone have more than a hundred million followers between them. You couldn't even dream of getting close to that many people with an advert these days.'

'I know social media is important, but you don't really think what you do is more powerful than what I do?' Charlie said, his hackles somewhat raised. 'I'm sure you're very good at arsing about on the internet, but we all know real advertising, real marketing is still what matters most. Everyone knows social media is the paid-for opinions of kids.'

'*Arsing about on the internet*?' I repeated, almost sure he must be joking. 'Paid-for opinions of kids? Is that really what you think we do?'

Charlie picked up a pink wafer biscuit and bit into it while responding to me with a very, very brave shrug.

'Annie is a goddess,' Miranda hurled a tea towel in Charlie's general direction as Martin winced. 'She could take any old man or woman off the street and turn them into a superstar. Or any tiny brand or business. She can get a million eyes on you without even trying, you write bad jingles and rip off movies to make shitty adverts for crap cars.'

Ooh, that one had to hurt. Fired-up Miranda wasn't always very kind and throwing a hangover and a bad bank manager meeting into the mix, was just asking for trouble.

'We had the idea for the talking raccoon first and you know it!' Charlie said, turning beetroot red. 'The only people who get famous online are either rich, fit or related to someone else who is rich and fit. Bonus points if you're rich *and* fit and can afford to have lots of photos taken on sandy beaches while standing in a yoga pose so people can crank one out over your feed at bedtime.'

Miranda gagged as I wrinkled my nose.

'Good to know what we'll find when the police go through your search history,' I muttered. 'Tell me you clear it every single night, please.'

Charlie looked unimpressed, Martin looked as though he would like to be literally anywhere else on earth and Miranda was ready to draw blood. I couldn't quite work out how things had escalated so quickly.

'You can make anyone famous, can you?' Charlie asked, steely eyed.

'Yes,' I said with all the confidence in the world. 'We can.'

'Fine,' he said. 'Prove it. Make me famous.'

'I could,' I replied. 'But even the internet doesn't deserve that.'

'Yeah, yeah, whatever,' he answered with a not-so-friendly chuckle. 'You talk a good game, I'll give you that.'

I pressed my lips into a tight thin line and planted my hands on my hips, fighting the urge to knock him out of the window. Charlie leaned against the fridge, a cocky smile on his handsome face that was seemingly designed to get me worked up in all the wrong ways.

'Is it me,' Martin muttered, breaking the silence, 'or did things just get very tense in here?'

'Oh, Annie, ignore them,' Miranda said, tugging on my shirt sleeve. 'Come on, you're going to be late.'

'I'm not done with this,' I warned them as I abandoned my cup of tea. 'Just so you know.'

Charlie threw me a thumbs-up as we left and my

heart pounded in my chest. I couldn't work out if I felt more insulted, furiously angry, incredibly turned on, or all three.

Life could be so confusing.

'I know, I'm sorry, I'm late. I've had the most ridiculous day,' I said, barrelling through the door without knocking. It was already ten past one, I'd lost ten minutes of my time, we could manage without the usual pleasantries.

Rebecca held out her arms for my jacket as I threw myself on her chaise longue.

'We'll get it out of the way,' I said as I stretched out. 'You've heard about Matthew, obviously.'

She nodded.

'Of course I'm happy for him,' I said, lying back and focusing on the same crack in the ceiling as always. One day, I was going to have to bring some Polyfilla with me. 'For both of them. Not that I know Karine at all, but she seems nice enough and Matthew is a good person. An OK person.'

I glanced over at Rebecca, who looked back in her steady, measured way with her notebook in her lap.

'Matthew is a person,' I said.

She pulled the cap from her pen and scribbled something down.

'I'm not jealous,' I insisted, running the pendant of my necklace up and down its chain. 'Just because she's younger than me and littler than me and she's got the most perfect nose I've ever seen in my life. It doesn't mean anything, my life is going brilliantly. I own my own company, I have amazing friends, I'm up for three big awards and what's she? She's engaged. Bravo, Karine.'

I rubbed the bare third finger on my left hand, I

gave a very heavy sigh and counted all the framed certificates on the wall. Bachelor's degrees, master's degree, certificate of this, certificate of that. Everything you'd want to see on the wall of a therapist's office.

'Did I tell you we've been nominated for three awards? Three! I think it's a record for a new company. I'm definitely doing so much better than when I was with Matthew. Don't you think?'

Rebecca made a non-committal sound across the room.

'Well? You're the therapist.' I sat up so I could see the expression on her face. 'What do you think? In your professional opinion?'

'In my professional opinion,' Rebecca replied. 'I thought you were bringing me lunch.'

I blinked at my sister before pulling two Prêt a Manger sandwiches out of my handbag.

'They were out of hoisin duck, sorry,' I said, chucking one of them in her general direction and unwrapping my own cheese-and-pickle baguette. 'Got you this instead.'

'They were out of duck so you got *tuna*?' my big sister wrinkled her nose and abandoned the sandwich. 'I can't eat that, you dickhead. I've got patients all afternoon and no one wants to share their innermost thoughts and feelings with a woman who smells like Flipper.'

'Sorry,' I replied, trading her for my cheese and pickle. 'I know you like tuna, I just didn't think.'

'Colour me shocked.' She unwrapped the sandwich and took a big bite. 'How many times do I have to tell you I am *a* therapist, not *your* therapist. You can't treat your little sister, no matter how big a nutcase she's turning out to be.'

33

'But you're so good at giving advice,' I said, covering my mouth with my hand. A courtesy not extended by my elder sister, who I knew for a fact was not raised in a barn. 'You're trained in it. You're a professional advice-giver. Advise me, please.'

'That's a lovely way to describe an agonizing five-year psychology degree,' Rebecca muttered. 'But since you asked, my professional opinion would be a diagnosis of FOMO. Get over yourself immediately.'

I swallowed and shook my head slowly. Becks loved to remind me her degree was far more advanced than mine. Me and my piffling BA in Psychology and English. Her with her fabulous doctorate.

'Six years at uni and the best you can come up with is FOMO?' I said, grinning when she finally cracked a smile. 'Becks, you're not even trying.'

'I don't even have to,' she reminded me. 'You're not my patient.'

'No, but I am your little sister and you're stuck with me, so help.' I gave her my best attempt at eyelash fluttering as I finished my sandwich. 'Why do you think no one has ever delayed the start of a massive sporting event to propose to me?'

'Oh dear god.' She picked a fleck of mascara from her cheek and sighed.

As big sisters went, Rebecca was far from the worst. Too clever for her own good, obviously, but there wasn't much I could do about that. She was five when I was born and she did not take the news of a little sister well. Apparently, she'd expressly requested a guinea pig. Instead, I came along to ruin everything. According to her.

'I haven't had sex in so long, I no longer own nice underwear,' I said. 'Shaving my legs above the knee does not occur to me. If I was confronted with a penis, I wouldn't know what to do with it.'

'If you are confronted with a penis, you should call the police,' Rebecca advised. 'And for your information, I have sex and I don't shave my legs above the knee.'

I pulled a face and spared a thought for her poor husband.

'Annie, if you really wanted to be in a relationship, you'd be out looking for one,' she said. 'I have never known you to fail at anything you set your mind to. Which isn't necessarily a compliment, by the way.'

I looked at her, my puzzled cheeks full of tuna.

'How is it not?' I did not understand.

'Are you still coming on Saturday?' she asked, throwing me a paper napkin. 'I'll have wine on Saturday. This would be a much easier conversation if I had wine.'

'I don't know, I might have to work over the weekend,' I replied quickly. 'I've got an event with one of our vloggers next week and I've a feeling it's going to take a fair bit of time.'

'And an event with a vlogger is more important than dinner with your family?' Rebecca asked, head cocked to one side. Definitely something she learned in therapist school.

'Please don't make me lie,' I said. 'Because you know the answer I'm going to give is not the one you want to hear.'

'There's something wrong with you,' she replied. 'You know that, don't you?'

'Is that your professional opinion?' I enquired. 'Because if it is, it's a shit diagnosis. I'm going to kill you on Yelp. My work is important to me. This event is important to me.'

'Of course it is, but work shouldn't be more important than spending time with actual humans who love you.'

Sometimes I wondered if we were even related at all.

'It would be brilliant if you could be supportive right now,' I told her. 'I've literally just walked out of an argument with two idiots in the office making fun of what I do. Making the company a success is very important to me and you know that.'

'As it should be,' Becks said kindly. 'But you need to find a balance. We both know how competitive you can be.'

'Don't exaggerate,' I said with a theatrical sigh. 'I'm no more competitive than anyone else.'

'Annie. You were banned from the school sports day for trying to take out that other girl in the sack race.'

I chomped into my sandwich and grimaced. 'It was the three-legged race, and why do people keep bringing that up?'

'You get it from Dad, you know,' she said, nodding confidently. 'This is classic Higgins behaviour through and through.'

There were some buttons that only family knew exactly how to push.

'I ought to be getting back,' I said, fishing for my phone in my handbag. Thirty-two unread emails in the last half hour. 'I'll text you about dinner.'

'Have you heard from Mum this week? I need to give her a call.'

'I talked to her yesterday, she's gone on that yoga teacher-training course,' I reminded her. 'No phones allowed.'

'Your worst nightmare,' Becks smiled. 'Please try to

make dinner on Saturday. The girls would love to see you and you know Dad always brings amazing booze.'

'Dad also always brings Gina,' I replied. 'Which is why you need the booze.'

'You need to be nicer to her,' my sister said, shaking her head. 'I think he's sticking with this one.'

Only time would tell.

I stood up, stretched and looked out the window. Fantastic. It was raining. It had been blazing sunshine when I left the office, not a cloud in the sky. Now it looked like I'd be treating London to a solo wet T-shirt contest on the way back to work.

'There's an umbrella by the door,' Becks said, finishing her sandwich. 'Take it.'

'Thank you,' I kissed the top of her head, ignoring her protests. 'You're a good sister. Terrible therapist but a good sister.'

'That's because I'm not your therapist,' she insisted. 'And please don't tell anyone that I am. I don't want to be considered responsible for what goes on inside your brain.'

'Love you too,' I called as I left. 'I'll text you about dinner.'

'You'll see me Saturday,' she corrected as I closed the door. 'You knob.'

I knew she loved me really.

When I walked back into the building, Miranda, Martin and Charlie were sitting together in the coffee shop, finishing their respective lunches. I'd managed to convince myself, as I power-walked through the rain, to let go of our argument earlier on. They'd caught me at a bad moment. I was upset about Matthew, I was stressed about our financial situation, I wanted a pizza and I was ready and waiting for something to set me off. There was no point in letting a man's ego get in the way of a little light flirting, was there? Besides, if everyone who got annoyed with the opposite sex stopped getting it on, the human race would be extinct within two generations. I knew how good I was at my job and I knew how hard I worked. I didn't need Charlie bloody Wilder or Martin dickhead Green to tell me so.

'Oh look, it's the Meryl Streep of social media,' Charlie said, wiping his mouth with the back of his hand. 'Afternoon, Professor Higgins. Been out racking up the likes?'

And then everything went red.

I dropped my sopping wet umbrella on the ground, splashing everyone in a ten-foot radius, and slapped both my hands on the table. Martin and Charlie looked up at me with wide eyes while Miranda just cleared her throat as she swept droplets of rain off her leather trousers.

'Pick anyone in this room,' I declared. 'And I will make them Instagram famous in thirty days.'

CHAPTER FOUR

'Are you sure about this?' Miranda asked as Martin got up to drag an extra chair over to our table. 'You're already working yourself to the bone.'

'It's nothing,' I said with steely determination. 'I could do this in my sleep.'

'If you're sure,' she replied, pulling a pen out of her pocket and grabbing a fresh napkin from the dispenser on the table.

'We'll need measurables,' Miranda said, scribbling down some numbers. 'There are roughly twenty million Instagram accounts in the UK and the average user over the age of twenty has three hundred followers.'

'That doesn't sound like a lot,' Charlie said as he pulled up the app on his own phone. 'Even I've got over nine hundred.'

'And you own an advertising agency,' she replied shortly. 'You should be ashamed of yourself. Are you even verified?'

Shamefaced, he put his phone away.

'Then to win the bet, you need to what?' Martin asked. 'Get them a million followers?'

'That's not possible,' I replied. 'Unless you're going to knock up Beyoncé while starring in a new *Star Wars* movie, that is an impossible number. Generally speaking, twenty thousand followers makes you an influencer, meaning you can start making money off your feed. A hundred thousand, you can make a living from it, but that can't be done in thirty days.'

'Sounds like you're doubting yourself, Meryl,' Charlie clucked. 'Twenty thousand is nothing.'

'Says the man with fewer than one thousand,' I argued. 'All you're doing is proving you've got no idea what you're talking about.'

'Before we agree to anything,' Miranda interrupted, snapping her fingers in front of Charlie's face. 'Other than wiping the smiles off your smug faces, what's in this for us, exactly?'

There was a reason she was in charge of driving the business.

'In it for you?' Charlie looked completely nonplussed. 'I don't know. When you lose, you buy me a pizza?'

'Or, when we win, we get a month's free rent?' Miranda suggested. 'Since you're so certain we can't do it.'

'A month's rent and a pizza,' I added. I wasn't about to turn down food.

'Agreed,' Charlie said, holding out a hand to shake on the deal. 'And when you lose, I get pizza *and* you have to do a month of social media for Wilder.'

'Hang on a minute, I'm the bloody landlord here, what's in this for me?' Martin yelped. 'Who's going to pay their rent if they win? I didn't sign up to free rent.'

'Keep your knickers on,' Charlie said with confidence, never once taking his eyes off me. 'They won't. And you can have some of the pizza.'

I narrowed my eyes and glared back.

'I'm not sharing it with you though,' he said to me.

'Ten thousand followers in thirty days?' I replied. 'Easy.'

'Fifty,' he countered.

'Fifteen.'

Charlie stared me out for as long as his contact lenses would allow.

'Thirty.'

'Twenty,' I said. 'We'll get twenty thousand.'

'Annie,' Mir whispered. 'Are you sure you're sure?'

'Positive,' I replied, even though underneath the table, my legs were shaking.

'Done,' Charlie declared. 'And I know you'd never do anything so underhanded, but for clarity's sake: no bots, no promoted posts and no paid-for followers.'

'As if I would,' I agreed, blood thumping through my veins. Either I was very excited or I was having a stroke, I really couldn't tell.

'Now we get to pick the victim.' Martin clapped Charlie on the back and the pair of them turned their attention to the world outside our table. The Ginnel's coffee shop, cleverly named 'Coffee Shop', was packed. Everyone was hungover after last night's game and stuffing themselves with tepid sausage sandwiches and floppy bacon butties. None of them looked as though they'd be a special treat to work with.

'What about Jeremiah, my graphic designer?' Charlie suggested, pointing at a small, angular man who was lining up sugar cubes along the counter and arranging them by size. 'He's . . . interesting.'

'No one from your office,' I said. 'It has to be someone who is an actual tenant but no one who works for you. That's cheating.'

'Fine, no one from Wilder.' He sulked and looked back out over the unsuspecting contenders. 'Carl, the bloke on the ground floor who makes those weird cartoon things?'

'Oh, the gorgeous Welsh artist guy?' Miranda said, mooning at the dark-haired man in the corner. 'Amazing pick.'

'No, not him,' Martin insisted, a flash of jealousy in his eyes. 'Who else?'

'I haven't got all day for this,' Mir said with an agitated sigh. 'We're doing it with the next person who walks through the front door. Agreed?'

Everyone sat up a bit straighter. Miranda could be pretty intense when she wanted to be.

Charlie and I locked eyes for a moment, each daring the other to protest.

'Fine with me,' I said.

'Fine with me,' he echoed.

We all turned to stare at the door.

I reached for Miranda's hand underneath the table but instead I got Martin's thigh.

'Sorry,' I whispered, wiping my palm on my jeans.

'Never apologize,' he insisted as the door flew open.

All four of us sucked in our breath at the same time.

It was Dave the Postman.

'Oh, bloody hell,' I grumbled, breathing out. 'Get out the way, Dave.'

'I think Dave could have a fascinating YouTube channel,' Charlie reasoned. His brown eyes were laughing. 'The Life and Loves of a London Postie. I might watch that. I bet he gets up to all sorts.'

Just as I was about to reply, Dave held the door open to let someone in. A strangely tall, skinny someone with an enormous beard and long blond hair, wearing baggy jeans and a grey T-shirt with a faded blue Jansport rucksack on his back. He paused next to our table as he passed, old-fashioned flip-phone in one hand, thermos in the other, then pushed his wire-framed glasses up his nose and kept on walking.

I opened my mouth then shut it again.

'I don't think I've ever been this happy,' Charlie said, crossing his hands behind his head and leaning his chair back on two legs. 'Game on, ladies. May the best man win.'

The room at the end of the hallway on the first floor had been empty for as long as we had been at The Ginnel. It was a tiny, awkward sort of space with a glass front and only one small, square window to the outside slightly above head height. It was too little to be a meeting room and too dark to be an office and, so far, no one who had been to look around had been interested in setting up shop.

Until today.

The first things I noticed as I approached the working home of my newest client were the panels of white paper that had been sticky-taped to the glass wall, effectively closing out the rest of his co-workers and pretty much defeating the object of being in a co-working space in the first place. The second was the sign on the door. It was a nameplate that appeared to have been pilfered from a 1970s polytechnic. Everyone else had identical signs in the same, slightly retro serif font but Dr S. E. Page MPhil PhD had got ahead of the game and glued a narrow blackboard with block white lettering onto the door himself.

Charlie and Martin had been positively joyous when our subject selected himself but what could they know

43

from one look? There was no reason to think, just because he wasn't some kind of Adonis he wouldn't be interesting. For all they knew he could be an amazing photographer or he might have a dancing dog or any number of incredible, Instagram-worthy skills. He already had more letters after his name than anyone I'd ever met and my sister knew some truly insufferable academic types who seemed to have been put on this earth solely to rack up qualifications.

'There could be any number of reasons he's covered up the windows,' I told myself, tracing the edges of the white paper through the glass. 'This space would make a decent dark room. Or he could be super light-sensitive.'

Inside the office, I heard papers rustling. I knocked, stepped back and waited.

The rustling stopped but he made no attempt to answer the door.

'Or he's an actual serial killer,' I suggested to myself. 'Making himself a nice skin suit for the autumn.'

I knocked again. Louder.

Still nothing.

'Once more for luck,' I said under my breath, rapping as hard as I could for as long as I could.

My hand was still mid-air when the door opened. The tall, skinny man had tied back his long hair in a man bun. His beard was still enormous, and not in a cool, hipster way and though it was huge, it completely failed to disguise the annoyance on his face.

'Dr Page?' I enquired with a forced, friendly smile.

'Is something wrong?' he asked, looking me up and down.

'No,' I replied. 'At least, it wasn't the last time I checked.'

'Right, you can go away then?'

He phrased it as a question but it definitely felt more like an instruction.

'I'm sorry, I'm Annie,' I said quickly before he could close the door again. 'We're office neighbours. I work upstairs? I came to say hello, welcome you to the building.'

He pushed his smudged spectacles up his nose with a long, slender finger.

'Right,' he said. 'Hello.'

And then he slammed the door so hard, I felt it rattle my fillings.

'Bugger,' I whispered, the door a fraction of an inch from my nose.

There was the slightest of chances this was going to be more difficult than I had hoped.

'That was quick?' Miranda looked surprised to see me back in the office so soon. 'How'd it go?'

'He only answered the door after I cut up my knuckles knocking for half an hour, asked if anything was wrong and then told me to piss off,' I replied. 'So not great.'

'So, he isn't a natural conversationalist,' Mir shrugged. 'How did he look?'

'Think Tom Hanks in act two of *Castaway*, only without the social graces necessary to make friends with a volleyball,' I said, punching the call button for the lift. 'He's the least likeable human I've ever met – and I've met Jeremy Kyle, Katie Hopkins and the man who plays the Fox in the Foxy Bingo adverts.'

Miranda grimaced.

'We'll work it out,' she promised. 'Or we'll call it off. It doesn't matter, it's only a stupid bet.'

'Oh, absolutely not,' I replied. 'There's no way we're not winning this. I'm not giving them the satisfaction.'

'You know you could just shag Charlie and get this out of your system,' she said, holding her hands up in front of her to create a human shield. 'Not saying you have to; just putting it out there as an idea.'

'I don't know what you're talking about,' I said primly, tossing my long ponytail over my shoulder. 'Don't worry, Mir; one way or another, we're going to win this.'

I walked over to the huge whiteboard in the corner of the room and uncapped a bright blue marker. On one side of the board, I wrote the word 'followers' and added a big fat zero underneath. On the other, I put down the number thirty. Thirty days to make this man the internet's latest leading attraction. Taking a step back, I folded my arms and stared at the board as though it might have the answers I needed.

'This is going to be a piece of piss for you,' Miranda said. 'A month is practically forever. You've got this.'

'Yeah,' I replied. Now I had the numbers literally staring me in the face, I was suddenly not quite as sure as she was. Zero to twenty thousand with nothing to go on. Inside thirty days. 'I've got this.'

Hopefully, the more times I said it, the more likely I was to believe it.

CHAPTER FIVE

Thursday, 5 July: Twenty-Nine Days to Go.
0 followers

'Are you planning on sleeping here?' Brian asked. 'Because, if you are, I'll get you a sleeping bag.'

It was late, again. I looked up from my laptop to see him stood in front of my desk, messenger bag slung over his shoulder, clearly ready to leave.

'I want to stay and finish this, my brain isn't working today,' I said, pointing to a half-edited vlog on my computer screen.

'You are allowed to leave and finish it tomorrow,' he replied. 'It's almost nine.'

I blinked at the time on my watch. So it was. The day had completely got away from me. I'd had a break-fast meeting with one of our mummy bloggers who was writing a book about her first year as a single mother then I'd run straight over to meet Miranda at Apple to discuss a possible TV show they were inter-ested in developing with one of our podcasters. By the time I got back to the office, I had fifty-seven emails to read, three videos to edit and a whole host of Twitter and Instagram posts that had to be checked and scheduled to make sure they came out at just the right time. Running Content meant wearing so many different hats at once, I really could have used an extra head.

'There's just a few bits and pieces I want to get finished,' I assured him, yawning bigger than Bagpuss. 'I've got that event with Lily Lashgasm in a couple of days and I need everything to be perfect.'

Brian gagged at the mention of our least favourite client.

'The joy of being the boss, amirite?' he replied, rubbing the top of his closely shaved head. 'Just don't stay all night. I'll be in The Cross Keys with Rob if you want to join us for a pint.'

I did want to join them. Brian's boyfriend Rob had once been in the chorus for *Cats* and I had not spent a single night in his company that did not end in someone singing *Memory*. Admittedly, that someone was usually me and it was possible Rob didn't like me nearly as much I as I liked him, but still.

I held up my own hand in a Brownie Guide salute. 'If I get this done, I'll be there with bells on,' I promised. Brian gave me a wave as he closed the door behind him, leaving me all alone in the office.

Once I was sure he was gone, I closed up my laptop and sighed. While I did have a date with Lily in the diary, I also had another challenging situation demanding my attention . . . I leaned back in my chair and pressed my fingers into my temples, staring up at the accusatory whiteboard that stared back at me across the office.

One of the reasons my brain was broken was because I just couldn't seem to concentrate. In between every single one of my tasks, I had run downstairs and knocked on Dr Page's door. I must have done it at least ten times over the course of the day and I was sure he was there. The light was on inside and I was certain I'd heard more than one tut and sigh combo, but he refused to acknowledge me. It was going to be very difficult to make him a social media superstar if I couldn't even get him to give me the time of day. I literally knew nothing about him. I couldn't find anything solid online. There had to be a hundred different Dr S. Pages in the world and, even with my advanced slightly stalky cyber techniques, I could not seem to narrow them down.

But there was one way I knew would definitely work and now that I was alone, I couldn't ignore the idea that had been prodding me all afternoon.

Right at the back of my desk drawer was a small, simple, silver key. A few months ago, I'd locked myself out of our office and needed to come in on a Saturday afternoon. Miranda was away and Brian was incommunicado, so the weekend security guard had let me use the master key to get in. He also said I could hold on to it until Monday because he wanted to nick off early and watch the FA Cup Final. Bloody football, causing problems for people, as per usual. I didn't have a specific evil plan in mind when I ran out to Timpson's to get a copy of the key made, it just felt as though a master key for the building in which I spent 75 per cent of my time could be a useful thing to have.

And right now, as devious as it seemed, I needed a helping hand. Was it wrong to break into a very anti-social person's office and have a little poke around to see what you could see? Well, yes, of course it was, but desperate times called for desperate measures and a quick peep around Dr Page's office might give me some pointers on who he was and how we could work together. And, it had also occurred to me that he might only be using the office as storage space, which would mean he wasn't really a tenant at The Ginnel which would mean I could probably convince Martin and Charlie to let me trade him for someone else. Anyone else, really, I wasn't fussy at this point.

The first floor was already empty when I stepped out of the lift. The strip lighting in the hallway buzzed quietly but the darkened offices were silent. Even though there was absolutely no need for stealth, something about the deathly quiet building demanded it and I tiptoed along, ignoring my racing pulse and screeching conscience. Once outside the doctor's office, I stopped in front of his papered-over windows and pressed my ear against the plywood door.

Silence.

Sliding the key into the lock, I opened the door very, very, very slowly. He seemed just the sort to booby-trap his office with some *Home Alone*-style shenanigans and the last thing I needed was a night in A&E. Even though the sun was only just setting outside, down here on the first floor with only one tiny window that faced our infamous alley, I couldn't see a blind thing. As dark as his office had been in daylight, it was pitch-black now.

Until something moved.

'Fuck!' I shrieked, grabbing for something heavy from the desk and hurling it in the general direction of the noise.

'Ow!' a voice grunted as my missile struck its target.

I fumbled frantically against the wall until I felt a click and the overhead light sparked into life. In front of me stood Dr Page, naked apart from a pair of boxer shorts, holding a heavy hardback awkwardly in front of his crotch.

'Sorry!' I cried, clapping my hand over my eyes and turning around. 'I'm sorry, I'm leaving.'

Before he could reply, I turned quickly, bumping into his desk and then his bookshelf, like a human pinball machine. I reached out to make a grab for the door and the bright lights of the corridor, but before I could make my escape, I stepped on a stray piece of cardboard and felt my right foot go skidding along the carpet while the left one stayed firmly planted. I was certain I could catch myself as I swayed back and forth on the spot, but the yoga class I'd taken that one time had done nothing to improve my centre of balance. Grasping at absolutely nothing, my legs went out underneath me and before I could right myself, I fell flat on my back in the middle of the room.

'Christ almighty,' I heard Dr Page gasp. 'She's dead.'

'Not yet,' I choked out, winded. 'But give me a minute.'

I wasn't dead but I was in quite a lot of pain. My backside throbbed and, as hard as I tried, I didn't seem to be able to sit up under my own steam. I turned my head to watch as Dr Page's feet padded towards me and spotted a blow-up mattress and accompanying tartan blanket wedged in behind his desk.

'Do you know what day it is?' he asked as he knelt down beside me and slid a hand underneath my head. A shiver ran down my spine as his fingers caught in my hair. 'Can you taste pennies? Do you know who is prime minister?'

'It's Thursday,' I said, forcing myself on to my side and shuffling into an uncomfortable sitting position, shaking his hands away from my head. 'No, I can't

51

taste pennies and honestly, I'd rather not talk about politics.'

Dr Page stared into my eyes but all I could see was beard.

'I'm calling an ambulance,' he decided. 'Do not move.'

'I'm fine,' I told him, sitting fully upright with a gasp and not at all enjoying the shooting pain in the bottom of my bum. 'Winded and bruised but fine.'

'Your pupils look normal and you didn't crack anything open, but you could have a concussion.'

He stood up and took a noticeably big step back-wards as I heaved myself up to standing. I pressed a hand against my bum and winced.

'You should go to the hospital.'

'I think a bag of frozen peas taped to my arse will do it,' I mumbled, unsure where to look. He seemed to have forgotten he was wearing nothing but a pair of Bart Simpson boxer shorts and some very elaborate red-and-green striped socks that looked as though they'd been knitted by someone's blind nan. Until he saw me staring. 'Sorry to bother you, I'll be off.'

'How did you get in?' He fumbled for an enormous V-neck jumper and pulled it on quickly over what looked like a surprisingly buff pair of pecs, a deep crimson blush growing in his cheeks. 'I'm sure I locked the door.'

We both looked down at the floor at the same time. A shaft of light from the hallway shone through the door, lighting up my ill-gotten key like a diamond.

'I heard a noise and I had to come and investigate,' I replied, reaching down on unsteady legs to pick it up and tuck it away in the pocket of my jeans. 'Because I am the fire marshal.'

I was a quick thinker but a terrible liar.

'You're the fire marshal?'

'A responsibility I take very seriously,' I confirmed in a grave voice. 'I was afraid there was a fire. Or a burglar.'

He did not look convinced.

'And you decided the best course of action would be to assault me with my own book?'

'What if someone had been stealing all your . . .' I looked around his office. Wall-to-wall, floor-to-ceiling bookcases. Nothing but books. More books than you could shake a stick at. 'Well. What if someone had been breaking in?'

He looked around at his mini library as we both tried to work out what anyone might want to break in for.

'Imagine,' he said, attempting to yank his jumper down over his boxer-short region in a casual fashion.

'We haven't been properly introduced,' I said, holding out a hand. 'I'm Annie Higgins, I work upstairs.'

'As you mentioned yesterday,' he replied, looking down at my hand as though I'd just offered him a turd on a stick.

'I'm sorry,' I said, gingerly poking at my lower back. 'I didn't catch your first name?'

'Because I didn't tell you,' he replied brusquely. 'In the event of a fire, where are we supposed to meet?'

'Down the road and under the arches,' I replied, absently waving a hand towards the door. It was almost as if he didn't believe I was really the fire marshal. 'I work at Content on the second floor. Co-own it, actually.'

He continued to stare at me. Red jumper, Bart Simpson undies, nana socks and a man bun. It was like a Fashion Wheel gone very, very wrong.

'We're a digital marketing agency, work with social media influencers mostly,' I said, trying desperately to start a conversation. 'Pair them up with brands, help them develop their content, that sort of thing.'

Nothing.

'And what do you do?' I asked in an encouraging tone of voice I usually reserved for actual children.

'I'm writing a book,' he replied with great reluctance.

'Ooh, that's exciting!' I exclaimed. He was a writer! Maybe there was something we could do with that.

'About a politician.'

'Oh.'

'In the eighteenth century.'

'Christ.'

'He's a fascinating chap, actually.' For the first time, something sparkled in Dr Page's eyes as he scanned across the assorted books, filled with bookmarks, that covered his desk. 'George Nugent-Temple-Grenville, the first Marquess of Buckingham. He was foreign secretary for four days in 1783. It's a hell of a story.'

'Sounds like it,' I said, feigning as much enthusiasm as possible. 'And what brought you to The Ginnel? Was he from around here?'

'Grenville?' he pushed his fist into his lower back as he spoke and squinted up towards the splinter of street light that snuck in from the window. 'His father was prime minister, so he certainly spent some of his youth in London, but he was educated at Eton and then Oxford, of course.'

'Oh, of course,' I agreed readily. Who wasn't educated at Eton and Oxford? Apart from everyone I'd personally ever met. 'Then what brought you to this particular office?'

He pushed his glasses up his nose.

'The man who showed me round promised me it would be quiet,' he replied. 'And that I wouldn't be disturbed.'

'Oh really?' I replied innocently. 'My aunt wrote a book.' I picked up one of the hardbacks from his desk which he promptly pulled from my hands, only to put it right back where it came from. 'But she worked from home. It wasn't the same as yours, mind, more of a *Fifty Shades of Grey* type thing. Really wish she hadn't given me a copy for Christmas.'

'I can't write at home, the last time was a disaster, too many distractions. Plus I'm preparing a lecture on Grenville for a PhD research symposium at my old university and I needed more space,' he said, finally giving up and taking a seat behind his desk. In his pants. 'We only have one bedroom and my books take up too much room. My girlfriend doesn't like the clutter. Or me talking to myself all night.'

He had a girlfriend? Knock me down with a red stripy sock.

'Then this isn't your first book?' I asked, wondering what she made of the man bun–Simpsons undies combo. It really would be quite the specialized fetish. 'You're already a published author?'

Dr Page half nodded, half shook his head and, if I wasn't mistaken, he was blushing.

'I self-published,' he replied, pulling a heavy hard-back book with a beige jacket from the shelf behind him and holding it up so I could see the cover: *Lord Lieutenants of Ireland 1171–1922*. 'It hasn't exactly been a blockbuster bestseller.'

'I don't know, I think it looks fascinating,' I lied. 'My grandad was from Dublin, on my dad's side. I bet he would have loved this.'

'Probably not,' Dr Page replied. 'The role was usually seen as a stepping stone to a more prominent position in British government, or a sort of punishment. And the Irish mostly detested whoever was in power as the people appointed to the position tended to abuse their role to control parliament. In 1777, when Lord Buckinghamshire was lord lieutenant, he promoted five viscounts to earls, seven barons to viscounts and then created eighteen new barons, all in one day.'

'I used to love Viscounts,' I sighed. 'The little chocolate biscuits, not the members of the aristocracy.'

Dr Page slowly placed the book down on his desk and picked up his glasses, unfolding them carefully and sliding them onto his face.

'You still haven't told me your name,' I reminded him.

With a very heavy sigh, he turned back to face me, pushing his glasses up his nose.

'Samuel. Dr Samuel Page,' he said.

Samuel. Sam. Sammy Boy. Doctor Sam. Hmm. I'd need to work on that.

'Do you go by Sam or Samuel?' I asked. 'I'll add you on Facebook.'

'Samuel. And I don't use Facebook,' he said, pulling a face. 'I don't use any of that, it's too distracting. Who cares what some random person they went to secondary school with is eating for lunch? No one, not really.'

I heard myself actually gasp out loud.

'I hope you don't mind me asking . . .' I peered around him at the airbed on the floor. The blankets were all upset and, given his ensemble, I was almost certain he'd been sleeping when I walked in. 'But why is there a bed in here?'

'Because, ah, as a writer . . .' Samuel replied, eyes

shifting from side to side as he spoke. 'Sometimes, for me, as a writer, it's easier for me, as a writer, to think like this.'

I sucked in my bottom lip and nodded slowly.

'In your office?' I asked. 'In your pants?'

He nodded, clutching at the edge of his jumper.

'On an air mattress?'

Another nod.

'Right,' I said, folding my arms in front of me. 'I thought maybe you were working late and it was easier than going home.'

'That would have made a lot more sense, wouldn't it?' he said with a low moan. 'This is what she's talking about, I make things too difficult.'

'She?'

'My girlfriend,' Samuel clarified. 'Ex-girlfriend now, I suppose.'

'Oh,' I replied, sucking the air in through my teeth. 'Bugger.'

'Yes, quite,' he said.

'Do you want to talk about it?' I asked.

'Absolutely not,' he said.

I couldn't say I was entirely surprised. He folded his arms and stared at me.

'Can you go now please?' he said bluntly. 'There's no fire as you can see and no one is breaking in, other than you.'

'I should probably get off home,' I said, gently massaging the sore spot above my bottom. 'Let you go back to . . .'

I gave his blow-up bed a half-hearted wave.

'Thank you very much for popping in,' Samuel said, picking up seemingly random books and stacking them on his shelves, as though it was exactly what he'd been planning to do before a complete stranger let themselves into his office in the middle of the night when he was fast asleep on the floor. 'And please don't be offended if I don't answer the door next time you knock.'

'Well, you don't always hear people, do you?' I said, still struggling with the idea of a man with no online footprint. 'When you're concentrating or if you've got headphones in, you can be off in your own little world.'

'No, I just don't answer the door,' he said, still busying himself with his shelves. 'Wouldn't waste your time.'

'So you were here all afternoon when I was knocking?' I asked, for some reason, surprised.

He turned and gave me a look as though I was the odd one.

'What if the building really was burning down?' I asked. 'You still wouldn't answer?'

'Perhaps you could push a little note under the door,' he suggested.

'And what if you don't see it?' I asked. 'And you die and the newspapers are all, Ooh, if only the fire marshal had tried harder to get him out?'

'I shall make an addendum to my will,' Samuel replied, turning his back to me. 'Goodnight, Ms Higgins.'

'Goodnight, Dr Page,' I said, quietly picking up his book from the desk and letting myself out of the office. '*So* nice to meet you.'

He was possibly the rudest, most insufferable man I'd ever met.

And somehow, I had to find a way to make him famous.

CHAPTER SIX

Friday, 6 July: Twenty-Eight Days to Go

'I still can't believe you agreed to this.' Brian leaned back in his chair, pointing an accusatory pencil at Miranda. 'The two of you made a bet with the idiot twins and now we have to find a way to make this creature popular? We've already got more work than we know what to do with, are you planning on adding a couple of extra hours into the day or something?'

My gaze wandered over to the picture on the back of Dr Page's book. A small black-and-white photo of the man himself squinted out at me from the back cover, a constipated expression on his face.

'It'll be a good exercise for us,' Miranda said. She was the queen of putting a positive spin on things. 'We've never had to work with someone so . . . social media averse.'

'In that we've literally only ever worked with people who are prepared to cut off a leg to be successful,' I agreed. 'Where's the fun in that? This is a challenge, it'll be great.'

An instant message popped up in the corner of my laptop screen. It was a gif of a dancing Leprechaun holding a pot of luck from Charlie. A second message popped up underneath it: 'Thought you might need this'. I closed the app and turned my attention back to the meeting.

'Whoever he is, all his accounts must be set to private,' Brian said, scratching his armpit. Boys were gross. 'I couldn't find him on Facebook, Twitter or Instagram. Not even LinkedIn. I hope he's hiding something good.'

'He's not hiding,' I replied, turning Samuel's book over in my hands. 'He's not on there. Or rather he's not using his account. At all.'

'This is ridonkulous,' he protested. 'Even my nana has Facebook *and* Twitter and she's eighty-nine.'

'I know, I follow her,' I told him with a regretful grimace. 'And I want to believe she doesn't understand what she's posting, Brian.'

'Oh, no,' he said, sadly shaking his head. 'She does.'

'I suppose he's not the only human being in the world who hates the idea of posting his entire life online.' I pressed my palms against my face, careful to cup my hands away from my mascara. We'd only just started and I was already exhausted. 'You don't see David Attenborough on Snapchat very often, do you?'

'I've heard he's got a secret Instagram account dedicated to snacks that look like Jesus,' Brian said confidentially. 'But you'll never prove it.'

'I think the social aspect of this is going to be a bigger challenge than the media bit.' I ran my hands over the dull beige dust-jacket of Sam's book. 'He'd rather be with his books than posting on Instagram. Or brushing his hair. Or talking to humans. Or possibly anything else in the entire universe.'

'This is truly all we have to go on?' Mir asked, taking the big, heavy book from me and flipping through the pages. '"The official residence of the Lord Lieutenant was the Viceregal apartments in Dublin Castle where the Viceregal—" Oh my god, I'm so bored I just went blind.'

'Maybe it's a horcrux?' I suggested. 'It definitely feels evil.'

'That photo is evil,' Brian agreed. 'Who took it?'

'Someone who really hates him.' Mir squinted at the unfortunate portrait. 'It's the most unflattering picture I've ever seen. Brian's racist nan could have done a better one with her phone. Photo copyright Elaine Gibson?'

I tapped Elaine Gibson, photographer, into Google and came up with nothing.

'Let me try Facebook,' Brian said, swiping up on his iPad.

Immediately, FB produced seven results for Elaine Gibsons in London. Four were considerably older than our new neighbour and none of the remaining profile pictures really screamed photographer. One was a cartoon of a flying pink elephant and one was an actual baby. Which just left the slightly artsy, half-face photo of what looked like a thirty-ish woman but could just as easily have been the Turin shroud for all the filters she'd applied.

'Info is private but her photos aren't,' Brian said, clicking through. 'Schoolboy error.'

Two seconds later we were seven years deep in carefully framed selfies and Snapchat filters. There was no way this woman was a professional photographer.

'Open that one,' I said, pointing at an album labelled 'The Worst Christmas Ever'.

And there he was, tagged as Dr S. Page, frowning

with a too small Santa hat perched on the top of his seemingly giant head. And there he was again, sat around the dinner table, still not able to crack a smile. And again, sulking under the mistletoe. This time wearing what was supposed to be an ugly Christmas jumper but in Samuel's case it looked to be much more stylish than the rest of his clothes.

If only it were closer to Christmas. These were comedy gold and I'd have made him a meme in five seconds flat.

I tapped on the tag but it went to a private page with literally zero content. Eurgh.

'His girlfriend took his headshot,' Brian said. 'Red flag, red flag.'

'Even she can't make him look good and she loves him,' Mir said, pressing her fingertips into her temples. 'Annie, this is giving me stomach ache. What are we even going to do with him?'

'Fitness blogger?' I suggested, fully aware of the straws I was clutching at. 'Body positivity?'

'I'm positive I don't want anything to do with his body,' she replied. 'Geek appreciation? Like body positivity but for nerds.'

'Maybe he's a gamer?' I said. 'That would be great.'

'Yeah, if that game is pontoon with your grandma,' Mir said. 'We saw him walk past the other day with a flip-phone.'

'How about a travel blogger?' Bri ventured. 'Long-distance, far-away-from-here travel?'

'We're not losing this bet, so we'd better come up with something,' I told them, setting my shoulders. 'What makes Sam aspirational and relatable?'

'He's certainly winning the 'Don't Give a Fuck Olympics', so that's something,' Miranda replied.

'It's the rest of the historians out there I feel sorry for,' I said. 'They can't all look like this.'

'He really leaned into the stereotype,' Brian said, pressing his hands against his face as he stared at a photo of Samuel posing next to a Christmas tree while the family dog beside him licked its own bum. 'He's more like a historical artefact than a historian. All we need to do is take a half a dozen photos of him and tag them #ICantEven. It'll be a million hits overnight.'

Miranda's eyes lit up in agreement.

'We only use our powers for good, remember?' I replied, pinching the coin pendant on my favourite necklace tightly between my thumb and forefinger. 'Content always takes the high road and that doesn't sound very high.'

'You're high,' Brian said, screengrabbing the shots of Sam from his girlfriend's Facebook page. I wasn't sure how it was possible, but each photo looked worse than the last. 'Bet's off, right? There's nothing we can do with this man, Annie.'

But I couldn't call off the bet. That would mean admitting defeat. Yes, I liked the sound of a month's free rent, but I liked the idea of rubbing Charlie Wilder's nose in our victory forever more even better.

'There's always something we can do,' I argued. 'All right, so he probably isn't going to be everyone's must-watch YouTuber by Monday morning, but that doesn't mean there isn't an audience for what he does. And don't worry about the girlfriend, they've broken up.'

Brian let out a sad 'pfft'.

'Can't imagine why it didn't work out. Is the man bun on purpose?'

'I think not.' I searched for the right words to

describe Sam's aesthetic. 'He's definitely a fixie short of a full hipster.'

'What's his message?' Mir stuck out her tongue as she delved into *The Lord Lieutenants of Ireland* with renewed commitment. 'What does he want people to know?'

I flicked through my own Instagram feed and pondered the question. What did I want people to know about me? My Instagram feed was full of pictures of me, Mir and Brian, my favourite views and a few carefully framed flat lays displaying my prized possessions, colour-coordinated, of course. That was the version of me I put out there.

'We need to find out,' I told them. 'Everyone wants something and we can help him get it.'

'So how do we lure him into social media?' Brian asked. 'What does he want?'

A bed, a proper pair of pyjamas, a sense of humour and some social graces.

'I think he needs a friend,' I said.

'I would have said a haircut and a good meal,' Miranda sighed. 'But a friend might be a good start.'

'Shall we go and talk to him then?' I closed my laptop with a happy click. 'Maybe we could all go for dinner. Isn't it two for ten pounds at the King's Head on a Friday?'

Brian and Miranda both looked at me.

'We?' Brian replied. 'I don't think so.'

'From what you've told us, I think this is going to take a gentler touch,' Mir agreed. 'One at a time. Me and Bri would only overwhelm him.'

'Just so you know, I hate you both,' I grumbled as they gathered their things and retreated to their desks.

'We believe in you, Annie!' Miranda cheered while

simultaneously ripping into a packet of Quavers. 'You can do this.'

'Bet you she can't,' Brian whispered loudly, a puckish smile on his face. 'Twenty quid says he tells her to do one again.'

'You're on.' Mir mimed shaking hands across the office. 'Money's as good as mine.'

'Have you already forgotten how we got into this mess in the first place?' I groaned. 'It's like you've literally learned nothing.'

'If I win the twenty quid, I'll buy you dinner,' she called after me.

'Fine,' I said, rubbing my grumbling stomach. 'The bet stands.'

'That's my girl,' Mir said with a grin. 'Go get him, tiger.'

'Knock knock.'

Just as I'd hoped and fully expected, Dr Page was hard at work behind his desk, all traces of his campout vanished.

'Did you unlock the door again?' he asked.

'Hello, Sam,' I said, slipping the key back in my pocket and ignoring the question. 'I brought you something.'

'No one calls me Sam.' His hair was back up in its man bun but his beard was running free and wild. He wore jeans at least four sizes too big for him and if I ever found out where he was getting all those awful shirts, I would have them in The Hague on crimes against humanity faster than you could say 'Nehru collar'. Thankfully, I had no way of knowing whether or not he was still wearing the Bart Simpson boxers.

'I like Sam,' I said. 'It's a good name. Solid. Friendly. Who wouldn't like a Sam?'

'No one calls me Sam,' he said again. 'They call me Samuel or Dr Page. Or in your case, that man down the hallway who is considering a restraining order.'

'I was in the coffee shop, trying to justify buying pastries and I thought, I wonder if Sam fancies a croissant.' I took a seat before he could ask me to leave and placed a small, white cardboard box and huge, steaming cardboard coffee cup in front of him. 'I don't know if you've had a chance to try the almond croissants yet but they are amazing. Life-changing, in fact. You can't have one every day because you'll get diabetes and die, but oh my god, what a way to go.'

I pushed the box towards him but he didn't move.

'Go on,' I kept pushing it with the tip of my finger until it was butting right up against his keyboard. 'You know you want to.'

'I'm allergic to almonds,' he replied. 'Please take it away before it kills me.'

'Noted,' I said, grabbing the box back and nursing it on my knee. 'You probably don't want the almond milk latte either then.'

I reached for the coffee cup with an apologetic smile. Sam did not smile back. Sam looked really quite annoyed.

'I have a fire marshal question,' I said. 'How many books do you think you have in here?'

'Three hundred and seventeen,' he answered without hesitation. 'Why is that a fire marshal question?'

'Fire hazard,' I replied. 'All those books, no second exit. It's important for me to know all this stuff.'

'I've got some very rare texts in here,' he said, taking off his glasses and pinching the bridge of his nose. 'Very old, very fragile. I can't even touch them without gloves. If there's a fire risk, I need to know.'

'Should be fine.' I turned to take in the sheets of paper stuck to the glass. They had been taped up with such care. 'Is that what the paper is for? To keep the light off the books?'

'What?' Sam looked puzzled. 'Oh no. That's to keep people out. I didn't realize the building would be quite so . . . social.'

'Did anyone explain to you what a co-working space was before you signed up?' I asked. He shrugged, unaware or unconcerned, it didn't matter. 'Most people here are pretty chummy.'

'I'm not most people,' he said bluntly. 'Now, is there anything else I can help you with? I'm quite busy.'

'Just trying to be neighbourly, given your situation,' I slipped the pastry box back in my tote bag, not entirely upset about the idea of eating them all myself. 'Where's your blow-up bed gone?'

'I'd rather not talk about it,' he said, tapping on his keyboard and refusing to make eye contact. 'And I'm really very busy, so if you're done—'

'When I broke up with my ex, I didn't really deal with it that well at first,' I said before he could finish. Sometimes the best course of action was to just keep talking until they gave in. Not often but sometimes. 'It wasn't until a few days after it really hit that we were over. It's the little things, isn't it? No one to go to the pictures with, no one to laugh at your in-jokes. Whenever we drove anywhere, whoever was in the passenger seat would always put their hand on the person who was driving's thigh and I remember the first time I went out in the car after he left, I got halfway to Tesco and had to pull over because I was sobbing like a baby.'

I pulled my fingers through the ends of my ponytail, combing out a stray knot, wishing he would do the same.

'That sounds terrible and I'm very sorry,' he said robotically. 'And now you've unburdened yourself, do you think you might let me get on with my day?'

I should have known he wasn't going to make this easy.

'I truly think you'd feel better if you talk about it,' I told Sam, taking a sip of the coffee I'd brought for him. 'Whenever me or Miranda are going through a tough time, we always feel better after we've talked it through.'

'Two questions I will surely regret,' Sam replied, taking off his glasses and pinching the bridge of his nose. 'Who is Miranda and why should I talk to you about my personal life?'

'Miranda is my business partner,' I said with a patient smile. 'And my best friend. Since forever. Well, since we were eleven, which is a very long time these days. And you should talk to me because I'm here and I'm nice and because spending twenty-four hours a day in your office is unquestionably unhealthy behaviour. I don't want to have to be the person on the *Ten O'Clock News* six months from now, saying "We're all so surprised, he was always so quiet and polite . . ."'

'I shall try to make a point of scheduling my rampage on a day when you're out of the office,' Sam said, 'Thank you for your concern, but I don't think it qualifies you to act as my relationship counsellor.'

'My sister is a proper psychologist!' I exclaimed, making him jump. 'Totally qualified and everything, she's very good.'

'And my brother is a brain surgeon, but that doesn't mean you want me rootling around inside your skull, does it?'

'Is he really?' I asked with suspicious eyes.

'No,' Sam replied coolly. 'He isn't.'

'That would be good though, wouldn't it?' I said, taking another sip of too hot coffee. Should have got it iced. 'Very *Grey's Anatomy*.'

He pressed his hands hard against his head and let out a surprisingly shrill shriek for a grown man.

'You're not going to leave, are you?' He peered out at me from between his fingers, without moving his hands away from his face. I offered him a winning smile and a thumbs up. Sam threw his hands up in the air and took a deep breath and I could sense victory.

'Get your coat,' I ordered. 'Let's go and get a coffee that won't kill you.'

He picked up a red-and-black plaid donkey jacket.

'Actually, leave your coat,' I said. 'Let's just go.'

In the bright, unforgiving light of a summer's day, Sam looked downright sickly, his baggy clothes hanging off his tall frame, giving the impression of a consumptive tramp. Blinking into the sun behind his glasses, he followed me through the streets, muttering, huffing and generally making noises you might expect to hear from your grandad's odd neighbour.

'It can't be a lot of fun, sleeping in the office,' I said as we turned onto the sun-speckled street. 'Couldn't you stay with a friend? Family?'

I tilted my head upwards to bask in the blessed rays as Sam shirked away, immediately moving into the shade.

'I don't want to be a burden to anyone,' he replied. 'My brother is away at the moment. When he gets home next week, I'll go and stay with him.'

'You haven't got a key to your brother's house?'

Sam shook his head.

'Why not?'

'Because I haven't. My brother and I are very private

people,' he said. 'As you might have noticed. But probably haven't.'

'I still think it's weird,' I said, checking the back pocket of my jeans for my debit card. 'I've always had a key to my sister's house.'

'He moved last month and he hasn't had a spare key made yet,' Sam said. 'He's recently divorced.'

'Oh, well that's good!' I said brightly, before immediately correcting myself. 'I mean, oh, that's terrible, I'm sorry. I only meant you could help each other through these difficult times. Or something.'

'Yes, perhaps you could send him a murderous pastry when he gets back from Japan,' he replied, pausing on the edge of the pavement to look both ways before he crossed. 'We're both allergic to penicillin as well, in case you really wanted to do us in.'

I wasn't entirely sure where we were walking but this was Shoreditch, we'd run into a coffee shop sooner or later, it seemed as if every other building was churning out caffeinated beverages these days. Bike shop slash coffee shop, Pilates studio slash coffee shop, gynaecologist slash coffee shop. You couldn't move around these streets for coconut milk flat whites. But my plan had more to do with getting him out of his office and seeing if I could loosen him up a bit than it was to caffeinate the shit out of him.

'Tell me what happened with your girlfriend,' I said, attempting to drag the conversation back on track. We were still some distance away from matching BFF tattoos. 'Can I help at all?'

Sam closed his eyes and opened them again as though he half-expected me to have disappeared.

'I shouldn't think so,' he said. 'I'm really not

comfortable talking about these things with someone I don't even know.'

'Me?' I threw my arms out into the air, accidentally slapping a passing bike courier. 'Open book. My name is Annie, I'm thirty-one, I grew up in South-West London with my mum and my sister. Child of divorce, dad's remarried, not keen on the new wife. I'm a Libra, favourite colour is blue, trainers over heels but boots over trainers. Sweet over savoury except when it comes to cheese, slightly short-sighted in my left eye but I don't need glasses unless I get really tired and, yes, this is my natural hair colour.'

He gave me a hard look.

'Perhaps you can explain to me,' he said, 'how any of that helps the fire-marshal sister of a psychologist help me with my relationship predicament?'

Well, at least he'd bought the bit about me being a fire marshal.

'Firstly, I am a girl,' I said, gesturing towards the front of my general T-shirt area. Sam looked away in mock or real distaste, I wasn't sure. 'And sometimes it helps to get another girl's perspective. Secondly, I also have half a psychology degree of my very own and I am prepared to put it to good use on your behalf.'

'How does someone get half a degree?' Sam asked.

'Because you do half psychology and half English and then graduate realizing you're not qualified for anything,' I replied swiftly. 'Now, spill: what happened with you two crazy kids?'

He walked on for a moment, taking long strides that spurred me into a half-skip to try to catch up.

'She said I was boring,' he replied, without looking at me. 'She said we don't have anything in common any more and that I care more about my books than I care about her.'

The easiest thing to do would have been to tell him what he wanted to hear but in this instance, I wasn't sure it would help. He did seem awfully fond of a lot of dead white men and a man who cared more about the lord lieutenants of Ireland than getting the bone was indeed a conundrum.

'How long have you been together?' I asked, treading softly. Press, don't poke.

Sam pulled his dimmed features into an almost smile. 'Six years,' he said. 'Almost six. We met when I was starting my PhD, she was doing her masters.'

'She's a historian too?'

'No.' He looked almost disappointed. 'She got a job in the finance department at the university to help pay for her programme and ended up dropping the degree to do that instead.'

He untethered the man bun, unleashing long, wavy blond hair that any self-respecting mermaid would have been proud of. A thirty-something-year-old man, maybe not so much.

'Your hair is very long,' I said as a statement of fact.

'So is yours,' he countered, caressing his ratty ends. 'And no one complains about that. It's double standards.'

'Yes, but my hair is long on purpose,' I pointed out. 'And I spend actual money to have someone style it. Your hair is just . . . there.'

He snapped the elastic band from around his wrist and twisted the whole thing back up behind his head.

'Elaine hates it,' he replied, scratching his beard. 'She says I don't care about the way I look.'

I blew out my cheeks, searching for the most tactful way to ask my next question.

'Not to be rude,' I said. 'But do you?'

'I'm clean,' he replied, sitting up straight. 'My clothes are ironed, I don't smell. Just because I don't want to waste money on expensive clothes I don't need doesn't mean I don't take pride in my appearance.'

A plan began to come together in my brain as we walked on in silence. Maybe I was going to be a sad, old spinster with many odd pets, but that didn't mean everyone had to die alone.

'You're so quiet,' I said, dodging a tag team of charity volunteers in neon tabards waving clipboards in our direction. I was already supporting every single charity you could possibly think of thanks to my crippling middle class guilt. Couldn't afford a settee but two quid a month to help ex-circus elephants readjust to life in Africa? Where do I sign?

'Not everyone has to talk all the time,' Sam said. 'I'm thinking.'

'What about?'

'Do we have to be out here?' He wrapped his jacket tightly around him as I led the way across the street to the square. Even though I'd told him to leave it. Even though it was boiling hot outside. 'Because I'd really rather not be.'

'Why not? It's grass, it's trees, it's flowers,' I replied, adopting a cheery tone. 'And hating on Hoxton is very 2007. Can you just go with it for now? It's nice to be outside.'

'Not for me, it isn't,' he grumbled. 'My hay fever is killing me. Car exhausts don't help. Everyone smoking those ridiculous electronic cigarettes.'

He crossed his arms over his hideous jacket and sniffed. I watched a ridiculously attractive man I vaguely recognized from The Ginnel walking a Boston

Terrier through the gates of the square, and sighed. Why couldn't he have walked through the front door behind Dave the Postman? Cheekbones that you could slice bread on that one. And an Insta-friendly dog! There was no justice in this world.

'So how did you leave things with your girlfriend?' I asked, deliberately slowing my pace now we were inside the square and forcing him to follow suit. 'Elaine, isn't it?'

'She said she needed time to think about things,' he replied tersely. 'And that she would be able to think more clearly if I wasn't in the flat.'

'But you don't want to break up?'

He inclined his head once in agreement.

'Correct.'

'So why aren't you banging her door down with a bunch of flowers the size of China and begging her to take you back?'

'Firstly, because I still have a shred of self-respect,' Sam replied, picking a speck of lint from his shoulder. 'And secondly because she isn't home. She texted me this morning to say she's gone away with her friends, on a . . .' he paused, looked around and then cleared his throat. 'A bitch trip.'

The very idea of this man being involved with a woman who would go away on a bitch trip was blowing my mind.

'If she's away, why don't you go home?' I asked, settling myself down on my favourite bench. He shook his head stiffly and reluctantly took a seat beside me.

'One of her friends is flatsitting,' he replied. 'Besides, she asked me to leave, I can't let myself back in while she's in another country. It wouldn't be right.'

74

Some men were too honourable for their own good. Not many, but at least one.

'On your own blow-up bed be it,' I said. 'Do you know when she'll be back?'

He pulled out his phone, an actual Motorola Razr that I couldn't quite believe still worked, and scanned his texts.

'She'll be gone for at least two weeks,' he replied. 'And she says not to call because she won't answer.'

Classic.

'Which means she wants you to call,' I said, holding out my hand for his phone. Rather than pass it over, he looked at me oddly, snapped it shut and slipped it back into his coat pocket.

'That doesn't make any sense,' Sam said, untying and retying his abundant ponytail. 'Why would she tell me not to call if really what she wanted was the opposite?'

'Don't ask me, I don't make the rules,' I replied. 'But if she really didn't want to talk to you, she'd just block your number or end your call when you tried to ring. This is a test, Sam. And you're failing.'

'I think you're wrong,' he said. 'And can you stop calling me Sam?'

I looked at him, sitting there on the bench in his baggy jeans, worn-out polo shirt and hideous, hideous donkey jacket, such a supremely sad look on his face. I hadn't just been given an opportunity to win a bet. I'd been given an opportunity to perform an act of extreme kindness, to do something good for another person, for the whole planet. The universe had dropped Sam in my lap for a reason and that reason had to help him back onto the path of true love. And possibly to set fire to that bloody awful coat while I was at it.

'She's away for at least two weeks, that gives us lots

of time,' I said, running the pendant of my necklace back and forth as my brain ticked over. 'When was the last time you and Elaine went on holiday?'

'Four years ago,' he said. 'We spent a weekend in Dorset in her aunt's caravan. It was dreadful.'

'Have you ever taken her for brunch?'

'It's a made-up meal,' he replied. 'And I won't waste money on it.'

'And when was the last time you bought her flowers?'

'No flowers. I have hay fever.'

Anyone else would have given up then and there. Anyone else would have washed their hands of this ridiculous situation, marched straight back into Charlie Wilder's office and admitted defeat. But I could not. At least, not without a fight.

'Dr Samuel Page, today is your lucky day. I am going to help you,' I said. 'As of right now, you are enrolled in the Annie Higgins School of Better Boyfriends,' I announced with a flourish. 'Boyfriend Bootcamp, if you will. I'm going to teach you how to be the best bloody boyfriend on the face of the earth. By the time we're finished, Elaine will be back from her holiday and you will be the living embodiment of her perfect man.'

His face looked . . . Well, who knew what his face looked like under the beard, but his eyes were not nearly as grateful as I'd have hoped.

'How are you qualified to run a boyfriend bootcamp, exactly?' he asked. 'Do you have a boyfriend?'

'Moving on,' I replied with a slap on the knee. 'We'll go through all the basics. Listening, doing nice things without being asked, planning ahead for special occasions, making the bed, putting the toilet seat down, accepting that sometimes it's nice to have throw pillows on the bed for absolutely no reason and you don't have to make a massive fuss about it.'

'And what's in this for you?' Sam looked extremely dubious about my plan. 'Other than some sort of sadistic pleasure, clearly. You don't even know me.'

'What makes you think I'm not offering out of the goodness of my own heart?' I asked, pulling on my coin pendant.

'Of course,' he nodded. 'How silly of me. What a wonderful, generous person you are. Do they still have the Pride of Britain awards? Let's get you one of those. Or perhaps we go all out and nominate you for a knighthood.'

I had a feeling he was being sarcastic.

'I did always want a Blue Peter badge,' I replied. 'Any chance you know anyone at the BBC?'

Sam ignored me. 'What's the catch?'

I truly was a terrible liar so there wasn't any point trying to pretend.

'Do you know Martin? Who owns The Ginnel?'

He curled up his bottom lip to make a not especially impressed face and nodded.

'What about Charlie from the advertising agency upstairs?'

'Haven't come across him as far as I'm aware,' he replied. 'But who knows who else has been letting themselves in my office without my knowledge?'

'Well, Charlie and Martin were being rude about my job and my company and so, we made a bet that I couldn't make a random person famous on Instagram inside thirty days,' I explained, holding out my hand to shush him when his mouth flew open. 'Before you say no, I won't ask you to do anything you don't want to, your involvement will be super-minimal and we won't post anything without your approval.'

'Absolutely not,' he said, getting up with a face like thunder. I didn't need to get to know him better to understand how completely averse he was to this plan. 'I hate Facebook and I can't even claim to understand Twitter. Why would I even consider this, just to help someone I don't even know win a bet?'

'Good news, this isn't Facebook or Twitter,' I said with accompanying jazz hands. 'It's Instagram.'

From the look on his face, that was not an improvement on the other two platforms.

'And before you say no, I reckon we can sell at least a thousand copies of your book in the first month,' I added quickly. 'If not more.'

That caught his attention. He stopped pacing next to the bench and held onto the back to steady himself.

'But I've only sold forty-seven copies of it,' he said, sitting down again. 'And it's been out for two years.'

'Really?' I asked, perplexed. 'And you're still writing another one?'

He nodded, then rested his forearms on his knees, folding his limbs as though he were trying to pack himself away.

'I could come up with any number of inspirational quotes right now,' I told him, shuffling closer but still keeping a safe distance. 'But the best thing I can do is exactly what I do every single day: get you online and sell the shit out of your book. And I'll help you get your girlfriend back at the same time. Doesn't sound like too bad of a bargain, does it?'

Sam considered the deal while I watched the handsome man from the office pretend not to see his dog taking a dump. Fine, they were all as bad as each other.

'How exactly was I selected for this bet?' he asked.

I smiled and pinched my shoulders together. 'You walked through the door at the right time.'

'Or the wrong time,' he said, rubbing his palms along his long legs. 'Fine. What would I have to do? To help you?'

'Practically nothing,' I replied, although the truth was I had yet to work that part out. 'Couple of photos maybe, nothing too sexy, no dick-pics.'

His eyes snapped open behind his glasses. I saw for the first time, they were a beautiful shade of almost cornflower blue. He looked lovely when he was terrified.

'I'm joking. Obviously.'

It was possible I'd gone too far too fast. It was also possible he had no sense of humour.

'I take what I do very seriously. I have to give lectures, I have to collaborate with other academics. I don't want to be turned into a joke and plastered all over the internet,' he said, breathing out heavily. 'The logic of social media is something that escapes me entirely.'

'You absolutely, one hundred per cent will not be a joke of any kind,' I told him, adding a conditional 'probably' in my head. 'We don't even have to put you in the pictures if you don't want to be.'

'I wouldn't have to be in any of the pictures?' he asked, interest piqued.

An unforeseen wrinkle but hardly a dealbreaker. There were lots of successful accounts that didn't show their creators.

'You won't have to be in any of the pictures,' I promised. 'I can work around that.'

'And if I agree to this, you won't be letting yourself into my office morning, noon and night, demanding I do this, that and the other? I do still have a book to write.'

'All right, Dad.' I hid my smile at his negotiation

tactics. 'But I am going to need some time and effort from you. Otherwise boyfriend bootcamp is going to be a bust, isn't it?'

He fell silent for what felt like hours. Point number one in his training programme was going to be easy. When someone says something to you, they usually want you to say something back in a timely fashion. It was called a conversation.

'This all feels like a terrible mistake,' he said finally as my phone vibrated. It was a text from Miranda, she needed me back at the office. 'Maybe Elaine was right. Maybe I should crawl back into my hole and stay there.'

I sucked the sticky summer air in through my teeth, suddenly wondering which part of this deal was going to be the most difficult.

'Crawling back into your hole is rarely the best solution to a problem,' I said. 'Trust me, I've done it loads. You can do better, Sam. Now, who wants to sell some books and get their girlfriend back?'

I thrust my arm high into the air.

'Hmm,' he said, standing up and shoving his hands deep into his baggy pockets. 'We'll see. I'm trying to get through my footnotes for the last chapter before the end of the week and they're hardly going to write themselves.'

'Sam?' I lowered my arm slowly to my side as he walked away. 'Don't leave a girl hanging. Do we have a deal?'

'I need to think about it,' he said, glancing back and then turning around and setting off without me. 'I'll give you my answer on Monday.'

I sank back onto the bench and watched him walk hurriedly out of the square onto the street, rapid-fire sneezes soundtracking him on his way.

CHAPTER SEVEN

Saturday, 7 July: Twenty-Seven Days to Go

East London was a strange place. When Rebecca and I were younger, it felt so dangerous to venture out past Old Street. When she was a student and I was still in secondary school, this was where we'd come to do things we couldn't tell our mum about. Gigs at the Macbeth, dancing at 93 Feet East, never-ending dumplings at the Drunken Monkey. But now the area was just a giant bundle of contradiction. Old and new, shitty and expensive. You want a bit of genuine exposed brick with your macchiato? That'll be five pounds, please, and yes we can do a babyccino, will that be with cow, goat, almond or oat milk? Where me and Becks had run full throttle down the dark streets just in time to catch the night bus, mums and babies strolled happily with their three-wheeler pushchairs on their way back from the gym. I could hardly remember a time when Shoreditch felt dangerous.

But West London . . . now there was a case for concern. I clambered up the steps at St Margaret's station, turning my head to avoid making eye contact with the Tesco Express in the corner. Too much temptation to fill my pockets with Haribo like I would on my way home from school. In East London, people were at pains to tell you everything about themselves from the very first time you laid eyes on them. Here, everything was camouflaged with matching sofas from Heals, Le Creuset cookware and the very finest ensembles Boden had to offer. I didn't even know where my top was from. I'd borrowed it from Miranda which meant it could be anything from haute couture or handmade. Hopefully no one would ask.

When we were kids, Becks was the rebel. She was the one who bleached her hair, the one who stayed out all night, got caught shoplifting, stole a full bottle of Malibu from the drinks cabinet, and yet here we were, twenty years later and she was living in a lovely three-bedroom semi, two roads over from where we grew up. Complete with a perfectly trimmed privet hedge, glossy red front door and a battered Cozy Coupe parked outside. She was living the suburban dream, just like the house next door and the house next door and the house next door and the house next door. And she claimed I was the one who had never dealt with our parents' divorce.

'Annie!'

Alan, Rebecca's perfect husband, opened the front door before I could knock and pulled me inside the dark hallway with a slightly manic look on his face.

'The baby is sleeping,' he whispered loudly, pushing me through the tastefully decorated house. 'Rebecca is in the back garden with your dad and Gina.'

I was twenty minutes early and I was still late. Brilliant.

'There she is,' my dad called from behind his giant Ray-Bans as I blinked, blinded, back out into the sunshine. 'What time do you call this?'

'Twenty to one,' I replied, leaning down for a half-hug and kiss on the cheek before smiling politely at my latest stepmother. She did not get the kiss or the half-hug. It had only been two years, I liked to wait until he'd made it past three years of marriage before I committed. I'd learned my lesson. 'Aren't I early?'

'Dinner was supposed to be at one,' Rebecca called from the outdoor dining table she'd set up at the end of the garden. 'I thought you'd be here earlier.'

My carefully set little sister smile did not budge.

'I brought wine.' I held up two bottles, one white, one red, both of which I'd nicked from the office. 'Shall I put it in the kitchen?'

Becks frowned, tucking her curly hair behind her ears. A morning slaving over the stove had left it frizzy, but this didn't seem like an opportune moment to mention the bottle of fancy hair serum I'd left in her bathroom last month.

Before anyone else could make me regret my decision to get up and drag myself across London on a Saturday morning, Alice, my wonderful niece and one of the top five people in the world, stuck her head out of her Wendy house and hit me with a massive, toothless grin.

'Auntie Annie!' she squealed, barrelling across the garden and spearing me into the grass. 'Mummy said you weren't coming.'

'I said you might not come,' Becks corrected on her way back into the kitchen. 'Not that you definitely weren't coming.'

'We were almost late ourselves,' Gina said, all confessional and apologetic when there was no need. 'There was a nasty accident on the A3. Sat there for half an hour, didn't we, Mal?'

My dad nodded his agreement from his fancy wooden lawn chair. My sister's garden furniture was nicer than anything I had in my actual living room, I realised with shame.

'At least we're all here now,' I replied, forcing my smile out wider from my prone position on the grass.

I'd promised Becks I'd try harder with Gina but, really, she didn't make it easy. You'd never seen a woman so basted with fake tan. You might think you had but it wasn't possible. In fact, I wasn't even sure there was any fake tan left in the world because Gina appeared to be wearing all of it.

'Is the baby still asleep?' she asked, dropping her voice an octave and over-enunciating each word, the way people do when they're talking about babies. 'I'm desperate to see him. We haven't been over since before Kefalonia, have we, Mal?'

My dad shook his head.

Worryingly, next to my dad, Gina looked quite pale only his tan wasn't fake. It had been a long time since I'd touched his face but I had to assume it had transcended skin and become hide some time ago.

'He's asleep,' Alice replied, still lying on top of me. 'He's always asleep. I'm not allowed to sleep as much as him, ever.'

'That's because you're a big girl,' Gina said, shifting registers to her high-pitched, little-girl voice. Incidentally, the same one she used with me. 'And Basil is still a baby.'

Basil. Thirteen months ago, my sister had given

birth and seen fit to name her baby Basil. Yes, I knew it was Alan's favourite grandad's name, but I had to assume if there was a heaven, somewhere above us, there was a kindly old man throwing his hands up in despair at the fact my nephew's life had already been ruined before he could even string together a sentence. Basil the Baby.

'Have you told Dad about the TechBubble awards?' Becks asked, hurrying back from the kitchen with a bowl full of freshly sliced baguettes. 'Annie's been nominated for an award.'

'Three awards,' I said quickly, sitting up as Alice scampered off down the garden. 'Best new agency, best boutique agency and best campaign. It's kind of a big deal to be nominated for best boutique agency the same year you're nominated for best new agency.'

'All I hear about these days is start-ups going under,' he said without removing his sunglasses. 'Would have been a better idea to stay at that big place you were at. Work your way up, think about your pension, get early retirement. That's what I did, and look at me.'

You couldn't not look at him really. He was positively radioactive. He was the most tanned man I had ever seen. In fact, was George Hamilton still alive? It was possible my dad was now the most tanned man on earth.

'But then I wouldn't have been nominated for three awards, would I?' I asked while googling the health and well-being of George Hamilton.

'When will you find out if you've won?' he asked.

'Start of next month,' I replied, brushing blades of grass off the arse of my jeans as I stood. 'The awards are on the second.'

'Shame you won't know earlier.' Dad pushed his

85

sunglasses onto the top of his polished mahogany head. 'I could have included it in the club newsletter.'

'Surely the tennis club newsletter should be about news from the tennis club,' I said. Gina took Dad's glasses, pulled a case out of her handbag, cleaned them with a little cloth and them popped them away. 'You could mention the nominations, if you liked?'

'But what if you don't win?' he asked.

'But what if we do?' I replied.

'But what if you don't?' he said again. 'And then I'm out with your Uncle Norman and he says, how did Annie do in those awards? And I have to say, she didn't actually win any of them, Norman, and then we're all going to feel foolish, aren't we?'

I pursed my lips and ran my tongue over my teeth. In for out, out for six.

'I love your top, Annie,' Gina said. 'Where's it from?'

Dinner was a blissfully swift affair. Lasagne, Dad's favourite; trifle, Alan's favourite; and wine, my favourite.

'Doing anything exciting tonight?' Rebecca asked, absently stroking Alice's hair as her daughter scraped a spoon against the bottom of her bowl. 'Seeing Mir?'

'She's got a date,' I replied. If that was what you could call her plan to 'maybe kind of probably get a drink with Martin if he's around or whatever'. Date was quicker. 'I have a load of work to catch up, I'll probably just do that.' The vague thought of Sam's unInstagrammed life gave me a small lurch in my stomach.

'No date for you?' Alan bounced Baby Basil on his knee, without even the decency to make eye contact while opening Pandora's box.

'Annie's too busy for boys,' Dad said, laughing as though he had just made the funniest joke in the world. 'Aren't you, darling?'

'Just busy in general.' I stared longingly at the sweaty bottle of white, still half full in the middle of the table, and briefly wondering what Charlie might be up to. 'You know me.'

'What about Matthew and that bloody stunt at the World Cup,' he said, looking across the table to Alan for support. 'Can't believe you let that one get away. Me and Alan could have been at the quarter finals right now if you'd played your cards right there.'

'I feel just terrible about the whole thing,' I replied, reaching for the wine bottle. 'Apologies, Dad.'

'Alice, have you shown Auntie Annie your new tree house?' Rebecca asked, taking the bottle out of my hand before I could fill my glass to the brim. 'I'm sure she'd like to see it.'

Alice stood and obediently held out her hand.

'It's at the bottom of the garden,' she informed me while her mother changed the subject. 'Up a tree.'

'Controversial,' I replied, throwing my sister a grateful glance as we skipped off down the garden.

'They make me go away when they want to talk about me,' Alice explained as I heaved myself up the steps and into her really rather nice tree house. Two chairs, an iPad and some lovely Cath Kidston curtains. If she could find her way to adding a mini fridge and corkscrew, I'd have been tempted to move in.

'I think they're probably too busy talking about me,' I told her, holding out my hand to accept a tiny plastic teacup that she filled with non-existent tea. 'Don't worry about it.'

Alice considered this and decided it was probably right as she poured herself a drink and made herself comfy on the second wooden chair.

'Now we can have a proper chinwag,' she said, a conspiratorial wink in her eye. 'Did Mummy tell you I put Persil in the fish tank?'

'No,' I replied, not sure what to be more afraid of, her use of 'chinwag' or the fact that I was alone in a tree house with a tiny sociopath. 'Why would you do that?'

She shrugged and sipped her fake tea.

'I was trying to clean it,' she said, as though it were obvious. 'But it didn't work and then we had to get new fish.'

Clever Alice, skipping over the part where they all died.

'Why haven't you got a husband?' she asked, opening an empty Quality Street tin and offering me an imaginary biscuit.

'Not everyone has a husband,' I said, taking care to select the right one. She'd tell me off if I took the imaginary Orange Club. 'Granny hasn't got a husband.'

'That's because Granny is too old,' she assured me. 'Daddy said so. And she used to be married to Grandad Mal, didn't you know?'

As my mum liked to say, Alice was six going on sixteen. I couldn't remember being quite so precocious when I was her age but, to be fair, the only thing I really remembered about being six was wetting myself on the way home from Alton Towers and my parents' divorce. Hardly a banner year for me.

'I did know that,' I replied, following her lead and nibbling on my fantasy biscuit. 'I don't have a husband because I haven't found anyone I want to marry yet.'

'That makes sense,' she said. 'I'm going to marry Kofi from my gymnastics class. He can do four somersaults in a row.'

I'd definitely dated people for less.

'I'll find someone when I'm ready,' I said, watching my niece cross and uncross her legs until she felt she'd found a suitably grown-up position. It would have been more effective if her dress hadn't ridden up in the process, revealing her pants to the whole world. 'There's no rush.'

'Daddy says you're getting old too,' she replied. 'And that you'd better get a move on because you're not getting any younger.'

'Did he now.' I pulled back the curtains and shot Alan a death stare across the garden. 'And what else did your daddy have to say?'

'He said everything started to go downhill for Mummy after thirty-five and that you ought to try to get a ring on it well before then.'

Note to self. Literally never open your mouth in front of a child over the age of one.

'Well, I know this is probably going to be a strange thing to say, but your daddy doesn't know everything,' I said. 'Especially about girls.'

'Oh no, I know,' Alice assured me. 'Mummy tells him that all the time.'

'Good,' I said, sipping my tea. 'Mummy is really very clever.'

'I know,' she replied happily. 'She tells me that too.'

She went back to her play kitchen for a moment, faffing around with pots and pans, making all the prerequisite not-quite-swears she'd heard from her own parents as she prepared our second course.

'I've done some sandwiches,' she announced,

turning around with a plate full of Matchbox cars. 'But you're not to have too many in case it makes you fat.'

'You shouldn't be worrying about things like that,' I said, the blood draining from my face at the thought of someone destroying my six-year-old niece's body image with one wrong word. 'Fat isn't a bad thing, you know. Some people are fat and some people aren't.'

'Yes, but you don't have a husband,' Alice repeated, in case I wasn't already aware. 'And getting fat certainly won't make finding one any easier.'

'Thank god your mother is a therapist,' I muttered, accepting a single red Hot Rod from the platter. 'You're definitely going to need it.'

Dad and Gina had to leave earlier than Rebecca had hoped. Lesley from badminton was having her retirement do at the club and they absolutely had to show their face, Dad explained, otherwise they might be a no-show at the end-of-summer party and she'd done the catering on exact numbers.

It took me longer to make my escape and before I knew it, I'd sat through bathtime, bedtime and bedtime story time. Alan was already flicking through Netflix by the time I started faking yawns.

'Stay,' Rebecca insisted. 'I'll make up the spare bed.'

'Yes,' Alan echoed with zero enthusiasm. 'Stay.'

'I'd love to but I can't,' I said, picking up my handbag, tote bag and refillable water bottle. The holy triumvirate of Modern Women's Things. 'I've got a really early yoga class in the morning and it'll be a nightmare to get across town at that time on a Sunday.'

'Oh, good for you,' Becks said, bundling me into a hug and a borrowed cardigan. It had turned cold after the sun had set. 'Do you need Alan to run you to the station?'

'I'll get the bus,' I said, much to Alan's relief. 'Or maybe I'll walk, burn off that trifle. Wouldn't want me getting fat, would we?'

He didn't even look away from the TV.

'I can't do lunch this week,' my sister said, buttoning up the cardi for me. 'But we'll see you at Dad's party next week.'

Of course. Dad's surprise sixtieth birthday party. So that was why Mum had nicked off to Portugal and gone completely incommunicado. We'd had quite the performance over his fiftieth birthday celebrations. She'd shown up at my halls of residence and refused to leave for a week. She spent most of it half-cut on Taboo and lemonades and in all honesty, I didn't even know they made Taboo anymore but it was amazing what a woman could find in a provincial off-licence if she was truly committed.

'Don't give me that look,' Becks warned. 'You're coming, end of.'

'Wouldn't miss it for the world,' I promised, patting myself down for my Oyster card and earphones. 'Talk to you later.'

'Text me when you're in,' Becks called as I headed out for the bus stop. 'And don't you dare think about missing that party.'

As if I would do such a thing.

CHAPTER EIGHT

Monday, 9 July: Twenty-Five Days to Go

'Are you ready?'

I popped out an earbud to see Miranda standing in the doorway. I'd been so busy editing an unboxing video, I hadn't even noticed her leave the room.

'Ready for what?' I asked.

'The ritual sacrifices are here,' she said. 'Waiting in the meeting room.'

'Then I'm ready,' I replied, grabbing my phone and following her down the hallway. I thought about leaving a note on my door to let Sam know where to find me but decided playing it cool was probably the safer option, I didn't want to scare him off with any more blatant enthusiasm.

Miranda had come up with a solution to our work-flow problem. Even though we had more clients than we knew what to do with, we were still owed so much money, we could barely afford to pay the staff we had – namely Brian – and so we had turned to the only option available to us. The most feared staffing solution this side of dragging people in off the streets. We were going to hire an intern.

'Are you sure about this?' I asked as we trotted down the staircase. 'We can barely manage ourselves.'

'What could possibly go wrong?' Miranda said, practically begging me to push her down the stairs. 'I remember doing work experience, it was brilliant. It's not like we're asking them to run entire campaigns for us, we just need someone who will make the tea, open the post and tell us how great we are. It's like a dream come true for these kids.'

'A dream where we pay them next to nothing,' I replied.

Mir paused on the stairs for dramatic effect. Mir did a lot of things for dramatic effect.

'We're paying them in opportunities,' she explained, sweeping her arm along the horizon. 'They will be rich in experience.'

I looked back, stony faced.

'And travel and living expenses and all the beauty products and computer games their little hands can carry,' she shrugged, opening the door to the ground-floor hallway. 'Lots of people don't pay anything, at least we're making sure they're not being taken advantage of. They're just kids, Annie. Enthusiastic kids who are dying to help. Nothing for you to be afraid of.'

Mir threw open the meeting room door and four cool, calm and confident human beings in much cooler outfits than I was able to put together at twenty (or now), turned to stare at us. Not a single one of them looked even so much as slightly nervous but they were young; true Monday Dread had yet to set in for any of them.

'What's the most important thing in the entire world?' Miranda asked, pacing up and down at the front of the room. 'If you had to pick one thing, what would it be?'

Very little time for pleasantries, had Miranda. I sat down on a chair at the top of the table. All three girls and the one boy sat forward at the same time like pre-programmed meerkats.

'Family,' suggested a twenty-nothing girl in a pair of inordinately large glasses.

'Nope,' Miranda replied.

'Friends,' a girl in what looked like her dead gran-dad's best suit asserted with undeserved confidence.

'Yes but no,' Miranda replied even more quickly.

'My dog?'

Silence.

'Is it love?' asked the bravest girl in the world. She looked to be about twelve and had such a hopeful expression on her face and all I wanted to do was give her a cuddle and then lock her in a cupboard so she would never know the dark truth about the cold harsh world outside these four walls.

'I meant a thing,' Miranda clarified before pointing at the only male in the room. 'You. A physical thing, what's the most important physical thing you own?'

'Me?' The floppy-haired boy dressed head to toe in black reared backwards as her gaze pinned him to his chair. 'Um, my grandad left me his watch, so I suppose, probably, if I had to choose one thing, maybe . . .'

'I'm talking about your phone!' Miranda didn't bother to let him finish.

They all made agreeing noises, as though it had been obvious all along and they were only testing her.

'Hi, I'm Annie,' I said, taking over as Mir collapsed into a chair, muttering to herself. 'I am the co-owner here at Content and we need an intern or even a couple of interns to work with us over the summer and possibly part-time after you go back to uni in September.'

All four faces stared back at me.

'The roles are starter level,' I carried on, ignoring a waving Charlie passing-by outside the window. 'We all appreciate ambition but we need someone who is happy to begin at the bottom and learn. It's mostly admin, but you would definitely be involved in team activities, planning, brainstorming, all that kind of thing. Any questions?'

'I'm already a YouTuber?' the girl in the glasses said. It sounded like a question even though I suspected it wasn't. 'And I've got seven thousand followers already, so I think I would be really helpful in a more active role?'

'Good for you,' Miranda said, giving me The Look. 'But right now we need someone who can help with admin.'

'Right,' the girl replied. 'So, could someone else do that?'

'I'll do whatever you need,' said poor, sweet girl who had yet to realize the world was in fact, Not Fair. 'I'm really happy doing admin.'

'Great,' Mir gave her a bright smile. 'Thank you.'

'Also, I really want to meet Zoella,' she carried on. 'Do you know her?'

Behind my back, I heard Mir sigh.

'We work with a lot of people,' I replied. 'But it's hard to say who will and won't be around the office at any given time.'

'Because I saw her on your Instastory once. You were, like, on holiday on a desert island together or something.'

'That was a brand trip we organized for a cosmetics company,' I nodded. 'But good memory.'

'I totally love her,' she said, addressing the entire room this time. 'I'm more of a Louise than a Zoe, so I think we'd get on so well.'

'I'm definitely more of a Tanya,' said the boy. 'Or maybe a Manny.'

'Does anyone here want to work in digital marketing or do you all just want to be YouTubers?' I asked.

No one responded.

'Are these the best people who applied?' I asked in a whisper. As soon as we stopped speaking directly to them, two of the four immediately pulled out their phones and started checking their email.

Mir nodded sadly. 'By a country mile.'

'The world is doomed.' I clapped my hands to get their attention. 'Moving on, I'm assuming you've all read the job description or you wouldn't be here, but does anyone have any questions about the actual internship?'

All four raised their hands.

'Questions that have nothing to do with Zoella?' Miranda clarified.

The boy and the Zoella stan lowered their hands.

'Questions that have nothing to do with specific YouTubers and directly relate to the position you're applying for?' I added.

The boy raised his hand again and I nodded for him to speak.

'Will we get a phone as part of the job?' he asked. 'Because I dropped mine in the toilet and I left it in a bag of rice overnight but it won't dry out and—'

'You and you,' Miranda cut him off and pointed at the girl in the big glasses and the girl in the suit, who by virtue of saying as little as possible, had won us over as the best candidates. 'Congratulations! You're our new interns.'

'And thank you for coming,' I said to the other two. 'It was great to meet you, let me show you out.'

'I don't understand, do we start Monday?' the girl asked as I hurried the failed applicants out of the meeting room, into the lobby and out of The Ginnel, never to return.

'No,' I said, as kindly as possible. 'No, you don't.'

It was hard to break the hearts of the young. Sometimes.

'Maybe you can apply again next year,' I suggested. 'When you've had a bit more experience.'

The pair of them stared at me like the creepy twins from *The Shining*, as I backed slowly into the building.

'Good luck!' I called as I closed the door on their confused faces. 'Great to meet you.'

And then I turned and bolted up the stairs.

'Were we too harsh on the others?' I asked from the queue in the coffee shop, after sending our official new interns, Zadie and Nat, home with goodie bags so big they could barely lift them. 'They're still so young and naïve.'

'Better they get crushed now,' Miranda said with confidence. 'If we toughen them up before they get to twenty-one, they stand a chance.'

'As if you're not the world's biggest secret softy,' I muttered, trying to convince myself I didn't really want a pastry when I was on such a tight budget. 'They're probably already better at this than we are.'

'Probably, but from now on, everyone who comes to work here has to sign billion-year contracts never to mention the word Zoella ever again, even if she's in the room,' she said without looking up from her phone. 'Actually, especially if she's in the room.'

I nodded in agreement before giving a big, greedy yawn.

'Today is going to be a good day,' I told her. 'I can feel it in my waters.'

'You're not wrong,' she said, eyes stuck to the screen of her phone. 'Annie, we've been asked to pitch to SetPics.'

I pressed my hands against my chest. It had happened. I was dead. I had died and gone to heaven. SetPics was one of the biggest entertainment streaming companies in Europe and they only worked with the best agencies, there was no way they'd asked tiny, little Content to pitch them.

'If you're making this up, I'm going to murder you,' I said, suddenly aware I was sweating. 'Kill you in your sleep and hide the body where people will never find it. Murder you.'

Mir was shaking and not because of my death threat.

'They want a social media campaign for a new show about four teenagers who discover a magic egg and develop the ability to travel through time and space with their unicorn guide,' she read from her phone. 'One of the boys from *Teen Wolf* is in it.'

'You're making it up,' I said. 'You know I love those poor, out-of-work werewolf actors.'

She looked up with bright, burning eyes.

'It's called *Uniteam 3000* and the pitch is due in three weeks from today.'

Even Miranda couldn't make that up on the spot.

'Mir, this is huge,' I said, blinking up at my best friend's gurning face. 'This is even bigger than the TechBubble awards.'

'I'm forwarding you the email,' she replied. 'Timing's tight. Maybe someone else dropped out?'

'Gift horse, mouth, don't look into it,' I said, my brain already racing into action. We'd have to come up with something shareable and fun, maybe a mobile game, maybe something with augmented reality. And while my heart beat only for the creative, my head swooned at the idea of a proper budget, real money coming in for once. 'Does it say who else is pitching?'

'Even better,' she said with a grin. 'It's us, PGC and Oz – that's it. We're going to get this.'

Oz. As in Gordon Ossington. As in my last boss before I quit to start up the company he told me would fold within six months.

'We have to get this,' I declared, squeezing her hands in mine. 'Suck it, Gordon Ossington.'

That decided it. I was definitely going to need a pain au chocolat.

'Excuse me.'

A tap on my shoulder made me jump out of my skin. I turned, hand on heart, to see Sam stood in front of me. Today he was sporting a delightful argyle jumper he seemed to have borrowed from my dad in 1986.

'I've thought about your proposal,' he said, completely ignoring Miranda. 'And I will accept the terms of your arrangement.'

'Today just gets better and better,' I said, hurling my arms around his neck in a hug. 'You won't regret this, Sam.'

'Samuel,' he said, disentangling himself from my arms. 'And I very much hope you're right.'

Working in a super-cool, super-creative co-working space was great until every meeting room in the building was occupied and you and your incredibly reluctant wannabe-Romeo ended up trapped in the 'Peace Room'.

A tiny little space chock-full of beanbags and prayer mats with all manner of pseudo-spiritual accoutrements. Yoga blocks, stretching straps, prayer beads, incense, candles and a number of plastic buddhas I knew for a fact Martin had bought in a job lot from the garden centre down the road that closed at Christmas.

An incongruous Sam sat in the middle of the floor, cross-legged on a purple silk cushion, as the wind chimes hanging in the open window filled the room with an unwelcome melody. It was like plopping a Teletubby down in the middle of the Gaza Strip; he couldn't have looked more uncomfortable if he'd been trying.

'Being a better boyfriend isn't difficult,' I said, wiping a giant NAMASTE off the blackboard at the front of the room with my sleeve. 'Whatever it is your girlfriend needs, if you're prepared to try to give it to her, I can't see why we wouldn't be able to work things out. So, tell me exactly what she said.'

'Must we do this in here?' he asked, switching the direction of his legs. 'I'm not excessively comfortable.'

'We're not doing it in your Gollum hole, so yes, we do,' I said, tapping a stick of incense against the blackboard. 'What did she say?'

'That she was bored,' he admitted. 'She said she was bored, that I'd changed and that we want different things out of life – which is ridiculous. I haven't changed at all and I still want exactly the same things.'

For a moment, I wondered if Elaine might be referring specifically to his outfits when she talked about the need for change.

'Perhaps it's more the case that she's been changing,' I suggested as kindly as possible. 'And maybe she's thinking you're stuck in a bit of a rut? And you don't realize it?'

'No, that can't be it.' Sam dismissed the theory out of hand and recrossed his legs once again.

'We'll come back to that,' I said, picking up a piece of pink chalk. 'Let's get down to business. The five steps of boyfriend bootcamp, your cannot-fail path to winning Elaine's heart back and becoming the perfect partner.'

He sucked in his cheeks and pulled roughly at a loose thread in his prayer mat.

'Step one,' I scribbled as I wrote. My handwriting was appalling, I'd never make it as a teacher. 'Listen. Which means—'

'Listening?' Sam suggested. I closed my eyes and took a calm, quiet breath in, the chalk hovering millimetres away from the board.

'Listening and not interrupting,' I replied as I continued to write, turning my back to my reluctant pupil. 'Listening isn't the same thing as waiting for your turn to speak. When she's talking to you, I want you to really pay attention, even if you don't especially care about what she's saying.'

Sam looked at me as though I'd gone completely mad.

'If she says she's had a bad day, ask her why it was so bad, don't just tell her how bad your day was,' I said. 'It's not about one-upmanship. Sometimes a woman just wants to be heard. If she says she's knackered, give her a hug, don't ask why she didn't take the rubbish out. If she says Maria from accounts has been a right old cow, agree with her. Never, ever defend Maria. You want to show her you're on her side. It's not just listening, it's empathizing.'

'I don't see how that is constructive if your theoretical Maria has done nothing wrong,' he said, shaking his head. 'Elaine does have a tendency to overreact—'

'No,' I said, cutting him off this time. 'Doesn't matter.

If she says someone's an arsehole, it doesn't matter. For now, you agree with her.'

Sam cast his eyes to the side of the room and motioned for me to move on.

'Step two, show her how much you care.' I added 'show her' to the blackboard. 'Start small. Buy her flowers, make the bed, fluff the cushions, get in some of her favourite treats. This needs to be everyday stuff, not once in a blue moon. It'll help her know you're thinking about her when she's not there.'

'OK.'

'Because you are, aren't you?'

'Unless I'm working,' he replied. 'Or thinking about something else.'

With an inward groan, I moved on; I didn't have all day. Thank god.

'Step three is a fun one.' In my best scrawl, I wrote down 'shared interests' on the board. 'I've been looking at Elaine's Instagram and it seems like she's got lots of different hobbies. Now, how many of these do you do together?'

Sam took off his glasses and gave them an aggressive clean on the corner of his shirt. 'Hobbies?'

'Yeah,' I said, kneeling beside him as well as my skinny jeans would allow and handing him my phone, pushing aside the slight separation anxiety that came whenever it left my person. 'Obviously she's a gym bunny.'

'She is?' he asked, peering down his nose at the screen. From this distance away, he didn't smell as musty as his beard suggested he might. In fact, he smelled quite nice. Especially for someone who had been sleeping on the floor for several nights.

'Every other picture is a gym selfie,' I pointed out,

trying to stop myself from giving him a second sniff. Maybe he was using a beard oil or something? Seemed unlikely. Sam poked at the phone screen with one unsteady finger, swiping up through photo after photo of his girlfriend's abs and truly impressive biceps. 'You don't wake up looking like that,' I said. 'She must practically live there.'

He was nodding, but I had no idea what the look on his face meant. Oiled or not, that bloody beard had to go.

'And it looks like she went to a documentary festival the other weekend.' I selected one of the pictures to enlarge it. 'Did you go to that with her?'

'I was working,' he said quietly. 'I wondered where she'd got to.'

I bit my bottom lip and kept quiet. Hmm.

'What's she doing in that one?' Sam asked, tapping away at one of the older pictures.

'Good god, man, never double tap!' I pulled my phone away quickly. 'Instagram cardinal sin. That picture is several months old and we do not go around liking ancient pictures unless we want to give ourselves away as a weirdo, all right? That's lesson number one.'

'Anything else I should know?' he asked, sitting on his hands.

'We don't slide into DMs and we don't send pictures of our genitals,' I replied. 'Ever. Even if they ask for it. You can delete that sucker all day long but once a picture has been taken on your phone, it is forever. Trust me.'

He blanched, eyes enormous behind his glasses.

'Never mind.' I unliked the photo. It had only been a split second, hopefully she hadn't noticed. 'OK, this is a picture from her last salsa dancing competition. Ooh, she came in second. She's good, is she?'

Sam unfolded himself and stretched his feet out straight in front of him.

'I don't know,' he said in a quiet voice. 'I didn't know she danced. Who's that?'

I enlarged Elaine's picture to see what he was talking about. There she was, eyes closed, head thrown back and draped across the arm of every man's worst nightmare. Tall, dark and gorgeous, in skin-tight black trousers and a white shirt unbuttoned to reveal what honestly looked like painted-on abs. I glanced at Sam and then back at the photo. It was the 'you versus the guy she told you not to worry about' meme, only in real life.

'Perfectly normal photo of someone dancing,' I said, swiping out of the photo as quickly as possible. 'Moving on to step four!'

I leapt to my feet, hopped over Sam's long legs and went back to the blackboard. 'Step four is going to be a fun one. Show her what she's missing. If she's not taking your phone calls and she's away on holiday, the best way to remind her you're alive is to make sure you're posting to Facebook on the reg. Consistency is key in social media, Sam.'

'Samuel.'

'Consistency is key,' I went on, tapping the word on the blackboard. 'She said she needs time to think, well, let's give her something to think about. You need to reactivate your Facebook account and you're going to post something funny, funny and relevant to Elaine's interests *at least once a day*.'

He actually gulped.

'Facebook is easy,' I promised. 'Keep it cute or keep it mute. You're not a troll, you're not trying to stir the pot. You just want to remind Elaine you're still here and how brilliant of a man you are.'

'What do I post?' he asked, scratching his beard.

'I'll help you for the first couple of days,' I suggested. 'And I know we said no photos on your Instagram but we might need to take a few pics for Facebook.'

Sam nodded absently as I tilted my head from side to side, trying to work out his best angle. Between the beard and the glasses, it was impossible to know what was going on under there.

'Is that it?' he asked, looking up from the floor like a naughty toddler. 'Smile, nod, follow her around like a puppy and post nonsense on the internet?'

'Well, when you put it like that, it does sound stupid,' I grumbled, adding the last step to the blackboard. 'You're going to have to put some effort in, Sam. The final step is going to be the real test. "The grand romantic gesture".'

He sighed, picked up a yoga block and knocked it back and forth against his head.

'Doesn't have to be expensive, doesn't have to be elaborate,' I said, not at all thinking about a certain someone's recent ridiculous proposal. 'Think of something meaningful. Something that will really show Elaine how much you care about her.'

Sam put the yoga block down and rested his elbows on his knees, chin in his hands.

'Sam?'

'I'm thinking,' he replied.

Apparently this was going to take a while.

'When's her birthday?' I asked.

'November,' he muttered.

'Hmm, Scorpio,' I noted. 'Any anniversaries on the horizon?'

'For as much as it is an anniversary,' he said, lifting his chin from his hands, 'it'll be six years since we met in a couple of weeks. On the twenty-fourth, I believe.'

'Perfect!' I added it to the chalkboard. 'That's still two weeks away. Plenty of time to come up with something amazing. Maybe you could take her on a minibreak, something that would be nice for both of you. What about a yoga retreat in Ireland?'

'What do you think I am, made of money?' he scoffed before stroking his beard and breaking into a thoughtful smile. 'Do you want to hear something funny?'

'For the love of god, yes,' I said, far too quickly.

'As you know, I'm writing my second book about the lord lieutenants of Ireland but I've never even been to Ireland,' Sam said in a whisper, dizzying excitement in his eyes. 'Elaine did suggest we go over once but I can't stand the ferry.'

'Brilliant,' I said, wiping a weary hand across my forehead, making a mental note to work on his sense of humour as well as his hair, his empathy and his ability to behave like a functioning human being. 'You're a laugh a minute, Sam.'

'Well, yes.' He dipped his head modestly. 'Is that it?'

'For now.' I nodded. 'So, what do you think?'

'I'm a thirty-five-year-old man with two PhDs,' he said, rising to his feet and stretching his hands up over his head so that the too tight T-shirt under his too big shirt rose up over his stomach. I looked away and added another note: new clothes needed. 'I think I can manage to follow a set of rather simple instructions.'

'Well, then,' I said, ushering him out of the room. 'Let's get to it then.'

I took one last look at the blackboard and sighed before bowing to the nearest plastic Buddha. I was going to need all the help I could get.

CHAPTER NINE

Tuesday, 10 July: Twenty-Four Days to Go

'And where are you running off to, Annie Higgins?'

I was already late when I heard my name. Charlie bounded up the steps of the tube station, two at a time. Instead of his usual office attire, he was wearing gym shorts and an Arsenal shirt. As much as I didn't care for football, he'd gone for quite a tight shirt and it did not look terrible. In this day and age, I hated to objectify anyone but he was already doing half the job for me.

'More like where have you been?' I asked, making a point of looking at my watch. It wasn't even noon. 'What's this? Casual half-day?'

Charlie laughed, lifting his gym bag onto his shoulder.

'I've got a knackered knee,' he said, lifting what I supposed was the knee in question. 'I had physio this morning. Getting too old to be dragging myself round the pitch every Sunday morning.'

'Exercising can be very bad for your health,' I agreed,

awkwardly swinging my bag in front of me. 'Going to the office?'

'Seems like it would be a good idea,' he said. His smile was practically blinding. There was no way he hadn't been on the whitening strips. 'You?'

'I've got a meeting,' I replied, gently pushing him out my way and starting down the stairs. 'And I'm late.'

'Always on the move,' he called after me. 'We should catch up, you can let me know how you're getting on with the bet.'

'I'm getting on just fine,' I assured him, even if it wasn't entirely true. 'But thanks for asking.'

'I can already taste that pizza,' he said, rubbing his tight stomach at the top of the stairs. 'Shame we won't be able to share.'

Before I could reply, he turned away and jogged off up the street.

I'd never been a museum person. Whenever I spent too long in the Tate Modern, I got my "museum headache", mental exhaustion brought on by straining to read tiny description plaques without getting in anyone else's way and one too many human beings in the same room. We'd done a lot of museums, growing up, mostly the free ones, mostly the rubbish ones; and there was a chance I'd held on to the sense of resentment that comes from being dragged away from the telly and dropped in a room full of fascinating things then being told you can't touch them. It's a cruel and unusual punishment for a child, when you think about it. And so I was already uneasy when we arrived at Hampshire House, the former home to one of Sam's beloved lord lieutenants and possibly the scene of my first ever murder.

'Can't you just feel the history oozing from the walls?' he asked as he let me in the front door. 'Then there's a smell. You can smell the power that thrived inside these four walls.'

'Fairly certain that's mould,' I replied, squeezing my elbows into my sides. In stark contrast to the museums I went to as a kid, here, I had no desire to touch a thing.

'So glad you suggested this,' Sam said, carefully placing his rucksack on the floor. 'I couldn't be more excited to share the story of the thirteenth Earl of Eglington with you. Unlucky for some, they say. Fairly unlucky for Archibald really, he died at forty-nine.'

'He died here?' I shuddered and clutched my bag closer to my body.

'Here?' he replied as I shrank away from the ancient wallpaper. 'Of course not. He died at Mount Melville House near St Andrews.'

'Was he born here?' I asked.

Sam shook his head and his beard shimmied in the morning light. 'He was born in Palermo, Italy. Interesting story.'

I believed him, thousands wouldn't.

'So he lived here, did he?' I did not care for the story. 'While he was Lord thingamabob of Ireland?'

'No. But he did once spend the night here on his way to oppose the Jewish Disabilities Bill.'

'Sounds like a right laugh,' I mumbled. 'I wonder if they'll ever turn my house into a museum.'

'The Ginnel should be in the national register,' Sam said. 'Heaps of history around that place. I'm rather surprised the management don't mention it more when people come around to visit.'

I followed him down the narrow hallway and into a sitting room that was equally as musty and unpleasant. 'Such as?'

'Jack the Ripper almost certainly hid out there from the police,' he said, a happy fever in his eyes. 'He met one of his victims right in our alleyway.'

'Oh,' I looked back over my shoulder to see whether or not he'd locked me in with him. He had. 'That's nice.'

'Odd that it's called The Ginnel when it's in East London. It's a term most often used in the north of England, even though its origins are found in the French word *chenel*, meaning passageway.'

'Fascinating,' I said with a big, supportive smile.

It was Miranda's idea to meet Sam somewhere he would feel comfortable and let him run around in his element, to see if I could loosen him up a bit. It was a beautiful, beautiful day and I thought perhaps he'd want to get a coffee or a snack or walk around Hyde Park or something, but no, of course not. He wanted me to sit on the tube for the best part of an hour and meet him in an entirely nondescript house that even your best friend's auntie's weird mum would be ashamed to call home.

'So when did your Lord Eglington visit this place?' I asked. 'Recently?'

Sam didn't even need to think about it.

'Relatively. May 1848.'

'And it hasn't been decorated since,' I marvelled.

And to think I'd given up my lunch hour for this.

He frowned at me from his position next to the fireplace. At least, I assumed he was frowning, it was so hard to tell from behind the beard. And the hair. And the glasses.

'How come you've got the key?' I asked, settling down on the edge of a stiff-looking chair. Sam remained next to the fireplace, resting his arm out on the mantle. All he needed were two very big dogs and a time machine. 'Oh my God, Sam, do you own this place?'

'I wish,' he replied, lovingly stroking the ugly fireplace. 'I'm one of the custodians. I help take care of the place, raise money for its upkeep. It's a very important house in terms of British political history.'

'Because people used to sleep over?'

'They weren't always sleeping,' he said with a theatrical and regrettable wink. 'Ah yes, many a scandal occurred in his house. If these walls could talk. . .'

'They would say, "Please remove this wallpaper, you're killing me,"' I suggested. 'Do you get many visitors?'

Sam looked aghast. 'We're not open to the public,' he gasped. 'This is a private house, a private museum. We couldn't have people just wandering in off the streets and touching things.'

I didn't have the heart to tell him there was nothing in this room worth touching.

'How are you getting on with your homework?' I asked. Sam cast me a dark look. I'd prepared him an All Elaine starter package, based on her interests, and played knock-a-door run the night before. Blu-Ray copies of *Step Up* one and four, *Strictly Ballroom* and *Dirty Dancing*, the original, not *Havana Nights*. Never *Havana Nights*. I'd also thrown in a couple of the documentaries she'd been to see at the docfest, a list of recent stand-up specials on Netflix, a book on mindfulness and half a dozen books listed on the website for Elaine's monthly book club. And just for my own personal amusement, both *Magic Mike* movies.

'I'm working very hard at being in the present as we speak,' he replied. 'I shall get to the rest of it when I have time.'

'As long as it's in the next two weeks,' I said, resting my elbows on my knees. Sam pulled a tattered white paper bag out of his jacket pocket and fished out a sherbet lemon. 'I wanted to talk to you about the other side of our bargain.'

'Go on,' he said, holding out the bag. Having no idea how long they'd been in there, I declined.

'Since your passion for history is . . .' I paused for a second, glancing around the manky old room. 'Infectious, I thought we really should share it with the world.'

'That's what I'm doing with my books,' he replied, folding over the top of the bag and storing it safely away for another decade. 'Are you going to tell people about them?'

'In a way, yes,' I said carefully. 'But think of your books like the main course of a banquet. They're a big, meaty main meal and people don't realize they're hungry enough for that yet. We need to whet their appetite, get their history juices flowing, so to speak.'

'Go on,' Sam said, sucking on the sherbet lemon.

'A great way to get people engaged is to give them something they want to share with their friends,' I explained. 'And the things that get shared the most are funny.'

'There are lots of funny stories in my book,' he said, tucking the boiled sweet into his cheek. 'Lord Eglington, for example, tried to establish a tournament in his name with jousting and the lot. Unfortunately, it rained on the day and the whole thing was a washout. Not to mention the fact it was 1839, hardly the Middle Ages.'

'In many ways, I am afraid of you,' I said. Sam continued to suck on his sweet, unperturbed. 'As hilarious as that story sounds, we're looking for anecdotes that are a bit more accessible to the everyday person. Something more soundbitey. Like Catherine the Great getting squashed by her horse when they were getting it on—'

'That's a common falsehood, there's no evidence to suggest she ever had intercourse with her horse,' Sam said, interrupting without hesitation. 'She died after she had a stroke on the toilet.'

'Like Elvis!' I replied, perhaps too enthusiastically. Sam didn't look nearly as pleased with the correlation. 'OK. What I'm thinking is, you give me a list of interesting facts, I'll illustrate them and we'll post them on Instagram. People will see them, they'll laugh, they'll click the link and boom, before they know it, they've bought your book.'

'But my book won't be about Catherine the Great,' Sam said with a frown. 'Won't they be disappointed?'

'Doesn't matter,' I assured him. 'It's all in the history ballpark, it doesn't have to be exactly the same. You're a historian, your Instagram should be about history. This is perfect.'

He looked confused. For a change.

'The posts don't have to be about my specific field of expertise?'

'Honestly, Sam, they just have to be good,' I said. There was no kind way of explaining the only person who gave a monkey's about Lord Eglington and his ill-advised tournament was him. 'The first thing we worry about is finding our audience; we can bring them all onto the lord lieutenant party bus later.'

Sam clutched his backpack closer to his chest.

'Figure of speech,' I promised.

'I went on one of those for my brother's stag party,' he replied, white as a sheet with recollection. 'Never again.'

My eyes lit up. 'Are there photos?'

'No, thank god.' He relaxed slightly, sliding his arms into the straps of his backpack so that it rested against his belly like a papoose. 'That's it then? All you need from me is a list of historical facts?'

'Interesting and preferably fun historical facts,' I said, with major emphasis on the interesting and the fun. 'And interesting to normal people, not just, you know, you.'

He looked down at his worn corduroy trousers. 'I'm normal. Aren't I?'

As if the trousers weren't bad enough, the sleeves of his white shirt billowed around his waist as though he was about to sail away. Thankfully the shirt was anchored to his body by a far too tight, V-neck sweater vest I assumed he'd had since secondary school.

'I should have said non-historian people,' I said kindly. 'Of course you're normal.'

I tried not to cry as I watched Sam pull another boiled sweet out of his pocket, inspect it, pick off a bit of dust then put it in his mouth.

'And then you'll expect me to inspect the pictures you selected to go with the facts, will you?' he asked. 'I'm not sure about this, I'm so busy at the moment, with my lecture and my book deadlines. Not to mention all of the nonsense you left in my office yesterday. Perhaps this isn't the best idea.'

'You don't have to check the images,' I insisted, very, very quickly. 'You don't have to do anything other than send me the facts. Trust me.'

'You keep saying that,' Sam said, eyeing me carefully. I held my hands behind my back and smiled broadly, my finest impression of a trustworthy person. 'And yet . . .'

'I'm a very trustworthy person,' I said, standing up before I was absorbed by the chair and wandering through to the back of the house. 'I've got spare keys to all my friend's houses and was routinely allowed to take the school rabbit home over the holidays.'

'Half-term or summer?' he asked.

'Summer once, half-term three times,' I answered, trying the handle on a huge wooden door and finding it locked. 'What's out here?'

'Quite obviously a garden.'

He took out a huge bunch of keys, holding each one up to the light in turn before settling on one that was long and shiny and so big it might have been filled with chocolate.

'We try to keep it as it would have been in the mid eighteenth century, but it isn't easy,' he said as he pushed open the heavy door. I ducked under his arm and gasped at what I saw. The inside of the house might have been musty and old and depressing, but the garden . . . the garden was something else.

'I must have walked past this house a million times,' I said, turning circles on the lawn, trying to get as much of the garden as possible into my eyes. Everything was so green and lush. 'Sam, it's gorgeous.'

'Samuel,' he said with a sigh. 'It was important to those who could afford it to keep a beautiful outdoor space. Life indoors could get awfully stuffy, sweltering in the summer and sooty and unpleasant in the winter back then, I imagine.'

'Back then, right now,' I replied. 'I can't imagine

having a garden of my own in London. I haven't even got a settee.'

'I haven't even got my own bed,' he reminded me, wandering over to a hydrangea bush, covered in soft purple and blue flowers. 'These were introduced to Britain in the nineteenth century. Flower arranging was very popular at the time. Lots of people decorated their homes with greenery from their own gardens.'

'Well, their homes were fairly disgusting,' I reasoned, leaning in to sniff the flower but resisting the urge to pick one. I didn't want Sam to faint. He was tall, I'd never be able to catch him. 'And I guess there wasn't much on the telly.'

'Just the three channels,' he said with a little laugh.

'Imagine not having Sky,' I commented with a sad cluck.

'I'm joking, of course,' he replied. 'The television as we know it wasn't invented until the 1920s and wasn't popularized until the 1950s.'

Gazing up into his eyes, I sighed at the task ahead of me.

'You'd be amazing on a pub quiz team,' I told him. 'Remind me to take you to the King's Head next Thursday.'

My phone was in my hand before I even realized it. Opening up the camera app, I squared the hydrangea in frame.

'Oh no,' Sam said, holding his hand in front of the photos. 'We don't allow photographs in the gardens or the house, not without prior consent.'

No wonder I'd never heard of this place; it wasn't just a museum about the nineteenth century, they thought it was still the nineteenth century.

'And who do I need to get permission from?' I asked,

wiping my camera lens on my sleeve. I couldn't touch his bloody books but he could put his mitts all over my new iPhone.

'Me, I suppose,' he replied.

'Then can I take the photo please, Dr Page?'

He considered the request for far too long.

'Yes,' he said eventually. I was amazed to see the flower was even still in bloom by the time he answered. 'But I'd rather you didn't post it on the internet. We don't want hordes of people running in here, traipsing around and breaking things.'

The man made no sense.

'Then why bother having a museum?' I asked. 'If you're not going to share it with people.'

'To preserve something important,' he replied, again talking to me as though it should have been obvious. 'Not everyone is entitled to everything. Some things don't exist solely to be exploited.'

'Sharing isn't exploiting,' I argued, lowering my phone. Was there really any point in taking a photo if I couldn't show it to anyone?

Yes, the devil on my shoulder answered. I quickly snapped a pic and saved it to my photo albums.

'Thank you for the grand tour,' I said, even though it had been far from grand and not really a tour. More like a sit-down, don't-touch-anything and no-you-can't-go-upstairs. It was Graceland all over again, only without the fried peanut-butter-and-banana sandwich at the end. Unless I went home and made one for myself.

'Here.'

I couldn't believe my eyes. Sam reached into the hydrangea bush and snapped off one of the pale, purple blooms.

'Thank you,' I said, cradling the flower in my hands. 'It's gorgeous.'

'It's only going to die anyway,' he reasoned, giving his beard a good scratch. 'You might as well have it die in your house.'

'Thanks,' I replied, not sure I wanted it any more. 'Nice positive thinking.'

Sam replied with a sneeze.

'My hay fever,' he said, snuffling into a white cotton handkerchief retrieved from his pocket. 'Might we go back inside?'

'We might,' I agreed, taking one last look at his secret garden before going back into the mouldy manor. Stuffy and unwelcoming from the outside but surprisingly beautiful once you were allowed in.

I looked back at Sam, hurrying inside the house with long, loping steps.

Maybe there was hope after all.

CHAPTER TEN

'I have learned so much from this bet already,' Mir said, blankly scrolling through her Instagram feed and pausing on the latest post from Sam's new account, @TheHipHistorian. 'What kind of attention-seeker has a state funeral for their amputated leg?'

'So extra,' Brian agreed. 'I kind of love it.'

The Hip Historian's Instagram account was on fire. Well, it was smouldering around the edges at the very least. We'd been up for two days, posting pic after pic along with some truly fascinating facts from the epic list Sam had provided. There was nothing that man didn't know about, as long as it occurred at least a century ago and the knowledge itself was utterly useless. I mean, who knew the Leaning Tower of Pisa was never straight to begin with? Sam. Sam knew. We already had over two hundred followers and it was growing every second. Zadie, my beloved new intern, had spent what seemed like every waking hour researching and following all the appropriate accounts, getting follow-backs, creating gifs and uploading our memes to every possible outlet. So far, so good.

'Mexico is a beautiful country, it's not like there was nothing to do there,' I said as I put the finishing touches to Lily's latest empties video. If it didn't upload on time, her fans would riot. 'General Santa Anna needed to get out more.'

'*You* need to get out more,' Bri commented, leaning back in his chair. 'Look at those glowing, pink cheeks. You're a girl in desperate need of a hangover.'

'No thanks,' I said, rubbing the life back into my dry eyes. 'Have you ever tried editing a YouTube video hungover?'

He gave me a look. We both knew full well that he had.

'He has a point,' Mir said, siding with the enemy. 'You've been killing yourself lately, between all your regular work, the bet, helping Sam, all the SetPics stuff. Why don't you knock off early, I'll finish Lily's video.'

I shook my head and smiled. 'As if you're not doing exactly the same thing. It's fine, this is temporary. Once we're incredibly rich and insanely successful, I'll be flat on my back on a superyacht in the south of France, Rihanna on one side, assorted celebrity Ryans on the other, I promise.'

'As long as it is temporary,' she replied, shaking three different Coke cans on her desk in an attempt to find a live one. 'All work and no play makes Annie a sociopathic shut-in.'

'Agreed,' Bri said with a sage nod. 'I hate to say it, buddy, but you've been on a dick-tox too long.'

Miranda spat out her Diet Coke.

'I know I'm going to regret asking, but can you run that past me again?'

'A dick-tox,' Brian repeated the word, as though it was an explanation in itself. 'Dick detox, like Dry January or Oct-Sober only it's more like a No-Peen-November. Or in Annie's case, a No-Dick-Decade.'

'Thank god the interns have gone home already,' Mir said, shaking her head sadly. 'Also, it's July.'

'It hasn't been a decade,' I argued, trying to remember just exactly how long it had been. 'More like a year.'

Brian gasped. Miranda sighed. I shrugged.

'What? It's not a big deal.'

'That's the problem with a dick-tox, once it's out of your system, you don't know how to get it back in,' Brian said. 'So to speak.'

'He's right,' Mir muttered into her can. 'Because, no matter what people tell you, it is nothing like riding a bike.'

Brian clapped his hands loudly. 'We've got to get you back on the horse. A Sandwich Man, a little snack to keep you going between meals.'

'A man-wich?' Miranda nodded approvingly. 'Maybe a nice French baguette.'

'I'm more likely to end up with a mouldy bit of Hovis and a floppy piece of plastic ham from Aldi,' I replied, holding up a hand to silence Brian before he could start. 'And don't start on Aldi. I know, I know, it's a perfectly good supermarket.'

'If you'd rather pay over the odds for fancy pack-aging, you go ahead,' he sniffed.

'So that's it, is it?' Mir asked. 'You're retiring from dating altogether? Stitching it up and calling it quits?'

I considered the question and all the existing rela-tionships in my life. Becks and Boring Alan, Miranda and Mess-Around Martin, my dad and his three iden-tikit wives. And that was before you thought about poor Sam, sat in his office, ploughing through all three *Fifty Shades* books in an attempt to keep his relation-ship together.

'Yes,' I replied. 'Do you know anyone who can do it for me?'

'Positive attitude, that's what I like to hear,' Brian replied. 'So, shall we kill ourselves now or later?'

'Later,' I said, going back to Lily's video. 'If this doesn't upload by seven, there'll be three million fourteen-year-olds on the street, screaming for my blood.'

'It's like working at Grey Gardens,' Brian said, closing his laptop with a slap. 'I'm off. I shall see you ladies tomorrow.'

Miranda rolled her eyes and grinned over her laptop as he kissed her on the top of the head, hit my high five and strolled out the door, whistling loudly.

'What can I do to help?' she asked, dumping all three empty cans in the recycling bin. 'You need me to set up links or anything?'

Before I could answer, Mr Mess-Around himself appeared in the hall outside our office. Mir straight-ened up and tossed her head, the angles of her face sharpening into an arched brow and a half-smile.

'Knew you'd still be here,' he said, holding up a hand by way of a hello. 'I've got two tickets to some rooftop film thing, starts in an hour or so. I wondered if you wanted them?'

'You're not going?' I asked, watching Miranda, watching Martin.

'Not on my own,' he replied. 'Should be fun though – there's drinks included.'

'Why don't you go with Miranda?' I suggested, a picture of innocence. 'I've still got loads to do, no way I'll be out of here in an hour and it'd be a crime to waste an open bar.'

The two of them looked at each other with wide eyes and blank expressions, neither wanting to seem too enthusiastic or too disinterested.

Martin spoke first.

'I'm in,' he said. 'I mean, if you fancy it?'

'What film is it?' Miranda asked. It was very impressive, I could tell by the way her hands were balled up into tight little fists she was chomping at the bit.

'Does it matter?' Martin replied. 'You can never concentrate on the film at these things anyway.'

Miranda swayed back and forth, deliberating.

'You sure you don't want to come?' she asked, looking back at me over her shoulder. 'Brian did have a point.'

'I'll go with you next time,' I promised, imagining the look on her face if I suddenly changed my mind, decided I wanted to go and sent Martin off on his Jack Jones. 'Have fun.'

She sighed at the pair of us, as though she was doing everyone a tremendous favour, then picked up her backpack and pushed Martin through the door with almost indecent haste.

'Don't do anything I wouldn't do,' I called as they vanished down the hallway, leaving me and my YouTube videos in peace.

I wasn't sure how it happened but the sun was going down by the time I closed my computer. Another late night, another rumbling stomach, another inevitable visit from my good friends at Deliveroo. Whoever was in charge of my account at the credit card company had to be worried about me.

The building always emptied out earlier in the evenings when the weather was good and, luckily for Martin and Miranda, it was a beautiful evening, a British summertime unicorn; warm without being sticky and a gorgeous sky that had been painted with the broad strokes of a sunset by the time I found myself outside.

'Pulling a late one?'

I looked to my left to see Charlie leaning against the building with his phone in his hand.

'They're all late ones at the moment,' I replied with a stifled yawn. My voice sounded croaky in my ears and the words scratched my throat. I fumbled around in my bag for my ever-present refillable water bottle.

'You look like you could use something stronger,' he said, nodding at the flask as I sipped the dregs. 'Fancy a drink?'

A drink? With a boy? On a Thursday? Spontaneity, thy name is Annie.

'Why not?' I said, smiling. A sudden fizziness replaced the rumbling in my stomach.

Charlie grinned, cancelled his Uber and put his phone back in his pocket.

'Come on then,' he said, leading the way. 'You can tell me how close I am to winning our bet.'

When we first moved into The Ginnel, Miranda and I had found ourselves locked in the King's Head after hours more times than I cared to remember. Actually, more times than I could remember. It was nice to have a work local to retire to after a long (or not so long) day in the office, it made Content feel more legit. If I told Mir I'd meet her in the pub, she'd know where I meant. But the last couple of months had been so non-stop, we'd barely crossed the threshold. Plus Brian was barred for standing on the bar and screaming at everyone for not supporting Taylor Swift enough when her last album came out. He was such a loyal soldier.

'I love a proper pub,' Charlie said, dumping his bag on a wooden bench outside the front door. 'Manky carpet, dark wood, terrifying locals. Exactly what a pub should be.'

'I'm surprised,' I said, waving to Maria, the landlady, through the window. 'I had you down as more of a private members' club kind of a man.'

He rolled up his shirtsleeves as he laughed. 'I am a member of Shoreditch House.'

'Of course you are,' I replied. 'What are you drinking?'

'I'll get them,' he insisted. 'What'll it be?'

'Gin and tonic,' I said with confidence. 'I've tried both wines, the red and the white, and they do not come recommended.'

'Noted.'

As he walked inside, I noticed a group of women at the next table give him the once-over before turning their attention to me. Two of them flicked their eyes away as soon as they realized I was watching while the other smiled, embarrassed, before they returning to their conversation. I wondered what it was that they saw. I knew exactly what they saw in Charlie. If you clicked on the hashtag 'hottie' on Insta, you'd even-tually find a photo of him, but what did they think when they looked at me? What was my hashtag? Without time to craft a clever caption, it was difficult to explain why I was a boss, why my life was goals.

All they saw was a tired brunette, badly in need of a filter.

'So.' Charlie sat back down with two glasses of gin in one hand and two bottles of tonic in the other. 'What's keeping you at work so late?'

'The inability to do ten things at once,' I told him. 'You?'

'We're working with an American company on a campaign,' he replied, pouring my tonic into the gin and then passing it across the table. 'They're based in LA. It's the strangest thing, everyone wants to work on the campaign but no one wants to stick around to do the late-night conference calls.'

'How peculiar.' I clinked my glass against his. 'To being the boss?'

'I should have got shots,' he said with a grimace. 'Some days I wonder if it's worth it. Must be nice to have a business partner, to not be in it alone.'

'It is,' I agreed, sipping slowly. Why was gin so delicious? 'When things get hard, it's good to have someone around to keep you going, but it's also a massive pain in the arse when you don't agree on something. We're usually on the same page but when we're not, it's tricky.'

He nodded, rubbing the two-day stubble on his chin.

'When I started up, I was planning to do the partner thing,' Charlie said. 'But it didn't work out. Probably for the best, I have enough trouble keeping relationships going.'

Something in my stomach dropped.

'Not that I've got a girlfriend,' he added quickly.

'It's hard to find a work–life balance,' I said, refusing to let on how happy I was to discover he was single. Brian and Miranda were right: I'd been off the wagon for too long. Perhaps it was time to jump back up on the horse and ride Charlie like a bike. Or something.

'Am I allowed to ask about the bet?' He stretched his long legs out underneath the table, bumping my knee with his. Whether it was on purpose or not, he didn't move it. 'Or is that off the agenda?'

I flushed, choking on my answer before clearing my throat with gin.

'God, imagine if you could actually agree to an agenda before a date,' I said with a skittering laugh, tucking my legs underneath my seat. 'Life would be so much easier.'

'A date?' Charlie leaned forwards across the table, backlight by the fading summer light. 'I thought this was just a friendly drink. Ms Higgins, are you trying to take advantage of me?'

'No!' I spluttered. 'You mentioned agendas and I thought it would be funny if you could have an agenda for a date, not that this is a date, and why are you laughing, you arse?'

'I'm sorry, I'm sorry.' He reached across the table to lay a hand on my forearm as his laughter settled and I noticed the girls at the next table watching us again. 'I'm just fucking with you. Seriously, how is the bet? Have I won yet?'

'I know a lot of women like confident men,' I replied, straightening myself in my seat. 'But there's a fine line between confident and cocky, Wilder.'

'She says, as though she isn't one hundred per cent betting on herself,' Charlie said, grinning as he raised his glass. 'Pretty sure it was your "confidence" that got you into this bet in the first place.'

'I'm pretty sure it was your arrogance,' I replied. 'But what would I know?'

I pulled my shirt out of my jeans and fanned myself underneath the table. Was it getting hot in here or was it just me?

'What I'm hearing is, you're not quite at twenty thousand followers just yet,' Charlie emptied the rest of one of the bottles of tonic into his glass. 'Don't worry, you've still got another couple of weeks.'

'I'm not worried,' I said, gently reminding myself not to get wound up. 'As soon as he finds his audience, Sam is going to be a sensation.'

Across the street, the front door to The Ginnel opened to reveal said sensation, wearing a cycling helmet over his long hair, one trouser leg rolled up to the knee and cuffed with an elastic band, as he fought with a reluctant folding bicycle.

'You have to be confident to get by these days,' Charlie said, shaking his head at Sam's ongoing struggle. 'But you also have to know when to admit defeat.'

'And you should know when to change the subject,' I said, sinking my drink. 'Don't count me out just yet.'

Charlie shrugged then nodded, a smile still playing on his lips. Having finally wrestled his bike into submission, Sam looked up and did a double take at the two of us. I waved, glancing down at Charlie, our empty glasses on the table, backpacks beside us on the bench. With a curt nod, Sam climbed aboard his bike and cycled off down the street, his long, Rapunzel locks flowing out behind him.

'I'm curious,' Charlie said as I watched Sam disappear into the sunset. 'What would be on your dating agenda?'

'Another drink,' I replied, climbing out of the wooden picnic-style bench with as much grace as my skinny jeans would allow. 'Same again?'

'Same again,' he confirmed. 'Thanks.'

I passed the table full of women on my way inside and offered them a vague smile. There was no point getting territorial over something that wasn't mine, or offended over a story I'd made up in my own head.

'I love your shoes,' one of the women said. I looked down at my knackered old Adidas and shrugged. Sure, why not?

'Thanks,' I said. 'They're so comfortable.'

'I love your boyfriend's shirt,' said another. 'Do you know where it's from?'

Ahh. The old 'finding out if he's your boyfriend by calling him your boyfriend' trick. Obviously, I knew I was not on a date. But still, that didn't mean I had to offer Charlie up to any old Tom, Dick or Harriet, did it? Flirting with him was fun, when he wasn't being such an arrogant tit. And weirdly, also when he was.

'Charlie?' I replied with mock surprise. They nodded, purring his name around the table. 'Sorry,' I said sweetly. 'He's gay.'

'Typical,' the first woman scowled.

'I should have known,' the second said. 'Such nice hair.'

The third just drank.

'Enjoy your evening, ladies,' I said, as they went back to sipping their ill-advised wine and prodding blindly at their phones.

None of them replied.

CHAPTER ELEVEN

Friday, 13 July: Twenty-One Days to Go
522 followers

'I honestly think this is going to be your favourite part of boyfriend bootcamp,' I said, knowing full well it would be mine. 'Everybody, meet Sam.'

I pushed Sam through the door of our office, to the tune of a fanfare playing on my iPhone. Across the room, Brian crossed himself while Miranda dropped a KitKat into her lap.

'It's just so much hair,' Brian breathed before remembering himself and rushing over to shake Sam's hand. 'Sam, Brian.'

'Most people call me Dr Page,' he insisted, raising a hand in what I assumed he believed was an appropriate human gesture. It was, just barely. 'Or Samuel. Actually, let's stick with Dr Page.'

After leaving Charlie and the pub, I'd sent Sam an email requesting his presence at our office at nine a.m. When he didn't reply, I knew he wouldn't come of his own accord. Unfortunately for Dr Page, it turned out if you were dedicated enough and prepared to sit outside the men's toilets for long enough, you too could catch yourself a hip historian. We'd been putting this off for long enough. Today was the day. Today we pulled out the big guns.

'Sam has very kindly volunteered to be a guinea pig for us today,' I announced. 'Brian, you told me you needed hair models for Coast this morning?'

'I'm not a model,' Sam whispered softly.

'He's not a model,' Brian whispered softly.

'But he will be,' I countered, steering Sam by the shoulders and kicking the door shut behind me. Now we had him, we had to keep him. 'Imagine what Coast could do with all this glorious . . . hair.'

'You're right,' Mir cheered. She was so good at putting a brave face on things. 'You, Sam, are a regular diamond in the rough. I can't wait to see what's going on underneath all that.'

'Annie said I'd just be getting a trim,' Sam said, turning to me, true fear in his eyes. 'That's what we're doing, isn't it?'

'You are in the best hands,' I promised, guiding him through the office and into the tiny meeting room where our client, Coast, was already set up with scissors, a spray bottle and the courage of a thousand men. 'And remember, you're doing this for Elaine. And hair always grows back.'

'Hair always grows back,' he repeated, gripping the arms of his chair as though he was about to shoot off into space.

'But that doesn't mean it should,' I added. 'Sam, meet Coast. Coast meet Sam.'

I waved my hand from one terrified-looking historian to one terrified-looking hairdresser. 'Coast,' Sam said slowly and deliberately. 'That's an interesting name.'

'Coast is one of the best stylists in London,' I said, actively ignoring the look of horror on said stylist's face. 'He's got a huge social media outreach and he's far too discreet to brag about it, but he does a lot of celebrities' hair.'

'If you'd consider the sixth person in line to the throne a celebrity,' Coast replied, eyeing his fingernails carefully. 'But as Annie said, I don't like to brag.'

'Thank goodness,' Sam said as Coast unleashed The Hair. I watched as it cascaded over Sam's shoulders with envy. My hair was a nightmare. Damp outside? Frizz monster. Central heating inside? Frizz monster. Humid, raining, snowing, anywhere above or below 16 to 18 degrees Celsius? You get the idea. I lived and died by my hair straighteners and as much as the style did nothing for him, I had to admit, when he set it free from that dodgy ponytail, Sam's hair was luscious.

'I think just a quick trim should do it,' he said with a brave smile.

'Leave it all to me.' Coast wound his victim's hair back into a ponytail and held it taut. 'This is my job, my friend, this is what I do.'

'I've had long hair since I was in uni,' Sam replied, waving a hand in the air as though that explained everything. 'It's part of my thing.'

I bit my lip, too scared to watch but too invested to look away.

'Friend,' the stylist said, yanking the ponytail backwards and taking Sam's head with it. 'It's time to let that thing go.'

He sliced right through his hair with one snip, shearing off the entire thing, and placing the poor ponytail in the palm of Sam's hand. I gasped, Sam gasped, Coast sighed. I very nearly needed a cigarette.

'My . . . my hair,' Sam was choking on his words as he cradled a decade of poor decisions in his arms. 'You cut off all my hair!'

'You are so welcome,' Coast said, grabbing a handful of Sam's new lob and pulling his head upright. 'Now the magic really happens.'

'Sam, you look . . .' I made an OK sign at a grief-stricken Sam as he stared at himself in the mirror Coast had placed on the table. 'I've got to make a quick phone call. Be right back.'

There was no phone call. There was only the complete and utter certainty that I was going to throw up with anxiety if I stayed in the room. Stood in the safety of the stairwell, I opened Instagram and landed on Elaine's feed. As if things weren't bad enough, she had spent the last twenty-four hours filling her Insta feed with hot dogs or legs pictures, alongside heavily filtered shots of cocktails, bikinis and sunsets. As Miranda would say, she could not have been more basic. The whole feed was a masterclass in basicality. Sam might be a lot of things but he could never be accused of being basic. At this rate, it was going to be easier to make Sam the new King of Instagram before I could convince these two crazy kids to get back together.

'Morning.'

I opened my eyes to see Charlie hanging over the handrail on the floor above me. He really was very tall and very handsome. I felt a pang of guilt for telling the three girls at the bar he was gay as I gazed up at him, but then he smiled and it passed, quickly. Maybe

133

after the bet was over and we'd won and I'd finished doing my victory lap of the building, I'd consider asking him out properly. Because men loved that, didn't they?

'How are your numbers looking?' he asked, a cheeky smile on his face as he came down the stairs, two at a time.

'Excellent,' I replied, pocketing my phone. 'Thanks for asking. How's your wrist?'

'My wrist?' he glanced down at his hand, confused.

'Just making sure you haven't got any injuries or RSI or anything like that,' I said. 'You know, anything that might stop you from signing our rent cheque next month.'

He shook his head and laughed. 'Annie, I'm a reasonable man. If you want to concede now, I'll take free social for two weeks instead of a month. You can't say fairer than that, can you?'

'I hope you've negotiated mates rates with Martin,' I replied, tilting my head up to look him in the eye. 'I really would feel awful if you had to find all that money.'

'You've got to love a girl with confidence,' Charlie said, taking a big breath in and then sighing loudly. 'You still think you can win with him, don't you?'

'I think I could win it with a monkey on roller skates.' I stood and moved up three steps until I was taller than him. Come to think of it, a monkey on roller skates would be far easier. 'But thanks for asking.'

A happy smile found its way onto my face and I turned, climbing the stairs back to the studio.

'I can't wait to see which filters you use on all my pictures,' he called after me. 'I can be a demanding boss, I hope you're ready for it.'

'I just hope you're not a sore loser,' I replied, glancing back down the stairwell, my heart pounding in my ears though my voice remained even and clear. 'Because I can be a terrible winner and someone's going to have to be gracious when all this is over.'

'We'll see,' he replied with a wink. 'I'm going down to the coffee shop, you coming?'

'I'm actually busy right now,' I said, opening the studio door with a shaky hand. 'But thanks.'

'You've got three weeks to find twenty thousand followers,' he reminded me as he jogged down the steps. 'I should think you are busy.'

'Shitshitshitshitshitshitshit,' I chanted as I let myself back onto the second floor. 'You're such an idiot, Annie. What are you thinking?'

'Oh good, you've gone mad.'

I walked straight into a bemused Mir.

'This bodes well.'

'I can't hear any screaming,' I said, almost too afraid to look into the meeting room. 'Has Brian killed him?'

'I think you'd better see for yourself,' she said. 'I don't have the words.'

It wasn't possible. I'd only been gone two minutes. What could have happened inside two minutes?

Preparing myself for the absolute worst, I watched my feet walk into the room before forcing my eyes up to see someone that used to be Sam, sat in Coast's chair.

'But, Dr Page,' I pressed my palm against my chest and gasped. 'You're beautiful.'

In my absence, a miracle had occurred. Chopping off Sam's long, sad ponytail had been revelatory. The waves sprang up into loose curls, and even though it had been cut short on the sides it was just long enough on the top for you to really get your hands in there. Should you feel so inclined. Best of all, the beard that had given me nightmares, was gone. His newly shorn stubble drew attention to a full mouth and a good, solid jawline and I had to assume neither had seen the light of day in over a decade. Maybe Elaine had been playing the long game all along.

'I hate it,' Sam said, still clutching his discarded ponytail. His blue eyes were anguished. 'I can't believe you did this to me.'

'How could you hate it?' I asked, walking around him, taking in every possible angle. Imagine having the potential to look this good but instead choosing to spend your life doing an impression of a 1970s cult leader. 'Sam, you look amazing.'

'I don't feel amazing,' he said, repeatedly touching his ears. It must have been a while since they'd been so exposed to the elements. 'I feel ridiculous.'

'I can't believe it's the same person,' Miranda whispered. 'Holy Hemsworth, Annie. Did you always know this was lurking under there?'

'I'd say he's more Hiddleston than Hemsworth,' Brian said, draping his arms over both of our shoulders. 'But either way, if I'm being brutally honest, I totally would.'

'You cut off my hair, not my ears. I can hear you both,' Sam called. 'Just so you know.'

'We know, we just don't care,' Miranda replied, shooting him a double thumbs up. 'You look fantastic, Sam.'

'Samuel,' he said. 'I feel ridiculous. How am I supposed to stand up and give a lecture in three weeks looking like this?'

'You're right,' Mir said. 'You need new clothes.'

'That's not what I meant.' He glared at her with indignation. It was so much easier to work out his expressions now we could see his face; before it had been like translating body language from Cousin It. 'What's wrong with my clothes?'

'Consider this a non-negotiable part of stage two of the boyfriend bootcamp,' I told him. 'We're giving you a wardrobe makeover as well as the hair.'

'I reckon the samples from the Dashell campaign will fit him,' Brian said, giving Sam a once-over. And then whatever you would call a second once-over. And a third. 'Coast, you really are worth all the hype, bro.'

'I love what I do,' Coast said with a great deal of forced modesty. 'And it would have been hard to make him look worse.'

Sam sucked on his teeth, making his cheekbones even more pronounced. Wasted on a man, they were. Utterly wasted. 'Am I supposed to sit here and take this?'

'Yes.' I nodded with sympathy. 'Another big part of boyfriend bootcamp. Knowing when to talk and when to listen.'

'So what now?' he asked, almost tearfully. 'Have I passed your tests?'

'Baby, you're just getting started!' Miranda replied as Brian took off into the samples cupboard and began hurling jeans, shirts and jumpers into a pile behind him. 'Rome wasn't built in a day.'

'Look at it like this . . .' I searched for the perfect metaphor as Sam disappeared under a pile of striped T-shirts and skinny jeans. 'Think of yourself as a really good cake.'

'I try not to eat sugar,' he replied as a pair of yoga pants landed on top of his head.

'Think of yourself as a really good book,' I corrected, ignoring Coast's eye-roll behind him as he packed up his things. 'The most important thing about you is the words, correct?'

'Yes,' he nodded. 'Well done, you understand how books work.'

'Before I give you a slap, let me finish,' I continued. 'The words inside the book might be utterly amazing. Mind-blowing. Life-changing even. But what if no one ever reads them? How do you get those words into the hands of the right people? You've got to come up with a brilliant cover. You've got to make sure it's in the shops. You've got to get people talking about it. You don't want to just be a book, you want to be a bestseller.'

Sam looked slightly overwhelmed.

'You got all that from cutting my hair?'

'She's very good at her job,' Mir shouted, clapping in between each word. 'What part of that do people not get?'

'I still don't understand how this is going to change the way Elaine feels about me,' he muttered, sadly handing off his discarded ponytail to Coast, who took it reluctantly between pinched fingers. There had been talk of giving it to a charity that made wigs out of donated hair but we weren't entirely sure whether it would be a kindness or an insult. 'If she cut off her hair, it wouldn't change the way I feel about her.'

'It's not about the haircut or the shave or the clothes or the fact you look like a completely different human being,' I explained, even though I couldn't help but think it might be at least a little bit about that when she got a look at him. 'You're showing her you're prepared to try to make things work, that you're prepared to change things for her.'

I had seen some great makeovers in my time but the new and improved Dr Samuel Page was a mind-blower. Gone was any evidence of an awkward shut-in, the weirdo who was one brown paper bag away from being someone you crossed the street to avoid, and in his place was a clean, handsome, well-coiffed man with Swipe Right written all over him. All that was left for me to do was get him into a pair of jeans that wasn't eight sizes too big for the first time since his mother stopped dressing him. Assuming his mother had ever stopped dressing him.

'Have you given any thought to what you're going to say when you see her?' I asked.

'I know exactly what I'm going to say,' he replied with a firm nod. 'I'm going to tell her I love her and I miss her.'

'Ahh,' I smiled over at Mir, who was standing behind him. She stuck her fingers down her throat. 'That's a good start. Who wouldn't want to hear that?'

'And then tell her she needs to stop being so ridiculous and that I need my hay fever medicine. I'm not paying for another prescription, they're exorbitant these days. Also, I very much miss my cat.'

'So, we'll work on that part,' I said as I walked him back into the office. 'But at least your hair looks really nice. Now, onwards to stage three.'

I smiled as I caught him messing with his hair, checking the style in every available reflective surface.

'What am I supposed to do next?' he mumbled. 'Write her a sonnet? Whisk her off to Tahiti? Fill the flat with flowers, get down on my knees and beg her to take me back?'

'Yes!' Brian exclaimed from inside the sample cupboard. 'All those things! Go, go now.'

'You're ridiculous,' Sam said, shaking his head at his own very good ideas. 'Flights to Tahiti are inordinately expensive, and that's before you even take the accommodation into consideration; I'm a terrible poet; and I don't know how many times I have to remind you about my hay fever.'

'I hate to be the one to break it to you,' I said, not really hating it at all. 'But at the end of all this, a grand romantic gesture will be needed.'

'You don't know Elaine,' he replied, still rubbing his naked ears. 'She's not that kind of girl.'

'Everyone is that kind of girl,' Brian said, emerging with arms full of shoes. 'Everyone wants to feel special, everyone wants to feel wanted, everyone wants to feel understood. Take a Claritin and get yourself down the florists before they've got nothing left but carnations.'

'What's wrong with carnations?' Sam asked.

'You're on your own.' Brian dumped the shoes on my desk and shook his head sadly. 'It's a wonder she stayed with him for this long.'

'Look, there's a beginners' salsa workshop tomorrow,' I said, fingers clacking against my keyboard as I googled local dance classes. 'Starts at one, it's right around the corner, they've still got spaces available. What have you got to lose?'

Sam looked at me with complete and utter disdain.

'My pride? My dignity?'

'Both overrated,' I replied. 'Imagine how impressed Elaine will be when you bust out a few fancy dance moves as part of your apology tour. If you can't force yourself through a single dance class to get her back, then why are you even bothering?'

'Maybe you should go with him,' Brian suggested. 'For moral support.'

'I have plans tomorrow,' I said, flipping my head between the two of them. 'Or of course I'd go.'

'Well, I'm certainly not going alone,' Sam replied. 'One would think if you were really serious about helping me, you'd be there.'

'Oh, Annie, one really would,' Brian agreed, biting his lip and clapping loudly. 'Aren't you supposed to be his mentor or something?'

The pair of them looked at me, Sam with a tightly set jaw and Brian with a massive grin on his face.

'Tomorrow, you said?' There was a definite edge of challenge to Sam's voice when he spoke.

'One o'clock tomorrow,' I agreed through gritted teeth as Sam paused by Brian's desk to pick up the assorted tote bags full of clothes and shoes he was holding out. 'Can't wait.'

With a firm nod, Sam trotted out the door and down the corridor.

'You'll be a marvel,' Bri said, resting his chin on his hands and beaming at me across the office. 'I'd actually give anything to see it.'

'You're in luck, there's still a spot open,' I said, sitting down at my desk and immediately booking three tickets to the dance class. 'You're bloody well coming too.'

CHAPTER TWELVE

Saturday, 14 July: Twenty Days to Go

I hadn't got to bed before midnight all week long, and when Saturday rolled around, the last thing I wanted to do was spend the day at a salsa dancing workshop with the main reason I'd been losing sleep in the first place. I knew my strengths and I knew my limitations. I was not a talented dancer or a graceful human, and the idea of being up and dressed when I could still be in pyjamas, scarfing a croissant and watching the Real Housewives of anywhere did not put me in the best of moods.

But there I was, martyr to the cause, outside the studio right on time with Brian by my side and two giant coffees already swirling through my bloodstream as I worked on my third.

'Watch out,' Brian said, nodding down the street. 'Here comes David Starkey does *Strictly*.'

'Oh, I would totally watch that,' I muttered as I waved to Sam.

He stopped in front of us, offering a short, sharp nod to Brian, who responded with raised eyebrows as he sipped his iced coffee.

'Sam,' I said, more than a little confused. 'Why are you wearing a giant coat? It's red hot.'

'I didn't want people staring at me,' he replied as sweat poured down his face. 'Are you two getting changed inside?'

'What are you talking about?' I asked, looking down at my perfectly respectable black leggings and off the shoulder T-shirt. Admittedly, it was a bit *Flashdance*, but there was no need for him to be rude.

'It's almost one,' Brian said, giving me a nudge. 'We need to get inside.'

'Come on then, Ginger Rogers.' I drained my coffee cup and dropped it in the bin beside the door. 'Let's see your moves.'

'Shouldn't you be Ginger?' Sam asked as we followed Brian inside the dance studio.

'As if she's going to let you lead,' Brian chuckled as he closed the door behind us.

'Good morning, class.'

We slipped into the brightly lit and aggressively chilled studio just as the instructor began. She was younger than I'd anticipated; clearly, I'd watched one too many dance competitions on TV. I'd been expecting an Arlene or a Bruno, an older, more worldly woman or a super-flamboyant man who'd at least make the day more fun. Brian wasn't nearly camp enough for my liking. He refused to indulge my obsession with #jelena and failed to give a single flip about the well-being of Britney Spears. But here I was, faced with a twenty-something stunner who really had no business walking around looking so good in a leotard. It was still early and some of us hadn't had time to put on makeup.

'I am so excited to see you all here for our salsa

immersion,' she said, rolling her 'r's with a purr. 'My name is Benita and today we will be learning all the steps you will need to go out and kill it on the dance floor. We'll be tackling the progressive basic, the side basic, a *cumbia* step, crossover step, and then we'll take on the turns.'

At the side of me, I heard Sam gulp as Benita's shiny T-strap shoes clicked up and down the classroom.

'Let's start by learning everyone's names.' Benita turned her beaming smile on me and Sam. 'My friends, we can start with you?'

'I'm Annie and this is Sam,' I said. My elbows were suddenly pinned to my sides and I felt very, very out of place.

'It's Samuel,' Sam said. 'Dr Page, actually.'

'We are so happy to have you join us, Dr Page,' Benita said with a little clap. 'Please take off your coat. You're making me think you don't want to stay.'

Resigned to his fate, Sam unzipped his Puffa jacket to reveal a spectacular pair of tight-fitting black trousers and a low-cut, red satin shirt I was almost certain he'd gone back in time to steal from my mum, circa 1989.

'What. Are. You. Wearing?'

Each word was punctuated by flashes from Brian's iPhone camera.

'A Latin dance outfit,' he replied, looking aghast at everyone else's standard workout clothes. 'I went to the dance shop yesterday and asked what I should be wearing; this is what they recommended. I wanted to do it properly, I didn't want to stand out.'

'Oh, don't worry.' I waved a hand at the rest of the room where literally everyone was wearing regular workout gear. 'You blend right in.'

'But the man said this is what you wear for salsa.'

He kept rolling up the huge, blouson sleeves and every time, they fell back around his wrists. 'Why is no one else wearing the right stuff?'

'Because no one else is going directly from here to the set of *Strictly*,' I said. 'It's a beginners' class, you numpty. That man in the shop was just trying to get you to spend money.'

'Someone needs to put Baby back in the corner,' Brian whispered. 'And leave him there.'

'I'm leaving,' Sam said, his shirt the only thing in the world redder than his face. 'I'm going straight back to that shop and giving that man what for.'

'You're going nowhere,' I said, grabbing his hand as Benita summoned the couples on to the dance floor. 'Besides, you look great. This is going to be exactly what you need when you're tearing up the dance floor with Elaine, isn't it?'

It wasn't a complete lie. Shiny, second-skin trousers and slashed down to here shirt was hardly the most forgiving ensemble but Sam had been hiding a pretty impressive bod under his baggy clothes. There was a part of me that would rather see him wear this ridiculousness every day if it meant getting rid of his massive jeans.

While I considered running back to the office and burning all his clothes, Sam's eyes were glued to the door and I could see him weighing up his options.

'Sam,' I said quietly. 'I think Elaine would be really impressed at how committed you are to this.'

With a resigned sigh, he dropped his shoulders and nodded. A few feet away, Brian smiled at me as he attempted to keep his septuagenarian dance partner's hands off his arse.

'Everyone team up with your partner and stand face

to face,' Benita called out. 'We're going to start by finding our frame. Leaders, place your right hand on your partner's back and clasp their right hand in your left.'

Regretting every moment of my life that had led to this, I turned to face Sam and assumed the position.

'Come on, Fred Astaire,' I said with an encouraging smile. 'We're here, aren't we?'

'We are,' he replied, clearing his throat and taking my hand in his. His palms were extraordinarily sweaty. 'Even if I am the only one in proper attire.'

'Time to show everyone else up,' I whispered, giving his hand a squeeze. 'You've already got the gear, it'd be rude not to be amazing.'

'I always ask my classes, does anybody have any dance experience?' Benita called over the music and people began to trip back and forth.

'We have never, ever salsa-d,' I stuttered, as Benita gyrated past. 'Or more accurately, I have never done any dancing of any kind stone cold sober, since I was seventeen.'

'Actually, I've got some experience,' Sam said.

'You have?' I asked, surprised. 'I thought you said you didn't dance?'

'Didn't, not couldn't,' he said, a dimple in his cheek appearing out of nowhere. 'And it's been a while so I'm certain to be rusty.'

'Well, who knew?' I said as his hips began to sway with the rhythm of the music. 'What else have you got up that enormous sleeve?'

'Annie, if you could be quiet and follow my lead, this will be a lot simpler,' he said, right in my ear. 'I know that won't be easy for you.'

I looked up from staring down at my own uncoordinated toes to see him smiling.

146

'You, sir, are full of surprises,' I muttered, stepping on his feet for the first, but almost certainly not the last, time.

'Quiet,' he reminded me. 'Concentrate.'

And against all laws of god and man, I did as I was told.

Three hours later, I could barely stand, Brian's phone was quite literally full of photos and Dr Samuel Page was a revelation.

While I struggled to remember my right from my left, from the moment the music began Sam picked the moves up like a complete pro. He flew around the room, hips swinging, seemingly independent to the rest of his body. Everyone else looked stilted and awkward but Sam looked born to it. Bright red, deep V shirt and all.

'I can't believe it,' I gasped, slumping against the studio wall, out of breath and swiping damp strands of hair out of my eyes. 'Look at him, Brian, just look at him.'

'I can't stop looking at him,' Brian said as Sam spun his latest partner around the dance floor. 'I have been hypnotized. Annie, those hips do lie, Shakira was full of it.'

He passed his phone to me and I clicked through the evidence. Caught in the moment and filtered into black and white, Sam looked like every woman's fantasy. Intense gaze, pursed lips and complete control. I stopped on one shot and zoomed in on his face, one perfect lock of hair falling into his eyes, mouth slightly open as he gazed down at his partner.

'Watch out,' Brian said, reaching over to wipe a finger over my chin. 'You've got a bit of drool hanging there.'

'Get off.' I knocked his hand away and passed him his phone. 'It's sweat. I'm sweating. Dancing is difficult.'

'Unless you're twinkle toes over there,' he replied as we both sank to the floor, cross-legged. 'Are we certain he's not actually an undercover spy?'

'We are no longer certain of anything,' I said, swabbing my face with my sleeve. 'Hey, how come I'm not in any of the photos?'

Brian knitted his eyebrows together in faux concern.

'Because you were shit?' he said, taking his phone out of his pocket and playing a video of me. It was all arms and legs and unflattering thrusting. 'See?'

'Why do I keep sticking out my tongue?' I asked, turning my head, trying to make sense of my erratic steps. 'And why am I always shaking my head?'

'Because you think you're a pony,' Brian suggested, leaning in beside me. 'If only you were the bet. This would get twenty thousand followers in a heartbeat.'

'You're not dancing.'

I looked up to see a breathless Sam stood over us, his feet still moving to the beat.

'What's wrong? Are you all right? Did you hurt yourself?'

'Just taking a break,' I said, pressing my hand into a stitch in my side. 'So, it turns out you're secretly the best dancer in the world. Do you have anything you'd like to tell the group?'

'Hardly the best dancer in the world,' he said, still jigging about as he spoke. 'I'm naturally inclined to pick up dancing quite quickly, that's all. It's muscle memory.'

'And what exactly are your muscles remembering?' I asked. 'That time you accidentally starred in *Step Up*?'

I noticed all the women in the class lined up on the opposite side of the studio, looking our way and

148

whispering to each other. It was like the adult version of my Year Seven Valentine's Day disco.

'*Step Up* is street dancing,' he replied. 'I did ballet, modern and tap.'

'So you have been doing your homework,' I replied, scraping my hair back into a ponytail. 'Interesting.'

'I took lessons when I was ten,' Sam explained, taking a small white towel from a giggling Benita and nodding his thanks. 'My grandmother bought them for my cousin, but she didn't like it; the lessons were non-refundable and my grandmother hated to waste money. I went instead. As you can imagine, it didn't exactly improve my popularity at school.'

'I think you'll find women love a man who can dance,' I said, looking away as he dabbed himself down with his tiny towel. Benita and the rest of the class did not afford him the same privacy. 'There are, like, at least seventeen films where that's the entire plot.'

'Women love Channing Tatum,' he corrected. 'They aren't interested in a late-blooming pre-pubescent boy dancing the Nutcracker in the Year Eight Christmas assembly. I jacked it in after a few years when I realized I was marginally safer from the school bullies in the library than I was on the stage.'

'Well, you're a natural,' I told him. It was true, he was magnificent on the dance floor. Even if the shirt was still ridiculous. 'Does Elaine know you can dance like this?'

He shook his head. 'As I said, my soft shoe shuffle has never been a big selling point with the ladies.'

'This is amazing!' I exclaimed, mentally deleting half my boyfriend bootcamp plans. This was going to be easy. 'The two of you would smash it on the dancefloor.

You should enter competitions together, when you get back together.'

Sam squeezed his face into an uncertain expression.

'Just because you're good at something doesn't mean you necessarily enjoy it,' he replied. 'This is it for me, Annie.'

'You could always try it in a different outfit,' Brian suggested. 'Then you might not feel like such a tit.'

'Appreciate the sentiment,' he said stiffly. He pulled at the cuffs of his shirt and shook his head. 'But perhaps we could try some of her other hobbies instead.'

Baby was officially back in the corner.

'But you're so good,' I said in my best wheedling tone. 'And I'm sure she'd be impressed, Sam. She posts about dancing all the time, I'm sure she'd love to share this with you.'

And I would love for my entire Saturday to have not been completely and utterly wasted.

'What were the other suggestions you had for me?' he said, resolute. 'There must be something else.'

'You could make her dinner?' I suggested with a sigh. 'But like, more than once.'

'Can't cook,' he replied. 'I once gave a group of friends food poisoning from bad mussels. I can't even begin to tell you how much I paid in dry-cleaning bills.'

'A proper party then,' Brian proposed. 'Get all her friends over, make a big scene. Even if she's not keen, she'll probably take pity on you out of politeness. Hard to turn someone down in front of a crowd. And you could work in the salsa if you change your mind.'

'I'm not really one for a large gathering where I'm the centre of attention,' Sam said. 'A dinner would definitely be better than a party.'

'A party?' I glanced up at the clock on the wall. It

was already past four, the surprise was scheduled for six. 'Oh Christ, I completely forgot my dad's birthday. I'm going to be late – my sister is going to be so mad.'

I hurled myself across Brian to grab my bag. My phone was full of messages from Becks, asking if I needed a lift, asking why I wasn't replying, asking if I was dead in a ditch. I frantically tapped out a reply to let her know I was on my way, even though that clearly was not even a little bit true.

'You can be a bit late can't you?' Brian asked, unfolding himself and climbing to his feet.

'It's a surprise party,' I explained, yanking my jumper over my head. 'We're supposed to be there for six, Gina is bringing him home at quarter past. If I'm not there, it'll be the end of the world, I will never hear the end of it.'

Brian winced in horror.

'Sounds hateful,' he said. 'Where is it?'

'Dad's house,' I said as I tied up my hair. 'Somewhere in the wilds of Hertfordshire. He likes to stay out of reach of the commoners. I'll have to get an Uber if I want to get there even nearly on time, it's going to cost me a fortune.'

'I can drive you,' Sam suggested. 'I've got a car.'

Brian and I looked up in surprise.

'It's a long way,' I replied, shifting the weight of my bag from hand to hand. 'It's going to be at least an hour in traffic at this time.'

'You can't take an Uber all that way,' he said with a certain sniff. 'They're not safe, I've read about it.'

Not to mention the fact I couldn't afford it.

'That's really nice of you but, like I said, it's so far,' I said, itching to take him up on the offer. 'And I've already taken up most of your Saturday.'

Another smile appeared on Sam's face as he folded his tiny towel up into a neat square.

'It's Saturday night, my girlfriend is god knows where doing god knows what and I'm sleeping on my brother's settee,' he replied. 'I would rather play taxi driver for you than watch a thirty-seven-year-old man bicker with teenagers on his Xbox for another evening.'

'Wow, your brother is even less cool than you,' Brian breathed. 'No offence.'

'None taken,' Sam said. 'He's an utter child. But what can you do? He's family. Now, Annie, you're in a rush, shouldn't we be leaving?'

I hopped from foot-to-foot, desperate to take him up on his offer but it just didn't seem right.

'You can pay for petrol,' he said. 'If that would make you feel better.'

'Only if you're sure,' I said, picking up my bag and practically running for the door.

'I wouldn't have offered if I wasn't sure,' he said as he pulled his huge padded coat on over his sweaty shirt. 'I'm parked round the corner. Shall we?'

'We surely shall,' I replied before turning back to give Brian a hug. 'Thanks for being so incredibly supportive today, buddy.'

'Have fun at your party,' he said, sending me off with a slap on the arse. 'Give my love to Becks.'

'I won't,' I promised, running back to the door where Sam was waiting to leave, much to the dismay of all the women who were waiting for their turn to dance with him. 'But thanks again.'

He waved us off with a one-fingered salute. Truly, I had the best friends.

CHAPTER THIRTEEN

'All I'm saying is, these are some really interesting musical selections,' I said, scrolling through Sam's song collection in the passenger seat of his Ford Focus. 'Nirvana, Oasis, even Guns N' Roses, all boy music, all to be expected. But I wouldn't have had you down as a Selena Gomez fan.'

'A good song is a good song,' he replied. 'If I hear something I like, I download it. I don't know who does what.'

'As long I don't find any early years Justin Bieber, we're OK.' I clicked on a Motown compilation as we pulled off the motorway. 'I still can't believe you've got the best of Britney on here.'

'Happy uni memories,' Sam said, something like nostalgia passing over his face for a moment. When he really, really went for it, there was a tiny dimple in his left cheek. 'And some of those songs are good to run to.'

'You're a runner?'

'I did the marathon last year,' he nodded. 'Never again, it nearly killed me. But yes, I like to run.'

I pulled one of seven lipsticks out of my handbag and set to work on my face. Going back to my flat wasn't an option if we wanted to make the party, so Dad was just going to have to cope with my T-shirt and leggings. Thank god my sweaty hair lent itself nicely to an up-do. The things you could learn from YouTube.

'Miranda runs,' I said, pressing the colour into my lips with my ring finger. 'I've never been able to get into it. I start thinking about things and then I get stressed out and then I give up. Too much going on in my head, I suppose.'

'That's why you need Britney,' Sam said, changing the music. 'You need a good beat to get started. Running lets me clear out all the noise, helps me to think.'

'About George Nugent-Temple-Grenville, the first Marquess of Buckingham?'

'Good memory. Yes, amongst other things.'

'What other things?' I asked.

'Not relevant.' he replied, turning up the music. 'Apologies in advance in case I start to sing along.'

I grinned and pulled my mascara wand out of the tube with a satisfying sucking sound. Baby steps, I reminded myself, at least he was talking to me. Sam might have been comfortable sitting in silence for an hour up the A1M but I just wasn't one of those people. Wielding my mascara wand, I pulled down his sunshade to look for a mirror. A mini Polaroid fell into my lap, Sam and Elaine hugging in front of the Eiffel tower, both of them younger, softer and happier than the more recent versions I had seen.

Sam tapped the brakes, just for a split second, and all my makeup rolled off my knee and into the foot-well.

'Sorry,' I said, trying to replace the photo. Every time I slid it back into its hidden pocket, the two of them floated back down, demanding to be witnessed. 'I didn't know it was there.'

'Neither did I,' he replied. 'I'm sorry, I could have caused an accident.'

'Not your fault,' I insisted. The easy peace I'd worked so hard for dissolved into a tense silence. Sam reached over and turned off the stereo.

'Almost there,' he said, eyes fixed firmly on the road, arms locked in a tense ten and two position.

'I've texted my sister to say we might be late,' I replied. 'It's fine, no rush.'

I turned my head to look out the window and slipped the picture into the pocket on the passenger side door, trying not to look at it. Instead, I tapped my phone into life inside my bag and opened up my phone Instagram: @TheHipHistorian had 1,500 new followers. I'd spent Friday night liking and commenting on what felt like millions of comedy accounts, most of which really stretched the definition of the word comedy but it was paying off. Sam's account was growing fast.

Two thousand down, only eighteen thousand to go.

'This is where your father lives?' Sam asked when we turned off the road and into Dad's driveway, fifteen long, awkward minutes later.

'This is where my father lives,' I confirmed. 'I know, it's weird.'

'It's not weird,' he replied, slowing down as we reached the end of a long line of stationary vehicles. 'It's a bloody mansion.'

Technically, it was not a mansion. It was an eight-bedroom red-brick monster of a house with a four-car garage, a swimming pool, a summer house and a croquet lawn set on two acres of land at the end of a private road. I knew this because my dad mentioned each and every specification of his luxury executive home in each and every one of his emails.

'I didn't grow up here,' I told him as I unbuckled my seatbelt. 'If that's what you're thinking. He only moved in here two years ago when he retired. Me, my mum and sister lived in a perfectly normal semi. One car, no pool. Well, we had a paddling pool one summer but there was a situation with my cousin's guinea pig and the less said about that the better.'

'I was going to ask if I could come in and use the loo,' Sam said, peering up at the looming stack of bricks. 'But I can wait. There was a McDonald's just before we got off the M25, I'll go there.'

'No one should have to pee in a service station if they don't have to,' I said, spotting my sister's Volvo parked directly across the driveway. I'd been instructed to park next to her. Dad thought we were coming over for a nice, quiet family dinner to celebrate this very important birthday. And no doubt he was furious about it. 'Don't you want to know how many toilets he's got?'

'The modern flush toilet is an ecological disaster, endless water wastage,' Sam replied as we climbed out of the car. 'Annie, is that a fountain?'

'Why yes, yes it is,' I nodded. 'You should see the waterfall in the back. Loves a water feature, does Malcolm.'

Sam had managed to find a knackered old black V-neck jumper in the back of his car and pulled it on over the top of his red satin shirt, giving him the look of a vampire about to teach an A-level geography class.

We were not going to win any prizes for best-dressed people at this party.

We skipped along, as quickly as possible. It was already after six and I wanted to get in and ideally get Sam back out before my dad arrived home. There was a brief pause while I fought with the door handle; for all the money they'd spent on this house, it never, ever opened first time.

'SURPRISE!'

As I threw open the door, confetti cannons fired in my face, balloons fell from the ceiling and a live band burst into a jaunty rendition of 'Happy Birthday'.

'Stop it, stop it!' I heard my sister shouting. 'Annie, what the flip are you doing here?'

Clearly there were children present.

'Just thought I'd stop by,' I replied, trying to gather as many balloons in my arms as possible as the band petered out, one instrument at a time. 'What do you think I'm doing here?'

'But you said you were going to be late.' She started kicking the confetti into piles, as though the cannons could be reloaded. I knew full well from watching several thousand YouTube videos, they could not. 'Dad's going to be here any—'

'What on earth is going on?'

We both froze, arms full of streamers, at the sound of Dad's voice.

'Surprise!' I exclaimed, throwing my balloons roughly one foot up into the air. 'Happy birthday, Dad.'

Gina stood behind my father, mouth hanging open, clinging to the doorframe and shaking. A single balloon fell down from the net suspended from the ceiling.

The band started up again and everyone began singing while I died where I stood. As if it wasn't bad enough that I'd forgotten about the party and I'd ruined the surprise, I'd also forgotten it was fancy dress. Everyone, from my niece and nephew to my Great Aunt Beryl had turned out in their glittery best, while I stood there in a pair of baggy-kneed Primark leggings and the off-the-shoulder T-shirt I'd stolen from Miranda.

Trust Gina to have chosen a *Saturday Night Fever* party for his sixtieth birthday.

'Happy Birthday, Dad,' I said, dying inside as I leaned in to kiss his proffered cheek. 'We got here late and there was a bit of a mix-up. I'm so sorry, Gina.'

'No harm done.' Her bottom lip trembled as she surveyed the sparkling carnage. 'We're just glad you're here, Annie.'

'I'm honoured you were able to grace us with your presence,' Dad said, looking Sam up and down. 'And who might this be?'

Behind me, Sam was scrambling to pull his jumper over his head. He chucked it unceremoniously behind the closest ice sculpture. There were several. Dad took his hand and pumped his arm up and down like he was hoping to win a jackpot.

'Dr Samuel Page,' Sam stuttered. 'I gave Annie a lift.'

'At least he bothered to dress up,' Dad replied, pushing up onto his tiptoes to throw an arm around Sam's shoulders. 'You need to take a lesson from your young man, Annabel.'

'He's not my young man,' I said as Sam raised an eyebrow at me. 'And he needs the toilet.'

'You know where it is,' Gina said, ushering my dad past us and into the welcoming throng of guests. 'Can you meet me upstairs in a minute?'

158

I nodded, even though I was quite certain I'd rather poke out my own eyes.

'I'm so sorry,' I said, pushing Sam away from the family and towards one of the downstairs loos. 'My dad can be a bit, you know.'

'Quite,' Sam replied, giving the front door a longing look. 'Annabel.'

'Literally never use that name again,' I warned him. 'He means well. At least, I think he does. Mum and Dad got divorced when I was six and sometimes he doesn't realize I've aged since the day he left.'

'Families are hard.' He pulled on the cuff of his shirt. 'I understand.'

'You should have been at my sixteenth birthday,' I told him. 'I'm there in my Doc Martens, showing off my nose-piercing to Stuart Danielson and Dad trots up to the village hall with an actual pony. A Shetland pony with a pink bow around it. We lived in a semi-detached in Twickenham – what was I supposed to do with a Shetland pony?'

'I don't know,' Sam said, smothering a smile. 'They're very small, seems like an appropriate-sized pony for a semi.'

'Don't,' I warned him, finding a smile of my own. 'I spent the rest of the party sulking on the back step, holding the reins of this tiny horse while Dad spent the entire night showing off his dance moves to my friends. I was mortified.'

'Perhaps I should get Elaine a pony,' he suggested. It took me a second to realize he was joking. 'Good to see you're not hanging on to childhood traumas, Annie.'

'You sound like my sister,' I said, a wave of dread washing over me when I remembered I still had to

159

apologize to Becks. 'I suppose I should be grateful he showed up at all. There were plenty of times when he didn't.'

'I envy people who had uncomplicated childhoods,' Sam replied. 'I can't even begin to imagine it.'

I brushed a renegade strand of hair out of my eyes. I wasn't used to people I didn't know very well being so sincere. 'Are you not close with your parents?'

'It's fine.'

It was quite clear that it was not.

'I don't believe I'm missing much,' he added. 'I have my brother, who is more than happy to embarrass me as and when necessary.'

'Oh good,' I said. 'As long as that's taken care of.'

Sam stood silently with a tense look on his face. It took me a moment, wondering what he might be trying to say, before I realized he just wanted to go to the toilet.

'Oh, God, sorry, go,' I said, stepping out of his way. I jumped as he swung the toilet door shut behind him. 'I've just got to go and find Gina,' I called, not especially keen to hang around and wait for him to use the loo. We weren't there yet. 'I'll be back in a minute.'

The party was in full swing. Dad's house was so unnecessarily huge, I didn't even know the proper names for all the rooms. There were the obvious ones – kitchen, dining room, living room, office – but then there were the more vague rooms that all ran into each other in some weird open-plan labyrinth: the den, the TV room, a second dining room and the enormous conservatory, which seemed to double for any and all of the above. Glitter balls were suspended from the ceiling and huge disco lights flashed and moved in time to the music as I skulked upstairs, hiding in the shadows.

'Annie?'

Gina beckoned me into her bedroom, a tiny blonde cloud of orange chiffon and Chanel No. 5.

'I am so sorry about spoiling the surprise,' I said, keeping my eyes on my stepmother and off their round bed. I didn't bother to ask if it rotated, I just assumed. 'You look lovely.'

'Are you getting changed?' she said, her massive hoop earrings jangling in disappointment. 'Because this is a lot more eighties than seventies, and I was quite specific in the invitation.'

'I kind of came straight from a work thing,' I hedged, pulling the cuffs of my sleeves down over my unmanicured fingers. 'Sorry, Gina.'

'It's your dad's sixtieth,' she said, taking hold of my arm and leading me over to her vast wardrobe. 'We can't have you walking around like that, can we?'

'Are you sending me to my room?' I asked, alarmed. 'Because you know I'm over thirty and I don't live here.'

'Oh, you,' she said with a tinkly laugh. 'Let's find you something of mine. I got a bit carried away shopping for tonight, so there are a few spares.'

My heart skipped several beats and not in a good way.

'But I don't think we're the same size,' I panicked. 'And I'm not wearing the right underwear. And also I don't want to.'

Gina turned to face me, fire burning in her eyes. She might have only been five feet tall and eight stone tops if she was piss wet through but in that moment she was truly terrifying. Or at least she would have been if one of her eyelids hadn't been weighed down by her false lashes.

161

'I know we're not best friends,' she said, crushing my fingers with an unearthly strength. 'But I'd like us to get along better, Annie.'

'OK,' I replied. Awkward familial confrontation. My kryptonite.

'And I think you'd look just fab in one of my dresses.'

'OK.'

'And I bet your boyfriend would like it.'

'He's not my boyfriend,' I said. 'Do you have anything in black?'

'You can't wear black, it'll wash you out,' Gina replied without looking at me. She flicked through a rack of dresses in a walk-in wardrobe that was bigger than my entire bedroom. 'Try this.'

I shook my head at the hanger in her hand.

'It's orange,' I said. 'I can't.'

'It's a good colour for you.' She held up a frothy concoction of pale peach chiffon underneath my chin. 'Brings out the blue in your eyes.'

'But I'm fine as I am,' I insisted. 'Really.'

'Try it on,' she ordered. Apparently we were no longer playing nice. 'And I'll see you back downstairs. We're doing the cake in ten minutes.'

Well. At least there would be cake.

By the time I'd wrestled my way into Gina's dress and found a pair of shoes that fit, I was certain that Sam would have left. But no, it was even worse. As I carefully made my way downstairs in my borrowed stilts, I saw him right away. He'd been cornered by the worst possible people: my aunt, my cousin and my Uncle Norman. Not that Uncle Norman was actually related to me in any way, shape or form. To the best of my knowledge, he was just a dirty old man who always seemed to hang around at family functions even though no one wanted to claim responsibility for having invited him in the first place.

'You changed,' Sam said, somewhat startled. I nodded, arms neatly folded underneath my chest. The dress did not allow for a bra. I needed a bra. This was not going to go well.

'Annie, don't you look a vision,' Aunt Helen said, clapping loudly as I arrived to draw as much attention to us as humanly possible. 'Wherever did you get that dress?'

'It's Gina's,' I said, hoiking up the tiny spaghetti straps. 'I borrowed it.'

The dress itself was actually beautiful, but I wasn't entirely doing it justice. A vintage, soft peachy silk disco number with an asymmetric hem and very low back, it moved when I moved, ruffles on the hem fluttering every time I breathed. And thanks to Gina's very high heels, I was breathing hard.

'That makes sense,' my cousin, Sharon, added. 'It's not very you, is it?'

I glanced over to see Uncle Norman's gaze safely resting on my cleavage. It was nice to see some things never changed. Oh wait, no, it wasn't.

'I won't be wearing it to work on Monday, no,' I replied. 'But it's fancy dress, aren't most people in costume?'

'This is vintage Halston,' Sharon gave a twirl that was met with a round of appreciative applause and a wolf whistle that seemed like overkill even for Uncle Norman. 'It was Mum's in the seventies.'

'I do like to take care of my things,' Helen commented, smoothing down her own liquid gold dress. She'd always been very thin. I would always remember the time my mum and Aunt Helen engaged in a silent Salad Off during a particularly traumatic family holiday to Menorca when I was five. They never did get along and, strangely enough, Sharon and I had carried on that tradition. Mostly because Sharon was a complete shit and always had been.

'Annie was never very good at looking after things,' Sharon told Sam. 'When we were little, she used to break everything. When we were seven, she broke the wings off my—'

'I broke the wings off her Flower Fairy,' I said, finishing for her before mouthing an apology at a bemused Sam. 'Accidentally. Unlike the time you cut the hair off all my Barbies because you said pixie-cuts were in.'

'Do you remember when you wet yourself on the way home from Alton Towers?' Sharon asked, colouring up. 'The car never smelled the same.'

'Remember when you ate all the profiteroles at my dad's wedding and threw up on your bridesmaid dress?' I volleyed back.

'Do you remember when you wrote that love poem to Marvin Somerton and he read it out in assembly and everyone died laughing?'

'Do you remember when you drowned a guinea pig?' I screeched.

I didn't realize I was raising my voice until everyone turned to look at us.

'I didn't know they couldn't swim,' Sharon said, white as a sheet.

'Everyone knows that,' I muttered under my breath. 'Everyone.'

'Dr Page was just telling us all about how you work together before you so rudely interrupted him,' Aunt

Helen said archly, squeezing his forearm as though her daughter hadn't just been accused of rodenticide and squeezing the forearms of strange men was acceptable behaviour.

Sharon took Sam's other arm. I knew she never cared about that guinea pig. RIP Rupert. 'Typical Annie,' she said. 'She's always been an attention-seeker.' She gave a little laugh.

So says the girl who once organized her own birthday parade, complete with fully choreographed dance number, three clowns and a pony. (Yes, the same one from my birthday party. It had to go somewhere once Dad realised it couldn't live in my back garden.)

'I don't think I quite follow.' Aunt Helen sipped a bright pink cocktail that matched Sharon's dress perfectly. 'If you're a historian, how is it you work with Annie? Aren't you still working for that chap who does the internet things?'

'No, I own my own business now,' I explained, choosing not to dwell on the fact I'd already explained this to her at length at Easter, Christmas and that one time I saw her in Tesco and couldn't run away and hide fast enough. 'It's a digital marketing agency.'

'She writes tweets for people,' Sharon explained, lowering her voice as though I wasn't standing right in front of her.

'I suppose anything can be a job these days,' Helen said, raising her eyebrows. 'So how do you fit in to this, Dr Page?'

'We work in the same building, we don't work together,' I replied, veering wildly between complete mortification and righteous indignation. So, really it was just your average family party. 'Sam's researching a book.'

'Mummy wrote a book!' Sharon said, brightening immediately. 'And it's so good.'

'Not nearly the same kind of thing,' I said, cutting her off quickly. There was something exceptionally wrong about hearing a daughter compliment her mother's self-published erotica novel. 'Sam's is non-fiction.'

'Yes,' he said, clearing his throat. 'It's about the first Marquess of Buckingham. He was foreign secretary for four days in 1783.'

No one said anything.

'I think it's jolly nice of you to bring Annie to this bloody thing,' Uncle Norman said, waving his glass in what was either a very odd toast or the first suggestion that he was already drunk enough to fall over. 'The poor mare always has to come on her tod, don't you, girl? Must be nice to have a chap with you for once.'

'It is, Uncle Norman, thanks for asking,' I said with a kind smile. 'For a moment I thought I was going to have to bring my lesbian lover but, you know, I didn't want to make a scene.'

'Oh gosh, I completely forgot to ask . . .' Helen let go of Sam to take my hand in hers and I was genuinely shocked when he didn't turn and start heading for the front door. 'How are you doing after the big news?'

'The big news?' I asked, eyeing a waiter with a tray of champagne. I had been sober for quite long enough.

'Matthew getting engaged?' she replied. 'To that lovely blonde girl? At the England game?'

Puffing out my cheeks to stop myself from speaking, I grabbed two glasses as she walked past. Sam held out his hand and I begrudgingly handed one over.

'That must have been such a shock,' Sharon said, holding her hand to her heart. 'I'd have died.'

'Well, we broke up a long time ago so it's not really a big deal,' I replied, draining the champagne in two mouthfuls. 'I'm really happy for them.'

'Yeah, OK,' Sharon snickered. 'Of course you are.'

'Annie, would you like to dance?'

'Dance?'

Sam held out his hand expectantly, nodding towards the dance floor.

'Sorry to be so rude but, well . . .' Sam said, searching the depths of his extensive vocabulary for the rest of the sentence. 'The truth is, I'm not sure if you realize but all these people are extremely unpleasant. Please excuse us.'

'Sam,' I said, following him onto the light-up dance floor, leaving my aunt and cousin gaping like goldfish behind us. 'That was bloody brilliant.'

Gina and my dad were spinning around the middle of the floor while Alice was waltzing around on top of Alan's feet. Becks bounced the baby on her hip, looking on happily. She tipped me the wink as Sam placed his hand on my lower back. I jumped as his thumb grazed the bare skin above my hips.

'It was unforgivably rude,' he said, a flush in his cheeks. 'I don't know what came over me. They were just so truly awful, Annie. Someone had to tell them.'

'It was magical,' I said, allowing him to move me around the room and hoping against hope that my boobs wouldn't fall out of my top. 'You just made one of my life-long dreams come true.'

He winced slightly as the music changed. The up-tempo number melted into something altogether more romantic, a song I only knew from the Destiny's Child cover version. Without even a hint of hesitation,

Sam changed tempo, holding my hand close to his chest, turning and twisting me around in small circles.

'I should apologize,' he said decidedly.

'God, no!' I exclaimed, trying not to trip over my own feet. This would have been difficult enough in trainers. In heels, I'd be lucky to get out of here without a broken neck. 'You didn't say anything that wasn't true. I'm only gutted you were the one to tell them off instead of me. Besides, you'll literally never have to see them again, so make the most of it.'

Sam's face lit up with an actual grin. Not the polite smile I'd seen come and go over the past few days but an honest-to-goodness, face-splitting grin. His blue eyes almost disappeared into the crinkles that appeared above his cheekbones and I spotted his hidden dimple somewhere inside his stubble. Without any kind of warning, he brushed a strand of my hair off the back of my neck. I shivered from head to toe. Suddenly, my flimsy dress felt inappropriate and the dance felt too intimate. We were barely even acquaintances, after all. I took a big step backwards and switched to a side-to-side shuffle, my arms moving awkwardly at my sides.

'Anyway, as much as I'm sure you're having the time of your life,' I told him, 'you can absolutely leave at any second. Don't think you have to stay.'

Sam looked back over my shoulder where my aunt was relaying his insults, complete with wild hand gestures, to anyone who would listen.

'I know they're your family,' he said. 'But you don't have to stay either.'

It was the craziest idea I'd ever heard.

'You've shown up, you've done your part,' Sam said,

cocking his head towards the door. 'It's not as if anyone's going to forget you were here, is it?'

'I can't leave,' I said, thrilled by the very idea. 'We've only just got here.'

But the thought of it . . . We could be back in London inside an hour. I'd be home before eight. I'd get an entire night to myself. And, more to the point, I wouldn't have to spend the next six hours explaining why I wasn't married, why I didn't have kids, a car or a proper job, and even better, I wouldn't have to listen to a Becks lecture on the way home, squished between two tired children tethered to car seats and a potentially shitty nappy.

'Annie!' Dad and Gina danced up alongside us, cutting off any potential escape route. 'You look a delight. You should let Gina give you a makeover more often.'

Sam scoffed before smothering it into a cough.

'And what about you?' I asked, taking in Dad's seventies ensemble. My step-mother was clearly enjoying her role as stylist and had changed him out of his neat polo shirt and into something altogether more. . . creative.

'Just look at you.'

'I know,' he replied, straightening his collar. 'Nothing like a sharp-dressed man.'

He did not look sharp. He looked like a sixty-year-old man called Malcolm who thought he looked like a twenty-two-year-old man called John Travolta. A little portly belly hung over his white flares and the long pointed collar of his black shirt opened to reveal an ostentatious diamond medallion, nestled in a bed of grey chest hair. I wanted to believe it was diamanté. I wanted to believe it so badly.

'Remind me again, when do you hear about those awards you're up for?' Dad asked.

'Two more weeks,' I said, bobbing up and down on the spot. It was against the law of physics to stand completely still on a dance floor, even if you were trying to hold a conversation with your fancy-dressed-Dad.

'Ah.' Dad nodded to Gina and gave her a spin. 'I thought maybe I'd missed them.'

'No,' I replied. 'If they'd happened, I'd have told you, wouldn't I?'

'Not if you didn't win,' he reasoned. I seized up, missing my footing and accidentally stabbing Sam in the foot with the heel of my borrowed shoe.

'We're going to do the cake,' Gina said, shouting unnecessarily loudly over the music. 'Before the oldies have to get off. I know Rebecca wanted to make a bit of a speech, but did you want to say anything, Annie?'

I shook my head and smiled. 'Becks is better at public speaking than me.'

'She's always been very good at it,' Dad agreed. 'I still remember that speech she gave at her graduation.'

With that, they dance-walked off the dance floor and over to the giant discoball-shaped cake on the other side of the room. I hadn't realized I'd completely stopped moving until they were laughing and hugging with my sister.

'I'll go and start the car, shall I?' Sam said.

Becks tapped the microphone and cleared her throat.

'Hi, everyone,' she started, Alice clinging to her ankles. 'On behalf of the entire family, I just wanted to thank everyone for being here today to celebrate Dad's big birthday and start off the speeches. But we

170

should probably start with a song, so join in if you know it! Happy birthday to you . . .'

As everyone started singing along, the urge to bolt became overwhelming.

'This must be why you have a PhD,' I replied, giving Sam the nod. No one would miss me. It was time to leave. 'Dr Samuel Page, you are a smart one.'

'It's a testament to your persistence that it is already too strange to hear you call me anything other than Sam,' he said as we shuffled slowly towards the door. 'It usually takes a minimum of twenty-one days for a human being to develop a habit. And I'm sure I told you I've got two PhDs.'

'Right,' I said as the band quieted down. 'Because what kind of loser only has one?'

'Quite,' Sam replied, reaching for his jumper from behind the ice sculpture as we made a run for it.

CHAPTER FOURTEEN

'Annie?'

'Go,' I ordered as Sam beeped his car into life. My sister was stood on the front step of Dad's house, hands on her hips, screeching my name.

'Annie! Where the bloody hell do you think you're going?'

'Sorry, Becks,' I called, waving as I went. 'We've got to get back to town. Save me a piece of cake, love you!'

Before she could try to stop us, I leapt into the passenger seat and Sam gunned the engine. Surprisingly aggressive for a Ford Focus. I glanced in the rear-view mirror to see her shaking her head as we tore down the driveway, leaving the party and, unfortunately, my bra in a literal cloud of dust.

The drive back to London was positively joyous. We blasted Sam's running songs, singing along as we circled the M25, even after whatever held us up by an hour we were still laughing. Sam, I assumed, high on sugar and me high on the look on Aunt Helen's face.

'Favourite pizza topping,' I said, popping a handful of Haribo, acquired at the service station, into my mouth.

'Hawaiian,' Sam answered, holding his hand out for more sweets. 'I know it's controversial, but I love pineapple on pizza.'

'Because you're a monster,' I replied happily. 'Everyone knows pepperoni is the only way to go.'

'I think it's because I spent my entire childhood eating cheese and pineapple on sticks,' he said as he chewed his fizzy cola bottles thoughtfully. 'It was the height of sophisticated cuisine when I was growing up.'

'You mean it isn't now?' I asked in mock shock. 'Kids today don't know they're born. OK, favourite superhero?'

Sam screwed up his face, whether it was at the sour sweets or tricky question, I wasn't sure.

'Favourite or best?' he replied. 'Because there's a big difference.'

'Hmm.' I swilled down my sweets with a mouthful of Diet Coke like the classy lady I was. 'Both, I suppose. Why would they be different?'

'Tell me yours first,' Sam said, switching on the windscreen wipers to wash away a sprinkling of rain that appeared from nowhere. I hoped it wasn't raining on Dad's party, Gina really had worked hard.

'Thor,' I said as I looked up at the suddenly grey skies.

'Why?'

'Because of the hammer and the Viking stuff and, you know.' I wrapped my arms around myself. It wasn't freezing but the clouds had blocked out the summer sunshine and it was suddenly too chilly to be sat in a car with a man I barely knew wearing a dress that covered next to nothing. 'Basically, he's really fit.'

Without taking his eyes off the crawling traffic, Sam reached into the back for a bright red Puffa jacket and laid it across my legs. I slid it around my shoulders, smiling a thank you.

'At least you're honest,' he said. 'But the best super-hero is Superman. He's got the best powers – he can fly, he's super strong, he's got that laser vision – plus he's a good man. He doesn't have to use his abilities to save humanity, but he does.'

'What about Batman?' I asked, unbuckling Gina's strappy stilettos and flexing my toes. They were like tiny torture devices. I had no idea how she wore them all day. 'Batman could be swanning around on a yacht with loads of supermodels but instead he's out saving the day, answering that bloody bat signal morning, noon and night and getting the shit kicked out of him by the Joker.'

Sam glanced over at me, a look of disbelief in his clear light-blue eyes.

'You're not serious?' he said, speeding up the wipers.

'Deadly serious,' I nodded. 'And how does the Bat signal work anyway? What if it's daytime? Or if he's having a bath? Or he's on the loo? Do they just hope he'll see people tweeting about it and get there in time? And don't get me started on how long it must take him to get the suit on. What if he hasn't shaved? Is he doing that while he's driving, because that definitely isn't safe.'

'Batman is a sociopath,' Sam replied, shaking his head and dismissing any of my other concerns out of hand. 'He might be cool but he's definitely not the best superhero ever. He hasn't got any powers, he's just rich.'

I didn't say anything but at that exact moment, it was a superpower I wouldn't turn down.

'Superman is the best superhero,' he insisted. 'But my favourite is the Hulk.'

'No one's favourite superhero is the Hulk,' I scoffed. 'You're just being awkward.'

'He's my favourite,' Sam insisted, resting the bag of sweets between his thighs. We were both starving, we hadn't eaten anything since the dodgy sandwiches Sam had brought with him to the dance studio and plastic ham sandwiches with curled up edges were no one's idea of fine cuisine. Except for possibly Brian's, because he had eaten nearly all of them. 'He's a world-class scientist, which would be entirely impressive enough on its own, he's got a dozen doctorates in different fields of research and yet he has to go about his day, saving the world, doing all his science, all while knowing that the Hulk could reappear at any second and destroy everything. He isn't like the others, his powers aren't a choice, he can't turn them on and off.'

'Doing all his science?' I said with a grin. 'Wow. So eloquent.'

'That is not the point.' He tapped his fingers on the steering wheel in time to the windscreen wipers. 'He's the true hero. He didn't ask for his abilities and he's still trying to save the world while living with the potentially terrible consequences of his powers all day every day.'

'Which must be a nightmare, considering he's doing all that science. Imagine trying to pick up a test tube with those fat, green fingers,' I said innocently. Sam grabbed a fistful of sweets and tossed them across the car. 'Hey! Don't waste sweets. Superman would never throw fizzy cola bottles at a woman.'

'With great power comes great responsibility,' Sam replied soberly. 'I apologize.'

It wasn't until Sam stopped the car that I realized we were home.

'That was fast,' I said, pulling his coat closer to me. 'Thank you so much for everything. I'm really, really sorry about my relatives.'

'You have nothing to apologize for,' he said, turning off the radio. 'As Britney once said, they're going to try to try you but they cannot deny you.'

'If I drop down dead in this very moment, I will die happy,' I said, completely serious. 'Perhaps your next book can be an oral history on Ms Britney Jean Spears.'

'At least that might stand a chance of selling,' he replied before rolling up the remains of the Haribo and handing them to me. 'Here, I'd hate for you to go hungry.'

'For your information, I happen to have half a turkey wrap in the fridge from three days ago,' I told him, retrieving my bag from the footwell of the car. Out of the corner of my eye, I saw the photo of Sam and Elaine, making the heart eyes emoji at each other in Paris. 'Sorry salsa dancing wasn't the thing. We can get back to work on boyfriend bootcamp on Monday.'

'Monday,' he echoed. 'The rain's not stopping.'

He was right; according to my weather app, it had set in for the night.

I began shrugging off his coat, goosebumps prickling my skin.

'Keep it on.' He lifted one hand from the steering wheel as if he was about to make a point. Instead he shook his head at himself and clapped it back into place. 'You'll get soaked otherwise.'

It was genuinely pouring down outside and the whole street was a blur of night sky and orange street lamps. It was late, it was dark, it was cold. All signs pointed to asking him up for a drink.

'See you Monday then,' Sam said, interrupting my awkwardly long silence and making my decision for me. 'Thank you, Annie, I think I had a fun day.'

'If you have to think about it, you probably didn't,' I replied with a wry smile. 'Have a good rest of the weekend.'

Safely under the porch, I watched him drive away before fumbling for my keys. It had, by all rights, been a terrible day. I'd hated the dance class, been mortified by my family and I felt sick when I thought about how much trouble I was going to be in with my sister . . . And yet I couldn't remember the last time I'd had so much fun.

CHAPTER FIFTEEN

Sundays used to be reserved for one of three things: hangovers, Sunday lunches (which led to hangovers) or lying on the settee in last night's pyjamas and revelling in every single filthy second of the night before. And yet here I was, fully dressed, stone-cold sober and armed with the company accounts. I had failed.

'Needs must when the devil shits in your teapot,' Miranda announced happily as we waited for the kettle to boil in my tiny kitchen. Even on a Sunday, even in her comfies, she looked super stylish. I was wearing jogging bottoms and a cropped black T-shirt I'd shrunk in the tumble dryer. Miranda arrived wearing neon pink leggings, white leather hightops and a little black T-shirt that was cropped on purpose. 'If we get through this quick enough, we can go for a drink after.'

'You can't just go for a drink on a Sunday,' I complained, popping two teabags into the teapot. 'You have to go out for Sunday lunch and then get drunk, it's the law. I think it's in the bible.'

'Ahh, Deuteronomy,' she said as she checked her bloodshot eyes in her powder compact. 'A classic. Now this is less likely to stand the test of time. Annie, what is this doing here?'

I looked over to see her holding Sam's book, a flyer for the local Indian restaurant poking out of the top as a bookmark.

'Just trying to understand my subject,' I said, snatching it out of her hands and placing it carefully on the coffee table. 'I know it starts off dry but when you get into it, there's some really interesting stuff.'

Mir stretched out a hand and pressed it against my forehead. 'Are you feeling OK?' she asked.

'Get off.' I pushed her away. 'Maybe I've been spending too much time with him.'

'You think?' she replied. 'Jesus, Annie, crack open a copy of *Take a Break* like a normal person, before I start worrying about you.'

The kettle clicked and I smiled at my best friend. I looked out the window as I poured the boiling water into the teapot, ignoring the drops of boiling water that splashed back and stung my skin. It was threatening to rain again. Another glorious British summer's day.

'Two sugars,' Miranda called, draped across my love-seat. Her head was propped up at one end while her legs hung over the other, almost touching the floor. 'I had one too many last night.'

'Where did you go?' I asked. One sugar always meant two, two sugars always meant three but none always, always meant none.

'Just to the King's Head,' she said in a suspiciously high voice. 'With Martin.'

'How interesting,' I replied, turning to see her covering her bright red face with a cushion. 'Now tell me, will we be going with something traditionally awful for my bridesmaid dress or are you planning to mix it up a bit?'

'Oh, cock off,' she said, resting the cushion on the top of her pulled-back curls. 'I went into the office to get my computer in the afternoon and he was there.'

'Just hanging around the office on his own on a weekend with nothing to do? Definitely not a red flag or in any way creepy,' I replied. Miranda fixed me with an unimpressed pout. 'Please go on.'

'We went for a drink,' she continued, a red rash I recognized climbing up her throat as she spoke. 'And some more drinks. Then there might have been a smidge of touchy-feely stuff. That was all, nothing you couldn't watch on TV with your dad in the room.'

'Your family is very different to mine,' I said as I rummaged for clean mugs. 'My dad couldn't even sit through the *Hollyoaks* omnibus the last time I stayed over at his house for the weekend.'

'And how old were you then?'

'Fourteen, but that's not the point.' I retrieved the milk and, in spite of myself, was desperate to get to the dirty details. 'Did you get the bone or not?'

'I did not get the bone,' she said, leaning backwards over the loveseat, flashing me an upside-down smile. 'But I was made aware of what bone is on the table, so to speak.'

'As long as I know which table it is so I can wipe it down with Dettol, that's fine,' I replied, watching as Miranda illustrated her point by pulling her hands further and further apart. 'Leave it out, I haven't had breakfast and I'm already queasy.'

'The one that got away,' she said with a sigh. 'For now.'

'You know I'm not against the idea of Martin,' I told her, attempting to sugar-coat my feelings to the appropriate BFF degree. 'But if he likes you, he should bloody well man up and be with you properly. We're not kids, he's almost forty, for god's sake.'

Miranda leant forwards and pulled off her shoes and socks; she'd always been a barefoot person and I had swept the floor accordingly.

'There's no rush, I'm playing the long game, Annie Higgins,' she insisted, balling up her socks and throwing them in the general direction of her bright blue backpack. 'If you build it, they will come.'

'I can't work out if that's dirty or not,' I said, kicking her socks closer to her bag before she left them behind and I added them to my excessive Miranda Johansson sock collection. I had it on good authority that it was the largest in Europe.

'It is,' she replied. 'It definitely is.'

'We had such very different Saturdays.' I coiled my hair into a knot on the top of my head, feeling around the kitchen counter for a hair elastic and finding one immediately. They were everywhere in my house, I was more or less keeping Boots in business. 'You actually got off with a boy and I had to endure the sight of my father dressed up as John Travolta.'

'*Grease* Travolta? Or *Pulp Fiction* Travolta?'

'*Hairspray* John Travolta dressed up as *Saturday Night Fever* John Travolta,' I said, shuddering at the memory. 'It wasn't something any daughter ever needs to see.'

'You don't seem as though you're in the best mood ever,' Miranda asked. 'Last night was that bad?'

Before I answered, I retrieved the biscuit tin from the cupboard above the microwave. If I couldn't drink, I could at least eat.

'Last night was confusing,' I replied, thinking back to the barrage of text messages I still hadn't answered. *WTF* from Rebecca; *That dress needs to be dry cleaned* from Gina; *You owe Mummy an apology* from Sharon; and best of all, a *Thanks for coming darling girl, best birthday gift of all* from my dad. The entire thing had passed him by.

'Confusing how? Did you push your horrible cousin in the pool? Again?'

Best to just rip off the plaster in one go, I decided.

'I went to a salsa class with Sam then he drove me to the party then he came in with me, then we were talking to my family and naturally they were awful but then he *told* them they were awful and then we danced and then he told me I could leave so we left and he brought me home and now—' I blurted out. 'Two sugars, you said?'

Miranda's eyes grew so wide, I thought they might fall out of her face. Instead, she looked over at the red Puffa jacket on the floor by my chair.

'Is this his?' she demanded loudly before immediately lowering her voice to barely a whisper. 'Is this his? Is he here? Did he stay over?'

'Yes, no and of course not,' I replied, turning the teapot and pouring the tea. Bit weak but I was desperate for a brew. 'I would never.'

She squeezed her mouth into a very unbecoming thin line.

'Because we shaved him down and it turns out he's the missing link between all the Hemsworth brothers? Yeah, I can completely see how that would turn you off.'

'Hot or not,' I said, spooning sugar into Mir's mug. 'Some of us don't go out with people we work with. And really, Mir, could you see me going out with an actual historian? Not to mention the fact he doesn't understand the first thing about what we do – and nor does he care.'

'I didn't think actual historians existed,' she said as she held her hands out for her tea. 'I thought it was a job they made up for films, like snake charmers or the man who stands around while they're drilling for oil and says "she's gonna blow".'

'I worry about you sometimes,' I said, settling down beside her on the settee, biscuit barrel in hand. I stared into the middle distance, thinking about Sam 'snake-hips' Page as I nibbled on a Hobnob and smiled. 'It was just a very weird day.'

'And absolutely nothing untoward went on?' Mir asked, raising one perfect eyebrow.

'Absolutely nothing,' I confirmed.

Apart from how I'd sat up until three a.m. reading his ridiculous book. Apart from the way I'd then laid awake, thinking about the look on his face when I got out of the car. And the way I'd shivered when he touched the bare skin on the back of my neck.

'Shall we start on this month's expenses?' I suggested.

Miranda clicked her tongue against the roof of her mouth.

'You took him to your dad's party though?'

'He gave me a lift. The salsa workshop made me late.'

'And he lent you his coat?'

'It was cold and raining and he is a gentleman.'

'Annie!' She leaned forward and clapped her hands right in front of my face. 'Wake up and smell the seduction. There's being a gentleman and there's trying to get into someone's knickers – the two are not mutually exclusive.'

'My knickers are the last thing on his mind,' I insisted. 'You've got such a mega horn for Martin, you can't think about anything else. Have you forgotten the part where I'm helping him win back his girlfriend?'

'The girlfriend who is clearly already getting it on with her dance partner?' Miranda asked, holding out her little finger as she sipped her tea.

'That's until she sees my masterpiece,' I reminded her. 'I'm helping him because he's helping us. Or at least he is in theory. If we can find him another seventeen thousand Instagram followers.'

I thought back to the post I'd put up earlier that morning. A fascinating little factoid about how Roman Emperor Gaius made his horse a senator. So far, only fifty-two likes. Sometimes I couldn't understand what was wrong with people. Our initial bump was beginning to wear off and things were slowing down. I didn't like it in the slightest.

'You'll get it.' Miranda dismissed my concerns with a wave that turned into a swan dive into the biscuit tin. 'You always get it. He ought to be kissing your perfect bottom for helping him so much. If you're into that kind of thing, obviously. Have we ever discussed that?'

'No and we're not discussing it now,' I said, tapping my foot against the laminate floor.

'Well, just because you're not into him, doesn't mean he's not into you,' she said, dipping a Hobnob in her tea. 'Bet you any money.'

'We've made enough bets lately,' I replied. 'And if

we don't win that one, we're going to be completely buggered.'

'We'll still be up a financial creek when I've finished asking all my questions,' she curled up on the settee, her gaze locked on me over the rim of her mug. 'Do you like him, yes or no?'

'Like him, yes,' I replied. 'Like him like him, of course not. He's thinks he's right about everything, he's obsessed with the past, he has the social graces of a goat and he likes pineapple on pizza. Why in the world would I be interested in someone like that?'

She raised her eyebrows and looked down at the floor.

'He hasn't even got a telly!' I exclaimed.

'Right, fine, I'm convinced,' Miranda said, dunking her second biscuit. 'Imagine not having a telly.'

'I can't and I won't,' I replied, turning my open laptop to face her. 'Now, on to the fun stuff. How did we spend this much in June?'

'It turns out running a business is expensive.' Miranda groaned at the negative figure at the bottom of the spreadsheet on my computer. 'We're doing everything right. We're signing new clients, we're winning accounts. Why are we still in the red?'

'Because people hate parting with their cash?' I suggested. 'Almost everyone owes us money, look how many payments are overdue.'

'We're doing everything right,' she insisted before chugging her tea. 'It will work out.'

'I really hope you're right,' I said, staring at the numbers until they stopped making sense. Not that they'd made an awful lot of sense in the first place. 'I'm starting to panic.'

Mir fixed me with a soft smile.

'What?' I asked.

'Oh, Annie, what are we going to do with you?' she said, getting up to refill the kettle.

'Me?'

'You don't even realize it yet.' She shook her head as she turned the tap. 'And to think he doesn't have a telly.'

'Just because you can't think about anything other than getting some doesn't mean the rest of us are the same,' I replied as my cheeks heated up. 'Can we get back to the accounts, please?'

'Whatever you say,' she said, flashing me a thumbs up. 'Whatever you say, babe.'

Never start a business with your best friend. It gets altogether far too messy every time you want to kill them.

CHAPTER SIXTEEN

Wednesday, 18 July: Sixteen Days to Go

Laptop, iPad, business cards, Tic-Tacs.

Laptop, iPad, business cards, Tic-Tacs.

Laptop, iPad, business cards, Tic-Tacs.

'Can you just leave already?' Miranda hurled a Twitter-branded stress ball across the office, narrowly missing my carefully braided head. 'You're even making me nervous.'

'I don't see why you can't do it,' I whined, checking the contents of my bag one more time. 'You know I hate it.'

'Because it's a panel for and about creative, not account management,' she replied. 'And you know I'd come if I could.'

'No, you go with your mum,' I said, zipping the zip and slipping the strap over my head. 'She needs you more than me.'

She didn't. She was a fifty-four-year-old woman who was afraid of the dentist and needed a filling. I was a thirty-one-year-old woman who was petrified of public speaking and had to give a speech in front of three hundred people. This was not fair.

'Call me when you're done,' Mir shouted. 'Break a leg!'

'I'll probably break them both,' I replied, holding my arms away from my body to avoid pit stains. I was already sweating and I wasn't even outside yet.

'Are you going somewhere?'

Sam appeared in the hallway, a very concerned look on his face.

'No, just walking up and down the corridor with my bag for larks,' I said, continuing on my way to the lift. 'What's wrong?'

'I've been trying to get to grips with your reading list.' He held a copy of *Fifty Shades of Grey* aloft. 'I have some questions. Firstly, is this a real book?'

'Technically, yes. Do you know what, you're just who I wanted to see,' I said, beaming from ear-to-ear. 'Can your books stand to spare you for the next hour?'

'No,' he replied.

'Brilliant, you're coming with me.' I laced my arm through his and pulled him into the lift. 'We're going on another excursion.'

'Why would Elaine be reading this?' Sam asked, still staring at the paperback in his hand as we travelled down to the ground floor. 'She's got a master's degree in Philosophy.'

'Just because you enjoy one thing, doesn't mean you can't enjoy another,' I told him. 'And she gave Christian five pairs of handcuffs out of five on her book club's Facebook page.'

Sam gulped as the doors of the lift opened, right in front of Charlie Wilder.

'Oh, hi, Charlie,' I said with a big smile. 'Could you hold on to this for us?'

I snatched the book out of Sam's hands and thrust it at Charlie with a wink.

'Thanks ever so,' I shouted back at him. 'Feel free to give it a read, you might learn a trick or two.'

'Where are we going this time?' Sam asked after we hopped into the waiting Toyota Prius and pulled away from the kerb. 'I haven't got my coat.'

'Well, it's July and we're not going to the Arctic, so I don't think you'll need it,' I replied.

Our car rolled through London, the narrow, brick-built streets of the east end giving way to the river, the river giving way to the City. There were people everywhere. Tourists in baseballs caps declaring they had in fact visited London or sweatshirts pledging allegiance to Oxford or Cambridge, as though they were rival football teams. The locals were almost as easy to spot. They moved faster, they wove in and out and they all had their heads down.

London on a proper summer's day was a wonderful thing. It almost made the rain and the grey worth it, almost. Bare legs and last year's sunscreen, the promise of wrestling for a seat at a picnic bench outside the pub after work. Even though you'd catch the sun on your shoulders, even though the Pimm's was watered right down, even though those wooden benches always gave you splinters, it was worth it.

'I always forget how many people still smoke until I go past a pub,' Sam commented, speaking for the first time as we slowed down at a traffic light. 'Why do they always have to roll up their shirt sleeves to smoke?'

A group of four or five men in matching, soulless

work wear stood in front one of those tiny, narrow pubs that only had room for two chairs inside, their pint glasses resting on windowsills and surely enough, all of them had their sleeves unbuttoned and rolled right up to the elbow.

'Impossible to say,' I replied. 'I've never smoked.'

'Good,' he said with an approving nod. 'Filthy habit.'

Typical Sam, I thought as I looked down at my lap and smiled to myself, checking the contents of my handbag one more time for luck.

'Where are we?' Sam whispered as we walked into a loud, buzzy hall, full of people carrying multiple devices and nodding seriously while their companions spoke, even though they clearly checking their emails and not listening to them at all.

'It's the TechBubble conference,' I replied, carefully combing my hair out from behind my ears. 'I'm giving a talk on how to run a successful social media campaign. How do I look?'

Sam looked me up and down.

'I could be reading the diaries of the Viscount FitzAlan of Derwent right now,' he responded, positively aghast. 'I thought this was one of my bootcamp obligations.'

'It kind of is,' I said, scrambling for a reason to have him here. 'You're supporting your friend. That's something a good boyfriend does.'

'Hmm,' he grunted, eyeing me with suspicion. 'You might have told me that.'

I blushed from head to toe.

'You asked why people love social media so much,' I replied. 'I'm on my way to give a talk about it, I thought you might be interested. And also I'm terrified of public speaking and thought it might be nice to have a friendly face in the crowd.'

He gave me one of his long looks.

'Really, Annie?'

'Yes,' I replied. 'Really. My comfort zone is sitting behind a laptop and making other people look good, not standing on a stage and answering random questions. What could be confusing about that?'

Sam sighed as though he was explaining a very simple concept to an even more simple human.

'It's illogical,' he replied. 'You're afraid that people will judge you and in some way find you wanting. If you're as good at your job as you so often like to say, I can't understand why you would be worried about speaking about it in front of a crowd.'

'There's just something about a room full of people that puts me on edge,' I said, breaking out in a cold sweat at the very thought. 'I am good at what I do, but that's because I do it in a room, on my own, with no one watching. Miranda is the mouthy one, she always has been.'

'Then why isn't she giving the talk this afternoon?' Sam asked.

'Because she's an arsehole,' I replied. 'And a good daughter or whatever. And it's about creative roles, not business development. That's my thing,' I grumbled on, aware of Sam's steady gaze and not entirely sure how I felt about it.

'Annie!'

Asher, the conference organizer and a sort of, kind of friend from uni, waved from the front of the room.

'Sit down and don't leave,' I told Sam. 'It'll be interesting, I promise.'

'More interesting than the personal diaries of the last lord lieutenant of Ireland?' he scoffed. 'I don't think so.'

'Remember that conversation we had about doing things for other people even if you might not really care about them yourself?' I asked. 'That's what this is.'

Sam shook his head. 'I thought that was about me not wanting to see *Les Mis* for the umpteenth time?'

'*Les Mis* and this,' I clarified. 'See if you can't learn something.'

'There you are,' Asher said, leaning in for a professional double-cheek kiss. 'I was looking for you.'

'Today was madness,' I said, my grip tightening around the strap of my bag and trying not to pay attention to the people milling into the room. 'Sorry, I should have been here sooner.'

'No worries, no worries,' he replied in his thick Australian accent. 'Listen, there's been a bit of a change of plan? We were running late so we've had to combine your panel with another?'

'But, I've got a PowerPoint,' I said shakily.

'It's going to be real low key, super casual, don't even sweat it,' Asher said. 'You know Gordon Ossington, right? He said you guys used to work together?'

'I used to work for him,' I replied, tensing up from head-to-toe. I did not care for Gordon Ossington.

'Yeah, so you're going to be on the panel with him now.' He paused and pressed a finger against the earpiece I saw poking out of his curly hair. 'I'll ask you some stuff about the industry, how you got started, what you're doing now. Easy.'

'But my PowerPoint,' I whispered again.

'Annie, you crack me up,' he said, slapping me across the arm. 'I've scribbled out some questions but we'll play it by ear. Jump up on stage, we'll get you mic'd up.'

It was illogical to be afraid of public speaking.

It was illogical to think all the people in the crowd would be judging me, thinking how stupid I was, talking about me afterwards, gossiping, laughing and telling all their friends.

It was illogical to even entertain the idea that this one panel could completely destroy my reputation, my company and my life.

And yet, as I made my way around to the three stairs that led up to the stage, that was all I could think about.

'I hope you don't mind me crashing your party.'

Gordon was already in place, seated on the first stool, of course. Smooth, suave, total tit.

'Nice to see you, Gordon,' I muttered as someone ran out from backstage to clip a mic pack onto my blue cotton shirt-dress. 'How are you?'

'Doing amazing,' he replied, unbuttoning his cuffs and folding up his sleeves. 'Thanks.'

Didn't bother to ask how I was doing. Because he didn't care.

'Welcome, everyone, to the last panel of the day!'

Asher jogged up the stairs and paced the stage while I tried to get comfortable. What kind of sadist put people on high stools on a stage? Gordon rested one foot on the floor and the other on the little bracing bar between the legs. I was too short to reach the floor and my shoes kept slipping off the brace, shaking my balance.

'Bit of a change of plan from what's in your

programmes,' Asher explained to the completely full room. As well as Annie Higgins from Content London, we're also joined by Gordon Ossington, owner of the Oz Agency.'

The crowd clapped politely although I could tell they were getting tired. End of the day, worst possible slot. All anyone wanted at this point was to get out of the panels and into a cheap glass of wine.

'I'm going to ask a few general questions, get the benefit of your expertise and then we'll throw it open to questions,' he said.

Oh good, questions from the crowd. What if I couldn't answer them? Or worse still, what if no one asked anything?

'Annie, I want to start with you. You're a woman.'

'Last time, I checked, yes,' I confirmed, recoiling at the sound of my own amplified voice.

The crowd gave a good-natured chuckle and I searched for Sam in the darkness but the lights shining on the stage were blinding and I couldn't make out any one particular face.

'Do you think being a woman has affected the way you approach your business?'

'I think it's hard to say,' I replied, blinking. 'I'm not sure how I would have approached it if I was a man because I'm not one.'

'From my perspective,' Gordon interjected, as he so liked to do, 'I'd say the women in my team definitely approach projects with more empathy. I think that's why there's a lot of women in social media: they're so good at seeing both sides of every story. Working out what people really want.'

Light applause from the audience. Mild annoyance from me.

'That's interesting, Gordon, that's interesting,' Asher rubbed his chin and moved on to the next cue card. 'Obviously, you've been on the scene in many different capacities for a long time but now you're heading up your own agency. How has it been, striking out on your own?'

'Exceeded expectations,' Gordon said, tenting his fingers underneath his chin. 'It's been a learning experience but so enriching. We've really hit the ground running, I couldn't have asked for more.'

He also couldn't have got more clichés into one statement, I thought, keeping the polite smile on my face as I nodded along. No wonder we'd won three out of the four clients we'd competed for in the last six months.

'And, Annie, Content is another new agency specializing in social media,' Asher said as I attempted to stay on my perch without flashing my knickers at everyone in the room. 'And your agency is entirely run by women. What was the decision-making process behind that?'

'The decision to have an agency run by women?' I asked. Asher nodded. 'There wasn't one. There was a decision to have an agency run by myself and my business partner, Miranda Johansson. It's not a no-boys-allowed club, we just both happen to be women.'

There was low chatter in the audience and I could feel the familiar red rash prickly around my neck. Why couldn't he just let me give my presentation?

'That's great, it really is,' Asher said, bobbing his head and scanning his cards for more questions. 'Gordon, there are so many different forms of social media now. How do you successfully target your audience without diluting your message?'

I sat on my stool, straightening my back and waiting

patiently while Gordon answered his question. This was so much worse than I'd imagined. Right now, I should have been on my sixth slide, comparing a good Twitter campaign to a pepperoni pizza. Instead, I was listening to Gordon Ossington talk absolute twaddle while everyone in the room dozed off.

'Annie, back to you. Why do you think it is that young girls particularly have embraced social media both as content creators and consumers?'

I wasn't getting a crack at Gordon's question, clearly.

'I think social media appeals to young people in general because it's so available and accessible,' I replied. 'A lot of industries are difficult to penetrate but all you need to be successful on social media is a good idea, a phone, determination.'

'And they're doing so well,' Gordon said, patting me on the arm. 'It's great to see the girls getting a turn.'

'One of the great things about social media,' I said, correcting him, 'is that you don't have to wait for permission to be heard.'

'Right, right, fewer gatekeepers,' Asher agreed, shuffling his cards. 'Gordon, the Oz Agency has been nominated for two Techies this year. In your mind, what makes a good social media campaign?'

'Well,' Gordon rubbed his palms against his jeans. 'You start by coming to my agency.'

A smattering of applause accompanied the audience's laughter as I realized I wasn't smiling any more.

'We've been nominated for three Techies,' I said, leaning into my mic.

'Which is amazing,' Gordon said, encouraging the audience to applaud as I slipped off my stool for the thousandth time. 'That's got to be a record for a woman-run agency – is it, Annie?'

'I don't know, Gordon,' I replied politely. 'We haven't been nominated for any "woman-run agency" prizes, just best campaign, best new agency and best boutique agency. Which one of those were you not nominated for?'

'Next question is for you, Annie,' Asher said, without waiting for Gordon to give his answer. 'We've definitely seen a boom in the number of women in the digital arena—'

A loud, clear voice called out from the audience.

'Excuse me, I have a question.'

'We'll take questions at the end of the panel,' Asher said, blinking into the spotlights. 'Thank you.'

'But I'd like to hear Ms Higgins' answer to the question about how to target an audience.' Squinting into the darkness, I realized it was Sam. 'So far, all of her questions have been about her gender, and that doesn't make any sense.'

The crowd whispered nervously, feeling each other out as a rumble of approving voices began to find each other.

'We're just making the most of Annie's perspective,' Asher answered. 'I'm sure lots of people in the audience are interested in what she's got to say about being a woman in the digital industry.'

'We'd also like to hear her answer the same questions as the male panelist,' a woman in the back called out to a rally of cheers.

'I think what the lady in the back is trying to say, is they'd like to hear a woman's take on the questions I've already answered,' Gordon said.

'Did you just mansplain my comment?' the woman shouted. 'Seriously?'

'I think it can be frustrating for women at things

like this when we have to spend half the time explaining to men what it's like to be a woman because, in the end, we won't have time to answer any other questions,' I said, my cheeks turning pink. 'You don't have to do the explaining because your experience as a man is already the status quo. We're still 'other'. It's like you guys have already started running a marathon while we're back at the start line explaining what it feels like to be a woman running a marathon. And honestly, I'm pretty sure all the women here already know how it feels to be a woman in digital because they're women in digital.'

A crash of applause silenced Asher's umming and ahhing as he flicked through his cards.

'Do you want to give them to me?' I asked Asher. He handed them over, head hanging low as I filtered through his questions and then handed them back. 'Just go with these.'

'Didn't know you were such a ball-buster, Annie,' Gordon whispered, covering his microphone. 'Remind me not to get on the wrong side of you.'

'Well, try to behave yourself and we won't have any problems, will we?' I said, patting him on the back as the smile slipped off his face. 'Now, who's got the next question?'

Half an hour later, after many questions, all of them for me, I walked out of the conference to find Sam loitering on the street.

'There you are,' I said, walking over with my hands deep in my jacket pockets. 'I thought you'd left.'

'No I just needed some fresh air,' he replied, kicking a stone with the toe of his lovely new shoes. 'I was thinking.'

I caught it with the inside of my left foot and kicked it back.

'About what?'

'You're a good public speaker,' Sam said, jiggling the change in the pocket of his jeans. 'You handled the situation beautifully. You shouldn't worry about things like that in future.'

'It helped to know you had my back,' I said. I was still on edge, still full of adrenaline. Too on edge to go back to the office. 'Do you want to get a drink? There's a nice little bar around the corner and I'm gasping.'

'A drink?' Sam looked at me as though I'd just asked if he'd like to smoke crack out of the carcass of a dead possum. 'I mean, I would like to, but I've got so much work to do and I really should get back to the office and—'

'That's OK,' I said, tossing my hair over my shoulder to show him just how breezy I was. 'Totally understand. I'd hate for you to get behind.'

'Right, yes,' Sam stiffened and gave a curt nod. 'You should stay and have a drink. I'm going to venture back. I'll see you at the office tomorrow.'

I stood still and watched him walk away. Something stopped me from chasing him down so we could travel back to work together, but I wasn't entirely sure what it was. I didn't move until he'd been swallowed up by the crowds headed to Trafalgar Square.

'I don't want to get into another conversation about *Fifty Shades of Grey*,' I told myself, fiddling with my headphones and slowly, very slowly, setting off in the same direction. 'Today has been rough enough as it is.'

Really, what other reason could there be?

CHAPTER SEVENTEEN

Friday, 20 July: Fourteen Days to Go

'Annie?'

I looked up to see Zadie in her giant glasses, blinking at me from the far end of the banqueting table.

'Yes?'

'Do the menu cards go on top of the napkins or are we tucking them into the napkins?'

'On top,' I replied, attempting to hang Lil's light-up neon logo on the wall without breaking it. Neon tubes shattered like nobody's business. I would know. 'And place the napkins on the plates so that the folds are downwards. Lily hates napkin folds.'

Lily hated a lot of things.

'And where does this go?' Nat asked, puffing underneath the weight of an enormous potted palm tree.

'Next to the flamingo and the cactus,' I instructed. 'And don't forget to wrap it in fairy lights. There should be loads of battery operated ones in that big box over there.'

It was the morning of Lily Lashgasm's annual

summer beauty bash. Lily was one of our first clients and one of the biggest beauty bloggers in the world. She was also a stickler for details and liked everything done a certain way which was a really polite way of saying Lily could be a massive bastard when she wanted to be. Every summer she had a huge party for all her friends, a few chosen followers and most importantly, her enemies. It was beyond me.

People loved to slag off YouTubers and influencers and the like but in my experience, they were some of the hardest working, most genuine humans I'd ever met. All our clients worked every hour god sent, they had to be brilliant writers, fantastic photographers and self-taught filmmakers all rolled into one while being amazingly creative, thoughtful, caring and collaborative sweethearts at the same time.

And then there was Lily.

It was like when people said they hated cats because they're all super anti-social and scratchy when really, they'd only encountered shit cats. I had to assume everyone who said influencers were all entitled, freebie-grabbing slackers with no real life skills had somehow come across Lily.

'The room looks sick,' Zadie said, slipping the last menu card into place.

'Lily's going to be furious,' I replied, comparing each place setting with my seating plan. It had taken hours to get it right and I wanted to trust the girls had everyone in the right seats but I couldn't not check. 'She wanted to hold the party outside this year.'

Zadie looked out the window, her confusion magnified by her massive glasses.

'But it's pouring it down.'

'And Lily is going to want to know why we couldn't

fix the weather,' I replied. 'Did you get the goodie bags?'

'Shit!' Nat exclaimed, pricking herself on the cactus. 'Miranda is bringing them over?'

'Fairylights on the palm tree, not the cactus!' I bellowed, beginning to lose my cool.

The day was not going especially well. Miranda, Brian and I had spent the morning working on the SetPics pitch but nothing seemed to be working. So far, the best idea we had was a 'turn yourself into a unicorn' filter that already existed on basically every platform ever or a time machine. At that very second, I would have taken the time machine in a heartbeat. On top of that, my mummy blogger had accidentally posted a shitty direct message, slagging off her potential publisher to Twitter so that was a lucrative deal down the toilet and somehow, without even trying, @TheHipHistorian had lost seventy-five followers overnight. There was no rhyme or reason to it, they were just gone. And now our summer bacchanal on the roof of Shoreditch House had become a cobbled together shindig in a meeting room. But as Miranda always said, if in doubt, throw fairylights at it and that was exactly what I was doing. So what if we didn't have the swimming pool? Who cared if there was no room for the photobooth? An automatic swing that created a gif that was sent straight to your phone *as you swang*? Swing-schming. We had enough strings of lights to illuminate the Eiffel Tower and enough rosé to get an elephant off his tits, it was going to be fine.

And if I said that another fourteen thousand times and drank some of the rosé myself, I might even begin believing it.

'Don't panic, I'm here, everything's going to be OK.'

I turned so quickly at the sound of a male voice, I slapped myself in the face with my ponytail.

It was Charlie, peering out from behind three big cardboard boxes.

'Miranda asked us to bring these over,' he said, dropping them next to the cactus and causing it to shed a shower of needles all over the carpet. The door slammed behind him and Zadie jumped, dropping a bundle of rose gold cutlery. 'Where do you want them?'

'There is amazing, thank you,' I replied, almost crying with joy as Nat instinctively picked up her Dustbuster. 'Where's Miranda?'

'She said she had to make a last minute call and asked me to run these over.' Hands on hips, Charlie surveyed the room. 'Nice. Very pink.'

'It's a "very pink" event,' I said. 'Thank you, Charlie, I appreciate it.'

'No big deal,' he said, picking up one of the menu cards and nodded as he read each course out loud. 'Girly party is it?'

'It's hosted by a woman and most of the attendees are women, if that's what you mean,' I replied. 'I really appreciate bringing over the boxes and don't want to be rude but we're very busy, I can't really chat right now.'

'I get it, I get it,' he replied with a wink. 'And you're welcome. You can buy me a drink and make it up to me later.'

'Excuse me, could someone open the door?'

Another muffled male voice called from the hallway.

Charlie gave it a push only for a tall, skinny blond man to stagger in, carrying twice the number of boxes.

'Oh shit, Sam!' I ran over to take the top two boxes off his stack before he dropped them all. 'What are you doing here?'

'Miranda asked if I could assist your friend here,' he said, pulling down his shirt over the waistband of his jeans as he set his boxes carefully on the floor. 'Is there anything else I can do?'

'I would love to stay and help but I've got an accounts meeting,' Charlie leaned in to place an unexpected and unprecedented kiss on my cheek. I jerked back slightly, stunned if not entirely displeased. 'Good luck with your party.'

'You don't have to stay,' I said to Sam, watching Charlie wander off down the hallway with his hands in his trouser pockets. 'Thank you so much for bringing the boxes over, I really appreciate it.'

'Well, I'm here now,' he said stiffly. 'If you could use a hand.'

'If you're sure?' I turned my attention back to the people in the room. 'Nat, I need you to make sure all the digital Polaroids are working. Zadie, can you put the decals on the mirrors in the loos?'

They both nodded and immediately went about their appointed tasks. Sam scratched his stubble, looking incredibly out of place in the middle of it all. Flamingos, palm trees, cacti, rainbows, flower crowns – it looked as though Coachella had thrown up in East London.

'Dare I ask?'

'We've got stickers that say hashtag Lashgasm2018,' I explained, holding up one of the stickers for his approval. He immediately gave it a thumbs up. 'And branded soap dispensers. And hand towels. And toilet paper. And napkins. And umbrellas. And tote bags. And tampons.'

He flipped from a thumbs up to a thumbs down.

'Everything is an Instagram moment,' I said with a

shrug. 'If you really want to help, I need to fill the goodie bags.'

'I can do that,' he agreed, clapping his hands and rubbing them together. 'Where do we start?'

I whipped a Stanley knife out of my toolkit on the table and tore into one of the boxes he had delivered.

'You sir, are my saviour,' I said, coiling my ponytail into a bun on top of my head. When I looked up, I saw he was blushing. Tipping the contents of the box out onto the table, I smiled.

'I'm not quite sure about that,' Sam muttered, opening one of the other boxes. Ahh, good. It was the branded tampons. 'But I do my best.'

There really was no arguing with that.

'You mean to say, you set all this up and then you disappear?' Sam asked, seemingly still confused about what I actually did for a living.

I nodded as I dropped the last eye shadow palette into the last goodie bag and placed it on the chair of a famously flamboyant makeup artist who I hoped would be able to stay sober long enough to get through the party.

'Amongst many other things,' I nodded. 'I plan the event, I organise the event, I make sure everything goes to plan. Brian designs everything you see with #Lashgasm2018 on it, Miranda orders it and then I put it into place. I make sure every part of the room is Insta-perfect and then I hide in the back corner and let Lily look like the host of the century, all while taking millions of photos, videos, Instagrams and Snapchats. I'll tweet as we go, we might even do a quick Facebook Live. I'll tag all the sponsors, thank the venue and at the end of it, I'll clear the place up.

Then go back to the office, edit together my videos to make the perfect vlog and post it for Lily's millions of followers tomorrow evening.'

'If they like her they must love you,' Sam commented as he tied a surprisingly perfect bow on the handles of Lily's special goodie bag.

'Most of them don't even know I exist,' I said with a smile. 'That's kind of the point.'

'All that work for so little recognition,' he replied, shocked at the very idea. 'That would be like me putting out a research paper I'd spent years on and leaving off my own name. It's utter madness, Annie.'

'I get recognition.' I crossed my fingers behind my back, hope hope hoping the TechBubble gods could hear our conversation somehow. 'Someone's paying attention to the work we've been doing or they wouldn't have asked us to do all this SetPics stuff.'

'If they saw this room, I'm sure they'd give you the account no questions asked,' he replied. 'I think it's marvellous.'

Even though I knew he had literally no frame of reference for what a good influencer event looked like, I was still pleased. There was nothing like a truly heartfelt metaphorical pat on the head for a job well done. And it wasn't just the Lashgasm event I was feeling smug about, my boyfriend bootcamp was really starting to show results. I couldn't imagine Sam coming out with such a thoughtful, spontaneous compliment a couple of weeks ago.

'That said, I'm not altogether convinced by the cactus,' he said, pushing his glasses up his nose. 'Could be a health and safety disaster.'

So close and yet so far away.

'Come on,' I said, grabbing my phone from the table.

'Let's get a photo of you in front of the flamingo. For Facebook, I mean.'

Shaking his head, Sam stood in front of his new inflatable friend, arms placed in front of him, one hand on top of the other.

'Oh, come on, loosen up,' I ordered. 'You're stood next to a massive pink flamingo in a meeting room in London in the pissing rain and you can't even crack a smile?'

'It's absurd,' Sam mumbled, rolling his eyes as I snapped away.

'Exactly,' I agreed. 'Now smile at Fred and give me something to work with.'

'Fred the Flamingo?' He looked the plastic bird in the eye and frowned. 'Annie, I don't want to alarm you but this is definitely a Florence.'

I looked at him through the lens of my camera.

'Is that right?'

'I'm one hundred per cent certain,' he confirmed. The flamingo's head bounced as he patted it.

'Two PhDs and a Masters degree in sexing inflatable flamingos,' I commented as I snapped the winner pic. 'Very impressive.'

Suddenly, the door to the room burst open, Zadie and Nat both running in with pink cheeks and the fear of god in their eyes.

'S-she's here,' Zadie stammered. 'She's early.'

'Oh, shit,' I muttered, dusting off my jeans and re-tying my ponytail. 'First time for fucking everything.'

Before anyone else could comment, a tell-tale clicking of high heels stopped right outside the door that was still swinging on its hinges.

'It's in here?' I heard her ask.

'Close your eyes,' I heard Miranda say. 'You're going to love it.'

Bless Mir and her confidence, she hadn't even seen the room herself yet. Mostly because she was three shitting hours late but still, it was nice to have your partner's full support in a time of need.

'But we're supposed to be on the roof?' Lily whined, still outside the door.

'It's hammering it down, Lily,' Miranda replied. 'And besides, this room is far, far fancier than the rooftop. It's not like you were planning on getting your extensions wet anyway, is it?'

Slowly, the door opened and I held my breath. Zadie and Nat were hidden behind the inflatable flamingo and truly the look on Sam's face was priceless. He looked more afraid than anyone.

A tiny, platinum blonde with flawless makeup and eyebrows that could have launched a thousand ships walked into the room.

'This,' she said, stepping right into the middle and taking it all in. 'Is nice.'

Me, Miranda, Zadie and Nat all exhaled at once.

'I like the cactus,' Lily added before looking Sam up and down. 'And I like him. Who is he? What does he do?'

'He's a historian,' I answered. 'And he's just leaving.'

'I should read more history books,' she said, openly licking her lacquered lips. 'My history teacher smelled like cheese and onion crisps and always tried to play football with the boys at lunchtime. He was totally sad.'

'I'm not a teacher,' Sam said, moving closer to me as Lily continued to look at him like he was a full, three-course meal. 'I'm writing a book on—'

'Sam's got to leave,' I interrupted, turning my back on her to give him my biggest, most grateful smile. 'Thank you so much.'

'Yeah, can you give me a minute so I can get some selfies before everyone gets here?' Lily said. It should have been a question but it wasn't. 'Don't tell me you haven't got a ring light.'

'There's four of them,' I said, as Zadie and Nat dashed over to the selfie stations, ready to spring into action. 'We'll just be outside.'

Lily perched herself on the edge of the windowsill and searched for her perfect angle as our interns descended on her with two halos of blinding light. She looked like a goddess.

'I think I will go back to the office now,' Sam said. It was fair, he'd seen a lot. 'Unless you need me to stay.'

'No, it's fine, thank you so much,' I said, reaching up to give him a huge hug. For the first time, he didn't even flinch. 'Couldn't have done it without you.'

He smiled tightly, nodding at Miranda before setting off down the corridor, whistling as he went. Miranda looked at me with one raised eyebrow.

'What?' I asked, flicking chunks of pink glitter off my black T-shirt.

'We're hugging now, are we?' she asked. 'You and your "project"?'

'It's all part of the bootcamp plan,' I told her, rolling my shoulders and trying to get them back down out of my ears. 'He's doing well, don't you think he's doing well?'

'He could very nearly pass for a normal human being,' Mir agreed, somewhat seriously. 'When I asked him to help Charlie bring the boxes over, he only had to think about it for three minutes.'

'That is improvement, believe it or not,' I said. 'Anyway, where were you?'

She groaned and I immediately knew it wasn't good news.

'I'll tell you later,' she said with a sigh, pulling out her headscarf and wrapping it around her wrist, her honey-coloured afro running wild and free. 'But to cut a long story short, the money that should have been coming in from Coast's Bear Beard collab, isn't coming in any time soon.'

'Is it coming in ever?' I asked, my heart sinking.

'It is not,' Miranda replied. 'They've gone under. Coast is furious.'

'Mir,' I said slowly. 'I would like to leave, go and find a dodgy old pub and get very, very drunk.'

'Soon, my love, soon,' she promised, squeezing my shoulders as she spoke. 'Shitting hell, Annie, it's like you've got a bag of marbles in here. You need a massage.'

'As well as some diamond slippers, an extra day in the week and a million pounds,' I agreed, flinching every time I heard Lily bark at one of the girls.

'When was the last time you took a proper day off?' Mir asked. 'A proper, honest-to-god, no-work-of-any-kind day to yourself?'

I looked up at the ceiling, cheeks puffed out with the effort of trying to remember.

'Ok, yeah, it's been too long,' Mir decided. 'You're taking tomorrow off, that's an order.'

'But I have so much to do!' I protested. 'There's the SetPics pitch for a start.'

'Annie, tomorrow is Saturday,' she reminded me. 'And you're no good to me exhausted. I want you to take a proper break. Why don't you go to the seaside or something? Get some fresh air, stuff yourself full of fish and chips, smack an annoying teenager with the test your strength mallet and pretend it was an accident.'

It was a tempting proposal.

'Maybe,' I said, rubbing my shoulder where she'd pinched it too hard. 'Where were you thinking? Brighton? I could go for some candyfloss if I put my mind to it.'

'Oh,' she flushed and tightened her scarf around her wrist. 'I would but I can't tomorrow. I said I'd go to this thing at the zoo, he's been invited by some charity or something and he didn't want to go on his own but I can totally cancel.'

I knew she would cancel if I asked her to but I also knew if I did, it wouldn't be an annoying teenager that would be getting smacked in the head with a mallet.

'No, it's fine, you go,' I said. 'I know you like the zoo.'

She didn't. She hated the zoo. Which only went to show how much she liked Martin.

'I bet you can't even remember the last time you did something that wasn't work,' she said, promptly changing the subject. 'Or at least work-related.'

Immediately, I thought of driving back to London from Dad's birthday party. With Sam. And then I thought about my after-work drink with Charlie. And then I thought about singing the score of *Cats* with Brian's boyfriend.

'Please, take the day off,' Mir pleaded as Lily starting shouting my name. 'Do it for me.'

'If we survive today, I'll consider it,' I said, taking a deep breath and preparing myself. 'But I'm not bringing you back a stick of rock.'

'You can be so cruel sometimes,' she said, pushing

211

me through the door. 'Oh shit, we should get branded sticks of rock that have Lashgasm running through them for next year's party!'

'Shut up,' I hissed, shoving her into the wall. 'She'll hear you and then she'll want to know why we haven't got them this year.'

Mir nodded, taking my hand in hers and pasting on her brightest smile.

'Here we go,' she said through gritted teeth as the lift door opened and a nuclear blast of artisan perfumes wafted down the hall. Everyone had arrived. 'Another day at the coal face.'

'Coal face doesn't sound so bad,' I said. 'My granddad worked down the mine. He said they ate lard sandwiches and wore massive man nappies.'

'And that's more appealing to you than this, is it?' Mir asked as the gaggle of guests turned the corner. I gave her a look as I braced myself.

'Never had a lard sandwich,' I whispered. 'But you know I'll try anything once.'

CHAPTER EIGHTEEN

Saturday, 21 July: Thirteen Days to Go
6,029 followers

Saturday was a glorious day. It was bright, it was sunny and, overnight, the Hip Historian had leapt from what felt like almost nothing to six thousand followers. For some reason, he was very big in Latvia and I couldn't help but wonder what they knew that I didn't. My latest post, a picture of Ryan Gosling winking alongside the caption 'Lord Byron kept a pet bear in his university dorm room' was turning in some spectacular traffic and I had a happy feeling in my tummy whenever I thought about the bet.

Less happy when I thought about the company bank account but there were other bright spots. Boyfriend bootcamp was coming along very nicely and a quick perusal of Sam's Facebook confirmed that his makeover was going just great. Even though it was killing him slowly from the inside out, he was posting every day. Links to funny news stories, thoughtful essays, cute videos of small children dressed as goats and crying while they danced to K-Pop. He was a natural. Still no likes from Elaine on any of his updated pictures but even if I didn't know her personally, I knew ex-girlfriends. There was no way she wasn't creeping all over that page after one too many late-night Sangrias with the girls.

'Annie.' I fumbled my phone away as Sam strolled into Victoria station. He was wearing his Dashell straight-leg jeans and a white T-shirt with black sleeves I vaguely remembered seeing in our sample cupboard once upon a time, but I also saw his donkey jacket peeking out the top of his backpack. Hopefully the weather would hold up and I wouldn't have to send it into the sea. Literally and figuratively. He looked fantastic – I had to applaud our makeover skills. Two girls were openly eyeing him up.

'What are we doing in a train station?' he asked.

'Hello, Sam,' I said, reminding him of general social niceties, once again. 'Nice to see you, Sam.'

'Yes, quite, but why am I at the train station?' he asked again.

'Because we're going on a day-trip,' I said, holding up two train tickets. 'How do you fancy Margate?'

'Never been,' he said with mild surprise. 'And you still haven't answered my question.'

'Step two of boyfriend bootcamp,' I explained. 'Show Elaine you care by spending time with her. And who doesn't love a spur-of-the-moment day trip?'

'But it's not spur-of-the-moment, is it?' he said, scratching his chin. 'You texted me last night and told me to meet you here at half-past nine.'

'As I was saying,' I continued, putting the train tickets away. He was not allowed to look after his own,

I'd gone through this too many times with Miranda and Brian and I was not putting another fine on my credit card. 'Next time you and Elaine have a day off, before she bogs herself down with dirty washing or the big shop, suggest a day out somewhere. Seaside, theme park, zoo – anything you wouldn't usually do with your day.'

Sam pondered the concept for a moment.

'Yes, all right then,' he said with a nod. 'Which platform are we on?'

'You're not going to argue?' I asked, shocked. I'd been expecting more of a fight. 'You're not going to tell me you have somewhere more important to be?'

'If it's for Elaine,' he reasoned, 'let's go.'

It was all going far too easily. 'You're sure you don't have research to do or skeletons to dig up?'

'You're confusing a historian with a palaeontologist,' he replied, following me towards the trains. 'At least, I hope you are. What is it exactly that you think a historian does?'

'Solve crimes with the help of a ghost?' I asked, pushing the button on the outside of the train and waiting for the doors to huff open.

Sam gave me a sideways look that held a hint of a smile.

'Yes,' he replied. 'That's it precisely.'

'I knew it,' I whispered, climbing aboard.

The train ride was uneventful. For a brief moment, I thought Sam might murder a teenage boy who insisted on sharing his love for Skepta with the entire carriage, but someone's nana gave him the scolding of a lifetime for not using his headphones before Sam could draw blood and the crisis was averted. Although, it did occur to me that would have been a very easy way to find twenty thousand Instagram followers.

'Why Margate?' Sam asked, looking up from his book for the first time in over an hour.

'Because I've never been either,' I replied with a shrug. 'Everyone says it's really cool. Maybe we can find some fun spots and then you can bring Elaine back before the end of the summer.'

'You're giving up such a lot of your time for me, Annie,' he said. His light blue eyes were fixed on mine, leaving me nowhere else to look. 'I can't thank you enough.'

'Well, you're helping me with my bet,' I said hurriedly. 'And you know how important that is to me.'

'Oh, yes,' Sam replied. 'How is that going?'

'Fine,' I turned to look out the window. 'It's fine.'

Out of the corner of my eye, I could see him studying me, book still held open in his lap.

'On the first of January 1877 a storm cut through Margate pier, or jetty as it was more commonly known back then,' he said, pulling the fact out of thin air. 'Somewhere between forty to fifty people were marooned on the remains of the pier until the next day.'

'And they still had a better New Year's than most people,' I marvelled. 'How do you know these things?'

'I retain knowledge easily,' Sam explained, worrying the strap of his backpack. 'And it's fascinating. Dozens of people, stranded in the sea by the savagery of Mother Nature on New Year's Day? Imagine what they must have been thinking, feeling. What conversations did they have over their longest night? Stranded, at the mercy of the elements.'

'I wonder where they peed?' I said aloud, much to Sam's chagrin. He shook his head in disappointment and looked back down at his book. And to think, they would have gone home with that story and everyone would have just believed them. Not a single person would have even thought to say 'Pics or it didn't happen'.

'Not to labour a point but, specifically, what will we be doing once we arrive in Margate?' Sam asked. 'Will we have time to visit the Walpole Bay Hotel?'

I brightened. 'For drinks?'

Sam shook his head. 'It's a museum.'

'I think you need a break – very important bootcamp lesson,' I assured him. 'So sit down, be quiet and bloody well learn how to enjoy yourself.'

And to think I promised Mir I wouldn't work on the weekend.

'Right.' I leapt off the bottom step of the train and followed everyone else off the platform and out the station. 'Where to go first?'

'You mean there's no itinerary?' Sam asked in a small, scared voice.

I shook my head and held up my phone.

'No, but there is Google,' I replied. 'When in doubt, ask the internet.'

'I don't believe you could get by for a single day without that thing,' Sam said, nodding at the phone in my hand. 'You'd be utterly lost.'

'Please don't try to goad me into a bet because it will not end well,' I said wearily. 'I can absolutely go a day without my phone, but why would I? We don't live here, we don't know what's good. We've only got a few hours, why waste them wandering around aimlessly?'

'Because that's what the human experience is.' He looked at me and held out his hand. I tried not to think about how depressing his statement really was.

'If we're going to be here, I want to truly be here,' Sam said, 'not spend all day following you around, while you stare at that tiny screen. Give it to me.'

'Absolutely not,' I said, breaking out in a cold sweat. Was he really accidentally preaching twenty-first-century mindfulness or was I being super-trolled?

'Then turn it off,' he ordered. 'I'm here, as requested, and I'll do whatever it is you want me to do, but you're not allowed to look at your phone all day. Deal?'

'Fine.' I put my phone away and prayed to every single deity I could think of to help me find the strength to leave it alone. 'Now what are we supposed to do?'

'We're at the seaside, how about we go and see the sea?' Sam suggested.

'And how are we supposed to find it?' I asked.

He pointed down the road to what was quite clearly, the sea.

'Yeah, OK, whatever,' I muttered, setting off down the road with Sam at my heels.

Wandering around the streets of Margate, seagulls cawing overhead and Sam smiling happily at my side should have been a lovely way to spend a Saturday. But I was anxious. I didn't know where I was, I didn't know where I was going and, quite frankly, if I didn't get an ice cream inside me in the next four minutes, I was going to flip out.

'Let's just go here,' I said, pointing at the ice-cream van parked up at the side of the street.

'We can do better than that,' Sam replied, turning

his nose up at the thought of a Mr Whippy. 'Look at that over there. Now that's an ice cream.'

He nodded towards a man sitting on a bench, merrily setting about an enormous ice-cream cone. Double scoops, raspberry sauce, sprinkles, the lot.

'That's got to be from somewhere round here,' I said, turning in a slow circle, seeking out the source of the world's most perfect ice cream. 'It's not like he's been walking around with that all afternoon.'

'I'll ask him,' Sam said, simple as that.

And now it was my turn to be aghast.

'You can't just walk up to someone and ask where they got their food,' I said. But it was too late. With a purposeful stride, Sam headed over to the man and stopped right in front of him, blocking his view of the sea as he lapped at his ice cream.

'Excuse me,' he said. The man looked up, mid-lap. 'May I ask you a question?'

The man looked past Sam to see me giving him a huge, all-teeth grin, desperately trying to communicate that we weren't planning to rob or murder him. He nodded slowly at Sam.

'My friend and I are looking for the best ice cream in Margate,' Sam went on. 'Where would you recommend?'

'This one's from the place on the seafront,' the man said, holding the ice cream slightly away from us, as though one of us might make a grab for it at any second. To be fair, it did look good, it wasn't beyond the realms of possibility. 'Can't remember what it's called.'

'Thank you very much,' Sam said, cheerful as you like. 'Have a lovely day.'

'Yeah,' the man replied. 'And yourself.'

I stretched my smile so wide I thought my face might split as I departed, trotting down the promenade after Sam.

'See?' he said to me, holding open the door of the ice cream parlour. 'And you're trying to teach me about human interaction.'

'He thought you were going to mug him,' I replied. 'Any money this is the first place that comes up on TripAdvisor.'

'And by the time you've checked, I'll be halfway through my ice cream,' he said. 'Now, what are you having?'

Ten minutes later, I was sitting on the beach, the remains of my homemade raspberry ripple ice cream in my hand and half a beach-worth of sand in my knickers.

'It's nice, isn't it?' I said, licking the sticky red sauce off the top of my cone before it could drip onto my hands.

'The ice cream or the location?' Sam asked as he tackled his pistachio and triple chocolate combo beside me.

'Both get top marks from me,' I replied. 'So, do you think Elaine would enjoy this?'

He shook his head. 'No, she's lactose intolerant, so it's not a regular occurrence unless we know there are decent facilities nearby.'

'Nice.' Not even another woman's toilet troubles could put me off finishing this amazing mother of an ice cream. 'I meant would she like Margate?'

'Perhaps?' he replied.

'And do you like it?'

'I'd like it more if I'd known I was coming,' Sam said, without the slightest hint of regret. 'I would have worn sandals.'

'Then I'm very glad I didn't tell you,' I replied.

'I don't think I'm a spur-of-the-moment person, Annie.' He fiddled with the shoelaces on the leather hightops we'd given him and dug his heels into the sand in protest. 'Some people just aren't.'

'I don't get it,' I said, chomping up my cone then leaning back to rest on my elbows, narrowly avoiding a football to the face. 'You seem like someone who would love the internet. I'd be scared to leave you alone with a laptop in case you fell down a Wikipedia hole and never came back out.'

'It's not a reliable source.' Sam shook his head, dismissing the theory out of hand. 'You can ask any credible academic, they'll tell you the same thing. You can't trust the internet.'

I shuddered at the thought of not being able to believe anything I read on Wikipedia. It was my number one source for all facts. Did that mean Ryan Gosling had never campaigned to stop dairy farms de-horning cows? This was a world of uncertainty and one I did not want to live in.

'The internet is useful for a lot of things though,' I argued, ignoring his non-committal pout. 'I listen to music on my phone, shop on my phone, I obsessively stalk celebrities on my phone. We would have found that ice cream place a lot quicker if I'd been able to look it up on Google Maps. When you shut yourself off from an entire section of life, you miss out on some amazing stuff.'

'And if you walk around with your nose glued to a screen, you miss out on life altogether,' he replied.

'Elaine was always on her phone. Whether we were in the car, watching a film, even when we were in bed.'

'And you didn't realize anything was wrong?' I asked, ignoring the slight lurch my stomach gave at the thought of them in bed.

Sam stared out to sea, I stared at Sam. For the life of me, I couldn't fathom the expression on his face. Unbuckling my sandals, I slipped them off and stood up, unravelling the hem of my sundress from my knickers.

'Fancy a paddle?'

'J.M.W. Turner said that Margate had the loveliest skies in Europe,' he said. 'He did not speak to the cleanliness of the water. There's at least three dogs in there right now, that I can see.'

A little knowledge was a dangerous thing. A lot of knowledge could be tedious.

'What are you thinking about?' I asked, holding out my bag out at arm's length. Sam took it without question, then stood up, brushing the sand from his bum and following me to the water's edge. As he stretched his arms high over his head, a tiny peep of tightly toned stomach appeared at the hem of his T-shirt. I really had to get that man some longer T-shirts. Or possibly not. Not terrible to look at. Hmm.

'What have you got against a quiet moment?' he replied, shielding his eyes against the sun. I was sort of surprised his glasses weren't sun-adjusting. He just seemed like the type to account for all occasions. 'Must you always have noise?'

'I have quiet,' I said defensively, my sandals swinging from my forefingers. 'I spent a fortune on noise-cancelling headphones so I wouldn't have to listen to Brian all day.'

'That's not true quiet,' he argued. 'Even if there's no noise, you're trapped in that deafening digital squall, constant communication. You're always in the middle of a conversation or an argument, it must be exhausting.'

I considered his point. My blood pressure had certainly gone up since we took over Lily's Twitter account. Some people needed their thumbs or their caps lock removing. My brain was never really off, I was either reading Twitter, checking Instagram stories or Snapchats, catching up on Facebook or watching YouTube videos. I couldn't even watch a film without googling the actors halfway through, and if the plot wasn't up to much, I was straight to Wikipedia to see if it was worth sticking with.

'What's the last thing you do at night?' Sam asked.

'Check my phone,' I admitted.

'And first thing in a morning?'

We were not close enough for me to admit the first thing I did in a morning was pee and we definitely weren't close enough to admit that, really, the first thing I did was check my phone while I peed. Everyone did it, literally everyone.

'I like knowing what's going on,' I said, stepping down to the water and letting little fresh waves wash over my toes. I felt a sharp shiver flash through my body and everything tightened at once. 'Stay on top of current events.'

'But how to filter through all the noise?' Sam frowned. 'No, I couldn't bear it.'

'You get used to it,' I promised, leaping out of the waves and wiggling my toes in the frigid sand. 'Although I'm not sure if that's a good thing or not.'

He stuck his hands in his pockets and wrinkled his nose. When his arms were at a slight angle, I noticed, his biceps swelled against the tight cuffs of his short-sleeved shirt. He must have been lifting some very heavy books.

'Shall we have a wander around?' I suggested. 'See what we can see?'

He answered with an agreeable nod.

'Where are you on your grand romantic gesture?' I asked as we made our way across the sand and back towards the promenade. 'Are we thinking ride a white horse over to her work? Have a million white roses delivered to the flat?'

'Why not go the whole hog and suggest an ostentatious diamond ring?' he replied.

I choked on the last part, coughing madly to cover it up.

'Sorry,' I said, gasping for air. 'Sand in my throat. There must be something more simple. Tell me about the day you met Elaine.'

He smiled. A true and proper smile.

'I was in the library at university and so was she,' Sam replied. 'I think it must have been a Thursday, because otherwise I would have been in lectures.'

'Right and more specifically than that?' I suggested. 'Did your eyes meet across the microfiche? Did your fingers brush against hers when you both reached for the same book?'

'It is quite a good story,' he said, smiling to himself. 'She was asking someone to be quiet and he told her to fuck off and I told him not to be so rude.'

'A meet-cute for the ages,' I replied. Definitely not one to tell the grandkids.

'I offered to buy her a cup of tea and we ended up in the Costa Coffee down the road, talking for hours.' He sighed, a happy, nostalgic sound that was too light for him. 'Then we went back to her flat and she cooked me dinner. I think we saw each other every day after that. That is, until she asked me to leave.'

'I'm sorry,' I said. There it was again, that same awful, gut-munching feeling. Maybe I was lactose intolerant too? 'Don't give up.'

'I remember she had her hair up.' He twisted his hands around behind his head to demonstrate. 'In a bun. And she was wearing her glasses even though she never wears them now. I loved those glasses, it always looked as though she was investigating something. She was just fascinating to me.'

My little black heart sang, even as it broke. It sounded as though he truly loved her.

And then a terrible thought struck me. What if this didn't work? What if I couldn't mend what was broken?

'She's always been curious,' Sam said, scratching his stubble. 'Always wanted to know everything about everyone. The two of you might get along, actually.'

'Do you think?' I asked, recognizing a slightly sour note in my voice I didn't care for at all.

'No, not really,' he said as he weighed up his own theory. 'You've very little in common apart from the fact you both find me insufferable.'

'I wouldn't necessarily call you insufferable.' I took my bag from him as we reached the promenade. I hadn't thought about it before but I didn't really have any specific hobbies. I had my friends, my family and my job and that was it. 'But I'm not one for the salsa dancing or the stand-up or the spoon carving. Maybe I need to be more adventurous as well.'

He nodded for a moment, hands on his hips as he looked out at the horizon.

'You seem to be doing all right. You're ambitious and you're bold. You're not afraid to try.'

I sat down on the edge of the promenade, sliding my sandals back onto sandy feet. I fiddled with the tiny gold buckle for a moment, not entirely sure what to say.

'That's good, is it?' I said, standing up and hitching my bag over my shoulder. 'What else?'

'You're funny.' He scrunched up his face, clearly giving his answer some real consideration. I was almost afraid to hear what he would come next. 'You're kind. And I think you probably care too much about what people think about you.'

'No I don't,' I lied. Of course I did, who didn't?

'Yes, you do but you shouldn't,' he replied, matter-of-factly. 'You're stubborn and you don't know when to take no for an answer. But you're also infectiously optimistic. One of those things is going to get you into trouble.'

'If you had any inkling about my relationship history, you would not call me optimistic,' I said, trying to kick sand out of my sandals as I walked. 'My sister always says I'm too competitive.'

'I haven't known you for very long, so my opinion is very subjective,' Sam said. 'But since we met due to you taking on a bet, I'd imagine she's right.'

'There's nothing wrong with a little healthy compe-tition.' I skipped a couple of steps to get ahead of him. Thank god he didn't know the Marie Brown hockey-stick story or I'd never hear the end of it.

'But who are you competing with?'

I turned to see Sam leaning carefully against the spiky, green railings, back to the clock tower, face to the sea.

'What do you mean?' I asked.

'Who are you competing against?' he said again as I took two steps awkwardly back towards him.

I frowned. 'Well, the bet is that I have to get you twenty thousand Instagram followers or—'

'Not for the bet,' he said. 'In general. Every single day, all the time. That's the part I don't understand. You're constantly going, it's as though you're scared to stop. When will you be satisfied?'

It was a question I didn't have an answer for.

We both stayed exactly where we were, forearms resting against the railings, full of sugar and new things to know about one another.

'This is the perfect place for a very important boyfriend bootcamp lesson.' I pawed through my bag, looking for my phone. 'I'm only using it as a camera,' I said when he began to protest. 'The ability to take a good couple selfie is an indispensable skill in this day and age. You're going to learn.'

'I don't see what all the fuss is about.' Sam folded his arms, hiding each hand in an armpit. 'Just hold up the phone and take a photo. Or better yet, don't be such a narcissist and wait for someone to take a photo of you at an appropriate time.'

'Take the phone,' I insisted, holding it out. 'Take it.'

'I'm taking it,' he said, holding the edges of my iPhone as though it were made of precious crystal. Which it could be for all I knew. 'Now what?'

'I'm going to stand here,' I stepped closer, forcing myself into his personal space and awkwardly nestled in under his left arm. His entire body froze. 'Don't worry, I'm not going to give you a wedgie,' I promised. He relaxed by a fraction and so I carried on with my instruction, focusing on the task at hand and not how nice and warm and snug I felt.

'Now hold the phone above your head, angle it down so we're both in the picture and then click, you're done.'

'I can't press the button on the front,' he said through a grim smile.

'You don't press the button on the front, you use one of the volume buttons on the side,' I replied. 'Much easier.'

'Why such a strange angle?' Sam asked, gurning as my phone fired off a million shots.

'Because it's flattering,' I replied, tilting my chin just so. 'You've got to trust me on this. A thousand Kardashians can't be wrong.'

'Excuse me.' A little old couple, resplendent in their Sunday best on a Saturday, stood in front of us, all smiles. They were both wearing hats and he leaned against a walker while she clutched his arm for support.

'Would you like us to take a photograph for you?' the old gentleman asked.

'That would be splendid, thank you,' Sam said, nodding for me to give them my phone.

'You just press this button here,' I said as I handed it over.

'Oh, we know,' his wife replied. 'We've got grand-children. I'm at level three thousand of Candy Crush.'

'That's bloody impressive,' I said, swearing under my breath as I stepped backwards and moved in closer to Sam.

'Language,' he replied, placing his arm politely around my shoulders.

'Go on,' the husband called. He held the phone out to better frame the picture. 'Give her a proper cuddle.'

Sam pulled me a little closer and I laughed, entirely

involuntarily. His skin was so warm, his hands were so big. I leaned towards him, my cheek resting against his chest.

'Say cheese!'

I looked up, as Sam did as he was told. Why couldn't I get him to follow an instruction so easily?

'I like your dress,' the lady said, handing me the phone as her husband rearranged himself with his walker. 'It's nice to see young people dressed properly. You make a very lovely couple.'

'Oh, we're not a couple,' I assured her, very, very quickly.

'Just friends,' Sam agreed. 'But thank you very much. Have a lovely weekend.'

They nodded, weaving themselves back together and set off slowly up the promenade while I checked the photos.

All of the selfies we'd taken were ridiculous. Sam looked like he was either crying or being goosed while I was laughing in every one of them. Me and my eighteen chins. But the picture taken by our new friend was something else. Sam was smiling straight at the camera, blue eyes clear and honest. I was in profile, chin lifted, laughing happily, smiling at Sam.

'Tell me that's not a better picture,' Sam stated, peering at my phone over my shoulder.

'It's fine,' I said, quickly closing the photo library and putting my phone back in my bag. He had captured something I wasn't quite ready to see. 'Can you believe they thought we were a couple?'

'Quite frankly, no.'

'Glad you took a moment to think about that,' I said, rolling my eyes and still clutching my phone through the fabric of my bag. 'Thanks, Sam.'

'It's a ridiculous concept,' he went on, not quite finished demolishing my ego. 'As if someone like you could be with someone like me. Imagine it, Annie. You come home with all your parties and Facebook and your internet stuff and I'm there working on an essay about the fourth Duke of Rutland. Whatever would we talk about?'

'I could stand to know more about the fourth Duke of Rutland,' I replied, stung. Just when I thought we were getting somewhere. 'But obviously I wouldn't want to burden you with the things I care about.'

Wisely or not, Sam decided not to reply. Instead, we walked on down the promenade without speaking, soundtracked by the sound of barking dogs, children laughing and whatever song came out of the next set of speakers.

'Seems to me we're making great strides with your so-called boyfriend bootcamp,' Sam began. 'Even if I do think I'm going to have to pass on the second *Magic Mike* movie.'

'It's better than the first,' I said, still not entirely ready to forgive him for his comment. 'Well, it's almost time for step five: the grand romantic gesture. And then you're done.'

He looked surprised.

'And then that's it, is it? I'm fixed?'

'You weren't broken,' I told him. 'We all need a bit of a polish sometimes.'

His hair fell over his face as he ducked his head and walked ahead of me. I paused for a second, watching him as he went. Sunny blond curls, square shoulders, narrow waist, long legs. He looked great. I'd done a good job with my makeover. My fingers found my phone in my bag and I took another look at our picture. He looked really good. But really, it wasn't Sam's face that stood out to me in that picture.

'I think that's where the pier was,' he called, pointing off into the ocean as I locked my phone and dropped it back into the bottom of my bag. 'Where all those people were trapped on that fateful January day.'

He carried on but I wasn't listening. I was still thinking about that photo. When was the last time I'd looked that happy? And when was the last time I'd felt the way I did right now? I wasn't altogether certain of the answer to either question and that would bother me a lot longer than the fate of forty people stranded on the Margate pier in 1877.

CHAPTER NINETEEN

We were twenty-one days into the bet and the Hip Historian still only had a little over nine thousand followers. Halfway to thirty days and not even a halfway towards hitting his follower target.

The account definitely had its fans but it was the same people hitting the like button every time. We weren't building on the initial audience and I couldn't work out why, no matter how long I spent running analytics and changing up the hashtags. It didn't make sense that the account had already peaked, we were still so new. I had to find a new boost and sooner rather than later.

'Annie?'

I looked up from my laptop to see the man in question standing just inside the door.

'Are you working?' Sam asked.

'Yes,' I confirmed, clicking out of an article on Emma Watson's style evolution. 'What's wrong?'

'Might I speak to you outside for a moment?' he

said, turning away from the whiteboard without giving it a second glance. 'I need to ask a favour.'

Without taking her eyes off her computer screen, Miranda sang out a couple of bars of wah-wah pedal guitar, evoking a seventies porno flick and massively entertaining herself in the process.

'She's a big Led Zeppelin fan,' I said, dashing out from behind my computer and dragging him into the hallway. 'What's up?'

'I wouldn't have had her pegged for it,' he said, with an admiring glance back at Mir. 'Are you doing anything this evening?'

My mouth went dry and I opened my mouth before I had words ready to come out of it.

'This evening I am not,' I said, marvelling at my own stupidity. 'I mean, I'm not doing anything this evening. Why?'

'Tonight's the night,' he said, beaming from ear to ear. 'Elaine's back.'

I stared at him with an open mouth. Already?

'Yay?' I tried. 'And wow.'

'I've spent a lot of time thinking about what you said and I've got my grand romantic gesture all planned out, but I want everything to be just so,' he said, pinching his fingers together. 'Will you help me?'

The last person who wanted to make sure everything was just so for me was the man who delivered my Chinese takeaway and even though he said he wanted to make sure I was satisfied, I had an inkling he didn't actually give a shit.

'What kind of surprise?' I asked in a high-pitched voice. What if he was going to propose? What if he wanted me to help choose the ring? What if he wanted me to officiate the wedding? What if—

'I'm going to cook her dinner,' he declared with great pride.

Oh. OK then.

'You're sure it's a good idea?' I asked, running my pendant up and down its chain. 'Surprising her with dinner in the middle of the week?'

'It's our anniversary,' he nodded. My heart lurched. Because I was so anxious for this to go well, I reminded myself. 'And according to your schedule, she has salsa class this evening so she'll be out until eight. I can let myself in, make the dinner and have it all ready for her coming home.'

Wow. Look at him, making thoughtful plans. It was almost as if someone had spent three weeks coaching him on how to be a better boyfriend.

'I've bought candles and I found a florist that sells bags of rose petals.' His entire face bloomed bright red on cue. 'But I was hoping you might help me with the meal. I'd really rather not poison her.'

'Of course,' I answered without hesitation. Because hesitation would suggest I didn't want to do it and why wouldn't I want to do it? 'I'm not the world's greatest chef but I can do one better than beans on toast.'

'Then you can do one better than me,' he said happily. 'Shall we leave here at six-thirty?'

'We shall,' I confirmed. 'See you then.'

He trotted off down the corridor while I hung around outside the office. What a success story he would turn out to be. From a disagreeable yeti into a considerate, kind fox in five easy steps. Someone get me a loaf and five fishes, I was officially a miracle worker.

'Oi, Higgins.'

I turned to see Mir giving me The Look over the top of her laptop.

234

'What's going on?'

'Sam wants me to help him make dinner for Elaine,' I explained, coming back inside and wandering around the office, too unsettled to sit. 'Tonight's the night.'

'Wow,' she replied. 'And you're going to do it, are you?'

'Of course,' I nodded. 'I can't wait.'

Mir bit her lip and frowned.

'Annie?'

'Miranda?'

'You can totally correct me if I'm wrong but it seems to me as though you've been putting a lot more energy into Sam's personal life than you have the actual bet.'

'Putting effort into Sam is the same thing as putting effort into the bet,' I replied, picking up a stapler then putting it down. Then picking it up again, snapping a few staples into my palm and putting it back down. 'I help Sam, Sam helps us, we win a month's free rent. What's so complicated about that?'

'I'm only saying, it looks like you're having a lovely time together,' Mir retied the pink bandana holding her hair back from her face as she spoke. 'While you're putting in all this effort.'

'You know I like a challenge,' I said with a sigh.

'I know you do,' she agreed. 'And I know you like Sam.'

No I didn't. No I didn't. No I didn't. No I didn't. No I didn't.

'Shut up,' I said as my neck and cheeks began to burn. 'And don't be so ridiculous.'

'Oh, you poor thing,' she whispered. 'You poor, poor thing.'

'I'm going to his flat to help him make a special dinner for his girlfriend while he fills the place with candles and rose petals and begs her to take him back and I'm completely and utterly OK with it.' I sank into my chair and dropped my head, face first, onto the desk. 'Completely and utterly OK.'

'Right you are, Annie,' Miranda replied with a salute. 'Whatever you say.'

'I'll get started on dinner and you concentrate on the set dressing,' I ordered Sam as he unlocked the door to a surprisingly nice flat in a surprisingly nice house in an unsurprisingly nice row of Georgian mews in Bloomsbury. I'd come to the conclusion that the best way to get through this was just to get through it and the sooner it was over, the sooner I could be at home, watching *Queer Eye* and inhaling the family-sized trifle I had in the fridge. I had to keep reminding myself this was a project. He was a project, nothing more.

'Sam,' I said, realizing he was not following me inside. 'What are you doing?'

Instead of following me in, he was hovering in the hallway, holding his key in one hand, staring past me, Sainsbury's bags clustered around his ankles.

'What's wrong?' I asked, putting down my own shopping bags and waving a hand in front of his face. 'Do you need me to invite you in? Oh god, are you some sort of reverse vampire? Because that really would make a lot of sense.'

'I haven't been here in so long,' he said, still hesitant to step inside. 'Something about this feels odd.'

I offered him the best sympathetic smile I could muster.

'Sneaking back into your own home to cook a nice meal for the woman who kicked you out? I don't know what you mean.'

'Yes, all right,' he said, breathing out and stepping over the threshold. 'Quite right.'

He looked around as though he was seeing the flat for the first time. As someone who *was* seeing it for the first time, I didn't know quite what to make of it. Sam and Elaine had a very nice home. Very, very nice. The flat wasn't huge but it was in a pretty swanky part of town and everything was tastefully done in that quietly expensive way. I couldn't spot even a single item of Ikea furniture. It was unheard of.

'It's a lovely place,' I said, watching as he picked up cushions and put them back down.

'It's Elaine's aunt's,' he replied. 'We're really just looking after it for her while she's in Spain. Only we've been looking after it for the last five years. I don't know what we'd do if she ever decided to move back to London.'

'Nice work if you can get it,' I commented, slipping out of my shoes and letting my feet sink into the thick beige carpeting.

It wasn't only a lack of Ikea furniture that was upsetting me. There was also a distinct absence of any evidence that Sam had ever so much as walked through the door, let alone lived here. No sign of him in the photos on the walls or the picture frames that lined the bookshelves. Either he still believed photographs stole your soul or he'd been removed. Already. 'She's changed such a lot of things,' Sam muttered, taking himself through to the kitchen. 'These are new pots and pans.'

'Sometimes it's nice to buy new pots and pans?' I suggested, trying not to panic him. None of this was a good sign. Elaine had completely erased him from her life.

'And all new plates. New mugs, even,' Sam re-appeared in the living room. 'She's bought new cushions.'

'Miranda is always buying new cushions,' I said quickly. It was true. I knew because I had all her old ones. 'It doesn't mean anything.'

But I was very, very worried that it might.

'Hmm,' he replied, his stance shifting slightly, stiffening until he looked completely at odds with the comfortable surroundings.

'Why don't I get dinner started,' I suggested, picking up as many of the shopping bags as I could carry. There was no way I could back out now. 'And you get to work with the candles and the rose petals and, god knows what else you've got in that bag.'

'It's cat food,' he said, producing an enormous sack of cat biscuits from his rucksack.

Of all the fetishes.

'My cat, Wellington, he's in here somewhere,' he explained as he got down on his hands and knees to look under the sofa. 'He doesn't like strangers, he might have hidden himself away when he heard your voice. This is his favourite food but Elaine doesn't like paying extra for it.'

'So I'm making dinner for your girlfriend while you make dinner for your cat?' I asked. Still crawling around on his hands and knees, Sam nodded. 'Good to know,' I said as I made my way into the kitchen. 'Good to know.'

If someone had asked me what was the most romantic meal a man could prepare for his lady love, I wouldn't have said Old El Paso fajitas but then I was the single one so if Sam insisted Tex-Mex be the food of love, I would cook on.

'It's all in the oven to keep warm,' I said, swiping

my forehead with the back of my wrist as Sam peered at the serving dishes from a distance. 'The guacamole and the salsa are in the fridge and the tortilla chips are in this bowl. Are you all done?'

'Yes, captain,' he replied with a salute. 'The red wine is open, the candles are ready to be lit – one scented and the others unscented, as instructed – everything else is where it needs to be.'

No one had ever covered a bed in rose petals for me. Matthew once put a rubber sheet down when I had food poisoning, but that really wasn't the same.

'Brilliant.' I wiped my hands down on the front of my jeans, ignoring Sam's grimace, and gave everything a once-over. It was ten past eight, Elaine would be home in ten minutes. Time for me to scarper. Or at least hang around in the bus shelter opposite and pretend to look at my phone until she arrived, which was exactly what I was planning to do.

'All you need to do is get changed and you're good to go,' I said, slinging my handbag over my shoulder.

Sam looked back at me blankly.

'Get changed?'

He pulled out the hem of his promotional University of Newcastle fresher week T-shirt, presenting it for approval.

'Remember how we're trying to show Elaine that you're prepared to change?' I said, exasperation creeping in to my voice. Just when I thought we were getting somewhere. 'What's the point in the fancy new haircut and thoughtful dinner if you're going to trot up in a T-shirt you should have been embarrassed to wear when you got it, let alone now?'

'But Elaine will think it's funny,' he insisted. 'Because I actually went to Durham.'

'I can't with you,' I said, holding up my hands in defeat. 'I can't even.'

'You can't even what?' he asked, following me out of the kitchen.

'You're getting changed,' I told him. Looking him up and down, it really was only the T-shirt that was a major issue. His jeans were the ones Brian had dug out from the Dashell collection and, thankfully, his bare feet were in pretty good nick. Impressive really, for any man. 'Have you still got clothes here?'

He nodded. 'My shirts are in the wardrobe in the bedroom.'

'Then let's see what we can do,' I said, pushing him down the hallway, hands on his shoulders and eyes trying not to look at his backside.

The options weren't great but we had what we had. I picked out a pale blue shirt that didn't look as though it would bury him and handed it over, politely turning my back when he pulled his T-shirt over his head. The bedroom was as nice as the rest of the flat and there were just as few hints that Sam had ever lived there. He'd scattered the petals over the beautiful new duvet cover we'd bought from the White Company and arranged them in a heart shape. A Jo Malone Red Roses candle waited patiently in the corner of the room and I spotted the ready-and-waiting post-coital chocolates I'd recommended on the dressing table. My knickers and my heart almost spontaneously combusted.

'Will this do?' Sam asked. I turned to see him glasses-less, buttoning up the next to last button on his shirt and gave him a thumbs up.

'I know I'm biased,' I said, straightening his collar slightly and smiling up into his worried eyes. 'But any woman who isn't impressed by this kind of effort would have to be crazy. She's going to love it, Sam.'

'I hope so,' he said, covering my hand with his.

'Sam,' I felt the skin on my neck begin to tickle and I couldn't stop myself. 'I don't know if it's going to help at all but I think you're brilliant. I realize all this started off with me trying to help you to change but, really, you're such a good man already.'

It was so quiet in the flat I could hear him gulp.

'And Elaine is lucky to have you,' I said, unravelling my hand from his and giving him a playful punch on the chin. 'Good luck, buddy.'

'Annie,' he said, catching my hand in both of his and holding it tightly this time. 'Thank you. For everything.'

It was only when I heard the key in the door, I realized I wasn't breathing.

'Fuuuuck,' I mouthed, snatching away my hand. 'Elaine?'

Sam looked around as she moved on to the second lock.

'Elaine,' he confirmed at the sound of a woman singing. 'In the airing cupboard,' he said, bundling me backwards. 'I'm sorry, I'll get you out in a moment, I'm sorry, I'm sorry.'

But not too sorry to shove me into a pitch-black cupboard barely wide enough and tall enough for me to stand up straight. Before I'd had time to squeeze myself into a safe space, I felt something warm and soft move over my foot.

'If that's a rat, I'm going to murder him,' I whispered before letting out a very restrained squeal as it moved again. Bracing myself, I looked down to see the outline of large, grey tabby cat looking right back up at me with

Total Eclipse of the Heart eyes. It sniffed my leg, batted the hem of my skirt with an enormous paw and then settled down on top of my feet, curling up for a nap.

'You must be Wellington,' I said quietly. 'Why don't you make yourself comfortable, pal?'

Sarcasm was wasted on cats.

The tiniest orange light on the hot water tank cast everything in the cupboard in shades of grey. Fuzzy outlines with no sense of perspective. The only sound was Wellington, who was having himself a time, purring on top of my foot.

Just as my eyes were beginning to adjust to the dark, the door to the cupboard flew open and I breathed in and pressed myself against the wall as a panting and confused Sam joined me, slamming the door shut behind him.

'What are you doing?' I gasped, shuffling up to make room, much to the annoyance of Wellington. 'You can't jump out at her, you'll give her a heart attack.'

'She isn't on her own,' he whispered. 'She's got someone with her.'

'So you're going to scare them both to death?' I asked.

'It's a man,' Sam hissed, his voice despondent. 'They were both laughing.'

'Lot of people laugh with other people, it doesn't mean anything,' I replied, my voice full of hope I didn't really feel. 'I've even cracked up at you once or twice, haven't I?'

He didn't say anything. Instead he slumped against the door, not even inches from my face. This was not a two-person hiding place. I could smell the warmth on his skin and feel every exhalation of breath. He shifted, just slightly, and suddenly my cheek was pressed against his chest and I could hear his heartbeat.

I opened my mouth to say something but nothing came out. *Think*, Annie, I ordered myself. Say something helpful, something nice. It can't be that hard. But every time I tried to find the words, my thoughts were drowned out by the rhythmic thud of Sam's heart. I rested my cheek against his shirt and closed my eyes just for a second.

'She's with a man,' Sam whispered, more to himself than me. 'Already. She's got someone else already.'

'We can't stay in here,' I said, finally breaking the spell. 'What if she finds us?'

'What if she does?' he replied. 'It's still supposed to be my home. It's not as though she can call the police.'

'Then why were you the one sleeping on your office floor?' I asked.

I could just make out his silhouette's response. An unconvincing shrug.

'I can't stand this, Sam,' I said, as Wellington began to wriggle around on our feet. The natives were getting restless. 'Open this door, walk out there and demand to know what's going on.'

'I don't want to look at him,' he said quietly. 'I don't want to see his face.'

'What if they come in here?' I said slowly. 'To the bedroom, I mean.'

'Oh no,' Sam mumbled. Outside, I could hear Elaine giggling away about something, as well as another voice, murmuring what, I couldn't tell. 'Absolutely not. What are we going to do?'

Luckily for Sam, I was excellent in a crisis. Just as long as it wasn't my crisis.

'I've got an idea,' I said. 'Just follow me.'

I reached down to the floor and scooped up a handful

of fur and claws, then let my handbag fall into the crook of my elbow.

'Keep your head up but don't look at them. And you don't have to say anything if you don't want to.'

I reached for the handle of the airing cupboard and turned it sharply, kicking the door open into the bedroom. Down the hallway, Elaine screamed as I marched Sam out into the living room and towards the front door. She was sat on the sofa, or rather her salsa partner was sat on her sofa and she was sat on him. Both half-naked and neither one of them expecting company.

'Evening, Elaine,' I said, holding up my hand as well as I could, given my furry cargo. 'Hello . . . you.'

Tall, dark and naked held up a hand in a confused greeting. Elaine stayed exactly where she was, her face set in a silent scream with, I noticed with not a little pleasure, mascara all over her face.

'We came for the cat,' I said, bundling Wellington into my bag, very much against his will. As if I want you in there with my MacBook Pro, I wanted to say. 'We'll let ourselves out.'

Sam was stood behind me, staring at his now definite ex-girlfriend.

It was too late, he had looked.

I was furious. Utterly enraged. How could she do this to him?

'There's chicken fajitas in the oven if you get hungry,' I said to Elaine, grabbing Sam's hand and pulling him out the door. 'And just so you know, I made the guacamole myself, so don't let it go off, avocados aren't cheap, you pair of complete bastards.'

Wellington miaowed in agreement as I flipped up my middle finger, yanked Sam over the threshold and slammed the front door shut behind us.

CHAPTER TWENTY

Before anyone could say anything else, I was shep-
herding Sam out onto the street and into a black cab
that was idling outside his next-door neighbour's house.

'I am so sorry,' I said, breathing hard and trying to
keep Wellington safely inside my bag. Matt & Nat totes
were not meant to be cat carriers. 'Are you all right?'

'Not particularly.' When I looked down at his lap,
I saw his hands were shaking. 'I can't take Wellington
to my brother's house. He's allergic.'

'You can both come to mine,' I offered as I gave the
taxi driver my address. 'It's not a problem.'

We drove on in silence for a moment, twisting and
turning around Russell Square before slowing down
at a red light.

'That's a very generous offer but I think I'd rather
be alone.' Sam finally spoke as we turned on to
Clerkenwell Road. 'But it would be a tremendous help
if you could watch Wellington for the evening. Until
I can make other arrangements.'

'Of course,' I agreed readily. Wellington seemed
perfectly happy to spend the rest of his life in my

handbag, how hard could it be? 'Shall we drop you off at your brother's house?'

'The office will be fine,' he replied, his voice stiff and far away, as if the last two weeks had never happened.

'Sam,' I said, one hand on the fur ball currently face down in my bag, the other resting on his knee. He looked down at my hand then up at my face as though I had just punched him in the nuts. 'You're not sleeping on your office floor tonight.'

'Please don't.' He kept his face turned away from me as we rolled on down the road. 'I'm not having this conversation.'

'OK, don't then,' I replied. 'But you're coming home with me and I will physically fight you if you try to suggest otherwise.'

He looked back at me, mild surprise in his eyes.

'Like I said, I didn't grow up in that mansion,' I reminded him, eyes forward, purposefully not looking at him. 'I will kick your arse if I have to, Dr Page.'

'Right, then,' he replied. 'Thank you.'

'Besides,' I muttered, keeping a firm hold of Wellington's neck. 'Someone's going to have to deal with it when this cat takes a dump, and it certainly isn't going to be me.'

'This is your flat?' Sam asked, peering inside my place as I opened the door.

'It would be weird that I had the keys if it wasn't,' I replied. 'Cup of tea? Or something stronger?'

'On a weeknight?' He looked positively aghast as I quietly stepped sideways into the kitchen to hide Monday night's wine bottle in the cupboard underneath the sink.

'You have a very nice home,' Sam announced as he

moved around, already looking more comfortable than he had in Elaine's fancy flat. 'It's very you.'

'I'm never really sure what that means.' I filled the kettle, shouting over my noisy taps. 'But I'll take it as a compliment.'

'It was meant as one,' he said. I glanced over my shoulder to see him studying the photos on my bookcase. 'You and Miranda have been friends for a long time?'

'Since the first day of school,' I confirmed. 'Some bright spark sat us next to each other in registration and regretted it for the next seven years. Best thing that ever happened to me. As long as we don't take into consideration the holiday to Ibiza between sixth form and uni – and we have actually had it written into law that we do not.'

Sam smiled politely and nodded, but his shoulders still sloped downwards as he walked around considering my trinkets. He looked defeated.

'It must be nice to have old friends,' he said, picking up a photo taken on Mir's twenty-first birthday. A *Rocky Horror*-themed party. In the background, if you knew where to look, you could make out half a Matthew, resplendent in his Burton's ensemble, refusing to join in with the fun. 'We moved around a lot when I was younger; hard to keep young friendships going back then. Penpals get bored after a while.'

'It must be weird now,' I said, eyeing Wellington with great suspicion as he nosed around my cardigan Uggs. If he peed on them, he'd be out the window. 'With Facebook and Twitter and Instagram and everything, it's almost impossible to lose touch with someone. Even if you want to. How come you moved around so much? Parents were super spies?'

'Possibly,' he replied. He rested on the arm of my

loveseat, not quite ready to commit to a full sit. 'My mum died when I was three and my dad really wasn't around an awful lot. I much prefer the thought that he was James Bond rather than your common or garden arse.'

'Oh,' I paused, holding one teabag aloft in each hand. 'I'm so sorry.'

'It was a long time ago.' Sam stood up again, gingerly picking up my framed graduation photo and studying it. It was the last time my mum and dad had been in the same place, at the same time and no crockery had been thrown. Possibly only because there was no crockery in the vicinity.

'We lived with my aunt for a while,' he added, 'but my uncle was in the army so there was a lot of moving – nowhere really interesting, just up and down the country. When they got posted abroad, I ended up with my grandmother.'

'It's a very good cover story,' I said lightly, closing my curtains on the fading sky and turning on a lamp, to stop myself running over to him and giving him the biggest hug in the world. I knew it wouldn't be welcome. 'But I'm almost certain your entire family were super spies. You too, for that matter.'

'I did go to public school for a while,' he admitted, fingering the spines of my little library. 'But I'd make a terrible spy. I can't ski for a start and martinis make me quite ill.'

'Then you're neither use nor ornament,' I told him. 'How do you want your tea?'

Sam stood in front of my bookcase, clashing with my lifetime of collected memories. Books, photos, bits and bobs. Tiny objects that stood in for momentous occasions, things I'd recognize blindfolded. And then, Sam.

'Touch of milk, tip of the spoon,' he replied, brushing his thumb along the spines, pulling one out at random. 'Obviously I already know your father is an evil mastermind and part of a global pony-trafficking syndicate. What about your mum?'

'Ah, Mum is fine,' I said. 'She replaced my dad with hobbies after the divorce. It's good, it keeps her off the streets.'

He looked at me with a half-smile.

'Isn't that something parents are supposed to say about their children?' he asked.

'That would be a very good question for my sister the shrink,' I replied, my mind suddenly on the trifle in the fridge. Whenever I thought about my relationship with my parents I thought about trifle. Or ice cream. Or chocolate. Or anything that wasn't my relationship with my parents.

'Is there a supermarket nearby?' Sam put down my book and picked up his tabby. Wellington immediately went limp and placed two paws on Sam's cheek before turning to me with a look that clearly said 'Don't you even try it'.

'Tesco Metro on the corner,' I said. 'What do you need?'

He rubbed Wellington between the ears until he dissolved into a rumble of purrs. 'I should probably get him a litter tray before he shits in your bath.'

'He does that?' I asked, eyeing my new nemesis.

'Oh, yes,' Sam confirmed.

'If Tesco hasn't got one,' I said immediately, tossing him my house keys, 'there's a Sainsbury's further up the road.'

'Do you need anything while I'm out?' he asked, patting himself down for his wallet. I pressed my lips together and shook my head as he let himself out the front door. 'OK, back in a mo.'

It was the strangest thing. I couldn't remember the last time someone had stood in my flat and asked if I needed anything. The simplest little gesture and I was practically in tears.

Out of nowhere, it hit me. I missed it. Someone picking up milk from the supermarket, someone to help me carry the Christmas tree home, someone to complain that I hadn't done the dishes again. Someone to pick me up from the dentist after they had to give me the laughing gas because I was too much of a puss to even get a cleaning without it. Miranda had flatly refused to do it again after the last time when I might have accidentally wet myself in the Uber on the way home. I'd paid her back for the cleaning fee, so I really didn't understand what the big deal was.

My heart broke for Sam. I couldn't imagine how hard it must have been for him, however lovely his relatives were. And now Elaine cheating on him. I was so sad, not just because I knew what he was going through but because I knew what was ahead. Time might heal all wounds but it was not an efficient course of treatment. And I felt bad for my part in it. He could have been two weeks along in the break-up process and instead he was right back in the middle of it, all because I'd convinced him I could help him win someone back who didn't want to be won.

What a tit I was.

I picked up my phone to text Mir and Brian. Clearly they needed to know the latest gossip. But when I opened my messages, I didn't know quite what to say.

This wasn't my news, this was Sam's and it felt wrong to share.

'Who even am I?' I whispered, putting my phone back on the kitchen counter and grabbing an unopened bottle of wine from the fridge. I worked the screwtop quickly and hit the second speed-dial button on my phone.

'I'm putting the baby to bed, what do you want?' Rebecca answered on the first ring.

'I'm having an existential crisis,' I replied, grabbing my mug, tipping the teabag out and filling it with wine. 'Help.'

My sister sighed down the line and then bellowed for her husband.

'Can you deal with Basil?' I heard her ask. 'I need to talk to the other baby.'

'Hello, Annie,' he called.

However did he guess it was me?

'What's wrong?' she asked, her voice bouncing as she jogged downstairs to her office. Becks was incapable of having a phone conversation unless she was in her comfy chair.

'I'm not sure,' I replied.

'Annie, it's nine o'clock at night, I'm knackered. All I want to do is have a bath and finish watching *Mindhunter*,' she said. 'Can you hurry this up?'

'Ooh, is that any good?' I asked. 'I've been meaning to watch it. I quite fancy Jonathan Groff.'

'I know that's not the problem you're calling about, but we should definitely discuss it when I see you next Wednesday,' she replied. 'Is this a work thing or a boy thing?'

I pouted and sipped my wine.

'Why does it have to be one of those two things?'

'Because it always is,' Becks said. 'And since you're

avoiding the subject even though you called me, I'd say it's a boy thing.'

'Might be.'

'The boy you brought to Dad's birthday party?'

'Might be.'

'Finally.' She let out a self-congratulatory exhalation before carrying on. 'What's the problem?'

'I honestly don't know,' I insisted. 'I've been trying to help Sam get his girlfriend back. They broke up a couple of weeks ago, he thought it was fixable, but now it turns out she's seeing someone else and he's really upset and I feel as though it's my fault. I know it isn't but I feel really weird about the whole thing. I feel guilty. But why?'

'Because you like him,' she replied.

'Not like that,' I said, tipping back more wine. 'He's my friend. Sort of. No, I think we're definitely friends now. We went to Margate.'

'The true marker of any friendship,' Becks said. 'And that was a statement, not a question. You like him. As more than a friend. You don't need a doctorate in psychology to see that, I could tell from the way you looked at him at Dad's party.'

A strange cold feeling washed over me and I struggled to swallow my wine.

'You feel guilty because you're happy his girlfriend doesn't want him back,' my sister explained. 'But you're anxious because, now he's truly available, you run the risk of rejection.'

'Nope,' I muttered into my mug. 'Not having that. I think we're just friends.'

'It's one thing to lie to me and Miranda, but it's quite another when you're wasting your time lying to yourself,' she yawned down the line. 'But, regardless,

I wouldn't advise you to tell him how you feel just yet. It's much too soon and you'd be running the risk of getting really hurt.'

'I can see why that would be a problem,' I replied, nodding at my phone. 'If I fancied him, which I don't.'

'Denial is exhausting,' Rebecca groaned. 'I've got to go. It sounds to me as though he needs a friend right now, Annie. Be that friend. Then call me when you've decided to stop being stupid.'

And then she hung up. At the exact same moment, the key turned in the lock and I flipped the switch on the kettle to heat it up again.

'Did they have what you needed?' I asked, necking my wine and putting the open bottle of wine back in the fridge. Drinking alone on a school night, I was a disgrace.

'They had the litter but not the trays,' he replied, holding up a plastic bag. 'Do you have a spare shoe box or something like that?'

I shook my head. Bloody KonMari method. My flat was still a shit-tip, only now I could never find anything I needed.

'Hang on, I might have something,' I said, rootling around in the built-in cupboard that demarcated the end of the kitchen and the beginning of the living room. 'Would this work?'

Sam squinted at the dusty box.

'What is it?'

'Foot spa,' I said, shaking it out of its packaging. 'Christmas present from my dad and Gina a couple of years ago. I think I've used it once.'

For the want of a better option, Sam opened up the bag of litter and emptied it into the two wells of the foot spa, before placing it carefully on top of three sheets of the newspaper he'd also bought at the super-market. Once upon a time I would have had at least one free paper hanging around but I hardly ever picked one up on the way home these days. Too busy looking at my phone to bother.

'Perfect.' I stood in the hallway with my hands on my hips. Becks didn't know what she was talking about. I stared at Sam and chewed on the inside of my cheek.

'What?' he asked, looking more than a little alarmed.

'Nothing,' I said, shaking my head at myself and taking two whole steps back into the kitchen. 'Tea's up.'

Sam emptied the rest of his shopping on the kitchen top. Toothbrush, deodorant and a bottle of whisky.

'I spoke to Elaine.'

I turned off the kettle and handed him an empty mug, which he promptly filled with single malt. So much for the tea.

'And?' I asked, fetching the wine back out from the fridge.

Sam slumped onto the loveseat, nursing his drink. 'Apparently, they're a thing,' he said in between swigs of whisky. 'Her and this Gianni. She said she was sorry and that she wasn't planning it and she didn't want me to find out like that.'

'You don't say.'

Though it seemed fair enough that she would prefer her old boyfriend not to be hiding in the airing cupboard with a stranger when she brought her new lover home.

This was the wrong time to ask whether or not they had eaten the guacamole.

'She said the guacamole was excellent.'

He was a mind reader.

Sam sat with his head down, swirling the whisky

around and around in the bottom of his mug. He was staring at it so hard, I thought he might fall in.

'I'm sorry,' I said, that same, strange gnawing feeling in the bottom of my stomach. 'I know there's nothing I can say that will make you feel better.'

He didn't respond.

'But if she was cheating on you, really, you're better off out of it.'

His head shot up and a shower of whisky splattered on his shoes. 'You think she was cheating on me?'

There was nothing I could say that would make him feel better but apparently there was something I could say that would make him feel worse.

'No!' I said right away. 'I misunderstood. I thought you meant they were a thing before you broke up. I'm sure she would never do that.'

I was not sure of that at all. In fact, if I had to put money in it, I'd bet the other way, but that wasn't going to help matters. What was I supposed to do with a recently dumped dude? I couldn't give him a tub of Ben & Jerry's, put on *Dirty Dancing* and stroke his hair until he felt better, could I? Or *could* I? I watched his face for clues but he was entirely inscrutable. Yes, he looked upset but I'd seen that same expression on his face a million times over the last fortnight, whether he was hungry, tired, or needed the toilet. His poker face had improved since we shaved off the beard.

Who knew how he was going to react? Who knew how hard he was going to take this? Who knew how long he would need to recover from such an ugly, explicit betrayal?

'What's done is done,' he announced, knocking back the rest of his whisky and then slapping his knees. 'Cheese toastie?'

He would need four point seven seconds.

'We can talk about it, if you want to?' I said, standing back as he strode into the kitchen, refilled his mug and delved into another Tesco bag to produce a white loaf and a bag of grated cheddar.

'Pre-grated cheese.' He held the bag up for inspection, shaking his head in wonderment. 'Best invention since sliced bread.' He patted the Kingsmill and laughed at his own joke. 'Where's the toaster?'

'Next to the microwave,' I said, shuffling out the way as he found his own way around my kitchen. 'You don't want to talk about it?'

'If I'm talking about it, I'll be thinking about it, and I've already lost hours doing that,' he replied, still busying himself with his dinner as he spoke. 'If it's done, it's done. Where's the good in dwelling on the past?'

'Said the historian to the digital marketer,' I replied.

Sam set about his task with as much care and attention as you might expect. He methodically placed each piece of bread in the toaster, opened the bag of cheese, turned on my grill and wiped down two plates he found on the draining board with kitchen towel. Once the first toastie was in the oven, he started on the second. He was halfway through scattering the cheese when the first tear fell.

I placed my hand gently on his back.

'Please don't,' he said. His gaze was focused on the toaster and his knuckles were tight around the butter knife in his hand. 'I'll be quite all right in just a moment.'

It was a lie but luckily, I knew exactly what to do. Without a word, I linked my phone to my speakers and quickly scrolled through my music library. Only one person could help us in times like these.

Sam almost dropped his knife as the music started, bass thumping underneath our feet. I saw a stray grey paw stretch out from under the loveseat and stealthily grab a crumb of cheese.

'Where is that coming from?' he said, shooing the scavenger away. 'Are you doing that? Is that you?'

I stood up and dimmed the lights before turning back to Sam. God, I loved a dimmer switch.

'That, Dr Page,' I said, holding out my hand, 'is the one and only Ms Britney Jean Spears. And she thinks you need to dance.'

I closed my eyes, threw my hands up in the air and waved them like I didn't care. About how silly I looked, about drinking cheap white wine on a Tuesday, about the nagging feeling that my sister was right.

'Come on, Sam,' I ordered with my eyes still closed. 'Otherwise I'm dancing on my own and I'm going to start feeling like a right tit.'

'That would make sense because that's what you look like,' he replied. I responded by turning up the music. 'What about your neighbours?'

'My neighbours are wankers,' I shouted. 'The ones on the left like to play video games in the bedroom at four a.m. on weekends and the ones on the right steal my post. Sod my neighbours, Sam. Besides, it's not even late. Get up and dance.'

I opened one eye just in time to see him shaking his head at himself and dusting crumbs off his hands.

'Sometimes you've just got to crank up the music and go with it,' I told him, gyrating my way into the middle of the living room as he began to step from side to side, elbows still firmly fixed to his body. I flailed around even more wildly, jumping in time to the music. 'Come on, Sam, Britney expects more from you. And we both know you've got it in you.'

He stopped. He picked up his whisky and took a long, deep drink.

And then the fun really began. First his hips started to move, then his shoulders, then his arms. Eyes closed, mouth open, he was all in.

'I don't know if it's Britney or the whisky,' Sam bellowed, punching the air as he jumped up and down. 'But this doesn't feel terrible.'

'That's the spirit,' I called back, moving away to give him room. Dear god, I had awoken a beast. 'Work it out, Sam, work it out.'

There we were, two idiots jumping around a dark living room, very slightly tipsy and singing at the tops of our voices. It was fantastic. I smiled as we locked eyes, mouthing the words to each other from across the room, throwing some serious shapes and chucking in some very important dance pointing. The space between us seemed to dissolve and soon we were face to face. I could hear him singing, I could feel the floorboards bouncing as he danced. Just for one moment, everything felt right.

Until the song ended.

'Right,' Sam panted, scraping his hair back from his face as his body came to a standstill. 'Excellent.'

'There's more where that came from,' I assured him, darting over to my phone to see why the next song wasn't playing. Hmm, texts from both neighbours. What a coincidence.

Sam's chest heaved and he studied me closely, both hands planted on his hips.

'Are you sure?' he asked.

'Never been more certain of anything in my life,' I replied.

'Maybe one more,' he said with a grin. 'I have to say, I do feel a little better.'

Deleting my neighbour's texts without reading them, I cranked up the bass and restarted the music. This time Sam didn't need any encouragement. Before I could even think to stop him, he grabbed my hands and began to twirl me around and around and around until everything was one big swirl of happy that I never wanted to end.

'You're never going to fit on that loveseat,' I said, hanging around the living room door as Sam puffed up his pillow. I hoped our dance-off looked just as becoming on me but I had an inkling my mascara had not been up to the job.

'Annie, I've been sleeping on an inflatable bed on my office floor,' he reminded me. 'This will be wonderful.'

He had a point.

'I'm just in here if you need anything,' I told him. Exhausted from our dance-a-thon and more than a little woozy from too much wine on an empty stomach and half a cheese toastie, I hung onto the door frame and stared. He'd put away the best part of half a bottle of whisky but it didn't even seem to have touched the sides. Impressive. 'Otherwise I'll see you in the morning.'

'In the morning,' he replied, clearly waiting for me to vanish so he could take off his trousers.

'Sleep tight then,' I said, flushing at the thought. 'Oh! Do you need a spare phone charger? I've got loads of different ones.'

'It's been dead for hours,' he said, producing the ancient artefact from his back pocket and practically giving me a seizure. 'I'll charge it up tomorrow.'

'At least you won't be able to send any regrettable texts.' I scrunched up my face as he set his ancient phone down on my coffee table. 'Are you really, really sure you're going to be able to sleep out here?' I couldn't see how he was going to fit his long legs on to that tiny Ikea loveseat.

'Quite sure,' he confirmed with a theatrical yawn. 'Wellington and I will make do.'

'OK, if you say so,' I said with a reluctant wave. 'Goodnight, Sam. And Wellington.'

An unseen miaow echoed from somewhere in the living room as I closed my bedroom door and smiled.

Maybe Sam could sleep without a fully charged phone but I couldn't. I changed into my pyjamas, tossing my clothes into the general vicinity of the wash basket, plugged my phone in beside my bed and shuffled myself under the duvet, exhausted. A quick check on the Hip Historian's followers and comments. Five hundred new followers and a hundred comments on his latest post. An old gif of Rihanna getting into a car with a single raised eyebrow along with the caption 'One of Russia's greatest rulers, Catherine the Great was a fraud. Her name wasn't Catherine, nor was she Russian'.

'Did not know that until today,' I muttered to myself.

My wine and dance buzz was beginning to wear off, the minty taste of toothpaste hastening my hangover, and I felt that odd feeling in the pit of my stomach hiccup into life again. I did feel guilty. And I did feel anxious. And I did like Sam. That didn't mean I was in love with him. You could be friends with a man without wanting to sleep with him, couldn't you? You could appreciate his personality without imagining the two of you on a beach at sunset, holding hands while your best friend officiated a small but tasteful wedding ceremony which you decided to do barefoot but bought a nice pair of Jimmy Choos for the party you were planning to have back in London a couple of weeks later.

'Ah, shit,' I whispered.

Just then, a god almighty crash came from the living room. I shot bolt upright, completely awake and aware.

'Sam?'

A quiet knock on my door came next.

'Sam?' I said, my heart thudding against my ribs as he opened the door. My bedroom never got completely dark and I could see the embarrassment on his face. I could also see his boxer shorts but that was neither here nor there.

'I broke your settee,' he said. 'I am so dreadfully sorry. All seemed to be well until I turned over and the legs just went out from underneath me. I thought I could fix it but I fear I may have made matters worse.'

'It's fine,' I replied, relieved he was not dead, we had not been invaded by murderers and almost relieved to have a reason to get rid of that bloody loveseat. 'Really, I'm sorry.'

Had there ever been two more English people? Arguing over who was more apologetic about a broken Ikea settee?

'I may be able to fix it in the morning,' Sam said. 'I didn't want to turn on all the lights and wake you.'

'Honestly, don't worry,' I insisted. There was only one problem. Where was he going to sleep?

'Right, good night,' he said, backing out of the bedroom. 'Sleep well.'

'You should sleep in here,' I said, pulling the covers up to my chin even as I offered up half my mattress. 'With me.'

He froze.

'I mean, you can sleep in here. In my bed. Not sleep-with-me sleep with me, but I am going to sleep in here as well so, er, you know what I mean.'

Sam stayed exactly where he was.

'What else are you going to do?' I asked. 'Sleep on the floor? You can't kip down on hardwood floors, Sam. We can put a pillow down the middle of the mattress if you really must.'

Muttering under his breath, he came into the bedroom and immediately tripped over my discarded clothes.

'Sorry,' I said as he recovered himself. 'My room is usually a bit of a mess.'

'A bit?' he replied as he climbed under the covers on the other side of the bed. The mattress gave under his weight but only slightly and I felt the sheets shift over my legs as they moved to accommodate him.

The unfamiliar sound of clicking claws tapped along the hardwood floor of my bedroom before another body made itself comfortable on my bed. From another night on my own to a girl-man-cat threeway, just like that.

'I hope you don't snore,' I joked weakly, taking off my watch and resting it on its charger, the light from the face briefly casting Sam's face in a green glow, like a superhero.

'I don't but Wellington does,' Sam said. 'I can shut him in the other room, if you'd like?'

'No, I don't mind,' I replied as I felt the cat taking a tour of the bed before turning three small circles around my feet and settling down. Now he was in the bed, I didn't want to give Sam a single reason to get back out.

We lay side by side in the almost dark room, not even nearly touching but so unbelievably close. Any chance of sleeping was long gone. Every flinch, every breath felt as though it were under scrutiny, as though I could somehow take a false step without even moving. I could feel Wellington snoozing at my feet, too hot in the sticky summer heat, but I didn't dare move him.

'Goodnight, then,' I said in a small, careful voice.

'Thank you, Annie,' Sam said, soft and sleepy. 'Can't thank you enough for all you've done.'

'What are friends for?' I replied, almost choking on my words. 'All in a day's work.'

'Your work is very different to mine,' he mumbled, before taking a deep breath and letting it out slowly. 'I'm very glad not to be alone tonight.'

'I'm glad you're here,' I whispered, daring each word out of my mouth.

'What would I do without you, Annie Higgins?' he murmured back.

That was it, I was done. My mouth was dry and my palms were sweaty and every word he whispered made my skin prickle from head to toe. But it was too soon, too soon, too soon. And I was tipsy and we'd been dancing and it would be such a terrible idea. But still. Here he was, in my bed, in his pants and saying the nicest things.

Maybe if I just stretched out a foot, I thought, just touch him with a toe and see what happened. My leg felt like lead. Why was this so hard? Steeling myself, I turned my head towards my bedmate, not even nearly ready for what could come next.

Sam's eyes were closed and he had a peaceful smile on his face. He was fast asleep.

Exhaling heavily, I rolled back onto my back, turning my head to look at him. He was utterly gone. Maybe that whisky had had an effect after all. I clasped my hands together under my cheek and watched him, listening to the rise and fall of his breathing. It began to slow, deep heavy sighs of sleep whispering out of his lips as he fell deeper and deeper.

It's nothing, I told myself as I memorized his profile. It's just a crush. It's been so long since there was a straight man in your apartment who wasn't here to fix the dishwasher, you're freaking out.

It made perfect sense when you thought about it logically. I was stressed about work, my ex just got engaged and we had been spending a lot of time together. I'd probably have developed faux feelings for anyone in this situation. Although I did spend an awful lot of time with Lily and I was a long way from feeling warm and fuzzy about her. The fact it was Sam was entirely coincidental. Sam with his flip-phone and history books, with his research and his sweet dance moves and unparalleled skill at hook-a-duck. Who wouldn't have a bit of a crush on his curly hair and blue eyes and that hidden dimple and the way he'd had my back with my family and at my presentation and the way he always frowned whenever he was really, really listening to me and, oh no.

Oh no.

Rolling over onto my back, I stared up at the ceiling, eyes wide open, heart pounding.

This would not do at all.

CHAPTER TWENTY-ONE

Wednesday, 25 July: Nine Days to Go

At first I thought I was having a heart attack. A heavy weight was planted in the middle of my chest, my breathing was shallow and I couldn't feel my right arm. My eyes snapped open only to find the back end of a tabby cat perched happily on my chest, backed right up to my chin and purring loudly.

Sam, however, was nowhere to be seen.

I squeezed the fingers of my right hand until the feeling came back to my arm and tried to work out how to remove myself from my own bed without upsetting my new bedmate. With a contented sigh, Wellington shuffled his backside even closer towards my face, slapping my nose with his long, fluffy tail.

The front door clicked open and Sam let himself in, red Puffa jacket over his jeans and shirt from last night, loaded down with a packed reusable shopping bag in each hand.

'Would you look at that,' he said, nodding towards my current cat situation. 'He likes you.'

'That or he's trying to suffocate me,' I replied through a mouthful of fur.

'One or the other,' Sam agreed. He held the shopping bags aloft. 'I'm making breakfast. Whenever you're ready.'

And then he disappeared.

None of my dates since Matthew had resulted in an adult sleepover. Even if they made it as far as shenanigans, they usually ended in me making excuses to leave, followed by an awkward but agreed upon taxi ride across London. I had no idea what to do with myself the morning after the night before. Why were there no articles on this? There were a million features on getting the man into bed in the first place and I could point you in the direction of a million more stories of what to do once he was there, but the morning after? A complete mystery.

I tried sitting upright, hoping the cat might move of his own accord but apparently that was not to be the case. Who needed a bikini body when you could be a cat bed instead?

'Sorry, Wellington,' I said, sliding my hand under his warm, furry belly. 'I have to get up.'

He protested softly before rolling onto the neatly made side of the bed his owner had vacated, circled once, twice and then curled himself up into a tidy pile and promptly went back to sleep.

It was so odd. To have someone else in my kitchen when I was still in my jammies. I stopped in the hallway for a moment, watching him empty his shopping bags on the worktop. He'd brought all sorts from the supermarket; bits and pieces I'd run out of, other things I wouldn't have bought for myself. I fit in my kitchen, every gap in my flat was Annie-shaped. Sam was moving around like a new piece in an old puzzle, but I had to admit, he fit in as though he'd been there all along.

I moved into the bathroom before watching him got weird, locking the door securely behind me. The Annie that looked back at me in the bathroom mirror had panic written all over her face.

'Shower first, inexplicable feelings later,' I mumbled, tying my hair up on top of my head and turning on the taps. Even though there was a locked door between us, I was embarrassed to strip off my PJs. Without warning, everything had become awkward. Clean my teeth, wash my face, step under the steaming hot stream of water and wash any trace of nonsense clean, clean away.

'You're imagining things,' I told myself, taking off the top layer of my skin with the scorching water and a spot of overly enthusiastic loofah-ing. 'The first time a straight man walks into your flat in twelve months, you're practically salivating over him. Get a grip on yourself.'

That's all it was. My poor hormones were confused by an entire evening's exposure to testosterone. And I felt so sorry for Sam. I felt bad about what had happened with Elaine. This wasn't love or lust or even like, it was guilt, masquerading as a crush.

'Easier to live with the horn than to feel responsible for what happened last night,' I reasoned. 'Classic compensation tactics brain, good try.'

I couldn't have a crush on Sam. I didn't care about his full lips, just inches from mine when we were locked in that airing cupboard. I wasn't even slightly interested in running my hands through his blond hair, even though it looked so soft, even though it curled around his ears just so.

Turning off the water and wrapping a towel around myself before I stepped out of the shower, even though the door was locked, I swiped the steam away from the mirror and gave myself a good, stern look. Damp curls that had fallen out of my topknot were stuck to my neck and my face was glowing from the hot water.

'OK, stop it,' I ordered with a determined point. 'You're being silly.'

Mirror Annie did her best to look ashamed.

'Good,' I muttered, wrapping the ugly, full-length dressing gown my dad had bought me for my last birthday over my towel and belting it tightly. 'This is why you should stick to computers. Real people are altogether too confusing.'

I slipped out of the bathroom and locked myself in the bedroom while Sam clattered around in the other room. I dried myself quickly under Wellington's slightly seedy, watchful eye. He rolled over onto his back and stretched out, baring his bright white belly before giving me a long, slow blink.

'Filth,' I stated, clambering into my underwear and pulling on the closest pair of jeans I could find. 'I thought you were supposed to be shy?'

Fully dressed, somewhat made up and hair half-dry, I walked into my kitchen to find Sam slathering something onto a piece of rough-looking toast.

'You didn't,' I said, walking around the breakfast bar and marvelling at his skills. 'Sam, is that avocado toast?'

'I looked up the recipe on the internet,' he admitted grudgingly. 'Turns out it isn't hard.'

'May I?' I asked, gesturing to one of the pieces of toast in front of me. He nodded eagerly, weaving his hands together as he awaited my feedback. 'It's delicious,' I said, holding a hand over my mouth as I talked and ate at the same time. 'Are you converted?'

He took a bite of his own and chewed for a while before he replied.

'It's no cheese toastie but the nutritional value is hard to argue with.'

I swallowed, laughed and choked all at the same time as the panic hit me again. Sam, stood in my kitchen, making me breakfast. Oh shit. This guilt thing really did feel an awful lot like love.

'I wanted to talk to you about Wellington,' Sam said, pushing a second piece of toast towards me.

'Wellington?' I replied, hoping I wasn't sweating through the thin white T-shirt I'd pulled on in haste. 'What about him?'

'It seems as though I won't be going home anytime soon,' he said gravely. 'And I can't take him to my brother's house because he's allergic. Until I resolve my housing issue, I was hoping he could perhaps stay with you? It does rather seem as though the two of you have bonded.'

He looked so sad, it was all I could do not to throw down my toast and wrap him up in a huge hug. But the thought of touching him had turned into something else and a hug wasn't just a hug any more. I wanted to comfort him and I wanted to keep a considerable distance at the same time. I wanted to brush his hair out of his eyes but I was afraid to even raise my hand from my side. Everything had become a contradiction.

If my brain had been an app, it would have quit unexpectedly.

'As long as he makes peace with his litter-box situation, I don't see why not,' I said, keeping my tone as light and carefree as possible and overthinking every word that came out of my mouth. 'And please tell him not to watch me getting dressed, it's creepy.'

Sam brushed his own hand through his own hair and I flashed back to the grey, early morning light of the dawn when I had laid on my side, staring at his face as it faded from black and white and into glorious Technicolor.

'I'll provide everything for his upkeep, of course. I wouldn't expect you to pay for anything,' he said. 'But it really would be a tremendous help.'

'It's a yes from me,' I said, suddenly very warm. The skin on my neck began to itch. 'Three yeses, Wellington is through to the next round.'

We stood on opposite sides of the breakfast bar and ate in silence. Sam finished his toast first and took a long sip of water from one of my red wine glasses. He didn't know where the water glasses were.

'And I will of course replace your settee,' he said, after dabbing at his mouth with a piece of kitchen roll. 'You've been so kind to me, Annie. I can't apologize enough for my imposition.'

'Don't be stupid,' I said, reaching out for the glass of water he had poured for me and trying very hard not to knock anything over. 'Accidents happen, that thing was long overdue for an upgrade.'

'I insist,' Sam replied. 'It's the least I can do, considering everything you've done for me in the past few weeks.' He looked down at his hands, the corners of his mouth downturned. 'And all for nothing. What a waste of your time.'

'Not for nothing,' I said, reaching a hand across the counter but stopping just short of his arm. 'It's never a waste to spend time with friends.'

He didn't look up but I saw the line of his mouth straighten a little. Not quite into a smile but it was something to see him become even a fraction less despondent.

'Friends,' he said at last with a loud clap. 'Right. Enough dillydallying. I'm sure you want to get dressed for work.'

I looked down at my jeans and T-shirt.

'I am dressed for work,' I replied, pulling nervously on the ends of my ponytail and wondering what was wrong with what I was wearing. 'Aren't I?'

'Quite.' He pushed his glasses up his nose, cleared his throat and quickly turned to move our plates into the sink. 'Ready when you are then.'

'While infatuation was once considered a sign of valour, in today's world a crush can be, in turns, fun, exciting, distracting and heartbreaking. Just thinking about the object of your affection causes a release of the chemical phenylethylamine which speeds up the communication between nerve cells and triggers the release of dopamine. The dopamine is what causes the feeling of bliss you so closely associate with your crush. At the same time, norepinephrine is released, stimulating adrenaline production. together, these three chemicals act as amphetamines, a kind of loved-up speed, which temporarily creates an addictive high, or a crush.'

I stood in line for a coffee, pretending to read emails on my phone but really, I was hoping Dr Johnson, host of my favourite podcast, *Live Life Love*, could talk me out of whatever madness my hormones were dishing up.

'The effects of this high usually lasts anywhere from

six months to three years. At which point the couple either decide to stick with each other and make things work or move on, chasing a new high.'

Great, I thought, pushing my fingertips into my temples. So anywhere from three months to six years from now and I'd be totally over it.

'If you're trying to end your crush,' Dr Johnson went on. 'You need to avoid spending time with the person you're making heart eyes at. Oxytocin, a pituitary hormone linked to human bonding, is triggered by the initial release of dopamine but increases with exposure and is especially enhanced by physical contact. So, if you want to end this crush sooner rather than later, no touching!'

So what she was saying was, spending twenty-four seven with a person followed by a night in bed together was also a bad idea. I inhaled sharply and exhaled slowly. Good to know.

At least boyfriend bootcamp was officially over, even if the results had been wasted on Elaine. There was no real reason for me to spend another second with Dr Samuel Page now.

'How did things go with Sam last night?'

I jumped as Miranda tapped me on the shoulder and replied with forced surprise. 'Sam? Last night? Why would I have been with Sam last night? What are you talking about?'

Her left eyebrow slid slowly upward.

'What are *you* talking about?' she asked. 'Weren't you helping him make dinner for his girlfriend?'

'Oh. Yeah. That.' It felt like a lifetime ago. 'Um, that didn't go very well.'

Mir's left eyebrow kept on climbing higher and higher.

'Turns out his girlfriend has a new boyfriend,' I

explained. 'Which put something of a kink in the plan.'

'I bet he is kinky,' she said, slapping my bum lightly. 'It's always the quiet ones.'

My cheeks turned pink at the thought of it. Stupid norepinephrine.

'He was very well behaved last night, can't say the same for Wellington.'

Someone hadn't fancied doing his business in a foot spa so he'd done it in Sam's shoe instead. It was an incredibly targeted dirty protest, there was no way it was a mistake.

Miranda added a muffin and a croissant to my latte order and carried them over to one of the little round tables next to the window. 'OK, I need all of the details. One, what do you mean he was well behaved last night? And two, who or what is Wellington?'

'One, it's a long story and we have a pitch to talk about and two, Wellington is a cat,' I replied, tearing into my croissant. 'Sam's cat and my new flatmate.'

Mir looked utterly incredulous. Or as incredulous as it's possible to be while inhaling half a croissant in a single mouthful.

'How come I'm only hearing about this now?' she demanded. 'This definitely feels like something that should have been texted to your best friend in real time. What happened with the girlfriend? What did Sam do? How come you went back to your house? Where did he sleep?' Mir bounced her palm against the tabletop. 'I am a details person, Annie Higgins, I need details.'

'We know his girlfriend has a new boyfriend because we saw her mounting him in their living room,' I explained. 'And no one wants to see their ex mid-shag, do they?'

Miranda shook her head and bit into her muffin, giving the kid from behind the counter a thumbs up as he delivered our coffees to our table.

'And then I took him back to mine. We'd also liberated his cat, the aforementioned Wellington, so we couldn't very well go anywhere else. Most pubs in London are not cat-friendly, you know.'

'Double standards, bloody full of dogs,' Mir replied, covering her mouth as she spoke. 'So you had a little sleepover party? With Sam and his cat?'

'Sam made me an excellent cheese toastie, we had a drink and then we went to sleep,' I said, fiddling with my necklace and leaving out the whole part with the dancing and the bit where I realized I was maybe, possibly a little bit in love with him. 'And then we got up and came to work. That is the end of the story.'

'Don't ask me why but I'm almost positive you're leaving something out,' she pressed. 'You're doing that twitchy thing with your necklace. Show me on the croissant where he touched you.'

'Shut up,' I said, leaning forward to press my leg down with my forearm. 'You're more handsy than he was.'

'Only because I sleep in the same bed as you,' she replied, peeling the paper wrapping off the bottom half of her muffin. 'Unless he's Mr Tickle, he'd have struggled to get his mitts on you from the living room.'

I didn't say anything.

This time both eyebrows shot upwards.

'Annie, where did he sleep?' Miranda asked.

'Please, please, please, please, please don't make a big thing of it,' I said, knowing it was a complete waste of breath. 'But he slept in my bed. With me.'

I waited for Mir's reaction, expecting something approaching nuclear levels, but instead she calmly sat in her seat, picking at the remains of her muffin and saying nothing.

'He's too tall for the loveseat. He tried to sleep on it but the leg broke!' I exclaimed. 'And I couldn't make him sleep on the floor, could I?'

Mir continued to chew in silence.

'Really?' I said, too impatient to wait for a reaction. 'Nothing?'

Miranda templed her fingers and considered the information.

'What's the point in me saying anything if you won't admit that you like him?' she replied. 'If you want to carry on pretending, that's fine. I'll be here to pick up the pieces, regardless. It's OK, I get it, I like him too.'

'You do?' I said, an unattractive streak of jealousy tearing through me before I could stop myself. 'What about Martin?'

'Not how you like him, you numpty,' she clarified, a massive grin cracking her face at the horror on mine. 'I like Sam in the same way I like Wotsits and videos of baby goats on the internet, I don't want to bone him. He's a very nice man who objectively happens to be very handsome and have an excellent bottom. You like him the way I like Martin and Ryan Reynolds and Ed Sheeran videos.'

'You know it's weird that you use them as porn, don't you?' I said, narrowing my eyes as she shrugged.

'The heart wants what the heart wants,' she replied. 'Speaking of which . . .'

'Morning, ladies.' Charlie sauntered over, three coffees stacked on top of each other. 'Plotting world domination?'

'As always,' Mir nodded. 'Trying to caffeinate your-self to death?'

'Big pitch,' he said, resting his chin on the lid of the top coffee cup. 'Fuelling the troops. Did Martin talk to you about our party Friday night?'

'Party?' Miranda looked at me, confused, but I had no idea what he was talking about.

'We're having a summer party,' Charlie elaborated. 'Wilder, I mean. But everyone in the building is invited. It's on the roof this Friday.'

'He didn't mention it,' she muttered, not very happy about the fact.

'We've got a pitch on Monday,' I replied, keeping my eyes on my own coffee cup. 'So we'll probably be working late.'

'Oh. That's a shame.'

I could tell without looking up he was disappointed. I felt a pang of guilt and bit my lip, concentrating on my croissant.

'I'm sure we'll make it up for one drink,' Miranda said quickly with a dazzling smile. 'See you there.'

'Sounds good,' he said, a smile appearing in his voice. Charlie was so much easier to read than Sam, every thought that ran through his mind was displayed on his face for the world to see. Why couldn't my stupid hormones have latched onto Charlie instead? 'And don't think I've forgotten about our bet. Do you think I'd make a good YouTuber?'

'Sure,' Mir replied sweetly. 'But I wouldn't think you'll have time to manage a channel. I'm assuming you'll have to take on a few more projects when you're paying our rent as well as your own.'

'See you Friday night,' he said, laughing as he walked away. 'Bye, Annie.'

'So, where are we on the pitch?' I pushed my cup to one side, ignoring Charlie and resting my arms on the table. Miranda looked back at me, gone out.

'Are you kidding me?' she replied. 'You're trying to change the subject to work right now?'

'We're not talking about Sam,' I reasoned, picking a piece of pastry out of her hair. 'And we're not talking about Charlie. Which only leaves work, doesn't it?'

'No, actually, it doesn't.' She stood up abruptly, any trace of a smile vanished from her face. 'There's what's going on with me, what's going on with Brian, the new series of *Love Island*. There are a million other things, Annie. Try to remember that from time to time.'

'Mir!'

I watched her walk off in a huff, silently reprimanding myself for being such a tit. There was never any point in running after Miranda when she was mad, she needed a moment to cool down, especially when she was right. I was putting so much energy into my job, my bet and my boyfriend bootcamp, I'd developed tunnel vision and completely forgotten about everyone else.

'No wonder the cat likes me so much,' I whispered in horror. It was so much worse than I realized – I wasn't just crushing on Sam, I was turning into him.

CHAPTER TWENTY-TWO

Thursday, 26 July: Eight Days to Go
9,532 followers

There were only eight days left in our bet.

Eight days to find the other ten thousand followers.

Thanks to a friend at Instagram, we'd been able to get @TheHipHistorian verified but, unfortunately, he wasn't able to drum up any imaginary people who cared that Hitler's nephew William served in the US Navy. Personally, I thought it was fascinating but there was no accounting for taste, especially when reality TV's first family kept churning out babies and naked selfies to disrupt my algorithms. I was this close to the end of my tether. Had I really got myself into an unwinnable bet?

Between coming up with clever @TheHipHistorian posts, editing videos, keeping up with our clients, slaving away over the SetPics pitch and soothing Miranda with BFF drinks the night before I had so many balls in the air, my life was starting to look like a particularly aggressive game of Hungry Hungry

Hippos. Everyone was desperately busy, so much so that even Brian jumped when Sam appeared, pressed up against the meeting room window at the end of our morning catchup meeting.

'Annie, you did a really good job on that boy's makeover but you've got to work on his manners,' Brian said, hand to his heart. 'If he carries on creeping around like this, I am going to shit myself and he's getting the dry-cleaning bill.'

Mir, Brian and the interns picked up their stuff and filed out of the meeting room, trotting down the hallway to our office space. Hiding my sweaty palms up the sleeves of my jumper, I smiled brightly as I scooped up my things.

'I was wondering how Wellington is doing,' Sam said, following me back to my desk. Miranda and Brian sat at their desks but I could tell they were fully tuned in to the conversation.

'He's great,' I said, swinging my hair around before peeling it off my lips. Attractive. 'Best flatmate I've ever had. Apart from the scratching, the peeing and the shitting everywhere.'

Even after I'd furnished him with the finest litter tray and scratching post a cat could ever want, Wellington decided his favourite place to sharpen his claws was on the back of the armchair and his absolute favourite place to take a dump was under my bed. Preferably in the middle of the night when I was sleeping and right under the centre of the mattress, making it as difficult to get to as possible. Not once had he even considered using his litter box for anything other than burying the scrunchies I kept in the bathroom to hold back my hair when I washed my face.

'He's anxious,' Sam stood by my desk, rubbing a hand over his face. 'I'm sorry. I can arrange to get the carpets cleaned.'

It was the sexiest thing a man had ever said to me.

'I haven't got carpets, but thanks,' I replied, brushing my hair behind my ear. And then flipping it out. And then brushing it back. 'No carpet for me. I'm all about the hardwood floors.'

Behind me, Brian coughed and spat water all over his desk.

'How's the pitch going?' Sam asked, tapping his fingertips on the top of a lightbox that used to say Content London but now, thanks to Miranda, said something obscene instead.

'It's going well,' I said, heart pounding at the thought of working for SetPics. 'I think it's going well. We're figuring it out. It's hard, it's good but it's hard. We really, really, really want to get it just right but we've never done anything this big before so it's tough, you know? I keep going over the ideas and it's like, what can I do to make sure it's perfect? And I don't know and—'

Sam's eyes widened slightly and he stopped tapping.

'It's going well,' I said, clearing my throat. Miranda, Brian, Zadie and Nat all smirked behind their respective computer screens. 'Thanks for asking.'

'You look nice today,' Miranda said, nodding at Sam's semi-fancy outfit. Slim-fit sand-coloured trousers rather than his usual jeans and a long-sleeved blue-and-white striped T-shirt. I wasn't sure he knew just how hipster he looked, but it was working for me. Shockingly. 'Great outfit.'

He hesitated, just for a second, before answering.

'It's one of the T-shirts you gave me,' he said, pulling

the fabric up at his waist revealing a glimpse of taut midriff that did not go unnoticed by anyone in the office. I immediately heard Zadie and Nat's fingers flying across their keyboards. 'I wasn't sure about it but Brian assured me it's definitely for a man.'

'More or less,' Brian commented. 'Looks hot.'

Sam pulled at the neck of his T-shirt and cleared his throat. 'If you're not too busy, I'd like to buy you lunch.'

Brian perked up immediately. 'I'm in. Anyone else fancy pizza?'

'Not you,' he clarified. 'Annie.'

Brian frowned. 'And after I gave you that nice women's T-shirt,' he sulked.

'As a thank you for taking care of Wellington.'

'Annie would love to get lunch with you,' Brian replied on my behalf. 'And she'd love to bring me a sandwich back with her so I can stay here and finish my work.'

'I'd like to,' I said, searching for an excuse. 'But I'm so busy, I don't think I have the time to go out today.'

That much was true. One minute I was matching quirky historical facts to Beyoncé gifs, the next I was coming up with a social media strategy for a CGI unicorn and his four best human friends. Life was confusing, my workload was overwhelming and I needed to get Sam out of my head.

'Annie, please get out of the office for five minutes,' Brian ordered. Miranda didn't say a word. 'You're starting to go grey.'

'No, I'm not,' I muttered, checking a strand of my hair just in case. 'And there's too much work to do.'

'Nat and Zadie have it covered,' Brian said, glancing over at the two girls lurking silently behind their laptops. Two pairs of eyes peered back at me, still tapping away at their keyboards. They literally never spoke out loud unless you made them but were constantly snorting and giggling under their breath as they exchanged iMessages all the live long day. Admittedly, they were very good and incredibly helpful but sometimes, they were beyond creepy.

'She'll meet you outside at one.'

'Annie?' Sam replied, looking to me for confirmation. I opened my mouth to protest but nothing came out.

You don't have to go, I told myself. You could just text him and tell him you're too busy. No one else is the boss of you and you don't have to do anything you don't want to.

'One it is,' I said. 'See you then.'

I was waiting outside the building at one on the dot. It was sunny but not as warm as it had been, bright enough for sunglasses but too cold for bare legs. Sam appeared in the doorway and I felt all the things I didn't want to feel. I was hot, I was sweaty, my mouth felt dry and all my words escaped me. Thankfully, it didn't seem as though Sam was much in the mood for talking either. We strolled down the street in silence as I fought with myself, trying to get back to the moment before I saw his face lit up by the tiny orange light in the airing cupboard. I wanted our easy banter back, this was too hard.

'How's the book?' I asked, digging my hands into the pockets of Miranda's pink satin bomber jacket and producing a pair of neon orange sunglasses. I was starting to wonder what she was getting up to at night, so much neon for one human being. 'Almost done?'

Sam nodded as he walked. I followed, no idea of where we were headed, slipping the shades over my eyes.

'And how are things at your brother's? Are you having fun?'

'No,' Sam replied. His shoulders began pinching up around his ears, the unreadable expression crossing over his face.

'And how are you getting on with your lecture?'

'Not very well.'

'Right.'

That was it. I'd exhausted every avenue of safe conversation in three seconds.

'OK, I'm just going to say it,' Sam said. My heart pounded against my ribs. Say what? Say what?

'I feel terrible about what happened on Tuesday and I'm very sorry for putting you in such an uncomfortable position.'

'Uncomfortable?' I replied in a tight, high voice. 'Why would I feel uncomfortable? Because we slept in the same bed? I sleep in the same bed as other people all the time. Men, women, cats as well these days. It's not even a thing. Who's uncomfortable? Not me.'

He slowed at the edge of the road, waiting for a Prius to pass.

'I meant the Elaine situation,' he said.

Right. That did make a lot more sense.

I flapped a hand in the air to wave away his concerns and promptly knocked Miranda's sunglasses off my face.

'Haven't given it a second thought,' I said, picking up the shades and checking for scratches. 'Perfectly average Tuesday evening for me.'

Sam's brow creased together underneath his curly hair. 'There's an excellent sandwich shop around the corner,' he said. 'Have you tried it? They do a very good coronation chicken.'

'All right, Grandad,' I replied, breathing out as I tucked the glasses back in Mir's jacket pocket. 'Do they have Horlicks to go with it?'

Sam smiled. Then I smiled. The tightness in my chest melted a little and I noticed the clear blue sky above me as we slipped back into a more comfortable routine. Gentle bullying was a safe space. It felt right.

'How are you getting on with the bet?' Sam asked in a lighter voice. 'Have we won yet?'

'I thought you didn't want to know about it?' I reminded him.

'I didn't say I didn't want to know, I said I didn't care,' he corrected. 'But I know it matters to you. So, I suppose, it also matters to me.'

Stupid, thoughtful man.

'It could be better,' I admitted. 'We're a bit behind where we should be, given we only have a week left. But I haven't given up yet.'

'If you need my help with anything, just say the word,' Sam offered. 'There are a million more fascinating historical facts where the others came from. Did you know, in 1911, the London Underground introduced escalators but people were too afraid to use them so they had a one-legged man ride up and down to convince people they were safe.'

'I don't think I'd find that especially reassuring,' I said with a frown.

'Well, did you know the nursery rhyme "Mary Had a Little Lamb" was based on a true story?'

'Shut up,' I replied. 'Really?'

'I will not shut up,' he said, indignant. 'It's disputed, but yes. Mary Sawyer, an eleven-year-old girl from Boston, was followed to school by a lamb in 1817.'

'Bugger me!' I took out my phone to make a note. That was a pretty good one. 'I can't believe no one ever wrote a song about what happened whenever a dog got into school.'

We walked on in silence until Sam stopped in the middle of the street and stood in front of me.

'Annie,' he said.

'Sam?' I replied, very happy to be hiding half my face behind Mir's giant specs.

He set his shoulders, lifted his chin and looked me right in the eye.

'A colleague of mine is having a birthday party on Friday night,' he said. 'Tomorrow night. And I told him I would go.'

'OK,' I said slowly. 'That is what most people do on their *friend's* birthday.'

'I definitely said colleague but I suppose he is my friend as well. I thought perhaps you might like to come with me,' he said, tall and straight and determined. 'To the party.'

Dr Johnson would almost certainly not approve of this.

'You want me to come to the party?' I repeated, twisting a piece of paper in the bottom of the jacket pocket between my fingers until it began to fall apart. I hoped it wasn't anything Mir actually needed.

'Yes,' Sam nodded. 'It won't be quite on the scale of your father's celebrations, but it should be fun.'

He was asking me out. He was asking me out on a date. Sam was asking me out on a date and I wanted to say yes but I couldn't say yes but if I said no there might not be another potential date but oh god, I should have said something by now.

'I know you're very busy and I wouldn't ask,' he added as he tried to stick his hands in his pockets, only to find they were still sewn up. It really had been a long time since he'd had new clothes. 'And I'm fairly certain Elaine will be there as well.'

Ding ding ding, of course he wasn't asking me out, he was asking me to be a human shield. No, I reminded myself, thinking of my call with Becks, don't be so selfish. He needs a friend. You're his friend.

'I'm sure it'll be fine once it all gets going but the thought of walking in by myself when everyone knows she and I aren't on entirely the best of terms,' he went on, trying to work his little finger into the gap in the stitching of his faux pockets. 'And it's in one of those ridiculous places that pretends to be a post office so you have to buy a stamp to get a pint or some such thing. I can't abide them. It's at six, tomorrow. Do you think you'll be able to come?'

I bit my lip before I could agree to it. It was a terrible idea, I said to myself, hopping from foot to foot in the street. A terrible, stupid, asking-for-trouble idea. Walking into a party with Sam, spending time with Sam. Meeting his friends, laughing, joking, touching his arm one too many times, making eye contact across the room, having one too many, sharing a cab home, ending up at mine, in bed, not sleeping.

'The thing is, I just said I'd go to Charlie's party,' I said, fighting with myself and the image of the two of us curled up together, giving Wellington a post-coital cuddle. 'Or of course I would.'

'Ah. I see.'

What? What did he see?

'You'd rather go to a party with Charlie.'

'Not with Charlie, to Charlie's party,' I corrected, already flustered again. 'Why don't you come to that one instead? I'm sure it'll be more fun than hanging out with your ex-girlfriend and someone you aren't even sure is your friend.'

'Really, Annie?' A tight smile took over his face. 'You think I would have fun at a party at The Ginnel?'

'You never know,' I told him, trying to imagine Sam bro-ing down with Martin and Charlie. In spite of my vivid imagination, it was a struggle. 'You might enjoy yourself. Stranger things have happened.'

'Never mind,' he said, setting off for the sandwich shop with renewed intent. 'I realize I've already asked quite enough of you as it is. I'll go alone.'

'You managed without me for a long time,' I reassured him. 'You'll manage without me again.'

'I don't know,' he said, that unreadable expression on his face again as he stopped and gave me a strange kind of smile. 'I do believe I've forgotten how.'

'You've got to go to this party with Sam,' Brian said through a mouthful of my abandoned coronation chicken sandwich. 'This is perfect. You show up looking hot AF, impress all his friends, show up the ex and then hit that thing. Boom, he's yours.'

'While he's still reeling from the break-up?' Mir countered. 'While he's emotionally vulnerable?'

'Especially while he's emotionally vulnerable,' he replied. 'How many men do you know who broke up with a long-term girlfriend and ended up getting married a year later?'

'Actually quite a few,' I said, going through my mental rolodex. 'Matthew, for example.'

'If he's done, he's done, and he's looking for the next thing,' Brian stated as though it was a known fact. 'Men who like to be in relationships don't stay single. If you wait too long, you'll miss your shot, Annie.'

'Disagree,' Miranda said, just as certain of herself. 'You're making massive, sweeping generalizations.'

'I was actually talking about myself,' Bri replied. 'But whatever.'

'I think Mir's probably right,' I said. It was too soon. Wasn't it? Probably? 'I don't want to be a rebound.'

'Straight men don't have rebounds. The only classifications straight men have are . . .' Brian paused for effect, holding out a highlighter-stained hand to count off his points. He'd been painting his nails with the Stabilo Boss pens again. 'Women they don't sleep with, women they sleep with once and women they sleep with more than once. You're the ones who love to go round slapping labels on things. How many times have we all watched *He's Just Not That Into You*? It's like you never learn.'

'You're like a gay, male Oprah and I hate you,' I muttered.

'If he likes you, he likes you,' he shrugged. It was so simple when you weren't part of the equation. 'Take your shot. If he doesn't, you're not going to change his mind by hanging around for long enough.'

Out of the corner of my eye, I could see Mir's mouth slowly disappearing, cat's arse style, into the centre of her face.

'I disagree. Timing is everything in relationships. Don't go, Annie. Come to the summer party instead.'

'The timing is perfect!' Brian insisted. 'He's hurting for a girlfriend and you could be that girlfriend. The

288

fact you want to be said girlfriend is another conversation altogether and should probably take place with you in a padded cell, but we'll deal with that another time. If you want that hot historian, you go get him.'

'You know I am forever Team Annie,' Mir said, covering my hand with hers. 'And if that means being Team Annuel, I'll ship it, but I feel like you're setting yourself up to get hurt and I don't want that.'

'I'm not sure about Annuel,' Bri said, rolling the portmanteau around on his tongue. 'But you can't be Team Sannie, can you? Sounds like a bad tampon commercial.'

I looked at my two best friends, willing one of them to say something insightful and profound.

Instead, Brian reached over and flicked my forehead.

'Hey,' I wailed, slapping his hand away. 'Pack it in.'

'Since when did you ever second-guess yourself?' he asked. 'What does your gut say?'

'It is uncharacteristically silent,' I replied, twisting my pendant on its chain. 'What does that mean?'

'That you should come to the Wilder party with us,' Mir said. 'I know Charlie would be happy to see you.'

'Brilliant,' I said, rubbing my face with my hands. 'Another way to make this even more confusing.'

'Just saying it would make my life more convenient if you went out with Charlie and I was going out with Martin and then we could all go out together.'

'Brilliant thinking, Miranda,' Brian commented. 'And maybe after playtime, we can all sit together in assembly and hold hands on the way home from school.'

'Piss off,' she replied, throwing a penguin-shaped eraser at his head. 'I'm trying to help.'

'No,' he said. 'You're trying to make your fantasy

weekend away in the Cotswolds more convenient. Annie, if you like Sam, tell Sam.'

I sighed and leaned back in my chair, staring out of the window while Miranda and Brian waited impatiently for me to make a decision. And I couldn't even put it to a Twitter poll.

'Annie,' Miranda said in her most serious voice, even as she hurled the rest of her novelty rubber collection at Brian. 'You know what you want to do. You're just waiting for one of us to tell you to do it, so you can blame us if it goes wrong.'

'And?' I replied blankly. 'Isn't that what friends are for?'

'Yes,' said Brian confidently. 'Go to Sam's party and tell him how you feel.'

'Or come to our party and give Charlie a chance,' Mir argued. 'What's it going to be?'

CHAPTER TWENTY-THREE

Friday, 27 July: Seven Days to Go

Even as I shuffled through the mass of bodies in the bar on Friday night, I wasn't sure I was doing the right thing. All I knew was, if I'd gone to Charlie's party, I'd be wishing I was here, with Sam.

Not that I was technically with Sam. It was as though we'd gone back in time, I had spent half the day hammering on his office door and sending texts that never reached their destination to let him know I'd changed my mind, that I was coming to the party. I'd even, pushed a note under his door to say I'd meet him here at six but I had no idea if he'd received any of my messages. Whether he had or hadn't, I didn't know that he would have replied. Sam was not one for unnecessary communications and if you didn't ask a direct question, you rarely received a response.

One thing I did know was that I looked as good as it was possible to look after a long week in the office. Miranda had done my hair and makeup, meaning I didn't look like I'd daubed myself in poster paints, always a good start. My jeans were tight in a good way and I'd replaced my work shirt with a cropped soft cardigan over a little white camisole. Sam was an academic, Sam's friends were academics and academics *loved* cardigans. All the way over, I'd been practising positive visualization, as suggested by the latest episode of *Live Life Love* and I could already see the smile on his face when I walked in the room. Now, if only I could stop sweating quite so much, everything would be perfect.

I stuck my head through a narrow wooden door at the back of the main bar, only to find another room, an exact replica of a 1980s village post office.

'Sorry, this is a private party,' a nice-enough-looking man in a nice-enough-looking shirt said, nicely.

'I'm meeting Sam?' I said, looking past him for a familiar face. 'Samuel Page, I mean.'

'Are you now? You've beat him here,' he replied, pumping my hand in welcome. I pulled my cardigan closed and smiled. My bra was not up to so much enthusiasm. 'Come on in, I'm Aggy.'

'Oh, happy birthday!' I said, following him to the bar. Or rather, to the woman waiting behind a little square window. 'I thought Sam might be here already.'

'Ever the man of mystery, Dr Page,' Aggy replied. 'I think the best thing we can do is get a drink, what do you reckon?'

'Sounds like a plan,' I said, looking at the menu and asking for a Postal Order. Or as it was more commonly known, a vodka soda. Here I was, not even two minutes in and already best friends with his best friends. I was amazing. I was a goddess. I was already a bit tipsy. Me and Miranda had sunk a sharpener in the office before I headed out. 'You're twenty-one again, I assume?'

So far, I couldn't tell an awful lot of difference between Sam's friends and my friends. There wasn't a single tweed blazer with leather elbow patches to be seen and no one was smoking a pipe. It was almost disappointing.

'How do you know Samuel?' Aggy asked, guiding me over to a table while I scanned the room for Elaine. Unless she was hiding under a table, which she bloody well should have been, I couldn't see her either. 'How did you meet?'

'We work in the same building,' I said, flashing a friendly smile at a small group of people already seated. 'I couldn't really miss him, could I? He's practically a giant.'

'I think I've forgotten what he looks like,' he replied. 'It's been so long since I've seen him. I nearly fell out my chair when he said he was coming tonight. Everyone, this is Annie, Samuel's new friend.'

There was an intonation on the words 'new friend' that made my stomach flip. I would have killed a man to be able to sit quietly in a corner and check my phone until Sam arrived.

'What do you do?' asked one of the girls sat across the table. She had bright red hair and light green eyes and was wearing a gorgeous blue sundress. 'Annie, was it?'

'I own a digital marketing company,' I nodded, keeping my hands on my knees and off my drink. Getting wasted was not going to improve this situation. 'What about you?'

She sipped a neon green cocktail before she spoke. 'I'm a senior lecturer on theoretical physics at Cambridge.'

'Sounds fun,' I said, grabbing my vodka and taking

a swig. I looked up to see more and more people piling into the room and heard each new arrival being briefed. There was a stranger amongst them and that stranger was waiting for Samuel Page. Given that everyone else here seemed to know each other, it wasn't hard for anyone to work out who the interloper might be. At any given point, there were at least five pairs of eyes on me.

'Sasha's husband, Ren, lived with me and Sam at Durham,' Aggy said, draping an easy arm around his friend's shoulders which she immediately pushed away. 'We're a pretty incestuous bunch.'

'You wish,' Sasha replied, tucking her short hair behind her ear. 'The only reason we're still friends is because we're all stuck in the lab or the library all day. Samuel clearly had the right idea. Get out, meet new people, stop hanging around with losers like you, Ags. It's hardly rocket science.'

'And if it was, she'd know,' I added.

Sasha laughed and held up her hand for a high five. I did not leave her hanging.

'I'm so impressed with Sammy,' Aggy said. 'He's never been good with meeting people. Are you sure he didn't pay you to come here?'

'Aggy, are you suggesting she's a prostitute?' Sasha asked as I reached for my drink.

'Prostitutes don't wear cardigans,' Aggy replied coolly. 'I would know.'

'I'm sure there's at least one sex worker who owns a cardi,' I said, stirring my vodka with a straw. 'It can't be all fishnets and ball gags.'

'So impractical,' Sasha agreed.

'And she's funny as well,' Aggy said with mock resentment. 'I thought it was my birthday, not Sammy's.'

'You're so rude,' Sasha threw a postage-stamp printed coaster at Aggy. 'She's already going out with Samuel, don't make the poor girl suffer any more than she already is.'

'I didn't say going out with,' I corrected quickly. Maybe this wasn't the best idea. Maybe I should finish this drink, have another one and then go.

'Sorry,' she said with an apologetic grimace. 'I've been married so long I forget the rules. He hasn't said it so you can't say it? Trust me, Sammy is such a private person, if he invited you here, he must like you. That, or he's punishing you for something, why else would he make you put up with this lot for the evening?'

The door opened and a stream of guests arrived, cheering and whooping. Aggy leapt to his feet to accept a bouquet of helium balloons decorated, for some reason, with Pokémon. But there was still no Sam and still no Elaine.

'We're all harmless, I promise. Well, except for Aggy, but we put up with him because . . .' Sasha screwed up her face as she tried to come up with a reason. 'Actually, I don't know why. He's quite rich. He's got a house in the South of France. Could be that.'

'It's as good a reason as any,' I assured her.

'We've had a group chat going about Sammy going AWOL on us for weeks,' she said in a quiet, conspiratorial voice. 'No one knew where he was or what he was up to since the break-up. Now we do.'

'I think he's just been busy working on his lecture and his book,' I told her, tucking my hair behind my ears. I should have tied it up. It was far too hot in that tiny room. 'I haven't been monopolizing him that much.'

'Monopolize away,' she said. 'It'll be good for him. Love him though I do, social graces have never been his strongest point.'

'But he's charming, in his own way,' I replied, thinking back to that first evening at The Ginnel and those awful, awful Bart Simpson shorts. 'I know he can be a bit awkward but he holds the door open, gives you his coat when you're cold. Who does that these days?'

'That's surprisingly sexy,' Sasha said, sipping her drink through her straw. 'I don't think I mentally tie that kind of chivalry to that amount of hair.'

'Oh, you haven't seen him in a while,' I bit my lip and smiled in spite of myself. 'Let me find you a photo.'

It wasn't hard. Once the photo albums on my phone had been full of cat gifs and well-lit selfies, now they were absolutely bursting with photos of Sam. Sam at salsa class, Sam on the beach in Margate, Sam at my dad's birthday party, Sam asleep in my bed. I quickly swiped past that one before Sasha could comment.

'Oh, Annie,' she laughed. 'Who's a smitten kitten?'

'Oh no,' I squeaked. 'It's not like that.'

'Love works in mysterious ways,' Sasha said, patting my hand and lowering her tone. 'How long have you known each other? If you don't mind me asking.'

'Only a few weeks.' It seemed impossible it had been such a short amount of time.

Sasha stroked her long neck with her forefinger and then nodded.

'And you know all about his break-up, I presume.'

'Hmm,' I muttered, keen to avoid awkward territory.

'That whole thing had been over yonks before they officially ended it,' she said, as though it was common knowledge. 'Elaine's been one of my best friends for years, I was so relieved for both of them.'

I almost spat out my drink. But that would have been a terrible waste so I choked it down.

'They were more flatmates than boyfriend and girl-friend in the end. I'm glad they dealt with it all so amicably.'

This was not good. Sasha was not my friend, nor was she Sam's friend. She was Elaine's friend. I looked around, looking for an escape route. No windows. Only one door. Stupid speakeasy.

'Lainey will be happy to know Samuel has someone; we were all so worried he'd hole up alone somewhere,' she declared. 'But here you are and you're quite clearly crazy about him.'

'Crazy is right,' I said, shaking my empty glass in her face. 'You know, I might pop back to the bar. Can I get you anything?'

Standing up before she could answer, I crossed the room quickly and hid at the busy bar to consider my options. This had been an incredibly stupid idea. I should never have come to the party without him. I should never have come to the party at all. How ridiculous, that I had shown up alone when Sam had clearly decided to give it a miss. I half expected to see a message from Mir to say he had shown up at the Wilder party. It was time for me to leave.

Decision made, I turned to make my way out, just as the door to the private room opened wide. It was Sam. I spied the top of his head over the crowds and felt my stomach lurch. And then the crowd of people between us parted and I saw he was not alone.

He was with Elaine.

'Well, I'll be a greased Jesus, is that you Samuel?'

Aggy declared loudly. 'Where's your hair? Who's responsible for this hatchet job? I'll have them.'

'You shush,' Elaine ordered, wrapping herself around Sam's arm as two red spots appeared in his cheeks. 'He looks gorgeous.'

In case I wasn't already hyperventilating, she yanked on his arm until he leaned over, bringing them face to face. Then she planted a kiss on his lips.

Everyone in the room turned to look at me.

'And how nice to see you together. Only, Sammy, your *other* friend is already here,' Aggy grinned and pointed over to the bar as I clutched my sweaty cocktail. 'We've all been having a lovely chat.'

'Annie?'

Sam looked more than a little surprised to see me.

But not nearly as surprised as Elaine. She tightened her grip on Sam's hand, staring daggers across the room.

'Just came by to say . . .' I necked my drink and shivered as the unmixed vodka in the bottom hit the back of my throat. 'Hi.'

'Don't I know you?' Elaine asked, narrowing her eyes with recognition.

'Let's say no,' I said, buttoning up my cardigan, post-haste. 'I had an important message for Sam. A business message.'

He just stared at me, utterly perplexed.

'Fire marshal business,' I added, words streaming out of my mouth in no particular order I could be sure of. 'They're turning the water off at work tomorrow morning at six. In case you were planning on going in early.'

'On a Saturday?' Elaine looked up at Sam. Her boyfriend. 'Why would they send someone out to tell you that on the off chance you'd be going to work on a Saturday?'

'Lovely to meet everyone,' I said loudly, throwing my handbag on my shoulder and slamming my glass down on the bar so hard, a long crack ran up the side. 'Happy birthday, Aggy, don't do anything I wouldn't do. Or anything I would do. Best not to even think about me at all. Happy bloody birthday.'

I sprinted through the bar and grabbed the door handle, pushing with all my might but it didn't budge.

'It says pull,' Sasha called from her seat at the table.

'So it does,' I replied, as cheerful as possible. I pulled the door lightly. It opened. 'There we go. Have a lovely evening, everyone.'

As soon as I was out of the party, I put my head down and pushed through the crowded bar, not looking up until I was back out on the street. How could I have been so stupid? Why were they there together? And how quickly could I get another drink?

I turned on my heel and ran down the street. An actual honest to goodness sprint. By the time I turned the corner, the tears began to roll down my cheeks, two at a time, hot, fat and fast. My mind replayed the moment when they walked in together over and over and over. Elaine looked so happy, so proud to be with him. Choking on my tears, I felt sick to my stomach, a rueful smile on my face. At least that was one good thing that had come out of his. I could officially say my boyfriend bootcamp had been a success after all.

CHAPTER TWENTY-FOUR

Out of all the different fantasies I'd entertained over the last few days, ending my Friday evening sitting on the roof of my office building, eating a Fray Bentos pie in floods of tears had never come up. And yet, that was exactly what I was doing.

'Why don't more people eat these?' I asked Brian in between mouthfuls. 'I feel reborn.'

'I would have run out and got you real food,' he said, pulling a most distasteful face. 'I can't believe you're eating that.'

'Neither can I,' I replied, sticking my fork back in the tin. 'Neither can I.'

The moment I arrived back at The Ginnel, my friends had welcomed me with open arms and an open bottle of wine and I had worked my way through the stages of rejection with no time to waste. The tears I dealt with on my own, Brian took the 'he's not even that great' phase, Miranda managed the 'why her and not me' bit and now the three of us were deep into my favourite part, the angry, righteous indignation, 'eff that guy' stage.

'Let her have him, that's what I say,' Miranda said,

waving her wine glass high above her head. 'More trouble than he's worth. Ooh, you're so tall, well done.'

'Lots of people are tall,' Brian agreed. 'Doesn't mean they're good people. Richard Madeley is tall. Donald Trump is tall. I'm tall.'

'Can't say I'm following that logic,' I muttered. 'I like Richard Madeley.'

'Tall doesn't make him special,' he continued. Brian was definitely slightly sloshed. 'And neither does a nice haircut and a decent pair of jeans. So what if he's got a PhD?'

'Two PhDs.'

'So he's twice as boring as we thought,' Bri shrugged and lay down on the floor, resting his head on Miranda's lady brogues. 'He doesn't deserve you, Annie. Let him go back to her, let him find out cheaters never change. Let him run around, trying to make her happy when she's just going to be shagging the first karate instructor that gives her a second look.'

'I went out with a karate teacher once,' Mir said. 'You'd be amazed at how long they spend washing those uniforms. Persil isn't enough, you've got to hand-wash it like, every time.'

'You, Annie, are a unicorn,' Brian announced. 'You're funny, you're clever, you're a wonderful friend. Your eyebrows give me life. I will not stand here and watch you cry when you deserve to have Justin Theroux's identical twin carrying you up the Eiffel Tower on his back and showering you in diamonds. You deserve the highest calibre of love possible and I won't allow you to settle for anything else.'

'Brian!' I was so touched. 'That's so lovely.'

'Or you need to get a bloody good seeing to,' he said, rolling over onto his stomach. 'Either or.'

'You started without us *again*?'

Charlie, Martin and everyone I had ever seen pass through the doors of The Ginnel streamed out onto the roof, carrying bottles of wine and cases of beer and bags upon bags of Doritos. The trashiest snack possible. I wanted it.

'We're trendsetters, what can I say?' Mir shouted, raising her cup in their direction. 'But we are running dry. Bring all that over here.'

And bring it over they did. The fairy lights went on, the music was turned up and I was surrounded. My pity party had been usurped by a real party.

'Might as well, since I'm already feeling shit,' I mumbled to myself, waiting until Miranda and Bri were both looking the other way and pulled out my phone, turning it on and waiting patiently for the screen to brighten.

I couldn't help myself. My first stop, Matthew's Facebook. Oh good, they'd had their engagement party tonight. Oh good, there were loads of people I used to think were my friends in the photos.

'Think of the money you'll save on Christmas cards,' I told myself as I scrolled through the happy event, mentally crossing names off one list and adding them to another. If only I ever actually managed to send Christmas cards.

I stared up at the darkening sky and tried to talk myself out of it. Unfortunately, I wasn't very convincing. Before I knew it, I'd already opened the app and found the account.

Elaine's Instagram feed was full of selfies of her and Sam. Absolutely full. A close-up of the two of them with their faces squished side by side. A team shot of her, Sam, Aggy and Sasha, taken just now at the birthday party. Elaine kissing Sam on the cheek, Sam trying not to look at the camera while he kissed Elaine. Toilet selfie.

But it was the last picture that killed me. Just a straight on photo of Sam, smiling slightly past the camera, his dark blond hair ruffled and one tiny dimple showing through his stubble in his left cheek and a caption that read 'This one' followed by an assortment of emojis. Heart eyes, a thumbs up, fire, a pair of scissors and because she was determined to fuck with me, the aubergine.

'Oi, professor.' I looked up to see Charlie standing in front of me, holding two bottles of beer. 'Need a drink?'

No, Dr Johnson and the *Live Life Love* podcast would have said, go home and meditate on your feelings, don't self-medicate with alcohol. And my sister would tell me not to start on wine and switch to beer. But Dr Johnson and the *Live Life Love* podcast had been a complete chocolate teapot when it came to dealing with the Sam situation and my sister was busy in the suburbs with Baby Basil so what was a girl supposed to do?

'I would love one,' I replied, taking the icy beverage in my spare hand and tipping it back. 'Thanks.'

I stood up, passing Miranda and Martin on the sofa, and walked over to the edge of the rooftop to my favourite shaded spot by the stairwell. Music started out of nowhere and the streets below us were swarming with people. London was officially off the clock.

'Long week,' Charlie said, following closely behind. 'Thought it might never end.'

'Tell me about it,' I replied as the beer settled onto a comfortable bed of pie. 'Happy summer party.'

He leaned over the wall that ran around the edge of the building. There was actually another low wall a few feet after that one but I wasn't sure why. It wasn't like someone who was determined to jump was going to climb over one four-foot wall and then think, you know what, I can't be bothered to do a second low-ish wall today, maybe I will go on with life instead.

'Any big plans for the weekend?' Charlie asked.

Sleep, work, possibly throw up a chicken pie, more work, more sleep and then maybe treat myself to a good cry and a *Dawson's Creek* marathon.

'Very exciting plans,' I replied, turning my back on the skyline and resting my elbows on the barrier that ran around the edge of the roof. 'You?'

'Probably end up working all weekend,' he said with a happy martyr's smile I recognized all too well. 'All those films I watched with my mum when I was growing up gave me seriously false expectations when it comes to the glamour of running your own business.'

'I'll drink to that,' I said, clinking the neck of my bottle against his. 'Sometimes I dream about turning my computer off on a Friday and that being it until Monday.'

'Sometimes I fantasize about not reading my emails before I go to bed,' said Charlie. 'Or waking up and actually getting out of bed before I check my inbox.'

'Inbox dread,' I groaned, managing a small smile at the same time. 'It's a modern epidemic. There's no cure.'

Charlie raised his beer to his lips, gazing out over London as he drank, king of the world.

'So,' he said, turning around so we were facing in the same direction, side by side. 'How are you doing with our little bet?'

I sniffed and shook out my shoulders, twisting the bottle around and around in my hand.

'I still have seven days,' I replied, wiping the condensation from the bottle on the backside of my jeans.

Charlie laughed and took a deep drink.

'It's going that badly? Oh, Higgins, I'm almost disappointed in you.'

'Don't be,' I replied with a sweet smile. 'Seven days is a long time in my world. A lot can happen in seven days.'

'If you say so,' Charlie replied, finishing his beer and resting the bottle on the ledge behind him. 'But I think the Wilder summer party would be a cracking place for you to graciously concede.'

Staring him dead in the eye, I picked up my beer and steadily drank until it was done.

'Oh no, I finished it,' I said with mock surprise, waving the bottle at him. 'Think I'll go get another.'

'Let me,' Charlie said, tipping back his own bottle and downing it in one. He took my bottle before lightly resting his hand on the bare skin of my forearm. 'Don't go anywhere.'

Ooh. Goosebumps.

Over on the sofa, I could see Miranda and Martin, already cosying up together. One of the girls from the Coffee Shop was trying to capture the perfect shot of Brian doing a star jump and everyone else was either starting on their second drink or saying their goodbyes. The end of the working week, the beginning of the weekend. Home to their families or off on adventures.

My phone vibrated in my hand. I had a new Facebook friend request.

Truth be told, I wasn't much of a Facebook user. Lurker, absolutely, but poster? Only on occasion. It took either an incredible gif or a generation shattering political event to drive me to tell Mark Zuckerberg how I felt and, generally speaking, I regretted it almost immediately after posting. The Facebook echo chamber was exhausting; give me Instagram's never-ending parade of highlight reels any day. Also, I found I was far less likely to have my day ruined by a beloved family member's casual racism on Insta.

It was a friend request from Dr Samuel Page.

His profile photo was one of the ones I had taken at Lily's party, complete with palm tree in the background. Lives in London, his profile said. In a relationship, his profile said. Decline, my heart said.

'Glad to see you're feeling better,' Brian said, appearing at my side. I shoved my phone in my pocket and tried to convince myself I hadn't seen it. 'Am I going to have to hold your hair back again tonight? Because if I am, I'm going to need a pay rise.'

'Yeah, I've been thinking about that a lot lately,' I replied, my hand on his arm, my voice super sincere. 'I'm concerned there could be a conflict of interests, you know, employing one of my best mates. So maybe you could pack up your things and fuck off? Thanks.'

'I'm one of your best mates?' he pulled a sour face. 'I thought we were bar friends at best. Barely acquaintances.'

'That's why I had to tell your mum you had food poisoning that time you puked on the bonnet of her Fiesta when we were seventeen, is it?' I asked. 'I suppose, technically, you were poisoned and technically, Long Island Iced Tea slushies are food . . .'

'We all made mistakes when we were young,' he volleyed back. 'And it looks like you're getting ready to make one any second now. What's occurring here?' He gestured back to where Charlie was making the universal 'bottle opener?' gesture of disorganised parties.

'Nothing in the slightest,' I said, accepting his offer of lip balm and immediately outing myself as a liar. 'He's just a flirt, he can't help himself.'

'Man-wich,' Brian whispered as he slipped the balm back in his pocket. 'He's the perfect palate cleanser.'

Maybe he was, I thought, watching as Charlie pawed through a bucket of beers, laughing with a co-worker. He made everything look easy, he was the complete opposite of Sam, who made everything difficult, every decision and action tied to the outcome of a million possibilities, all of them running through his head at the same time. Yet the thought of him being back with Elaine ate me up. I felt hollowed out, I felt bereft. And the only person who would truly appreciate my appropriate use of the world bereft was bloody Sam.

'My lady,' Charlie said, handing me my drink and a packet of Hula Hoops. 'My ears are burning, were you two talking about me?'

'Annie was telling me how great it is to have another dedicated, ambitious entrepreneur in the building,' Brian lied smoothly. 'And also how your thighs are like, really, really nice.'

He clinked the neck of his beer bottle against mine and walked away, whistling as he went.

'Wow,' Charlie replied, wide-eyed. 'I don't think I've ever felt so objectified.'

'I didn't say that,' I said quickly, flustered, trying not to look at his thighs. 'I didn't. The thigh part, I mean.'

He considered my response for a moment.

'But you did say the other part?'

I shook my head. 'Sorry. I suppose it is true though.'

'The thigh part or the dedicated and ambitious bit?' Charlie asked, launching into a series of squats. 'Come on, Annie, you can tell me the truth.'

'Stop it,' I laughed. 'People are looking.'

'It's my thighs,' he insisted as he squatted even lower. 'They can't help themselves.'

I turned away, covering my eyes with my hands, still laughing. I actually felt a bit better.

'Calm down, I've stopped,' Charlie said, pulling my hand away from my face and ever so casually keeping it in his. 'If I carry on they won't be able to control themselves anyway and I can't expect you to fight off every woman in the building.'

'You're so kind,' I flicked my eyes down to my hand in his. It was nice. I let it go.

'So, Annie Higgins. What's your secret?'

I pushed all thoughts of Sam out of my mind and focused on other, more immediate concerns. Like whether or not I should tell Charlie his fly was coming down and just how much I smelled of pie.

'Secret to what?' I asked, arranging myself to look as nonchalant as humanly possible.

'Modest as well,' he laughed, making sure I noticed his bicep as he brushed his hand through his hair. Charlie's hair was a lot lighter than Sam's. Not as curly. Not that I was thinking things like that. 'Owns her own company, nominated for a very important award, clever, ambitious, gorgeous.'

On any other day, I would have rolled my eyes and walked away. On any other day.

'Nominated for three awards, actually,' I said before taking a sip of my beer. 'Since you're so interested.'

'Oh,' he said, a small smile playing on his lips. 'I'm interested.'

He was flirting with me. If only I'd kept all those back issues of *Mizz* magazine, I'd know what to do now. Somewhere in the dark recesses of my brain, alongside Spice Girls lyrics and the application instructions for Sun-In, a voice told me to move towards him, to stroke my hair and touch his arm.

I cocked my head to one side and gave him the old once-over. He was tall. Not as tall as Sam, who was an actual human beanpole, but definitely over six foot. Richard Madeley tall for sure. And he really did have very nice thighs.

'So, no big plans for the weekend?' Charlie asked as he moved ever so slightly closer. Maybe he'd grown up reading *Just Seventeen* too. 'Doing anything later tonight?'

I shook my head and sipped my beer slowly.

Don't tell him you have to go home and wash cat pee out of your mattress.

'Nope,' I whispered. 'No plans.'

'Good,' he said, flashing the full force Charlie Wilder grin. 'You can stay and talk to me.'

'So you can try to talk me out of the bet?' I asked, returning his smile.

'I would never,' he replied. 'Because, when I win, you're going to have to hang out with me all the time.'

Licking my lips, I rearranged myself, copying his body language and laughed. *Sugar* magazine definitely said you were supposed to laugh.

'You could just ask me, if you wanted to hang out,' I said, tossing my hair out of my face only to tweak a muscle in my neck. My spine was a mess. Too many hours spent hunched over a computer. I was this close to giving up and moving to Notre Dame.

'You always look so busy.' Charlie sipped his beer as I dug my forefingers into the sharp pain and tried to make it look seductive. 'And I used to get the feeling you didn't like me very much.'

Annie Higgins, putting men off without even trying since forever. I shrugged, faux nonchalant, biting on my lip as I tried to straighten my neck.

'Glad to hear that isn't the case.' Charlie rested his bottle on the low wall and smiled at me. A real smile. A clear, clean, all-signals-are-go grin.

I gazed into his brown eyes and couldn't think of a single reason not to kiss him. Better to be with someone than no one, I thought. And, I realized, taking a step towards him and grabbing the collar of his shirt, I was just drunk enough to give this a go.

'Just so you know,' I whispered, breathless, as he took me in his arms. 'I just ate a Fray Bentos pie.'

'Marry me,' Charlie replied before pulling me in for a kiss.

Only it wasn't so much as a kiss as a headbutt with lips.

'Sorry,' I murmured, pulling away and rubbing my forehead. 'Let's try that again.'

'Yes, please.' He brushed my hair behind my ear and touched his lips to mine but once again, we couldn't quite get it right.

'Ow,' I winced, pulling away as the crown of his watch got stuck in the fine hair at my temple. 'Ow ow ow, that really hurts.'

'Hold still, I've got it, I've got it.' He pulled back, unfastening his watch, turning it this way and that, trying not to scalp me. 'There we go.'

'Thank you,' I said, watching him rebuckle the strap. I smiled, Charlie smiled, I laughed and looked away. What an adorable story we'd have to tell our couple friends over all the couples' brunches we'd be invited to.

'Third time lucky,' Charlie said, cupping my cheek gently in his hand and guiding my face toward him. We both closed our eyes and our mouths met, soft and warm and full.

And I didn't feel a thing.

I pulled away, breaking the kiss and leaving a breath between us.

'Is it me,' Charlie said quietly. 'Or is this really weird?'

'It's weird,' I confirmed, wiping my mouth with the back of my hand. 'Sorry. That was awful.'

'Maybe we should try again,' he said with admirable determination. 'Just relax.'

Was there anything less relaxing than someone telling you to relax?

'Nope,' I said, pinching his face between my thumb and forefinger and craning my neck away from his fish lips. 'For the first time in history, this really is an "it's not you, it's me" situation.'

'Huh,' Charlie shuffled backwards half a step and stuck his hands in his trouser pockets. 'I don't think this has ever happened to me before.'

'First time for everything,' I told him, clucking my tongue while I searched for something to say. The teen mags had not prepared me for this situation. Another feature that needed writing; what to do when the office hottie plants one on you and it feels like you're kissing your second cousin.

'No hard feelings,' Charlie said, finally accepting defeat. 'Wasn't in the stars for us, was it? Probably best we keep it professional anyway. For when you lose the bet.'

'Thank you,' I said, leaning in to plant a peck on his cheek and taking a deep breath. 'Thank you very much.'

'For what?' he called as I walked away.

'For reminding me who I am,' I shouted as I jogged across the rooftop, in search of my friends. 'For a second there I forgot.'

CHAPTER TWENTY-FIVE

Saturday, 28 July: Six Days to Go

Some people were perfectly capable of dealing with a hangover. They woke up in their own homes, they took an ibuprofen, maybe scarfed down a bacon butty and then they were fine. But not me. That would be too easy.

'Morning, princess.'

I rolled over to discover I had at least made it to my own bed.

But I was not alone.

Brian beamed back at me, pulling down the duvet to reveal his outfit. To be fair, my black satin pyjamas did look good on him.

'You brought me home?' I said, rubbing my head as though I could stop the throbbing from the outside.

'I did,' he confirmed. 'Me and Mir tossed a coin for the privilege.'

'She left with Martin,' I began putting the pieces of the evening together.

'She did,' he confirmed. 'Do you remember sticking your tongue down Charlie Wilder's throat?'

'I remember giving him a chaste peck and it feeling like I was getting off with my nan,' I corrected. 'Super weird.'

'Maybe he's gay,' Brian speculated with bright eyes. 'Or maybe you're definitely in love with a certain Ginnel-based historian who shall remain nameless.'

I rolled my eyes and rested my head back on the pillow.

'Don't be so vague,' I groaned. 'However am I supposed to work out who you're talking about?'

I fumbled on my nightstand, reaching out for my phone but it wasn't there.

'Do you remember where I put my phone last night?' I asked, rolling out of bed. If Brian was wearing my pyjamas, what was I wearing? I looked down to see the same white camisole I'd been wearing the night before and, for some reason, my swimming costume over the top.

'You said you wanted to wear something waterproof in case you wet yourself,' Brian explained. 'Seemed pointless to argue with logic like that.'

Summoning all my energy, I peeled the straps down over my shoulders and shucked off the swimming cossie. It didn't really make any sense for me to still have my knickers on underneath but I was grateful nonetheless.

'I remember having it in the bathroom,' I said to myself, retracing my steps. It wasn't hard in a flat this size.

'Probably texting on the toilet, you filthy mare,' Brian shouted. 'Can you make me a coffee please?'

'I don't think I was texting.' I stood in the middle of the bathroom, looking for something to jog my memory. Toothpaste on the sink, used face-wipes on the floor. Shoes, jeans, cardigan in a pile by the bath while my bra was draped over the glass shower screen. But where was my phone?

'I was working,' I realized. 'I came up with something really good for the Hip Historian but I can't remember what it was.'

'That old chestnut,' Bri replied, standing in the doorway. 'Did the dog eat your homework as well?'

'No, I came up with something really great,' I said, moving from the bathroom to the living room. My bag had been upended in the middle of the floor and my notebook sat open on the loveseat. 'I was looking at my phone and I was getting really upset about Sam.'

'You were complaining that she only wants him now he's hot,' Brian said. He filled the kettle and began rifling through the fridge. 'And if he was happy with that then sod him.'

'I am prepared to bet you any money I didn't say "sod him",' I replied as I leafed through my notes.

He turned to me, a prim expression on his face, a packet of ginger nuts in his hand.

'You did not,' he said. 'But my delicate ears can't stand to hear that torrent of filth again this early in the morning. Are these seriously the only biscuits you've got?'

'Check the freezer,' I said. 'I have to put the chocolate Hobnobs in there to stop me eating them all.'

Wait, the freezer!

I scampered to my feet, pushing Brian out the way and delving right into the back of my freezer compartment. There it was, wrapped up in a freezer bag between the potato waffles and the fish fingers.

'You put your phone in the freezer?'

'It's an old tech trick,' I told him, opening the bag

and taking out my precious, precious phone. 'People do it to reset the operating system.'

'Does it work?'

'No. But it does stop you from texting people you shouldn't when you're drunk and angry.'

Now I remembered.

I'd been looking at Elaine's Insta feed again after I got home, when she posted a new photo. The basic bitch pièce de résistance, a fake sleeping pic. Sam might have been properly asleep but Elaine's faux snooze was completely given away by the shadow of her own arm falling across her face in the picture and you know, the fact someone had to be taking the actual photo. I opened Instagram and there it was, still her most recent picture and it was racking up the likes. I wondered how Sam would feel when he saw it. If he ever saw it.

My notebook was covered in angry looking scribbles that began to make sense. But could I do it? Did we have the time? Would it make Sam incredibly, incredibly angry?

He didn't care about my feelings, why should I care about his? I was just a shallow, social-media-obsessed airhead after all.

Wellington poked his head out from underneath my armchair, stretching out his front paws and pushing his butt up into the air with a shudder.

'Brian, I think I've worked out how to win the bet,' I called from the living room floor.

'Does that mean I can stop looking for a new job?' he asked.

'It means we'll be able to pay you at the end of the month,' I said. 'But you should keep looking anyway, you're very annoying.'

'I think I'll stick around,' he replied, heaping instant coffee into two mugs. 'Annoying you is fun.'

'If this doesn't do it, nothing will,' I said to Wellington, taking one last painful look at the photo of Sam's sleeping face. The cat purred, looking up at me with almond eyes. I was almost certain I could see a smile on his face.

'Please don't wee on my bed again,' I whispered.

He agreed to nothing.

CHAPTER TWENTY-SIX

Monday, 30 July: Four Days to Go
13,002 followers

'Morning,' I said, dropping my handbag on my desk on Monday morning. 'How was everyone's weekend?'

'We were eaten by a giant space alien that came up out of the Thames,' Mir replied. 'Thankfully it swallowed us whole and we were able to slay the beast from the inside, find a way out after a very thrilling adventure. You didn't see it on the news?'

'Must have missed it,' I replied, updating the numbers on my whiteboard. Four days to go. 'Sounds fun.'

'You haven't replied to a single one of my text messages all weekend,' she said, closing her laptop to give me the full weight of her stare. 'I thought you were dead. Did you finish the pitch?'

'I was at home,' I replied, as if that was going to be an acceptable answer. 'I was working. And yes, of course I did.'

'I told you we'd have heard about it if she'd gone

on a murderous rampage,' Brian said before picking up his coffee. 'You are a drama queen.'

'Have you looked at Sam's Instagram today?' I asked.

Miranda, Brian, Zadie and Nat all picked up their phones at the same time and smiles spread across their faces.

After Brian left on Saturday, I'd spent the entire weekend putting my new plan into action. Editing photos, researching captions, tagging, retweeting and collaborating and we were already up three thousand new followers. It was a social media miracle. The original plan had been to mix random historical facts with random celebrity pictures and gifs but we'd peaked and stalled at ten thousand fans. No matter what I tried, I couldn't get us past that. There were only so many times people could watch Dawson ugly cry after all, regardless of the fascinating historical titbit attached.

The new plan was beautiful in its simplicity. I'd replaced all the random photos of celebs with not so random photos of a post-makeover Sam. My very own Hot Historian. The first new post was a close-up of Sam taken right after his makeover scratching his stubble and staring straight into the camera. The portrait was accompanied by the text 'The Anglo-Zanzibar war of 1896 lasted only 38 minutes' and it already had a thousand likes. I had four more days to find seven thousand new people who liked learning useless factoids and looking at hot men. It couldn't possibly be that difficult.

'I like the one where he's holding a Chihuahua,' Zadie said with admiration. 'The dog looks so excited to find out Alexander Hamilton founded the *New York Post*.'

'And you can't even tell it's Photoshopped,' I said proudly. 'That Chiahuahua started out as a nineteenth century thesaurus.'

'That one picture already has two thousand likes,' Mir gasped. 'How did you come up with this?'

'This is going to be massive,' Brian said, eyes on his phone. 'Everyone's going to love it.'

Everyone except for Sam, I added to myself.

I ignored the sick feeling in my stomach. If Elaine could litter her Instagram with photographs of him, so could I. And besides, he had said he wanted me to win the bet. That's what I was doing. Winning the bet. Even though I had promised not to use any photos of him on the Instagram account . . .

'You're so good you scare me sometimes, Annie,' Miranda muttered, gathering her things and chucking them all into a tote bag. 'Don't suppose anyone's got any Tums, have they?'

'Sorry, nana,' I said. 'We can get some on the way. What's up?'

'My mum made this Peruvian stew for Sunday lunch and it was terrible,' she said as she rubbed a nervous hand against her stomach. 'I definitely shouldn't have had seconds.'

I picked up my backup printout of our SetPics pitch. Yes, we were a digital agency but one of the most important lessons I'd learned working in tech was that tech fails. All the time. And given that this was the most important meeting of our careers, that simply would not do.

We arrived at the Devitt Building ten minutes before our meeting. Long enough to pull ourselves together but not long enough to psych ourselves out. We were good at meetings, Miranda and I. She gave the spiel while I smiled, nodded and made sure all the slides played in the right order. We were a slick team.

Or at least we usually were.

'Annie, I don't feel well,' Mir muttered as I checked us in at reception. 'I'm going to pop to the loo.'

She'd been uncharacteristically quiet all the way over, even when I'd relented on our no cab rule and let her book an Uber, but I'd put it down to nerves and the fact she'd spent most of the weekend getting more sex than food or sleep.

'Do you need me to come with you?' I asked, suddenly worried. I grabbed the black leather laptop bag she thrust at me.

'No, stay here,' she replied, pawing at a suddenly sweaty forehead as she turned and ran. 'I don't think you want to be part of this.'

I took a seat on the little cube sofas in the lobby while Mir walk-ran into the bathrooms, dodging assorted men in suits.

'Annie, how nice to see you here. Twice in one month, how lucky am I?'

'Gordon,' I replied, scratching the side of my nose with my middle finger. He couldn't see but it made me feel better.

'What brings you south of the river on a Monday morning?' he asked, two lackeys from the Oz Agency hovering behind him with matching grins on their bearded faces.

'We're here for the *Uniteam* pitch, as you well know,' I said, not wanting to show him how much he annoyed me but struggling to hide it. 'I hope your meeting went well.'

'Exceptionally well,' he confirmed, nodding. 'I have

to say, I think it's fantastic that they're still seeing you. It's important for small businesses to pitch above their level, helps you to grow, doesn't it? I mean personally of course, not work-wise. Because I'm going to win this.'

I smiled pleasantly, trying to think of something clever to say.

'Fuck off, Gordon.'

Sometimes you didn't need to be that clever.

'It's a shame you're not still working for me, Annie,' he commented, shifting his man bag onto the other shoulder and pretending not to have heard me. 'I would have had you on this account. You'd have been good at it. You always did have a knack at knowing just how to communicate with people.'

'Well, we'll be hiring when we win,' I said sweetly. 'Maybe you can come and work for us?'

He took a sharp inhale, as though he was about to say something particularly unpleasant but instead he smiled, turned away and walked out, tossing his security pass at the girl on the front desk as he went, his two helper monkeys scurrying after him.

'Annie Higgins?'

A young man wearing a Mark Zuckerberg-approved hoodie and jeans combo appeared from nowhere.

'I'm Annie,' I said, standing to shake his hand. 'My partner Miranda is just in the bathroom.'

'We're running a bit tight on time, will she be long?' he asked, glancing down at an iPad Mini.

'Let me go and check on her,' I said, leaving my bags on the sofa. 'Won't be two secs.'

But we were going to be two secs. We were going to be considerably more than two secs.

'Miranda?' I called, bending over to peep under

the closed stalls in the ladies' loos. 'Where are you? They're ready for us.'

'Annie.' A weak, raspy version of my best friend's voice called from the last stall on the line.

'Mir? Are you OK? Open the door,' I ordered, pushing against the lock. 'Let me in.'

'Babe, I can't do that to you,' she said through the door. 'You don't want to see this.'

If it looked anything like it smelled, she was quite correct.

'Do you need to go to hospital?' I was starting to panic. What if she was really ill? What if it was a bacterial infection or a parasite or—

'I'm puking up Peruvian stew,' she interrupted my chain of thought, reading my mind like she always did. 'I'm sorry, I'm a twat but I'm not going to die. You're going to have to do this one on your own.'

She may have spoken too soon on the 'not going to die' part.

'Please, Annie, we might never get another chance like this,' Mir said. 'You don't need me.'

'But I do,' I wailed, catching sight of myself in the mirror. My neck, my chest and my face were flame red. 'We'll postpone. I'll ask them if we can come back tomorrow.'

Miranda's foot suddenly shot out from under the stall door, kicking me in the ankles.

'You're going to go in there, you're going to give this presentation and you're going to win,' she was very assertive for someone who was currently turning themselves inside out in a public toilet. 'Never give up and never give in.'

'I hate when you use my own words against me,' I

said, dodging the foot as it came back for a second swipe. 'Are you sure you'll be OK?'

'Can you hand me some toilet paper?' she asked, one hand appearing where the foot had been. 'Like, a lot of toilet paper?'

Wrenching the cover off the dispenser in the next loo, I pushed the whole roll under the door.

'Thank you,' she said as it disappeared into the stall of despair. 'I love you.'

'I love you too,' I said, squeezing her hand for just a second before standing to wash my hands under an aggressively hot tap. 'Shall I see you back at the office?'

'You'll see me back here,' she mumbled. 'I'm going to be here for a while.'

'OK,' I said, wincing as someone else walked into the loos, a sudden look of shock crossing her face. I mouthed an apology as I held the door open. 'I'll be back down as soon as I can.'

'That's my girl,' Mir called weakly.

'We'd like to thank you for putting this together at such short notice,' said Harry, the head of SetPics communications, as he filtered through a stack of pitches in front of him, looking for the one from Content. He sounded friendly enough, but there was certainly a sense of someone desperate to press on with their day. Probably because he'd already decided to give the business to Gordon, whispered the devil on my shoulder. I pushed the thought out of my head, it wasn't helpful.

'Your work has been very impressive, far and away the most creative campaign we have seen,' Harry went on, scratching his stubble. 'I can't imagine what you'd have come up with had you had the same amount of time as the other agencies but, to be honest, you did the best at getting to grips with the DNA of *Uniteam 3000*.'

I nodded and tried not to drip sweat on anything electrical. Harry's IT guy was busy hooking my laptop up to their system while I stared up and down the table. Two people, maybe three, Miranda had said. Or alternatively, I'd be presenting to seven people. Seven unsmiling, bored people who had already sat through god only knew how many presentations so far that morning.

'Thank you,' I said slowly and deliberately before giving them all a big, bright smile. Not too big, you don't want them to think you're mental, I reminded myself. I dimmed the megawatt grin by fifty per cent.

'While we loved the work you sent over, you are the least experienced of all the agencies we're talking to.' Harry gave my forced smile a brief look of concern before turning to his notes on our pitch. 'Which leaves us with some uncertainty. We can all see you're very talented and you've got solid ideas, but you can understand why we'd be wary of committing such a huge project to a relatively untested agency.'

'OK,' I replied. I was unsure what I was supposed to say to that kind of backhanded compliment. 'We know we could do it though, or we wouldn't be here.'

They all looked at one another, not talking but definitely communicating in some kind of telepathic language which I had to assume translated to 'ridiculously cocky for a small agency'.

'I get that there's a comfort factor in going with a more established agency but I don't think you want comfort, I think you want new subscribers,' I said as, against all odds, our presentation appeared on their pull-down screen. 'Shall I walk you through the pitch?'

'We've read the pitch,' Harry said, speaking on behalf of all the silent judges around the table. 'We want to get to know you. Talk to us, Annie.'

It was literally the worst thing they could have said.

'What do you want to know?' I asked, throwing open my arms and knocking over a stack of paper cups. 'I'm an open book.'

This should have been Miranda's time to shine. Everyone knew I talked either far too much or not nearly enough when I was nervous, and my incredibly sweaty palms suggested I was definitely nervous. I'd done my bit, I'd written the slides, I'd come up with the ideas. Miranda was the one who did speaking, that was the deal. Stupid bloody Peruvian stew.

'We have brilliant in-house PR and marketing,' Harry said, leafing through a print out of our presentation as he scratched his head. 'But we've struggled with social media. We just can't seem to get it right. Looking at where we've been, what would you do differently?'

'It's not as easy as it looks,' I said carefully. Somewhere in the back of my mind, I heard Sam's voice. There was no need to be nervous, I knew what I was talking about and I was prepared.

'Social media is its own language,' I said. 'And you need to be fluent. You can make yourself understood without that, but if you really want people to listen, you've got to talk to them in their own language.'

This was the truth. The number of times my sister had texted me asking for definitions of online abbreviations. And truly, I rued the day I set up my mum's Twitter account. No one should have to spend a Saturday afternoon talking their sixty-year-old mother out from an Urban Dictionary click hole. I would never forget the moment she explained to my grandmother that she was a proud PAWG at the Easter dinner table.

'We know where people are and we know how to talk to them,' I said. 'And we make it fun. You can't expect people to engage with something if they're not enjoying it or if it doesn't make them feel anything. Like anything else in life.'

I reached out for a glass of water with a shaky hand and raised it slowly to my mouth.

'What else would you like to know?' I asked as I set it down successfully.

Harry leaned back in his chair, his face interested.

'And what about you, Annie?' he said. 'Why should we want to work with you?'

'Because I get nervous when I care about something and I'm incredibly nervous right now,' I answered, trying to laugh. Everyone else went with a polite chuckle. 'So I must care about this an awful lot. Also, people keep telling me I'm incredibly competitive and I suppose that could work in your favour.'

'A lot of people say that like it's a bad thing, but I don't think that's necessarily the case,' a woman across the table in an actual Steve Jobs polo-neck jumper said. 'Do you think you're competitive?'

'Competitive people want to win,' I said slowly, feeling out the truth in my words before I said something I might regret. 'And I think that used to be true of me. Win at all costs, add another tick to the tally. But now I'm thinking winning might not be as important as getting it right. I wouldn't want to win this account if I didn't think I could do it well. That wouldn't help me, not in the long run.'

No one said anything so I did what I do best in these situations, I just kept on talking.

'I'm not trying to sound like an inspirational Instagram post,' I said, fiddling with a stray highlighter in my lap. 'Because I'm sure I've done things in the past that I wouldn't put on Father Christmas' nice list, all because I wanted to get a win.'

Clocking Marie Brown with a hockey stick, for example.

'But ultimately, you want to start a conversation with people and conversations need to be honest,' I said, satisfied I was finally getting to my point. 'You can only fake it so many times, you can only apply so many filters. For this campaign to work for you, you need trust and you need the truth.'

Harry and all Harry's colleagues looked at me, then looked at each other and then looked back at me.

'It's easy to throw the words "sincere" and "authentic" around, but honestly, they don't mean anything any more. Chances are, your audience is going to find it condescending. This is a teen show and Generation Z, the post-millennials, they grew up with social media. They know if it's real or not. It won't matter how cool your graphics are or how sophisticated your bots might be, they'll sniff out a fraud at a hundred paces. We can do it right, and we can do it well. No bullshit, no faking – real honest conversations with the people you want to talk to.'

There was some encouraging nodding as I talked and, much to my delight, everyone looked interested. I finished with a breathless 'Any questions?' When no one replied, I gave my best professional smile. 'That's really all I have to say.'

'So, we're going to take a couple of days to go over all the presentations,' Harry said slowly, keeping one eye on me. Everyone else pulled their papers, pens and phones into little piles and made noises to excuse themselves. I clicked the cap on and off the highlighter in my lap, impatient for this to be over. 'And we'll get back to you soon. I saw you're up for a couple of TechBubble awards. Will you be at the do on Thursday?'

'Yes,' I replied, slyly wiping my hand on my chair before I stood to shake his hand. 'You must stop by our table.'

'Then we'll see you there,' he said, looking down at my white skirt and immediately pulling his eyes back up. 'It was very nice to meet you, Annie.'

I glanced down at myself. The highlighter had leaked everywhere, leaving a very attractive yellow stain in my lap.

'Can I see you out?' the man from the lobby asked.

'Probably best,' I said, following him out the door.

'What I don't understand is how I spent the last hour turning myself inside out from end to end and you're the one who walked out of a meeting looking like she'd pissed herself,' Mir said as we arrived back at the office. 'Wait here, I want to get a Coke.'

'Shouldn't you be nil by mouth for twenty-four hours?' I loitered at the bottom of the stairs.

'Coke'll help. Food poisoning is like a hangover,' she said. 'You have to replace the sugar.'

'What if you've caught something dreadful from Martin,' I suggested, a lurid look of joy on my face as she blanched again. 'What if it's literally eating its way through your insides right now?'

'Oh, hello, Sam,' Miranda said loudly over my shoulder. 'What can we do for you today?'

No. Nope. No way. I pushed out my bottom lip and shook my head at my friend.

'I was hoping to speak to Annie,' he replied, some-where behind me.

'Brilliant, we've just finished our pitch, she's all yours,' she said, clapping me on the shoulder. 'I have to go and make sure something isn't eating my insides away.'

Some people had short memories and no loyalty.

I turned around to see Sam standing outside the Coffee Shop, cup of tea in one hand and a huge hard-back book in the other.

'Trying to hide from me?' he asked.

'Yes,' I said, too weary to lie. 'Sorry.'

'What, why?' He pushed his glasses up the bridge of his nose with the back of his wrist and I looked for a speedy way out of the situation that didn't involve throwing myself under a passing bus.

'I've been really busy,' I told him, clinging to my tote bag. I didn't want to use my very pricey laptop as a weapon but if needs must . . . 'Spent all weekend working. On the pitch. Still busy, to be honest. I should get back up to the office.'

'I thought you'd want to know officially, Elaine has said she'll give me another chance,' he called as I started to walk away. 'There's no way she would have considered it if you hadn't helped me so much.'

'Yay,' I replied weakly. 'I'm so happy for you.' I started walking away. I couldn't face going up to the office and dealing with Miranda, so I headed down the corridor towards the back of the building.

'I'm still a little confused as to what happened at Aggy's party last week,' Sam said, trailing after me. I was trapped. There was nowhere to go but out into the tiny smoker's courtyard at the end of the alley, behind The Ginnel. He caught the door when I didn't

329

hold it open for him and followed me outside. It was a terrible hole of a place, it stank of bins and, because it was always in the shade, it always felt damp and cold and miserable. It was absolutely the right place for me to be at that exact second.

'Don't know what you're talking about,' I said, hoping he would realize I didn't want to talk to him before I really did have to batter him to death with a MacBook Pro. They were so expensive these days and I'd have to sell one of Brian's kidneys to replace it.

Even in the dim, half-light of the courtyard, it hurt to look at him.

'I thought about what you said, about Aggy's party, and I decided the best thing to do was to clear the air with Elaine before I went. Head the awkward confrontation off at the pass, as it were,' Sam explained, tucking his book under his armpit. 'I convinced her to meet me and . . . I suppose she decided she wanted to try again.'

'That's nice,' I said, wondering if it wouldn't be easier to just drive my own head through the brick wall than listen to the rest of this story.

'She was very impressed with my new look.' He reluctantly set his mug on the ledge covered in the least amount of visible bird shit. 'I even told her about the salsa class. And I've agreed to work harder at being more present. If everything keeps going well, I'll be moving back in next week.'

He, looked upwards as he spoke the last line, as though he was remembering something very specific.

'And what did she agree to work on?' I asked, crossing my arms over myself. 'Given the fact she was cheating on you even though she tried to make you feel like the break-up was your fault and you'd spent the best part of a month attempting to completely change your entire self for her?'

Sam looked perplexed, as though the thought had never crossed his mind.

'What exactly did Elaine put on the table?' I pressed.

'Well, she explained about that,' he replied. 'I pushed her into it by not being around. Emotionally unavailable, is what she said. She didn't want to cheat.'

'Right, brilliant,' I shook my head, amazed. Between us, Elaine and I had really done a number on the poor boy. 'You take all the blame, offer to completely change your life and she agrees to do nothing other than let you move back into your own home. That sounds fair.'

'Why are you angry with me?' Sam said, placing his book next to his mug. It was a biography of William Wilberforce. A name I hadn't heard since GCSE History and, had I never gotten involved with Sam, might happily never have heard again. 'And why is the front of your skirt yellow?'

'Don't look at my skirt!' I ordered, my last nerve fraying into nothing. 'Why do you even want to get back together with her, Sam? I don't understand what was so great about this relationship that you of all people are literally prepared to give up every single shred of dignity just to have this woman back in your life.'

'Because I liked my life before,' he replied, the closest he'd ever come to raising his voice to me. 'I liked knowing how every day was going to be. I liked my work, I liked my home, I liked my cat. I didn't need day-trips to the seaside or fancy haircuts. I just want things to go back exactly how they were before. You wouldn't understand, trapped in your little bubble. I know it can't possibly have occurred to you

331

that I was happy before you came along and tried to fix me, but I was.'

I felt as though he'd slapped me in the face.

'I wasn't trying to fix you, I was trying to help you,' I argued. 'And how am I the one trapped in a bubble? You're literally locked in a tiny room with a load of old books and a cheating girlfriend.'

'I preferred my cage to yours,' Sam shook his head sadly. 'I knew the limitations of my universe and I liked them. You can't even see the bars on your cage and you put them there yourself.'

My breath was coming hard and fast and a million words were rushing around inside my head, fighting to get out my mouth first. I kicked a stray stone across the yard, unsettling something that was rootling around the bins.

'I'm very sorry I caused you so many problems,' I said, my fists clenched so tightly I could feel my fingernails digging into the palms of my hands. 'And I'm happy you've got your shitty life back. Hurrah, you can go home. Hurrah, you don't have to stay at your brother's or sleep on the floor any more. I'll bring your cat back tomorrow and you can take him home to your perfect flat and your perfect life and everything will go back to normal for you, as if nothing ever changed. But you're wrong about my life; my life was great until you came along and confused everything.'

Sam's eyebrows drew together, the hurt look on his face melting into something else.

'What does that mean?' he lowered his voice to all but a whisper. 'How have I confused things for you?'

I bit my bottom lip and glanced around, wondering if the rats or the pigeons might have a ready answer.

'Forget it,' I said, walking towards the door. 'I've got to get back inside.'

But Sam stepped in front of the door, blocking my way.

'Annie, what're you talking about?' he pleaded. 'I never thought I'd have to beg you to talk to me.'

He slipped his hands into his pockets and looked away as I fought the tears that began to blur in my eyes. Perfect. Now he could write me off as an overly emotional female and go on with his day.

'Things have been very complicated in general,' I mumbled in a thick, unsteady voice. 'What with you and with work and Mir and the bet with Charlie and everything—'

'Ah. So this is about you and Charlie, is it?' Sam said, poking around at the assorted debris on the concrete flagstone floor with one foot. 'That makes sense.'

'Now I have no idea what you're talking about,' I said, genuinely confused.

'It's nothing to do with me,' he said, taking off his glasses and rubbing them on the hem of his T-shirt. 'And obviously I have no right to pry into your personal life, but I am a little surprised you chose to keep your relationship with him a secret from me. You've been very happy to talk about literally everything else, in the truest sense of the word.'

'I don't know what you're talking about,' I said, getting very, very close to my limit.

'Annie, I know everything about you,' he replied, almost smiling. 'From your place of birth and middle name to your preferred brand of sanitary protection and your feelings on every contestant to have ever appeared on something called *Love Island*.'

'It's not physically possible to watch it and not get involved,' I pouted. 'But what are you talking about, me and Charlie? There is no me and Charlie.'

'Annie, I have seen you together, you know, in the pub across the road. I've seen the way he looks at you. Not to mention this utterly inane bet. It might surprise you to know this, but I'm actually quite bright. He might as well be pulling your pigtails in the playground.' There was the unreadable expression in his eyes again. He took a step towards me and I took a step back, the stench of the bins overpowering his Samness. 'Tell me what's got you so upset.'

'I'm not upset,' I said, wiping away one stray tear. 'I'm not.'

'Annie,' he said softly, taking a step towards me. I took another step back and trod in something soft and squishy that didn't stand to be looked at. Don't be a rat, don't be a rat, don't be a rat. 'When I was upset, you told me I'd feel better if I talked about it.'

That was it, the final straw. Everything began to build up inside me, all at once and all I could see was red. Every late night, every early morning, all the almosts and the nearlys. The bank loan, the bet, the non-kiss, Matthew's engagement, clearing up after bloody Wellington and, on top of everything else, realizing I was in love, completely and utterly and undeniably in love with a man I had spent the best part of a month training to become the perfect boyfriend for someone else, only to discover he'd been perfect for me from the beginning.

'Fine, I'm fucking upset,' I exclaimed with a primal wail that sent the pigeons scattering in every direction. Sam stayed where he was, stalwart and true and very slightly frightened. 'I'm upset, I'm angry and I'm tired.

'I'm tired of everything being so difficult. I'm tired of having to work harder, of having to prove myself and never being allowed to make a mistake. I'm tired of other people getting the things I want and I'm tired of convincing myself I didn't want those things in the first place.'

'Then don't,' he replied, moving closer. This time there was nowhere for me to go unless I was prepared to dive into the wheelie bins. 'Tell me what you want.' I couldn't look up at him, couldn't meet his eyes.

'I can't,' I said, smiling at the absurdity of it all even as the tears began to fall. 'Because it would only make me feel more stupid and I already feel quite stupid enough.'

'Annie,' Sam murmured.

I held my breath as he said my name. Was this it? Was this our moment?

'You're not stupid, you're wonderful.'

Oh, oh, oh, oh. So what if Karine got her magical moment in front of millions of people at Wembley Stadium? I was more than happy to settle for out the back, behind the bins.

'And you're far too good for Charlie Wilder.'

I breathed out all at once in a heavy, angry sigh.

'I can't decide if you're being deliberately dense or you're truly this stupid,' I pushed him out of the way and knocking his book onto the filthy floor as I passed. Childish but satisfying. 'I'm glad you and Elaine are trying again, I'm glad all our hard work paid off. Good luck with it all, I think you're going to need it.'

If he said anything after that, I didn't wait to hear it.

CHAPTER TWENTY-SEVEN

Tuesday 31 July – Three Days to Go

After talking to Sam, I walked directly out of The Ginnel, down the street and did not stop until I got all the way home. On Tuesday, I did the unthinkable. I called in sick.

It was an odd situation, playing hooky from your own company. In theory, I had no one to answer to but myself, but it didn't stop the guilt. Curled up on my uncomfortable loveseat, having hacked off the one remaining leg, I was too weighed down by all the feels to move. Wellington and I were halfway through *Loose Women* when a knock at the door reminded me I hadn't even bothered to get dressed.

My heart began to flutter as I tiptoed over to the peephole, trying to make it across the floor without stepping on any of the creaky floorboards. I hadn't ordered anything, I wasn't expecting anyone, but what if it was him?

'Open the bloody door,' Miranda bellowed. 'I can hear you, I know you're home.'

It was not him.

'This might be a good time to remind you I've got a key,' she called. 'And I will use it if I have to. I'm not having that cat eating your face if anything really has happened to you.'

'I'm fine,' I muttered, opening the door and letting her and her hair into the flat. 'You didn't have to come over.'

'I know I didn't have to come over but still, here I am,' she said, waltzing through to the living room as Wellington made a dash for his preferred hiding place, under my armchair. 'Are you dying?'

'I had a migraine,' I said, rubbing my temple in what I hoped was a convincing fashion. 'I feel a bit better now. How about you?'

She nodded, poking at the pile of books on the floor with the toe of her boot. My phone was underneath a cushion where I couldn't see it. When it was in my hand, I couldn't help myself. The previous night had been a never-ending merry-go-round of Sam's Facebook page, Elaine's Instagram, Matthew's YouTube channel, Gordon Ossington's website. For the first time in my life, the internet had completely turned against me. The only safe place was in the pages of my books. It was so good of Charlotte Brontë not to interrupt every fifth page with a Facebook notification. St John likes your profile pic. Mr Rochester has poked you. Bertha is now broadcasting live from the attic.

'I'm fine now, never eating another one of my mother's culinary experiments.' Mir walked over to open a window. 'Annie, you do know your flat stinks of cat piss, don't you?'

'I do,' I confirmed, pulling a blanket round my shoulders. An outward expression of my inward despair. 'He's working through some separation anxiety.'

'Because you're holding him hostage?' she asked.

Two green eyes peered out from underneath the armchair, fully aware we were talking about him.

'To give him back, I'd have to speak to Sam and I really don't feel like doing that,' I replied, tightening my ponytail with an aggressive tug. 'Did we hear from SetPics?'

'We did not,' she replied. 'Don't think about it. A watched pot never boils and all that jazz.'

'Hmm,' I rubbed my dry, sore eyes with tightly balled fists. 'Do you think I should email Harry?'

Mir shook her head, stopped in front of the broken loveseat and settled down on the armchair instead. Wellington sniffed the back of her boots with great suspicion.

'I really don't think it'll make any difference,' she said, picking a cold Pot Noodle up from the table and giving it a cursory sniff. Nope, definitely past its best. 'If I had to guess, I'd say they invited us to pitch to make up the numbers. They were probably curious. I don't think they ever had any intention of giving us the job.'

'But they haven't said no yet,' I reminded her, snatching my breakfast/lunch/dinner out of her hand as she gagged. 'It could still happen.'

'Annie the optimist.' My best friend said with a smile as I draped my blanket over my head. 'I hope you're right. Now throw that nasty shit away before you get food poisoning as well.'

'As long as they don't give it to Gordon, I'll survive,' I replied, settling into my rut on the loveseat. I'd been sat there so long, I'd created quite the nice little dent for myself. 'If Oz gets the account, I might have to burn the building to the ground.'

'It's nice to see you've got a handle on your competitive nature,' Miranda clucked. 'How's that meditation app working out for you?'

'Deleted it,' I said, turning off the TV. 'Thanks for coming over.'

She pulled the long strap of her handbag over her head and dropped it on the floor and kicked off her boots. She was here to stay.

'What else was I going to do? Stomp around the office while you sulk in your pit of despair? Lame.' She automatically pulled out her phone and rested it on the arm of the chair. We were who we were. 'You've never, ever called in sick as long as I've known you. What happened yesterday?'

I was not going to cry. I was not going to cry. I was not going to cry.

'Nothing,' I said with a squeak.

'You talked to Sam then?'

I nodded, pressing my lips tightly together.

'And did you tell him how you feel?'

I shook my head, squeezing my eyes closed.

'Do you think that might be a good idea?' she asked. 'In that anything other than what's going on right now would be a good idea?'

I was not going to cry. I was not going to cry. I was not going to cry.

'He's back together with Elaine,' I wailed, hot tears pouring down my cheeks. 'So what's the point? I can't even be upset about it, Mir. I have been actively *trying* to get them back together and now it's the only thing I have successfully achieved in the last month. We're not going to win SetPics, we can't win the bet, we won't be able to pay Brian, the business is going to go under and I'm stupid in love with a man I can't have. I have fully shafted myself on this one.'

'You're in love with him?' She climbed out of the chair and crawled across the floor to bundle me up in a hug, my face pressed against her chest. 'I thought you just fancied the arse off him? Why didn't you tell me?'

'Because it's stupid,' I choked out in between heaving sobs. 'I'm stupid, he's stupid. It's all so stupid. I don't want to be in love with him, how did this even happen?'

'I know you're used to being in charge of everything but you don't always get a lot of say in this kind of stuff,' Mir said, stroking my hair as I tried to stop my ugly cry. 'What did you do last night?'

'I sat in the bath looking at my phone until it died,' I replied, gulping in big breaths. 'And then I listened to my power ballads Spotify playlist for about five hours. And then I lay in bed, staring at the ceiling until it got light and now you're here. I'm OK. I'll be over it tomorrow.'

'Yes, it sounds like you've got this completely under control,' Miranda said. 'Apart from how it sounds like the complete opposite of that. Annie, you've got to tell him how you feel.'

'But I can't,' I argued, wiping a sniffy nose on the sleeve of my pyjamas. 'Because he loves her. I don't want to put him in that position.'

Nor did I want to put myself in that position. The only thing worse than believing someone didn't love you was *knowing* they didn't love you.

'And what if he doesn't love her any more?' she suggested. 'What if he loves you?'

Shaking my head, I stretched out a hand, trying to

340

lure a reticent Wellington from his hiding place. He chirruped under the armchair before shuffling backward until all I could see were two, narrow green eyes trained relentlessly on Miranda. My little watch cat.

'He doesn't,' I replied, quite certain. 'He could never be with someone like me, he said it himself. We have nothing in common, he hates what I do for a living and it would never work. Ever. In a million years.'

'If that's all true, how come you're in love with him?' Miranda asked, stroking my head over the top of my blanket-shroud. I clutched the ends tightly together under my chin, like a considerably less virtuous Mother Theresa.

'Because I'm stupid,' I reminded her with tear-stained cheeks. 'Completely and utterly stupid. Finally found a challenge I couldn't win.'

Mir sighed and shuffled me along on the broken loveseat until we were both squished in, side-by-side, rib-to-rib.

'So you're just going to avoid him forever and never tell him how you feel?' she asked. I nodded. 'Can't say that's the best idea you've ever had.'

I closed my eyes and saw Sam in front of me in the courtyard. The look on his face, the hurt in his eyes, the sad slope of his shoulders.

'I don't know what to do,' I admitted at last. 'Why can't men be more like women? Why can they only see what's black and white and right in front of their face? You would know, wouldn't you, if I liked you? You have the basic mental and emotional functions necessary to put two and two together and come up with four, why hasn't he?'

Miranda's eyes almost rolled back in her head.

'If we're going to start on "what's wrong with men"

341

we're going to be here all day,' she groaned, yanking my blanket off my head. My hair frizzed up around my ears in a halo of static. 'But I will give you that Sam is a super-stubborn example. He spends far too much time locked up with books about dead white dudes for you to expect him to understand nuanced emotional behaviour. Human interaction kind of seems like a challenge for him, Annie, do you not remember how you met? He didn't even know his girlfriend was cheating on him. You didn't make this easy for yourself.'

'It's just so infuriating,' I said, shaking my fists in front of my face. 'It's a mystery to me how the human race has lasted this long, it really is. Stupid feelings.'

'Right but we still have to figure this out,' she reminded me gently. 'You've got to come back to work at some point and we can't make him move out of his office—'

'That's it!' I said, sitting up too quickly and hitting my head against one of her boobs. 'You can get Martin to kick him out. Not that I'd ever ask you to use your sexual powers for nefarious ends, but come on, Mir, what choice do we have?'

'I don't think he can cancel a lease as easily as that,' she replied, pulling her face into a frown. 'Or at least, I hope he can't. We should probably check our contract if he can.'

'You haven't even asked,' I said, sulking. 'What's the point in going out with your landlord if you can't bully him into evicting people?'

'We're still not officially going out,' Miranda said. I could tell by the way she stifled her smile she was stopping herself from talking about him. She sat on top of her excitement like it was a bomb about to go off. 'Anyway, back to Sam.'

'Anyway, back to Martin,' I countered. 'If you want me to ever believe in love again rather than superglue my vag shut, I'm going to need a reason. Tell me what's going on with you two immediately.'

'I don't know,' she said, the smile slowly painting itself all over her face. 'But he does want me to come over for dinner tonight, and I was with him practically all weekend, so whatever. I don't need to see him again, it's all a bit much. I'd rather stay here with you.'

If I was a grey, grubby blanket, Miranda was a rainbow. Everything about her was Technicolor, and even in my heartache, I was happy.

'Mir, you've been waiting six months for him to be a bit much,' I said, finding a smile for my friend. 'You absolutely do need to see him again.'

She covered her face with a cushion and gave a smothered squeal.

'I don't know,' she replied, still behind the cushion. 'Do you not think I'm rushing in? What if it's just shagging for him and I'm getting ahead of myself?'

'It's not shagging if it's dinner,' I said, snatching up the cushion and tossing it across the room, much to Wellington's dismay. 'He wants to cook food for you. On a weeknight. Like a proper boyfriend.'

'He's not definitely my boyfriend,' she said, fussing with one of the three different necklaces she was wearing. 'I don't think.'

'Maybe you'll know after dinner,' I said. The human race was truly hopeless. Sam didn't know what to say to Elaine, I didn't know what to say to Sam and Martin and Miranda didn't know what to say to each other. No wonder online dating was so popular. 'And maybe it's a good idea not to commit either way until we've seen what his cooking is like.'

Mir considered this for a second and then nodded.

'Can't be worse than mine. If he can boil an egg, he'll do.'

'And if he can poach an egg, propose,' I said, managing to muster up a happy hug even though it was hard to move at all, we were wedged so tightly into the loveseat. 'I'm serious though. You really don't have to stay here with me, I'm fine. I don't actually have a migraine.'

Miranda gasped. 'You don't say? Doesn't matter, you silly cow, I'm not going anywhere just yet. The business won't go under if we miss one day.'

'Or it might go under anyway,' I suggested brightly.

We both stared blankly into the middle distance and I felt my tears threatening again.

'I think I might have another bath,' I said.

'No way, you are not going to wallow around like a grumpy hippo,' she said, stroking her thumbs across my cheeks to wipe away the fresh tear tracks. 'Annie, I honestly don't think you were this upset when you broke up with Matthew. What is going on?'

I dug out my phone and swiped it into life. The photo Sam had taken of the two of us in Margate, standing with the seaside in the background lit up.

'Matthew was terrible and we all knew it,' I said, my words thick with feelings. 'Sam is something else. Sam is . . .'

Mir waited patiently while I searched for the right words.

'There's no one else like him,' I said finally. 'He's one in a million.'

All out of fight, I sank back against the cushions at my side just as Wellington slunk out from underneath the armchair and crept across the floor to leap up onto my lap. He purred madly, rubbing his head against my hand and kneading his paws on the edges of my blanket.

'You're far too fond of that cat, I can still totally smell where he pissed on the floor,' Mir said, picking up the remote and settling in. I smiled and scratched him between the ears. 'What's on telly?'

'Nothing?' I answered as she flicked through the channels.

'Perfect,' she said, pulling my blanket over my legs.

And for just a moment, even though it wasn't, it was.

CHAPTER TWENTY-EIGHT

Thursday, 2 August: One Day to Go

It was three days since I'd last seen or spoken to Dr Samuel Page. Three days and I was completely over it. That's if you consider 'over it' to mean creeping up the fire stairs at the crack of dawn and back down again on stroke of midnight to avoid him, and re-organizing the entire office so I could hide my desk behind a little den made out of filing cabinets. We'd even instated an official Dr Page drill. At the first sign of him entering the office, someone was to shout 'cheese-and-onion Pringles' and I would go to ground. I don't think the interns appreciated knowing that was Brian's safe word but still, so far, so good.

Not sleeping was playing havoc with my hair and my skin but it had really helped me put a dent in my to-watch, -read and -organize lists. Never had my Netflix queue looked so empty and my underwear drawer hadn't looked this good since I'd first filled it. On top of that, I was way ahead on all my work projects. Well, all of them except for one.

'The Surligner Cosmetics event that Lily is hosting is a week from today,' Zadie said, scanning her notes in our team meeting on Thursday morning. 'I've got RSVPs back from everyone, personalized pyjamas are all ordered, the printed tote bags are coming in tomorrow, I've got everyone's train tickets and except for Beauty by Bee, who is driving herself.'

'Lily hates Bee,' Mir said with a frown, scanning the guest list for the event. 'Did we invite her?'

'Lily doesn't hate Bee,' I corrected. 'Bee hates Lily. But Surligner really wanted her there and I've explained it to our gracious host so it's all OK. I've put them at opposite ends of everything, don't worry. They won't even have to breathe the same air if they don't want to. Have you invoiced Surligner?'

I realized I was actually shaking, waiting for the answer. Overnight stays for fifteen people at five-star countryside hotels did not come cheap. I really was on the wrong end of my own business.

'We've invoiced for half the fee and they've actually paid,' Mir nodded. Brian and I immediately high-fived. 'We'll invoice the rest when we get back.'

'I feel all funny and lightheaded.' I could barely believe someone had paid an invoice without so much as a threatening phone call. 'What's next?'

'Uh, the Hot Historian?' Zadie the intern read from the agenda on her iPad. Literally, her iPad. We'd offered her Brian's old one so she'd brought in her brand-new iPad Pro from home.

'Sorry, Annie, I meant to take that off,' Mir waved it away. 'What's after that?'

Everyone around the table looked anywhere but at me while I stared over at the whiteboard on the wall. The words 'Hot Historian' had been doctored to read

347

'Shit Shitstorian' which was very thoughtful but not especially helpful, and the numbers hadn't been updated since last week. It still said we had ten days left before the end of the bet. We didn't, we had one.

'It's OK,' I said, forcing strength I didn't feel into my voice. 'What numbers are we on?'

'Fifteen thousand,' Brian confirmed. 'Which is incredible, Annie. He's doing a roaring trade in Scandinavia.'

'Hotties before hygge,' Mir said, reviewing the stats. 'They love that freaking idiot. According to our Amazon affiliates link, we've sold more than fifteen hundred copies of his book.'

'That's insane,' I breathed, a tiny flash lighting up my heart as I imagined the look on his face when we told him. Only I couldn't see him so I couldn't tell him. 'So, we just need five thousand more Scandies to join Instagram in one day to win the bet.'

'Don't even think about it,' Miranda said, leaving no room for debate in her voice. 'It's a stupid bet, we're forgetting it ever happened. All Charlie's fault, really.'

'Fairly certain it's my fault to be honest,' I pointed out. 'I can't believe we're going to lose this thing.'

'You just need people to follow the account?' Zadie said, flicking up and down through what felt like thousands of photos of Sam on her iPad. 'You don't care who they are, you don't need them to do anything?'

'At this point, it's not a particularly targeted campaign, no,' I replied. 'The only rule is, we can't buy followers.'

'I could ask my friends to follow? And like, post about it?' she suggested.

'And I can put some new posts up, refresh the content,' Nat, our second intern, offered. 'Looks pretty straightforward to me. Hot dude, dumb fact, hey presto.'

I looked over at Miranda, who shrugged. 'Up to you,' she said. 'Otherwise I'm just as happy to drop Charlie Wilder into the Thames.'

'She's joking,' I assured them.

She shook her head, staring at them with threateningly wide eyes.

'She's not joking,' I muttered.

I bit down on my lip. Had I ever felt so conflicted? On one hand, I did not want to spend another second of my life scrolling through photos of Sam looking like a verifiable fittie but at the same time, the idea of letting go of one of my projects? Giving up control? Handing it over to *interns*? I didn't even like letting Miranda hold the remote of an evening.

'Chicks before dicks,' Miranda confirmed, slapping the table to end the meeting and making the decision for me. 'For the next twenty-four hours, you two are officially in charge of the Hot Historian account. If you get him up to twenty thousand followers by this time tomorrow, you get a prize.'

'The new iPhone?' Nat guessed feverishly.

'A French bulldog?' Zadie gasped.

'I was thinking a Kinder Egg, but who knows?' Mir gulped at the potential cost of their suggestions. 'But I think it would be easier to feed the five thousand than to win this thing at this point so, sure, whatever you want.'

'If we do need to make with the loaves and fishes, I've got a recipe for a lovely breaded lemon sole at home,' Brian said, checking the time on his phone. 'Can you manage the rest of the meeting without me? I've got a meeting with Coast in half an hour.'

'You can all go,' Mir waved them away. 'We'll finish up. Thanks, guys.'

Zadie and Nat followed Brian out the meeting room, leaving us alone with our bottom line.

'We're going to have to manage without him for more than the team meeting if we don't sort this out sooner rather than later,' I said, sifting through our outstanding invoices. 'If things don't change in the next twenty-four hours, it's a choice between paying Brian at the end of the month or paying the rent.'

'What if we don't pay us?' she asked, hopeful as ever.

'That's already assuming we don't pay us,' I replied. 'If you want to take home a salary as well, you'll be working on your own, in the street. I've gone over the books so many times, we're owed so much money. How is this possible?'

'It's possible because we need bigger clients with deeper pockets,' she said, turning my computer screen so she could see. 'They can't give us what they don't have and we shouldn't have spent what wasn't in the bank.'

'It's not like we pissed it up the wall on caviar and champagne,' I said, pressing my fingers into my temples hard. 'It went on wages and rent. I know it's early days but is there any chance you could marry Martin and become our landlady before the end of the month?'

'No,' she replied. 'Because my life isn't a Jane Austen novel.'

'Well, at least you won't die of consumption,' I sighed. 'I suppose there's still a chance the SetPics job could happen?'

'There's a chance,' she agreed. 'But it's not money we can rely on. Even if we got the gig, they wouldn't be paying us for a while yet.'

'Right then, it's threatening phone call time,' I said, rolling up my sleeves. 'Do you want to go first, or shall I? Or I could pay some people a visit in person, I think I look more frightening than I sound at the moment.'

'Tell you what,' she said, closing my laptop and almost taking my fingers off in the process. 'Let's save that for tomorrow when we're hungover. We'll be that much more monstrous. Let's bin the rest of the day and fancy ourselves up for the awards tonight. If this all goes tits-up in six months, I want to go out with a bang. It's "go big or go home" time.'

'I can go home?' I asked, yearning for my miserable pit and my sad woman's blanket and Sam's incontinent cat.

'You know what I mean,' Miranda said sternly. 'You need an MOT, my love. Nails, hair, makeup, the whole lot. Do you even know what you're wearing tonight?'

I shook my head, stretching my arms to not-so-covertly sniff the pits of my T-shirt only to catch the eye of three people waiting outside to use the shared meeting room.

'Can't I just go like this?'

'Annie, I didn't want to be the one to tell you,' she said reached across the table, taking both of my hands in hers. 'But you've become the female version of pre-makeover Dr Page. And it's not pretty.'

I turned my eyes towards my ghostly reflection in the meeting room window. Lack of sleep had left me tired and drawn, my skin was genuinely grey and I'd taken gender-neutral dressing to a very dark place. While I'd always enjoyed a Mark Zuckerberg-inspired work wardrobe, my outfits were always smart and at least marginally cute. Cool jeans, cute shirts, fun tees, the odd funky dress to mix things up. But not today.

My skinny jeans had gone baggy at the arse and the knees and my once-white T-shirt looked like it had come out of the lost-and-found in a particularly rough A&E department. It wasn't even worth getting into what was going on with my hair because I had no idea.

'Where did I even get this?' I asked pulling on the material, trying to remember. 'Christ on a bike, I'm a mess.'

'You are,' Miranda agreed. 'But we can fix it. Cinders, you shall go to the ball.'

'The only thing is, Cinders wanted to go to the ball,' I said, swinging my limp ponytail over my shoulder. 'And I'd rather stay home and work. Why are all those princesses such extroverts? They always say they want to be cuddled up with a good book, but that never stopped them swanking along to every possible party in the kingdom, did it? Everyone would have been saved a lot of hassle if they'd paid attention to their parents and stayed at home.'

Miranda stood up and gestured for me to do the same.

'Enough's enough, Higgins. I want no more sulking from you today. We need to put our best foot forward tonight; it's not just a party, it's work. Lots of potential clients, lots of potential mon-ay. I want you shiny and bright and working it like the rent is due on Monday. Because it is.'

'Maybe you could just put me in a bin bag and keep me under the table,' I said, reluctantly rising to my feet and letting her march me out of the meeting room. I nodded politely at the people waiting to go in. They all recoiled in terror, hustling around each other to avoid touching me. Things were even worse than I realised. 'Save some time and energy.'

'You're not beyond saving just yet,' Mir promised.

'But you're close. Come on, we don't have any meetings this afternoon, no one's going to be doing any work anywhere else because they're all going to the thing tonight. Please, for once in your life, do as you're told, Higgins.'

'Yes, Miranda,' I said with a sigh. 'Whatever you say, Miranda.'

'That's my girl,' she said, slapping me on the arse as we went.

In our office, a long white envelope with my name written in elegant script was waiting for me on my desk.

'What's this?' I asked, holding it in the air and waving it like I really did care. 'Who left it?'

Brian and the interns all shrugged, clueless, while Miranda busily tapped away at her phone.

'None of us,' Brian reasoned. 'Nice handwriting.'

My face fell. I gave it a sniff and then held it in front of my face, eyes clouding over with unwelcome tears.

'Hand it over.' Brian jumped up from his desk and sprinted around the filing cabinets to snatch the letter out of my hand. 'That sneaky bastard, he must have brought it in while we were in the meeting.'

'Why wouldn't he email you, like a normal person?' Miranda asked, joining Brian to carefully examine the outside of the envelope. There wasn't much to see, just the word 'Annie' written on the front. The back had been sealed.

'Because he isn't a normal person,' I replied, numb from head to toe.

'Can I open it?' Brian asked.

'No,' I said, snatching it back. 'No one is reading it.'

Holding it made the tips of my fingers fizz.

Sam had written me a letter.

When was the last time anyone had written me a letter? Not counting the note my neighbour shoved under my door the morning after our dance party. That only had two words on it and neither of them were pleasant, so I wasn't sure it counted.

Was he upset, did he miss me? Perhaps he'd realized the error of his ways and he was running away to join the French Foreign Legion. If there was still a French Foreign Legion. That was something to Google later. Or maybe the letter was from Elaine, who had more than likely realized I had a massive crush on her boyfriend, even if he hadn't. In any case, the odds of it being a longer version of the note from my neighbours far outweighed the possibility of a handwritten declaration of love. While it was still safely in its envelope, it was full of possibilities. Once I tore it open, there was a real chance it was only full of goodbyes.

'You're not reading it?' Mir asked. Zadie and Nat busied themselves at their desks, pretending not to listen while whizzing loaded looks at each other over the tops of their computers.

'I can't,' I said, swallowing a lump the size of a dinosaur egg. 'I need a minute.'

'Well, you don't have a minute,' Miranda said, pinching the letter out from between my fingertips and tucking it away in her handbag. 'I just texted my mate down at Hershesons, we've got to leave right now if they're going to fit us in.'

'You're worth it,' Brian whispered as he bundled me up in a quick hug. 'Fuck him, Annie.'

'We'll see you at the Haighton Hotel at seven,' Mir shouted. 'Black tie, clean shoes, brush your hair. And everyone on time, please.'

Everyone called out their promises, hollering with excitement as we left, completely unaware we could all be out of a job in less than a month. Meanwhile I traipsed along behind Miranda, thinking about nothing other than the crumpled white envelope peeping out the top of her handbag.

The candlelit ballroom of the Haighton Hotel was full of people by the time we arrived. Everyone was hugging, shaking hands, raising their glasses and generally pretending they didn't spend five days out of every seven desperately trying to run each other out of business. It was only four weeks since we'd found out we were nominated for our TechBubble awards but it might as well have been a lifetime ago. I glanced around, looking for familiar faces and fighting the urge to do a Cinders. It was only seven o'clock, I realized, plenty of time to be home and in bed by midnight.

All around us, people had polished themselves up spectacularly. There wasn't a single hoodie or pair of Converse to be seen. There was still a pretence of professionalism but it was early – a work awards do was basically a wedding reception without the bride or groom. I had yet to attend a single event like this that didn't tick off at least three items on the Formal Function bingo card – shagging in the toilets, puking in a plant pot, crying on the boss, a regrettable resignation or, my personal favourite, proper drunken fisticuffs.

'Annie!' Brian grabbed my hands and held them out in front of me before spinning me around on unsteady high heels. 'You look amazing.'

'Thank you,' I said, tossing my carefully arranged casual curls over my shoulder before immediately putting them back where I had found them. It was unlikely I would ever look this good again; I didn't want to cock it up before the evening even started. 'You scrub up all right yourself.'

'Please,' he said, dusting his own shoulder. 'I always look amazing. But you should live in that dress. Who knew you had such nice tits?'

'Me?' I replied, looking down. Miranda had put herself in charge of my wardrobe while I was getting my hair done and raided the showrooms of a PR buddy. She chose a black silk dress printed with beautiful red roses, something I would never, ever have picked for myself and quite frankly could in no way afford. From the second I'd slipped it over my head, I was in love. I was also under strict orders to only drink clear liquids for the duration of the evening. The V-neck of the dress was held up by delicate double spaghetti straps that ran over my shoulders all the way down my bare back to meet the nipped-in waist, and the skirt poufed out with a romantic ballgown silhou-ette, ending a little bit above my ankles to show off my simple black sandals. Through some feat of spec-tacular engineering, the slender straps held up my boobs without a bra, even when I gave them a proper shake in the privacy of the office toilets. Even if I did say so myself, I looked really, really nice. My dad always said you had to dress for the job you want. According to this dress, I wanted to be Meghan Markle. And actually, I did so that was perfect.

'You smell nice,' I said, giving Brian a sniff as we pushed our way through the crowds to find our tiny table right at the back of the room. 'What cologne is that?'

'I ran out so I sprayed some Febreze in the air and just ran around in it,' he whispered back. 'Tell no one.'

'It goes to my grave,' I replied, pulling out a chair at our table.

'Are you ready for some good news?' Mir asked, hurrying over from the bar. Her kohl-lined eyes were wild and bright and even in the dim lighting of the ballroom, her silver dress shone. Zadie and Nat stood behind her, awkward in their semi-formalwear, both clutching their phones in one hand, a Diet Coke in the other.

'Zadie got Buzzfeed to feature Sam's Instagram and their tweet has been retweeted six thousand times already,' Miranda said, waving her own phone right in front of my face. 'He's got two thousand more followers!'

'You're kidding me?' I grabbed the phone out of her hand and tried to focus. There it was, the Top Ten Facts from the Hot Historian. And there was our follower count – seventeen thousand. 'Zadie, you did this?'

'I sent it to my friend, she's an intern at Buzzfeed,' she nodded, seemingly unaware of how amazing her achievement was. 'She's always looking for stuff like this.'

'And I got my cousin at Instagram to put it on the main search page,' Nat offhandedly added. 'They won't be able to do it every time, but now and then, it's cool. Except for how I have to dog sit for him when he goes to Ibiza at the end of the month.'

'Nat, that's amazing,' I said, clicking through the slideshow.

'Yah, I guess it's a pretty good dog,' she said. 'He's a puggle. He has his own YouTube channel.'

'Well, I meant the Instagram thing, but that's pretty great too,' I replied. Every time I went back to Sam's profile page, the numbers just kept going up and up. 'This is so, so incredible.'

They looked at each other, shrugged and sat down.

'Oh, and a man called from *This Morning* wanting to know if the fittie in the photos was doing TV appearances. I said I'd let them know,' Nat added. 'I have always wanted to go on *This Morning*. Can I go with him, please?'

I looked at Miranda to check I hadn't gone mad but she was too busy staring at the girls with her mouth hanging open.

'French Bulldogs and iPhones for everyone,' I shrieked, throwing my hands in the air. 'And hands up who wants to spend the weekend at Disneyland?'

'Even if we win the bet, I say we sack Brian and give these two a job immediately,' Miranda whispered as everyone put up their hands.

'We'll talk about that tomorrow,' I said, stuck on the last picture in the slideshow, one of Zadie's latest posts. It was one of the first shots we'd taken of Sam, right after Coast cut his hair and Brian dressed him up and he was still that weirdo from down the corridor, only with a better haircut. Before I knew him. Before I loved him. I closed my eyes, concentrated on my deep, calming breaths.

'I'm ordering champagne,' Miranda announced, snatching her phone out of my hand. 'The company card can take it for one night,' she promised. 'Although, if it gets declined, are you able to run in those heels?' She threw me a wink as she headed to the bar.

'Annie?' I was still standing by the table with my eyes closed when I heard someone say my name. I opened one eye slowly and saw Harry from SetPics, all suited and booted in his tuxedo, smiling my way. 'I thought that was you.'

He leaned in for the obligatory double-cheek kiss

and I slipped the phone back into Miranda's bag, only to notice the crumpled white envelope nestling next to her lip gloss, credit cards and house keys.

'Sorry it's taking so long to get back to you on the *Uniteam* pitch,' he said, glancing over my shoulder at the rest of my table. 'Do you have a moment to talk?'

I nodded, and followed him away from the table. I didn't want to cry in front of my team. Again.

'I'll be straight with you,' he said, propping himself up on the back of a chair and folding his arms high on his chest. 'We liked your pitch a lot but we're not going to give Content the job.'

The universe gaveth and the universe taketh away.

'Feels as though that could have waited until tomorrow,' I replied as my stomach fell through my tasteful sandals, through the floor and through to the centre of the Earth. I wanted to argue, I wanted to fight but this wasn't the time or place. 'Can we discuss this later?'

When I was least expecting it, Harry smiled.

'Content is too small, the company isn't big enough to manage the account,' he said. I frowned, there was nothing like negging a girl's beloved company to convince her to crack a bottle over your head. 'But we were impressed with you. I want to offer you a job.'

Clearly I hadn't heard him correctly.

'I want to offer you a job at SetPics,' he repeated, grinning from ear to ear. 'Head of UK digital marketing. Reporting to me, complete control over all our properties. Interested?'

'I don't know what to say,' I said, very much wishing I was wearing something else. It was hard to have a serious conversation when your heels were so high you could see his bald spot.

'You're good, Annie. You're ambitious and talented,' Harry said. 'And this is a big job for an exceptional person. Content could grow, in time, but it could also disappear like so many other start-ups. I'd hate to see someone like you wasted.'

I looked down to see my hands were trembling. Also that I was revealing altogether too much cleavage for this conversation.

'I don't need an answer right now,' he said. The chair he was leaning against wobbled slightly and he threw out his arms to maintain his balance before turning his slip-up into a shot with the finger guns. So slick. 'I wanted to speak to you before things got crazy. Whether you win or not, I want you to know, we at SetPics know your worth. Give me a call tomorrow, we'll talk.'

He stood up, straightened his bow tie and walked straight over to the Oz table to shake hands with Gordon Ossington, leaving me standing and sweating in my nice dress. I couldn't leave Content. I would never leave Content. Even if we weren't doing so well and might all be out of a job in six months anyway. No, it was my baby and mothers never left their babies. Except this was a huge opportunity. I would never have dreamed of getting a job this big before we started our little company. Head of digital marketing. Corner office, squishy sofa, minions upon minions upon minions. I'd even heard a rumour they had a hot tub and executive ball pool in their basement . . .

'Earth to Higgins?'

I spun around to see Miranda brandishing a bottle at the head of the table.

'Are you with us?' she asked.

'Yes,' I nodded in response. No, I wouldn't even

consider it. I could buy a paddling pool on the weekend and get myself down the Harvester if I wanted a ball pool that badly. 'One hundred per cent. Now where's that champagne? I thought we were celebrating.'

We didn't win campaign of the year or best boutique agency, so by the time they were ready to announce best new agency, everyone at the table was properly sloshed. Everyone but me. Try as I might, I couldn't stop thinking about Harry's offer. Not that it was even a real offer. Not that he'd put money on the table or a job description or anything.

I pasted a smile on my face and laughed along with the rest of the table. Brian's boyfriend Rob had made an appearance and Miranda was feverishly tapping away at her phone with a look on her face that let me know she was only texting one possible person.

'What's Martin up to tonight?' I asked.

She looked up suddenly, as though she'd been caught out.

'Tell him to come,' I said as a grin found its way onto her face. 'He should be here.'

'He's on his way,' she said, biting her lip. 'You sure you don't mind?'

'Your boyfriend should be here,' I said pointedly. 'I'm glad.'

And I was. For her. For one night at least, everyone should be happy and with the people they loved. Even Zadie and Nat seemed satisfied, constantly streaming every second of their evening on Instagram stories.

My phone buzzed on the table and I snatched it up before anyone could see who had sent the message.

Good luck tonight, luv Dad & G xoxo

There was no way my dad had sent that message, I realized, putting it down without answering. Becks was right, I had to be nicer to Gina. After all, she had to put up with Dad all the time, she did not have an easy life.

Out of the corner of my eye, I saw Sam's letter, peeking out of Miranda's little handbag as it swung from the corner of her chair, probably thinking I would drunkenly demand to read it once I'd had a couple. She knew me so well. Only I had no intention of waiting a second longer.

I flexed my fingers, ready to make the pinch but instead, I saw something far more troubling than a letter from Sam. Gordon Ossington was making a beeline for our table, beaming from ear to ear. I looked all around, trying to work out the quickest way to the lavs, but every route was blocked with people.

With no better option, I grabbed the bottle of champagne from the ice bucket, slid out of my seat and disappeared underneath the table. Thanking the sartorial gods for everyone's decision to wear knickers, I nursed the bottle and made myself comfortable, surrounded by a circle of crossed legs and shiny shoes. Miranda's heels were off her feet and under her chair, while I noticed with not a small amount of curiosity that Nat was actually wearing two mismatched black stilettos. I wondered whether or not it was on purpose.

With a swig out of the bottle of Veuve Clicquot, I made myself as comfortable as possible, preparing to wait Gordon out. It was actually quite nice under the table. Five minutes off from forcing a fake smile and laughing at another of the host's terrible jokes. Besides, I'd already eaten everything on offer, we hadn't won anything and my feet were killing me. What was the point in hanging around?

'Good evening, Content London.'

Somewhere above me, I heard Gordon's insufferable, nasal voice.

'Don't let him see me, don't let him see me, don't let him see me,' I whispered into my bottle of bubbles.

'Bad luck tonight,' he said. 'Just wanted to stop by and make sure you weren't too disappointed. You're only babies, you've got time.'

'I'm a thirty-year-old grown woman and I'm at least a foot taller than you,' Miranda replied. 'Also, I don't remember seeing you up on stage.'

I raised a silent toast to her from my hiding place. Have that, you bastard.

'We were robbed,' he answered smoothly. 'I'm sure we'll make up for it next year when we enter the *Uniteam* campaign.'

'We'll see,' Miranda replied. 'Aren't you a bit old for this one-upmanship?'

'He's nearly fifty,' I muttered to no one. 'He lies about his age but I've seen his passport.'

'Please give my condolences to Annie,' he said. 'I always thought she'd do well for herself. Maybe she still will. After Content.'

I watched his footsteps retreat to his own table and concentrated my rage into drinking as much champagne as possible without hiccupping. The man was bulletproof. It didn't matter what anyone said or did, it all rolled off him like water off a duck's back. As much as I hated to admit it, perhaps that was something I could stand to learn from him.

And then I saw it again. A tempting glimpse of a white square, peeking out of Miranda's open bag. I crawled over on my hands and knees, keeping as far away as I could from my friend's bare legs and tugged at the envelope, inching it out until it was free from the bag and safely in my hands.

I crossed my legs and spread my skirt out all around me, crouching low, and carefully, carefully opening the envelope without tearing the paper.

Annie.

I saw his handwriting and heard his voice and the room went silent.

While I am not sure what I've done to upset you so much that you will not see me or speak to me, whatever it is, please believe I am deeply sorry. Although we have only known each other for a short time, you have become very dear to me and I feel your absence greatly.

'Who writes like this?' I whispered to myself.
It was fantastic and I loved it.

One possible reason comes to mind and even though it seems utterly absurd, the possibility persists. Even though it causes me great discomfort to even suggest it, you have already made it quite clear that you want no more to do with me and so, I stand here with nothing left to lose.

Might it be possible, Annie, that you have developed feelings for me?

I gulped and took another shot of champagne.

It seems so very unlikely that someone like you could ever feel any kind of romantic affection for someone like me, but since the thought entered my mind, I cannot stop myself from wondering whether or not it could be true. My dearest Annie. In the words of the great American poet, Britney Spears, don't let me be the last to know. You were there for me when I didn't even know I needed someone. When others wanted me to change, you showed me all I needed was to be myself. And, as I must at last admit, a haircut.

I turned the empty bottle upside down and groaned. This was a fine time for the champagne to run dry.

I am sorry for my rudeness when we first met and, more than anything, I'm sorry I did not have the courage to tell you how much I truly, truly adore you.
   Annie Higgins, I miss you.
   Always,
   Your Sam

I read the letter over again, one more time, pinching the tender skin on the inside of my arm to make sure I was dreaming and hadn't gone mad. He adored me. He said he adored me.

Well, that did it.

Clambering onto all fours, I crawled out from underneath the table, pushing over my chair in the rush to get out.

'Annie?' Miranda exclaimed, jumping up out of her seat. 'How long have you been under there?'

'And, more to the point, what were you doing under there?' Brian asked. 'You can't be too careful these days. Lurking around under tables like that will get you in trouble.'

'I've got to go, I've got to find him,' I said to Miranda, waving the letter in front of her face. 'I need to leave, I'm sorry.'

'Leave?' she grabbed my arms to calm me down as the people closest turned our way. I was vaguely aware of someone talking on stage, of the tables around us, but none of it mattered. I was in love and I was drunk. 'Babe, what are you talking about?'

'Sam!' I said, waving the letter over my head like a white flag. 'The letter from Sam. I've got to talk to him now, while my hair still looks nice.'

'You can't go,' Miranda insisted, grabbing my empty hand and pulling me down next to her. 'It's our last chance.'

On the stage, I realized the host was holding an envelope of his own. I reluctantly paid attention, this was it, the last award.

'And the TechBubble best new digital agency award goes to . . . Content London!'

'Annie!' Miranda shrieked, pulling me up and leading me through the tables. 'We won!'

The lights grew brighter as we neared the stage. Brian, Nat and Zadie all swarmed around us, carrying me along on a wave as the whole room applauded. Almost the whole room. I had to assume Gordon Ossington wasn't exactly bringing the house down. All around the room, various Content clients were displayed on the big screens in real time – Dashell's first fashion collection, Lily's latest YouTube video, a selection of Coast's Snapchat shots. It was real. We'd really, really won. Somehow, I made it up the stairs as the music played and someone handed me a huge block of glass with our company name engraved into the base. Best new digital agency.

The host, some C-list celebrity I vaguely recognized from a BBC 2 quiz show, patted me on the back. I stared at the award, our award, for a second, blinking as a blinding spotlight shone right into my eyes. Barely able to take in what was happening, I realized I was still holding Sam's letter. Through the glass, I could see his handwriting, magnified in my hand. The letter. The most important thing. Someone put a microphone in front of Miranda and the deafening music died down, leaving the two of us in the spotlight while Brian cheered and danced behind us. Even Nat and Zadie, hovering at his side, looked genuinely excited.

'Thank you so much,' I heard Miranda say as I passed the trophy to Brian who immediately started using it to do goblet squats. 'Content London has been such an exciting journey for us and we can't thank you enough for recognizing all our hard work. Obviously, none of this would have been possible without my amazing best friend and business partner, Annie Higgins, who I love and am grateful for every single moment of every single day. Annie, do you want to say a few words?'

A tearful Miranda thrust the mic under my nose.

'Thank you?' I said.

I could hear people laughing – with me, I hoped.

'This is wonderful,' I said, picking out familiar faces that weren't washed out by spotlights. Harry, smiling, Gordon, fuming, and Martin and Charlie whooping loudly at the back of the room. 'Everything Miranda said. We very much appreciate this but, um, I have to go and see a man about a cat.'

'Wait!' Miranda yelled, pulling me aside. 'Where are you going?'

'Sam,' I said, waving the letter in front of her face. 'I have to go and find Sam.'

'Annie, no, wait! Look!'

Scrambling off the stage as fast as my high heels would carry me, I followed her gaze towards the back of the room. Why was it so much harder to get down stairs in heels than it was to get up? Behind Martin and Charlie was another face I recognized. Dr Samuel Page. Black dinner jacket, bright white shirt, crimson cheeks.

'I told him to come,' Miranda confessed, holding me up before I could faint away with surprise. 'While you were getting your hair done. I called him and told him to get his arse over here and talk to you. I didn't know if he'd come, so I didn't say anything.'

'But you didn't know what was in his letter?' I said, my heart in my throat. Thank God this dress was sleeveless, the last thing this moment needed was sweat patches.

'I took a punt.' She stood in between me and whatever came next, smoothing my hair out of my eyes and wiping a fleck of mascara off my cheek. 'Felt like the safest bet I've made in a long time.'

'You're amazing,' I said, meeting her brown eyes and seeing nothing but love. 'Thank you so much.'

'Go get him, tiger,' she whispered, kissing me on the cheek.

I walked around the edge of the room, so aware that everyone was watching but only caring about one pair of eyes. Sam came towards me, Charlie and Martin hanging back by our table, Charlie resting his chin on Martin's shoulder and throwing me a thumbs up.

'Hello,' I said, not knowing whether to laugh or cry.

'Hello,' he said, brushing his curls out of his eyes.

He was clean-shaven and his dimple was very much in evidence.

'I got your letter,' I showed him the crumpled piece of paper in my hand. He took it and began to smooth it out.

'This is why you can't have nice things,' he muttered, folding it back into three perfect pieces. 'You don't look after them.'

'I don't really want to ask,' I said, biting my lip. 'But what about Elaine?'

'There is no Elaine,' Sam replied. 'Not any more.'

'Oh my god,' I gasped, looking around to see who might have heard him. 'What did you do?'

'She's not dead,' he said, sighing at my reaction. 'We ended things. Properly this time. You were right, we aren't suited any more and I was just too afraid to face the facts. Besides, she isn't the person I want to be with. Annie.'

'Right,' I said, stepping closer to him, pulling him out of the spotlights and into the shadows. 'And at the risk of being a bit forward, who do you think that might be?'

'And you say I'm the one who's obtuse,' he replied, leaning down as I pushed up onto my tiptoes, my arms circling his neck as his hands circled my waist and—

'What is that?' Sam said, jerking his head away from me.

'What's what?' I asked with an expectant pout.

I turned around to see every screen in the room, covered in photographs of Sam. Or rather, the Hot Historian. I looked back at Sam to see an expression I'd hoped had been retired.

'Annie,' he demanded, pushing his glasses up his nose. 'What the bloody hell is going on?'

CHAPTER TWENTY-NINE

'What's that?' Sam asked. 'Why is there a picture of me on the screen?'

'Nothing,' I said, trying to get in between him and the monitors. But it wasn't possible, they were everywhere. 'Ignore it.'

'Ignore my face plastered all over this room full of strangers?' he countered.

'OK, the thing is . . .' I started to talk but when Sam looked back at me, I opened my mouth and nothing came out. 'Can we talk about this somewhere else?'

'You promised you wouldn't use any photos of me,' he said, his voice getting louder as the photos kept on scrolling. Sam on the beach, Sam dancing, Sam sat in our office, Sam walking down the street. It was like they'd pulled up the beloved family album of an actual stalker.

'I didn't!' I replied. He looked back at me, utterly bewildered. 'At first. And then I did.'

'I don't understand,' Sam said. 'Was this the plan all along? To drag me out here and make me a laughing stock?'

'No!' I insisted, scrabbling for an explanation that would take that awful, hurt look off his face. 'Not at all. The other pictures weren't working and we had all these great photos of you, and you and I weren't talking so I thought why not and—'

'We weren't not talking, you weren't talking to me,' he reminded me in a low but unmistakably angry voice. 'I can't believe this, Annie. The whole thing has simply been one big joke to you.'

Everything stopped and I felt my heart seizing up in my chest.

'I don't think you're a joke,' I said, grabbing hold of his hands, desperately trying to make him understand. 'Sam, I think you're everything.'

He paused for a moment, staring deep into my eyes and as I searched for the right words, the words that would make him laugh and smile and stay. Over his shoulder, I saw the follower number on his account: We had hit twenty thousand, we'd won the bet. And it meant nothing.

'Your letter was beautiful,' I said, holding it aloft, trying to remind him how he had felt not so long ago. If he didn't believe my words, perhaps he could at least believe his own.

'I am very, very sorry I came here tonight,' he said. 'For a man who supposedly knows so much about history, all I seem to do is repeat it.'

And then he left.

CHAPTER THIRTY

Friday, 3 August: Deadline Day

Reports show that the average person checks their phone eighty-five times a day but after Sam walked out of the Haighton Hotel ballroom, I must have checked mine eighty-five times a minute.

Miranda, Martin, Brian and Charlie closed ranks around me as I watched Sam leave, never once slowing down or never once looking back. I called and I called and I called but it went to voicemail every time. All my text messages went unread. My Facebook friend request was dismissed and I was blocked. When we got back to my flat, we found Aggy on my doorstep, stony-faced and ready to collect Wellington. Miranda herded him into the cat carrier Aggy brought with him while I locked myself in the bathroom and cried. When we got to The Ginnel the next morning, the door to Sam's office was closed, a padlock hanging from the door and his nameplate removed.

'Annie, I'm so sorry,' Zadie said, nervously playing

with the arm of her enormous glasses as I floated over to my desk. 'Someone from TechBubble called on Monday and asked for a list of Content's clients. I didn't know I wasn't supposed to send Sam's stuff.'

'It's not your fault,' I assured her, even though my heart was breaking at the thought of me taking that phone call instead. 'Who knows? It might have been a factor in us winning the award.'

'His account is doing spectacularly well,' Miranda said, resting her bum on the edge of my chair and stroking my head. 'I'm so sorry, babe.'

'It's still up?' I asked from inside my jumper, bundled up against the beautiful day in sloppy, unseasonable layers. If I had to turn up the air conditioning, I would do it. No one should have to be this unhappy in nice weather. 'Take it down. Delete it.'

'But Annie, he's got nearly thirty thousand followers,' Brian said, turning his phone screen to face me, trying to obscure everything but the numbers at the top with his hands. And yet, all I saw was Sam peeking out at me from between his fingers. 'He's a phenomenon. Everyone's been in touch, BBC, ITV, Channel Four, Sky. YouTube called this morning. YouTube. Called. Us. They want to talk to us about developing an online history show with him. And his book sales are through the roof. You can't mean it?'

I pushed my hair up off my face, fastening last night's curls in a terrible topknot and glared across the office.

'I'll delete his account then,' he said grimly, turning his screen back around.

I stared out of the window, vaguely hearing all the noise around me as Martin walked through the door, weighed down by a giant white cardboard box.

'Doughnut delivery,' he said, laying them on my table and popping a quick kiss on Miranda's cheek.

'They smell so good,' Mir replied, immediately digging into the box. 'You shouldn't have.'

'I didn't,' Martin said, handing her a small gift card. 'They're from SetPics.'

My ears pricked up at once. SetPics. Harry. Oh god, the job.

'They're from Harry,' Miranda read, eyes sparkling. 'It says congratulations on the win last night, nothing about our pitch. It looks good though, doesn't it? They must be impressed by us? They wouldn't send doughnuts if they weren't at least considering us.'

'Maybe,' I said, recalling my conversation with Harry. I watched the team descend on the box of sweet treats and felt a new pang of guilt. Oh good, just when I thought I couldn't feel any worse.

'Knock, knock.'

Wherever Martin went, Charlie was never far behind.

'Congratulations, Content London.' He raised his coffee cup towards me in a toast with an awkward smile. We hadn't really spoken since the world's worst kiss but he'd seen everything at the party and I was sure Martin and Miranda had filled him in by now. 'Very well deserved.'

'And congratulations on winning the bet,' Martin said, nodding at the whiteboard on the wall. 'Thirty days, twenty thousand followers. You did it.'

'Twenty-eight thousand, four hundred and sixteen, as of just now,' Miranda said through a mouthful. 'Not that it matters, only I want to make sure you two know how badly we trounced you.'

Charlie hid a smile behind his coffee while Martin mooned in her general direction. The man was done for.

'Thank you,' I said, tightening the strings on my hoodie until I began to choke. 'But we have to delete the account. So technically, we're back down to zero.'

'No way,' Charlie said. He set down his coffee and wiped out the numbers on the whiteboard, replacing it with the words 'Content Wins'. It was the first time in my life I wasn't excited to see those words. 'You one hundred per cent won. When I'm wrong, I say I'm wrong. You did it, Professor Higgins. Now, what pizza am I getting in?'

'Don't feel much like a don at the moment,' I mumbled, searching for some spark of satisfaction. I'd won a bet even I thought was unwinnable. I'd been offered a huge and powerful job. But I felt nothing. Who even was I?

'I might pop upstairs for a bit,' I said, picking up Miranda's sunglasses and digging my handbag out from underneath my desk. 'Get a bit of fresh air.'

'Want me to come with?' Mir asked. I shook my head and waved for her to sit back down.

'I won't be long,' I said. 'Save me a doughnut.'

'I'm promising nothing,' Brian shouted as I went.

The rooftop was empty. It was only eleven, no one was up for lunch yet so there were only the pigeons to keep me company.

I settled in on the comfy sofa, staring at the space where the TV screen had been thirty days earlier. A whole month ago. Really, when you thought about it, what had changed? Nothing. We didn't have the SetPics job and I didn't have a friend called Dr Samuel Page. The only difference was, instead of not knowing he existed, every fibre of my being missed him. I missed his voice, I missed his smell, I missed the way he pushed his glasses up his nose whenever he was nervous. You could delete an Instagram account or block someone on Facebook, but how did you turn off a feeling? I couldn't forget him any more than I could forget the lyrics to my favourite song. For the last thirty days, he'd been on repeat in the background, even when I wasn't paying attention and now I couldn't get him out of my head. All I wanted was to feel like myself again.

Picking up my phone, I scrolled through my emails until I found the number I was looking for.

'Harry Francis.'

'Harry, it's Annie from Content,' I said, grinding up an abandoned cigarette butt with the tip of my trainers. There was no smoking at The Ginnel, Martin would go spare if he saw it. 'How are you?'

'Bit worse for wear,' he replied, laughing. 'And yourself?'

'Same,' I admitted, pinching myself as I spoke. Was I really going to do this? 'Thank you so much for sending over the doughnuts, you really didn't have to do that.'

'Happy to, happy to.' I could tell he was keen to cut to the chase. 'Did you really call to say thank you or were you wanting to follow up on the conversation we had last night?'

'Well, yes,' I said, straightening up. This wasn't a hunched over, feeling sorry for myself conversation. This was an Annie Higgins, arse-kicker-extraordinaire conversation. There was no need to be nervous this time, I had nothing to lose.

'As I said, we've been looking for a director of digital marketing,' he began. 'And I think you'd be perfect for the job. We can talk about the money further down the line, but you'd manage the budgets, the creative—'

'Would I be able to bring in my own people?' I asked, cutting him off.

'Absolutely,' he replied. 'It's a new role so we don't have anyone else staffing the department at the moment. Did you already have people in mind?'

'Yes,' I said. My voice was clear as a bell and even though I wasn't sure when I'd started the call, now I was absolutely certain. 'Harry, I'm turning down the job.'

A pigeon cooed on the edge of the roof while Harry processed the information.

'You are?'

'I am.'

'Why do I get the impression that's not all you have to say?' Harry asked.

'Because it isn't,' I answered. 'You said you didn't want to give Content the Uniteam account because we're too small and too inexperienced and yet you want to bring me in to run the entire digital marketing team.'

'It's a different job,' Harry explained. 'A different fit. You'd be part of SetPics, not a separate company. We want your entire focus, Annie. You're so weighed down with everything else going on over there, we want SetPics to be your priority.'

Here it was. Time to bet on myself.

'And what if it was?' I asked. 'What if I were to strategically manage the digital media for SetPics within Content? I'm prepared to hand over my current responsibilities to other members of my team and work exclusively on the SetPics account. This way you get me and you get the expertise of the rest of Content and you don't have the pressure of setting up an entirely new division inside your marketing department.'

'I don't understand how it would work,' he said slowly. 'Just take the job, Annie.'

'Let me explain it to you.' I could tell he was curious and I was not about to give up without a fight. I never did. 'You hire Content on retainer for three months, I'll be in charge of creative across all your brands, Miranda will execute the strategy. Honestly, Harry, if you'd been able to meet Miranda at the pitch, we wouldn't be having this phone call. You'd be begging her to take your job, which she never would because she's too dedicated to Content. This way you get both of us. If it doesn't work out after three months, we both walk away, no harm done.'

He breathed heavily down the line, deliberating. Somewhere across the river, I could hear him tapping his fingers rhythmically on his desk.

'I don't know,' he said. 'It's not the way we've done things in the past.'

'The way we did things in the past isn't always the best way to do them in the present,' I pointed out. 'Let us take you for lunch on Monday. If I haven't sold it to you, Miranda will convince you in five minutes flat.'

Or at least she would as soon as I explained it all to her.

'And what if it doesn't work out in three months?' Harry asked.

'Then you hire a digital marketing director,' I said. 'If I don't take the job, do you have anyone else lined up to start on Monday or will you have to start recruiting properly? We both know how much fun that will be.'

'Lunch on Monday then,' he replied. 'Roast in Borough Market at one. Don't be late.'

'We won't,' I promised, heart pounding with the thrill of a gamble that had paid off. 'See you then, Harry. Have a lovely weekend.'

I ended the call and dropped my red-hot phone on the settee by my side. I was sweating from head to toe. Fighting my way out of the hoodie, I lay back, staring up at the blue, cloudless sky. There was a solution to every problem. I couldn't turn off my feelings without the use of some very inadvisable class-A drugs and just forget Sam had ever happened with a lobotomy. There was a chance my sister could help with the latter and Brian could most likely get hold of the former, but I was looking for a more constructive solution. If I could win the unwinnable bet, if I could get a second chance at a dream job, why couldn't I think of a way to get to Sam?

Two minutes later I ran back into the office and snatched up my handbag.

'Hi,' I called to the assembled doughnut eaters. 'Bye.'

'Oh, she's off again,' Miranda sighed, jumping to her feet and following me down the corridor. 'What are you doing?'

'We don't give up and we don't give in,' I reminded her, grabbing my handbag. 'I'm going to see Sam.'

'Oh shit.' Mir grabbed her own bag and followed me out the door. 'On second thoughts, I think I prefer "Yes, I will have another".'

'This might be the perfect opportunity for both mottos,' I said, squeezing her hand. 'Oh and, I need to talk to you about something on the way.'

No need to be nervous, I reminded myself as Miranda threw me a suspicious glance.

I had nothing to lose.

CHAPTER THIRTY-ONE

Traffic in London was never not terrible and every second we sat in the back of the black cab, my heart pounded faster, taking seconds and minutes off my life.

'What are you going to say to him?' Mir asked.

I pulled my seatbelt out as far as it would go and then let it ping back. Pulled it out as far as it would go and let it ping back.

'No idea,' I replied. 'But I had no idea what I was going to say to Harry until I started talking and I've managed to get a foot in that door. Let's see what happens.'

'About that, you're insane, by the way,' she said, peeling a stray strand of hair off my sweaty forehead. 'Do you think he'll go for it?'

'It'll save the company,' I said. 'And I honestly think you could talk the hind legs off a donkey, so we'll see how it goes on Monday.'

'No pressure then,' Mir said, yanking on her own seatbelt as we pulled around the corner into Bloomsbury.

I paid the taxi driver and ordered Mir to stay exactly

where she was, quiet and out of sight. Sam spooked easily, we didn't need to make this any worse. I couldn't think of any reason why Elaine would be at home in the middle of the day on a Friday and our last two interactions hadn't gone especially well, so I was very much hoping she would be at work. All I needed was two minutes. To tell him I was sorry, explain I'd only posted those pictures to make him a success, to tell him how many books he'd sold, how people shared his love of history. He would understand eventually. He would have to.

I pressed the doorbell but no one answered.

I pressed it again. Nothing.

'One more go,' I whispered to myself, the butterflies in my stomach settling down as I started to accept that he might not be home. Still no voice on the intercom. Instead, a face appeared at the bedroom window.

'Oh, bollocks,' I muttered as Elaine's face registered mine. I turned quickly, crossing my arms wildly in front of myself. 'Mir, run for it,' I shouted. 'Abort mission, abort mission!'

'Oi!'

Elaine was considerably faster than me. Must have been all those Crossfit classes.

'It's you, you're the girl who showed up to Aggy's birthday party,' she said, grabbing hold of my hood and yanking me backwards. I ran on the spot for a moment, almost choking myself. I watched as Mir disappeared around the corner and silently screamed for help. 'You're the one who's responsible for all this shit.'

'I don't know what you mean,' I choked, rubbing my throat. 'I'm just the office fire marshal.'

'Yeah, pull the other one,' Elaine said, dropping my hood as if it were on fire and folding her hands under her armpits. She looked embarrassed. 'You're the reason he left.'

'He left?'

Now I looked at her, I saw her eyes were red and puffy, her nose was red raw. She'd been crying. I hadn't noticed at first, I'd been too busy looking at her abs. Actual visible abs peeking out the top of her waistband. I didn't think I'd ever seen any IRL before.

'I didn't even want him,' she said, a certain edge of hysteria in her voice. Behind her, I saw Wellington slinking out the door, rubbing himself on the door-frame. 'I dumped him. I had already moved on. And then he turns up with his speech and his haircut and his new jeans and I think, yeah, I'll give it a chance. And then all of a sudden, he's changed his mind? I don't think so.'

I puffed out my cheeks and shrugged. 'People change their minds all the time,' I said, keeping my eyes on Wellington. 'Who's to say he won't change it back again?'

Elaine scoffed. 'No man leaves a warm bed for a cold one,' she said. 'There's something going on with you two.'

'There really isn't,' I promised before nodding towards the cat. 'Should he be outside?'

She looked confused.

'Samuel?'

'Wellington,' I replied as the terrible tabby made a run for it across the garden.

'Oh shit,' she muttered, dashing after him. 'He's not allowed out, Samuel is going to go spare.'

The cat stopped in front of an oak tree and started circling, eyeing us both as we approached.

'You go left, I'll go right,' I said, slowing down my steps and crouching down, offering Wellington a handful of nothing. 'All right you tart,' I whispered. 'Don't you dare go up that tree.'

He immediately went up the tree.

'OK, enough's enough,' Elaine said, pushing her dark brown hair out of her face. 'I'm not standing here with *you*, waiting for his cat to climb out of a tree. You can have him. I never wanted him in the first place.'

'Sam?' I asked.

'Wellington,' she replied. 'But you can have him as well. Wherever he is.'

'He's not home?' I asked as Miranda reappeared, pressing her hand into her side. 'Sam, I mean?'

'This isn't Samuel's home any more,' Elaine said coldly. 'He left yesterday, said he'd be back for the cat. He can have him if he can find him, or you can take him – I don't care.'

'Do you know where he went?' I had a feeling she wasn't going to be in a rush to help me locate her two-time ex, but it had to be worth a try.

'Nope,' she replied, looking down at her watch. 'And I don't care. I have a dance competition tonight with Gianni, my new boyfriend. When you see Samuel, make sure you tell him that.'

'Will do,' I promised with a squint. 'Break a leg.'

Or both of them, I thought to myself as Elaine walked back inside, throwing me a one-fingered salute as she went.

'I was halfway back to the office and I turned around and you weren't there,' Miranda gasped, jogging over. 'Wasn't that—?'

'Yes.'

'And isn't that?'

'Yes.'

I looked up at Wellington, who was perched on all fours. The second Elaine's door slammed shut, he leapt down out of the tree and into my arms.

'So Sam wasn't home?' Mir asked.

'He wasn't.' I scritched Wellington underneath the chin and he purred approvingly. 'And if he didn't take this little bugger with him, I'd assume it's because he's gone to his brother's.'

She nodded, giving Wellington a sweet pat and getting a nasty swipe for her trouble.

'And where's that?' she said, giving Wellington the frowning of a lifetime.

'I have no idea,' I said with a sigh. 'But I'll bet we can find him.'

CHAPTER THIRTY-TWO

Saturday, 4 August

'I can't believe we can't find his brother,' I wailed, twenty-four hours later. 'Why is this so hard?'

'I can't believe Sam was savvy enough to block us all on Facebook,' Brian groaned. 'I mean, all of us. Even Nat and Zadie can't find the mysterious second Mr Page.'

'All we gave them to go on is he's divorced and he's got a brother named Samuel,' I said, collapsing on the floor of my flat. 'How many divorcees are there in London with a brother named Sam? We don't know he's even in London. Sam never said.'

Brian gave me a sad smile from his spot at the breakfast bar. 'We'll get there eventually,' he promised. 'Or I'll get you so drunk we'll destroy all the brain cells that remember him. Don't worry, I've always got your back.'

Miranda kicked my foot from her spot on my armchair.

'He's right,' she said. 'People don't just disappear, he'll turn up eventually.'

Even Wellington threw in a supportive chirrup from the broken loveseat.

'I hope you're right,' I said, poking him with my big toe.

We'd spent what felt like all night searching for Sam, and his brother, online. I'd tried calling his mobile, Miranda had tried calling his mobile, Brian had tried calling his mobile. We'd even convinced the Indian restaurant down the street to let me try ringing him from their landline but five poppadoms and ten tries later, he still wasn't answering. At almost lunchtime on Saturday, I was about ready to call it a day and go back to bed. It turned out I could do anything I put my mind to except for the most important thing of all.

Across the room, Brian's phone rumbled across the breakfast bar with a message.

'It's Zadie,' he said, turning around excitedly. 'She says Nat's found him.'

'You're kidding.' I sat bolt upright while Brian enlarged an attached photo. 'Where? How?'

'They've been following the Hot Historian hashtag on Insta, this just came up in someone's stories,' Brian said. 'Looks like he's giving a talk or something?'

He handed me the phone and there he was. Sam, my Sam, standing behind a lectern in a shirt and tie, a heart eyes emoji vibrating in the top corner of the screen.

'It's his lecture,' I realized, my brain fog starting to clear. 'Today is his lecture on the lord lieutenants of Ireland. But I can't remember where it is, ULU, UCL, Kings? One of the universities. Why can't I remember this? He talked about it all the time.'

'Brian, google it,' Miranda ordered. 'Don't worry, Annie. This, we can find.'

'And what am I supposed to do?' I asked, scrambling to my feet and dancing up and down on the spot.

'Brush your hair and clean your teeth, for a start,'

she replied. 'Go! If he's already started, we haven't got much time.'

'I don't know, he does like to go on,' I said, running for the bathroom. 'Brian, any joy?'

'He's at ULU and we've got forty-five minutes to get there,' he replied. 'I'll call a taxi.'

'Call an Uber!' Miranda exclaimed as I fumbled for the toothpaste with shaky hands.

'You know I'm morally against them as a company and—'

'Then call a fucking taxi!' I shrieked. 'Just get me a car and get it right now.'

I had forty-five minutes before he vanished off the face of the earth again. There was no way I was letting him get away this time.

'There's nothing I can do about your hair,' Brian said with a sniff in the back of the cab. 'Better leave it up and pretend it's supposed to look like that.'

'It's fine,' I said, pushing him away as we pulled up outside the university. 'Miranda, can you sort the taxi? I'll pay you back.'

'Yes, Miranda,' Brian said, following me out the cab. 'Please sort the taxi.'

'I don't want to miss anything,' she called after us as we spilled out of the shiny silver Prius and into the ancient buildings, looking for the right lecture hall. 'Don't start without me.'

'Excuse me,' I said, stopping short in front of a startled student. 'Do you know where the historical symposium is being held today? I'm looking for the lecture on the lord lieutenants of Ireland.'

He pulled a skinny white earbud out of his ear and blinked slowly.

'What?'

'Kids today, you mean excuse me,' Brian corrected before physically pushing him out of the way. 'Annie, over there.' He pointed at a small square sign with too much writing on it. 'This way!'

We raced across a bike path, narrowly avoiding a Boris bike, into the foyer of what looked like a cathedral. Through the crosshatched glass windows in the door, I could see Sam stood in front of a lectern, just like he was in the video the girl had posted, hundreds of heads turned to face him as he gave his lecture.

'Are you ready?' Brian said as Miranda staggered up the path to meet us, panting and out of breath.

'You really need to hit the gym,' I told her, straightening my dress. I was too dressed up. I was too hot. I hadn't thought enough about what I wanted to say. 'And no, I'm not. Is this a terrible idea?'

'Yes,' Brian replied before opening the door and shoving me through it. 'Now go.'

I clattered into the room with all the grace of a colicky elephant, the heels of my sandals clacking loudly against the worn-down stone floor, shattering the silence of the room.

Two hundred anonymous heads all turned at once while one recognizable face looked up. Every single pair of eyes on me.

I cleared my throat and stood up straight.

'Hi,' I said, holding up my hand in a salutary wave. 'Don't mind me, I'll wait until you're done.'

At the end of what seemed like a terribly long aisle, I saw Sam's expression changing like the colours on a mood ring. Blue, green, red, black. He would be the worst poker player ever.

'As I was saying, Edmund FitzAlan-Howard was

born on the first of June 1885 and died on the twenty-eighth of May 1947 and was the first Roman Catholic to be appointed to the position since 1685, during the reign of James II and I'm sorry but you are distracting me terribly if you have something to say, can you just say it, please.'

'Me?' I asked from my seat in a pew at the back of the room.

'Yes, you,' he replied. 'Everyone else is here because they're interested in Irish history.'

'I actually got lost on my way to the refectory,' said one meek voice in the third row. 'But it seemed rude to leave once you started.'

'Do you want to leave now?' Sam asked, one hand in his hair and the other on the lectern.

'If you don't mind?' the man replied. 'I'm starving.'

With a grim set to his jaw, Sam waved him away and the room murmured with unrest.

'Now everyone here is here because they're interested in Irish history,' he said. 'Apart from you.'

Another hand went up. 'Actually—'

'If anyone else wants to leave, please leave now,' he said, cutting him off. The man cowered in his seat and bowed his head. 'You included.'

'I can wait until you're finished,' I said, looking over my shoulder to see Brian and Miranda's faces pressed up against the glass. 'I think it's all very interesting.'

'No, you don't,' Sam huffed. 'You think it's all a joke. Just like you think I'm a joke.'

'That's not true,' I protested. 'I messed up, I know I did, but you were never a joke. I was an idiot, but no one was ever laughing at you.'

'That's where I recognize him from,' a girl whispered to her seatmate in the front row. Very, very slowly, they pulled out their phones and started taking photos.

'It's not good enough, Annie,' he replied, casting a very dark glance at his admirers. 'You thought it was OK to make me the subject of a bet before you even met me, and you thought it was OK to tell me I needed to change everything about myself before you even got to know me. I would never judge someone like that.'

'That is categorically untrue!' I stood up and marched down the aisle to meet him. 'You judge everyone. You judge me all the time. For starters, you think social media is ridiculous.'

'I'm not a fan of the medium,' he said stiffly. 'But I respect how hard you work.'

'And what about all that "I could never be with a girl like you" nonsense in Margate?' I asked. 'How is that not judgement?'

'I didn't say I could never be with a girl like you, I said a girl like you would never be with someone like me,' he said, turning pink. 'The thought beggars belief.'

'But I do want to be with you,' I said. He stayed behind the lectern, keeping a safe distance between us. 'I know I made a huge mistake. I did something incredibly stupid because I was angry and jealous and competitive. Not my favourite characteristics about myself, but I know it was wrong and all I can ask you to do is forgive me.'

I took a deep breath, ready to start the next round of begging.

'Are you quite finished?' he asked.

'I've got loads more actually,' I said, pressing my hands against my chest. 'Unless there's something you want to say?'

He stood still, towering over me.

'If you'd asked me if you could post those pictures, I would have said yes,' Sam said, correcting his sliding glasses. 'But you chose not to.'

'I know.' Out the corner of my eye, I saw at least half the audience on their phones, recording our confrontation or searching for Sam's hot pics, I wasn't sure. 'I'll never forgive myself.'

'And you did such a good job with my makeover,' he looked down at his smart trousers, his slim-fitting shirt. 'How will I ever know if it's really me you care for? Inside, I'm the same old Samuel. A new haircut and different clothes can't truly change the person inside.'

'That's the person I want,' I insisted. 'If you want to grow your hair back down to your arse and wear your grandad's clothes all around town, that is entirely up to you. I will still be here. Not here, exactly, that would be weird, but I'll be wherever you are. Unless that would legally be considered stalking?'

'Yes,' shouted one very gruff voice in the crowd. 'It would.'

'Right, OK, well, the point I'm trying to make is, I want to be with you, however you come packaged,' I declared. 'I know now, you should never judge a book by its cover.'

A woman in the third row put her hand up but did not wait to speak. 'I work in book design,' she said. 'And we actually work very hard so that people can make a judgment based on the cover.'

'You're not helping me,' I told her. 'But I'd be very interested to hear more about that afterwards.'

'You've asked me to trust you so many times,' Sam sighed. 'I just don't know.'

'You've got to give me another chance,' I pleaded,

climbing up to the lowest step. 'I think you're the cleverest, funniest, most interesting historian I've ever met and quite possibly the best man there actually is. Please, Sam?'

He kept his eyes down and I watched as his fingers curled around the edge of the lectern, squeezing tightly.

'Go on,' the gruff-voiced man shouted. 'Give her another chance.'

'Yes,' I said, turning and clapping as the man stood up. 'Listen to him, he seems very clever.'

Sam took a deep breath in and focused his attention on the papers in front of him.

'Annie, I have to finish this,' he said, refusing to make eye contact. 'I've been working on it for months and it's really incredibly unfair of you to walk in here and distract me like this.'

'Yes, of course,' I said, tiptoeing lightly down the steps and gesturing for the people in the front row to move along and make room. 'I didn't mean to interrupt. I'm actually very keen to hear it. I'm sure it's fascinating.'

He looked up and his light blue eyes immediately met mine. I slid my pendant up and down on its chain as he stared, saying nothing. Doing nothing.

'Where was I?' Sam muttered to himself, running his finger along his notes.

'FitzAlan-Howard,' someone behind me called politely. What a memory.

'That's it, thank you,' Sam said, and I threw an appreciative thumbs up into the air. 'Edmund FitzAlan-Howard, born first of June 1885 and died on the twenty-eighth of May 1947, was the first Roman Catholic to be appointed to the position since 1685, during the reign of James II and the last lord lieutenant of Ireland. Thank you.'

He stepped back and inclined his head slightly and everyone in the room began to applaud.

'That's it?' I asked, looking around me at the clapping masses.

'You came in rather towards the end,' Sam replied, eyes down. 'So unless you think there's something I missed, yes.'

'Well, I don't like to brag, but I did finish your book which makes me something of an expert in the field, I should think,' I said, the skin on my neck heating up. If he was finished, it was time for The Talk. 'I wish I'd heard the whole thing.'

He nodded, staying exactly where he was as everyone began to file out. Everyone except for the two girls who were clearly live streaming us from the back of the room.

'I am so sorry,' I said from my empty pew. 'Tell me what you want me to do and I'll do it. Brian suspended the account, no one can see it any more.'

'Then put it back up immediately,' he replied, his expression indignant. 'Have you any idea how many books I've sold? A month ago there would have been fifteen people in this room, today we had a full house.'

Sitting directly in front of him, I watched Sam's face change as he filed his papers away into his backpack. There was something new there, something I couldn't remember seeing before. He was desperately trying to stifle a smile.

'Wait, you're not angry?' I asked, gripping the edge of the wooden bench as he made his way down the steps towards me, clutching his backpack in front of him. 'You want those photos up there?'

'I was upset,' he admitted, sitting down beside me, backpack by his side. 'Because you did it behind my back. And I was embarrassed to see all those pictures on those enormous screens in front of all those people. But I didn't even let you try to explain, I simply reacted – which was very wrong of me. Very rash.'

'I wasn't trying to hurt you.' I took my hand out of my lap and rested it on the pew, just inches away from his leg. 'I made a mistake.'

Sam nodded.

'If I could go back and change it, I would.' Here it came, the verbal vomit. 'I don't care if we have nothing in common, you've shown me so many new things, you taught me so much about myself. I can't imagine my life without you.'

Be quiet, Annie, I told myself, shut up. Sam had his hands in his lap and he was so close I could feel him. This was the quiet part. This was the bit where I sat and waited until he was ready to talk. My knee bobbed up and down on the spot, fingers dancing along the pew.

'You're dying to say something else, aren't you?' Sam asked, that almost-smile reappearing on his face.

'Me?' I replied, tugging on my necklace. 'Not at all. Love a bit of peace and quiet, I do. Please feel free not to fill a perfectly good silence with senseless chatter, Samuel.'

'My friends call me Sam,' he placed his hand over mine and I exhaled slowly. 'You know, you've taught me a lot of things too. And I wouldn't say we don't have anything in common, apparently, an old dog can learn some new tricks.'

'You do take an excellent selfie,' I said in a whisper, curling my fingers around his, slowly at first until I was squeezing them as tightly as I dared, never wanting to let go.

Sam turned to face me. His blue eyes were almost grey in the dim light of the hall but they were so wide and so bright and so honest, I could barely breathe. I'd spent hours upon hours upon hours staring at his face over the last month but in that moment, it was like seeing him for the very first time. He was Dr Samuel Page PhD, he was an expert salsa dancer, a terrible family mediator, a Britney Spears aficionado, a bad cook, a cat lover, the world's leading authority on the lord lieutenants of Ireland. He was all those things and a million more that I couldn't wait to discover.

He leaned towards me and I inhaled sharply as everything else went soft at the edges. My insides were melting but my skin was on fire, lips tingling with anticipation before he could even touch me. His lips on my lips, his hands holding my hands. And then it was happening. The kind of kiss that demanded fireworks and a swelling orchestral soundtrack and an audience of a hundred thousand people cheering us on, except this kiss was ours and only ours. Nothing else was real, just for that moment and I didn't want to share it with anyone.

'So,' I breathed as I broke away, my heart pounding as I caught my breath. 'What now?'

'Firstly, I imagine the university will be wanting this space back,' Sam replied, nodding towards a gaggle of people, peering in through the door with wide eyes.

I bit my buzzing lips and smiled. 'I sort of meant about us.'

'Oh,' he muttered. 'Yes, that makes sense. What would you like to do?'

We both blushed on cue. Sam pushed his glasses up his nose while I immediately reached for my pendant.

'Maybe we don't make a plan?' I suggested. 'Maybe we just see what happens?'

'Sounds good to me,' he said, leaning towards me again.

'What about the people outside?' I whispered, not protesting nearly hard enough. Once you've kissed someone you really, really want to kiss once, it's very difficult not to keep doing it over and over. A month ago I hadn't even known that he existed and now I couldn't imagine a day without him in it.

'They can wait,' Sam murmured. 'I've waited long enough.'

It was like I always said: every once in a while, the universe steps up and, for a single day, everything in your life is amazing. Fortunately, this was one of those days.

EPILOGUE

Friday, 11 August

There was peace and quiet and there was peace and quiet.

I leaned over the edge of the wall to watch the waves sweep in, swell and then break along the cliffs below. The spray spritzed my skin but the sun was shining, the sky was blue and so I didn't really mind. I tucked my hair behind my ears in an attempt to keep it away from my lip balm, but it was a futile effort. When I closed my eyes, all I could hear were birds and the wind. When I opened them, it was all sea and sky.

London felt very far away.

'You're not going to jump, are you?'

'Unlikely,' I replied, shielding my eyes from the sun. 'I know it's August, but I reckon it'd still be a bit nippy.'

'Around fifteen degrees at this time of year.' Sam peered over the low limestone wall and into the ocean. 'Give or take.'

'The walking, talking human Google,' I said with a

grin. 'He can't name a single Kardashian but he knows the average sea temperatures off the coast of Ireland.'

He screwed up his face as he wracked his brains. 'Karen? Is there one called Karen?'

'Who knows?' I replied, smiling at his thinking face. 'Probably is by now.'

We stood side-by-side, not quite touching, and stared out to sea. The waves were choppy, just like Becks had said they would be. I turned my head to look at Sam. His curly hair blew around as he pushed his glasses up his nose and smiled at nothing. The very definition of contentment.

'What are you thinking about?' I asked.

'How nice it is to be here,' he replied. 'With you.'

'Aww,' I beamed happily. 'Sam.'

'And how I do hope you're not going to spend the entire weekend talking about nonsense.'

'But of course, sir, you need your quiet, sir, I understand, sir,' I said, bowing and scraping as I backed away. 'I'll be right over here, sir.'

I spotted a little wrought-iron bench across the yard and ambled happily across the patchy green and yellow grass to take a seat. We'd been travelling for what felt like forever, but Sam insisted on 'clearing out the cobwebs' before we accepted the landlady's offer of a cup of tea and freshly baked scones. I had saddled myself with a monster. My stomach rumbled as I pulled the sleeves of my soft, grey jumper over my hands.

Given Sam had never stepped foot on Irish soil before, he looked right at home. He was all walking boots and ruddy cheeks, curls blowing around in the breeze. I was prepared to overlook the red, quilted gilet but it wasn't easy. In fact, he looked so good,

I wanted to take a picture. Without thinking, I reached into my pocket to check my phone but it wasn't there. I'd left it inside, in my backpack, without even realizing. I lifted my wrist to check the time on my Apple watch but the screen was blank. The battery was dead. I hadn't charged it the night before.

'Sam,' I called, heart beating just a fraction faster. 'What time is it?'

'Must be about two?' he replied without turning around. 'I'm fairly certain I just saw a puffin. I wonder if there's a breeding colony here.'

I wanted to Google it so badly.

Running my thumb over my fingernails, I stood up and walked back over to Sam. The view really was gorgeous. Maybe not as impressive as my beloved rooftop view of London but still, very pretty.

'Have you got your phone?' I asked.

He patted himself down, checking all available pockets until he produced a brand, spanking new iPhone from his inside chest pocket.

'I hope you don't need it for anything,' he said, handing it over without question. 'There's absolutely no service.'

Absolutely. No. Service.

'How will we know where to eat tonight?' I attempted to open a search window and saw that he was right. 'How will we know what time the ferry leaves on Monday? How will I check the weather?'

Sam shook his head with pity.

'You'll check the weather by looking out of the window,' he replied. 'We'll know what time the ferry leaves by asking someone, and we'll know where to eat because there's only one pub on the entire island.

Honestly, for someone who's supposed to be bright, I worry about you sometimes.'

'Don't give me that,' I said, my fingers curling around the weight of his un-encased phone. 'How did we even find this hotel in the first place? Online. How did we book the ferry to get here? Online. We wouldn't even know this island existed if it wasn't for the internet.'

He pursed his lips for a second and I knew it was as close as he would come to admitting I was right. At least about that.

'It was your idea to come here,' Sam reminded me. 'You were the one who proposed "an escape from it all". You could be sat at your desk right now.'

'Plenty of time for that when I get back,' I replied. 'Maybe Deliveroo comes over here. People can't be expected to live a pizza-less existence just because they were born on an island.'

'You know this island was once inhabited by Gráinne O'Malley, a pirate queen from the sixteenth century?' Sam said, holding his hand out for his phone. 'Fascinating woman. Irish revolutionary who successfully met and negotiated with Elizabeth I.'

'Sounds to me like the kind of woman who might have appreciated having access to a ten-day weather forecast,' I grumbled, passing over my technological contraband.

'Come here.'

He wrapped his arm around my shoulders and pulled me in close. My heart stopped pounding at the lack of connectivity just long enough to flutter. It was still so new and different, the closeness of him. The kind of connection I'd almost forgotten.

Sam held his phone up above us, tilting it up and down until he found the perfect angle. My heart soared at what I saw on the screen. Heads pressed together, his blond curls meshed with my tangle of windswept hair, both our faces glowing. No need for a filter here.

'Now, smile,' he commanded, awkwardly adjusting his grip until he found the right button to take the picture.

As if I needed any encouragement.

'Perfect.' I beamed at the digital proof of us. This was it, the first proper photograph of the two us togeth-er-together. 'If only I could post it.'

'The internet hasn't been cancelled,' Sam reminded me. 'It'll still be there when we get back.'

We were a "we" now.

I tucked the phone away in his pocket. It was only three days. I could survive for three days. Once I was back, we'd be rushed off our feet. Sam had his new book to finish and all his YouTube meetings. I would be handing over my clients to Brian, Zadie and Nat, setting strategy for SetPics, meeting with the new team, washing Wellington's wee out of the mattress.

'Maybe we keep that one just for us,' I said, turning in towards him, winding my arms around his neck. 'Just this once.'

'That sounds like a fine idea,' Sam said, his mouth curling into a smile, inches away from me. I tipped my head backwards, felt his kiss on my lips and knew I was exactly where I was supposed to be. 'But I'll bet you can't do it.'

'It won't work, Page,' I whispered, nestling happily against his chest. 'I'm officially out of the betting business.'

'Look at you,' he laughed, holding me tightly and kissing the top of my head. 'You're a changed woman.'

'Maybe,' I replied, snuggling in. 'Just a little bit.'

'Well, for the record, I happen to think you're fairly close to perfect,' he said, blue eyes meeting my green ones. 'Right now, off the shelf, as you are. No alterations needed.'

'That's the nicest thing anyone has ever said to me,' I said with a smile. 'I am hashtag blessed.'

'And I am hashtag starving,' Sam replied. 'Shall we go and see about those scones?'

I nodded and took his hand, following him back inside the hotel. No one could really say where this was going but for once, my heart and my head were in complete agreement.

This was the start of something real.

ACKNOWLEDGEMENTS

To Lynne Drew and Martha Ashby, ten years down – how do you feel about another decade? Because I *literally* have nothing else to do. Thank you for everything you do for me, it is hugely appreciated.

To Charlie Redmayne, Kate Elton, Lucy Vanderbilt, Hannah O'Brien, Emma Pickard and everyone else at HarperCollins, there isn't enough paper left in the book to apologize to/thank everyone who deserves it but trust me, I feel so terrible/incredibly grateful for everything.

That said, I do have to give a special thanks to Felicity Denham for being the tour partner of dreams, thank you for being so amazing and patient and for always making sure there's time for a nap. You're a champion.

To Rowan Lawton, Eugenie Furniss, Lucy Steed and everyone else at Furniss Lawton/James Grant, you make everything so easy and keep me going. Thank you so much for all that you do.

Big huge mega thanks to Sunil Singhvi for his sage advice and wise counsel. As a sign of my appreciation,

I appoint you Hand of the Queen (please note people in this role don't usually live that long but still, you get a nice badge).

So many people held me up during this one and you all deserve a hug from the Marvel Avenger of your choice. Unfortunately, that is not within my power and all I can do is say thank you, so, for putting up with my nonsense/plying me with booze/talking me off the ledge/humouring my cat videos/making excellent online content and/or books/not delivering the next Game of Thrones book so I had time to get my own book finished*. THANK YOU to Rebecca Alimena, Della Bolat, Ryan Child, Kevin Dickson, Giovanna Fletcher, Emma Gunavardhana, Harry Hadfield, George RR Martin, Karl Morgan, Mhairi McFarlane, Louise Pentland, Paige Toon, Terri White, my brother, my boyfriend, my aunt, other people's pets and the entire WWE roster. Except the ones I don't like.

*delete as appropriate

A Q&A WITH LINDSEY KELK!

1. What inspired you to write *One in a Million*?

It was a perfect storm of procrastination. I was watching *My Fair Lady* on the TV and Instagram stories on my phone at the same time and the story just appeared for me. I started thinking about the way people choose to represent themselves today and how they transform themselves to fit an online ideal. The idea of a modernized version of *My Fair Lady*, tied into social media made perfect sense. I really wanted to write a story about the way social media impacts our lives without judging it too much. Social media definitely isn't the bad guy in the story, it's more a warning about how to use it responsibly. Also, Wellington is clearly the bad guy.

1.b. So how many times did you watch *My Fair Lady* for research??

At the beginning of writing, I only watched it once because I didn't want to copy the story structure or anything like that. It was more inspiration rather than a straight update/modernization but I did listen to the soundtrack a lot. Once the first draft was complete, I went back and watched it a couple more times. It's actually incredible at how they managed to retain so much heart in a story that actually treats its heroine pretty shabbily. Eliza fights to keeps her dignity and sense of self, which is so important, and I love that the ending is still somewhat ambiguous. In *One in a Million*, Annie and Sam are both equal parts Henry Higgins and Eliza Doolittle, their dynamic changes a little more than it does in the movie and I loved that about them. They're much more open to learning new things from each other (even though they both think they know best).

3. Annie is not the only one bossing social media – you've got a pretty great social presence yourself and you were an early adopter too – what was it about social media that appealed to you? And what do you like most (and dislike most) about it?

To me, social media is just another way to communicate and tell stories. I really try not to over-think it, I'm just trying to keep in touch with people I care about. It's hard being over in the US, I sometimes feel very detached and alone but if you've got Twitter and Instagram, you're immediately connected. People can make friends and find the support of a community they might never have otherwise met and that's an amazing thing. But at the same time, you have to be strong enough to know how to filter out the more negative aspects, and that's not always easy. Also, you have to be able to use your judgement and question as to what's true and what isn't, another thing you can only learn over time. What we have created is incredible; real time communication with people all over the world. I just wish we were able to keep it a more positive place.

4. What's your favourite social platform and why?

It's too hard to choose between Instagram and Twitter. I can watch Instagram stories all day long, it's such a dangerous time suck. But I rely on Twitter for my community – I'm able to talk to other authors and other book lovers, all while I'm sat behind my laptop at home, by myself. That's an incredible gift to a writer.

5. You've lived in the US for nine years now, what do you miss about home? And has the internet changed the experience for you perhaps?

Everything. I've been incredibly homesick recently and have a real love/hate relationship with the internet right now! On one hand, I love that it keeps me so close with everyone but at the same time, I have epic UK FOMO. Every time my friends post about something they're all experiencing, I'm dying over here! But having that connection has made like over here much easier in the long run.

6. What's next on the cards for you, both book-wise and non-book-wise?

There's no such thing as non-book-wise! I'm already working on my next two projects and yes, one of them is a new *I Heart* book...

And now some questions from readers!

7. lisajade_wg: Which of your characters would you say is most like you?

There's part of me in all the characters but right now, I'm probably most like Annie. I can be competitive (although I have never hit anyone with a hockey stick) and I'm terrible at pushing myself too hard. I'm also definitely addicted to social media, just try tearing me away from my iPhone and see what happens. Obviously, I'll always be an Angela but our lives are *very* different these days!

8. georgieljames: Do you ever want your books to be turned into films?

Yes, I would love that! I think it would be really fun to see them interpreted into another format although I'm sure I'd have trouble giving up control. Because as we've established, I'm a bit of an Annie.

9. onceuponabookdream: You, Paige Toon and Giovanna Fletcher are my favourite three musketeers!! What do you love the most about those girls?

They're the best, seriously. As I've mentioned, life as a writer can be very isolating — you're literally in another world while you're writing. Having good friends who understand exactly what I'm talking about helps so much. They're both so supportive! I always know I can text them when I feel like I've gone a bit book mad and they don't think I'm a weirdo. Hopefully they feel the same way (because it'll be really awkward if they don't).

10. Emily Ashdown: Who's your favourite super-hero and why?

Much like Annie, I'm going to have to choose Thor. Because he's Thor.

11. emilyswhitelies: Who was your first book boyfriend?

I had a lot of flirtations but the first BB I fell completely in love with was probably Troy Tatterton in Virginia Andrews' *Casteel* family books. He was so brooding and tortured and yet, so very handsome. This explains a lot of the problems in my adult life. And no, I know it's not the coolest answer ever given but that's how you know it's true.

12. ravija_m23: Name one thing that you always wanted to do but still haven't done

Visit Japan! It's on the list.

There are lots of ways to keep up-to-date with Lindsey's news and views:

lindseykelk.com

facebook.com/LindseyKelk

@LindseyKelk

@LindseyKelk

LindseyKelk